Praise for Miranda Dickinson

'Brilliant, brilliant, brilliant! Your book was the complete pick me up I needed and for that I thank you from the bottom of my heart.' **Jayne Simmons**

'It is the very best read I have had in a long time. It was true romance & intrigue.' **Joy Jones**

'The tone is optimistic, sincere, funny and sometimes, I felt like it was talking to me.' **Nathalie Kennedy**

'Just finished reading this book . . . I can't even let the book go off my hand this whole week! It's amazing :D' **Hanna Insyirah**

'I really enjoyed this book it made me feel part of the story and it's a book that I couldn't put down.' **Lindsey Middleton**

'Thanks for such a heart-warming tale. You are an inspirational author, and have made me smile today. Thank you :)' **Allena**

'I love the main character of Romily, So optimistic and strong (though she has no idea!) she makes you want to live everyday with a broad smile and a "we can do it" mantra chant!' **Anika**

'Loved, loved, loved this book. Read it in a day as I couldn't put it down! Loved the twist at the end, and the romance was perfect!' **Julie Hodgkinson**

'A fantastic read. It was refreshing, exciting and romantic.' **Liz Stead**

'Your books are so uplifting and romantic that each time I finish a book I feel inspired to make the most of life and that is a true gift.' **Mallory**

'Best book I have ever read! I enjoyed it so much, some parts even moved me to tears! I literally couldn't put it down when I was reading it.' **Jess**

'The unravelling of the plot, impromptu meetings and characters who you'll instantly love, make *When I Fall in Love* an easy and heartening read.' **Caroline Smailes**

'*Welcome to my World* is a fabulous book filled with heartwarming charcters, mouthwatering food and lots of romance and it will make you want to book your next holiday right now!' **Amanda – One More Page**

'I know a Miranda Dickinson tale is the perfect story to snuggle up with on the couch, with a cup of tea and a couple of free hours.'
Jody – A Spoonful of Happy Endings

'I loved the modern touches; the emails, tweets and posts from the blog community that Romily relied on. But most of all I loved reading about a girl on a singular mission who attacks it with passion, enthusiasm and . . . a hint of madness. If you want to read about a happy ending, go out and buy *It Started With a Kiss*.'
Cesca Martin – Novelicious

'The story is amazing, the characters are so warm and so witty and loveable and Miranda's writing just flows so naturally. Miranda Dickinson just gets better with every book. *It Started With A Kiss* was a triumph in every sense of the word.' **Leah – Chick Lit Reviews and News**

TAKE A LOOK AT ME NOW

Miranda Dickinson has always had a head full of stories. From an early age she dreamed of writing a book that would make the heady heights of Kingswinford Library. Following a Performance Art degree, she began to write in earnest when a friend gave her The World's Slowest PC. She is also a singer-songwriter. Her first four novels, *Fairytale of New York*, *Welcome to my World*, *It Started with a Kiss* and *When I Fall in Love*, have all been *Sunday Times* bestselling titles. She lives with her husband Bob in Dudley.

To find out more about Miranda visit www.miranda-dickinson.com and find her on Twitter @wurdsmyth.

By the same author

Fairytale of New York
Welcome to my World
It Started with a Kiss
When I Fall in Love

MIRANDA DICKINSON

Take a Look at Me Now

AVON

AVON

A division of HarperCollins*Publishers*
77–85 Fulham Palace Road,
London W6 8JB

www.harpercollins.co.uk

A Paperback Original 2013

1

A catalogue record for this book is
available from the British Library

ISBN-13: 978-1-84756-235-7

Set in Sabon LT Std by Palimpsest Book Production Limited,
Falkirk, Stirlingshire

Printed and bound in Great Britain by
Clays Ltd, St Ives plc

MIX
Paper from
responsible sources
FSC® C007454

FSC™ is a non-profit international organisation established to promote
the responsible management of the world's forests. Products carrying the
FSC label are independently certified to assure consumers that they come
from forests that are managed to meet the social, economic and
ecological needs of present and future generations,
and other controlled sources.

Find out more about HarperCollins and the environment at
www.harpercollins.co.uk/green

Dear reader

You hold in your hands my fifth novel. I'm still amazed that I got to write more than one, so five books is incredible! I hope you enjoy this story: I wrote it for you.

Many thanks to the amazing Avon team – Sammia Rafique my lovely editor, Claire Bord, Caroline Ridding, Rhian McKay for awesome copy-edits and Anne Rieley. To my wonderful agent Hannah Ferguson – thank you for your support, enthusiasm and emergency chocolate supplies! Thanks as ever to my family – the Dickinson, White, Smith, Davies and Ellis clans – my fantastic friends including The Peppermint massive and my church family. Your support and love means the world. Special thanks to Kim Curran Goodson for being my biggest encourager and my lovely husband Bob for being the love of my life.

I love collaborating with lovely people on Twitter and Facebook, who make the writing and editing process far less lonely and much more fun. Massive thanks to my #getinvolved winners, whose brilliant suggestions are in this book:

Apollo the taxi driver named by @bookminxsjv
Vintage dress from Well Beloved chosen by Melissa Denny
Java's Crypt named by @bear_kp
Wonder Woman in Lizzie's flat chosen by Willow and Anne Streeter
Autumn (Ced's girlfriend) named by Kayla Oliver
Rooster on a motorcycle statue chosen by Cathleen Holst
Pablo the Goldfish named by Nikki @Promyelocyte13
S-O-S Club popcorn cupcakes created by Kate @MeMyBooksandI
House coffee blend at Annie's named by Claire Scott
Xiu Min (Eric's girlfriend) named by Nancy Mac

We're living in uncertain times, when jobs are shaky, money is scarce and the future is uncertain. This story is about kicking back at the bad stuff and daring to dream of more. Life has a funny way of coming good, eventually. Sometimes, you just have to take the chance . . .

Miranda x

For my lovely Bob

Thank you
for believing in my dream,
for keeping my dream alive
and for doing the washing-up.
I love you xx

'Our brightest blazes are commonly kindled
by unexpected sparks.'
Samuel Johnson *(1709–1784)*

CHAPTER ONE

The day that changed my life

When the thing that was going to change my life arrived, it didn't look anything like I'd expected.

Had you asked me before – say, for instance, when I was wedged into the unfamiliar armpit of a fellow commuter on the bus into work that morning, trying my hardest not to retch at his unique aroma of onions soaked in B.O., and *wishing* for something in my life to change – I'd have predicted it to look like a priceless object. And I would have expected it to arrive with a *Hallelujah* chorus and a dramatic, edge-of-your-seat voiceover by that bloke from *X Factor*:

'*Nell Sullivan has been waiting for something to change her life. And NOW. This. Is. IT . . .*'

What I *didn't* expect was for it to be a three-line message scribbled on a lime-green sticky note, stuck to the screen of my computer at work. Especially not from Aidan Matthews – my line manager in Islington Council's Planning Department and, perhaps more importantly, the man who had been the on-off love interest (and nearest thing to a steady relationship) in my life for the best part of five years.

Hi Nell
Any chance you could find an excuse to pop into my office this morning? Things I need to tell you. A x

As soon as I saw it, I knew my wish from the B.O. bus seat that morning was about to bear fruit. Aidan wanted me back. Until now I hadn't realised quite how much I wanted to resolve things with him. When we had broken up last time it had been a mutual decision – both of us tired of navigating the problems we'd never been able to solve. But as my finger traced his familiar handwriting on the note, my heart began to race. Maybe we'd both known this would happen: it always had done before. We were destined for each other; it was evident in the chemistry that still sparked between us even when we weren't together. It had been building for a while: with the lime-green message I now held his intentions were obvious.

Avoiding the suspicious stare of Connie Bagley, the sour-faced secretary who perched like a bitter owl at the desk next to mine (and would happily run to management with the merest whiff of accusation against me), I sauntered nonchalantly across the grey carpet to see Vicky Grocutt, Assistant Planning Officer – and my best friend.

'Morning, Vicky,' I said, making a point of raising my voice enough for Cranky Connie to hear. 'Do you mind if we go over the applications for Domestic Works?'

I saw her eyes light up at the promise of potentially salacious gossip.

'No problem, Nell. I'm afraid there's *quite a few* to get through.' She gave a knowing smile and stood, grabbing a large armful of files. 'Perhaps we'd better take this into the meeting room?'

'Excellent idea.'

Smiling innocently at the repressed rage of our colleague, Vicky and I barely managed to keep our giggles at bay until we were safely behind the closed meeting room door.

'I've got to hand it to you, Nell,' Vicky laughed, tossing the files on the oval beech meeting table and flopping into a leather office chair, 'you certainly know how to wind that woman up.'

'She's her own worst enemy. If she didn't take so much pleasure in ratting on everyone it wouldn't be as much fun to annoy her.' I filled two mugs from the coffee machine, which was permanently on duty to satisfy the caffeine needs of the department.

'And you do it so well.'

I grinned as I joined her at the table. 'Thank you.'

Vicky sipped her coffee and shuddered as the thud of caffeine hit her. 'My *life*, who's on percolator duty this morning?'

'Terry, I think.'

'Oh well, that explains it. He's trying to give up smoking. *Again*. Must need caffeine to fill the gap.' She pushed her mug aside and squared herself at me. 'So come on, what's the real reason for our meeting?'

'This.' I enjoyed the shiver of anticipation as I pulled Aidan's note from my suit jacket pocket and handed it to her. 'It was waiting on my screen this morning.'

Vicky picked it up and screwed up her eyes to scrutinise it. I smiled to myself. Even though everyone around her insists she needs glasses, Vicky Grocutt remains a defiant squinter, the thought of visiting an optician's just too horrific to consider after being brought up in a family of them.

When she realised who the note was from, she blinked at me.

'*Nell* . . .' she breathed. 'Do you think . . .?'

I shrugged and it was all I could do not to squeal out loud. 'I'm not sure. But what else could it be?'

She appeared to be as excited as I was, having become an expert in my love life by living it vicariously over the years. 'I knew it! I told you he was giving you the eye yesterday in the briefing meeting. I *knew* I hadn't imagined it!'

Yesterday afternoon I hadn't wanted to believe it, especially as things had been decidedly cool between Aidan and I over the last couple of months. But then I'd caught him glancing in my direction as our superiors droned on about planning objections and schedules, his stunning blue eyes causing the same army of butterflies to lay siege to my stomach as always. Gorgeous Aidan Matthews, with his closely cropped fair hair, square jaw and body to die for . . .

Aidan's ability to melt my resolve with one look had long been my undoing since the first day I met him in the office kitchen, six years ago. I lost all power of rational thought when he was around. Over the years the effect he had on me had covered a multitude of disappointments, broken promises and bad timings, leading me to reach the conclusion that we were probably destined to end up together. I believed that our other failed attempts had simply been a case of both of us not being ready: sometimes he'd backed away, sometimes I had. But we always ended up in each other's arms, and that had to mean something, surely?

'I don't know what else it could be,' I replied. 'I think he wants us back together. And I think this could be it for us. We're both tired of this stop-start thing going on. This could be where we get serious.'

'And not before time,' Vicky grinned. 'Greg and I had met, moved in and were expecting Ruby by the time you guys were on your third round of "will-they-won't-they". You both need to stop being so feisty and settle down, in my opinion. But how do you feel about it?'

'Good,' I said, my mind still abuzz with the revelation. 'I mean, it's unexpected, for sure, but now I've had time to think about it, I think it could work.' I could feel tears prick the corners of my eyes. 'Oh who am I kidding? I love him, Vix!'

My best friend scooped me into a hug, knowing exactly what this development meant for me.

'Oh babe, I know you do. I want you two to get back together, have lots of hot sex and babies!'

Since becoming a mother, just over two years ago, Vicky had decided that everybody's life was more interesting, sexy and exciting than hers. While I knew she loved her partner Greg and adored their daughter Ruby, it seemed that she still mourned for the excitement of her single days when she was the terror of bachelors across London and the Home Counties.

She let me go. 'So, when are you going to see him?'

I took a deep breath. 'Now.'

When I'd wished for something to change on the bus that morning, the prospect of rekindling my relationship with Aidan had been the furthest thing from my mind. It wasn't going to change my life – not in the way I expected – but it was a start. A more settled relationship might set me up to make the changes I really wanted to make, changes that might take a few years to bring them into being. For unbeknown to anyone – even my best friend – I had been cradling a dream for years. I dreamed of running my own business. It had begun as an idea for a restaurant but when Vicky and I visited New York for a Christmas shopping trip two years ago my dream had changed. Instead of a café or restaurant, which were ten-a-penny in the capital, I began to dream about establishing a truly authentic American diner, serving pancakes, waffles and French toast for brunch and all manner of burgers, calzone, pizza and BBQ cuts for dinner. Everything prepared fresh, everything made to order. I dreamed about it when stuck in boring Council meetings, sketching doodles of interior layouts and signs on my work memo pad. In my mind it was so clear: baking fresh bread, scone-like biscuits and cinnamon rolls every morning, and crafting banana cream pies, deep-dish apple pies and batch upon batch of pancake batter every day. All of my daydreams were a world away from the never-changing schedule of procedures, plans and paperwork that my current job entailed. When Aidan and I rekindled our relationship, maybe this time I would share it with him. Besides, Aidan was lovely and whenever we had been together, we'd always been happy. Our version of happy, anyway . . .

Vicky left the meeting room first, making an expert job of engaging Connie in conversation. Seeing the coast was clear, I ducked out and sprinted through the main office to Aidan's door at the other end. Outside, I paused, checking my reflection in the darkened window of the empty office next door. *Not bad, Sullivan*, I told myself. My dark-blonde hair was neatly back from my face, making the most of my cheekbones and deep green eyes, and the suit I'd thrown on in a hurry after sleeping through two snoozes of my alarm that morning didn't look too creased. Aidan wanted to see *me*, I reminded myself, not my choice of outfit. Straightening the hem of my jacket, I knocked.

'Yes?'

I pushed the handle and peered around the door. 'Hi. You wanted to see me?' *Play the game, Nell. Enjoy the chase . . .*

Aidan's blue eyes sparkled and he rose from his chair. 'Yes. Yes, I did. You look . . . great, Nell.'

Yes I do, Aidan. 'Thank you. As do you.'

'Quick, come in and shut the door.'

I did as he asked, willing my heart rate to slow as images of the last time we'd got back together flashed across my mind – the passionate kisses, the locked door and the pot plant by his desk that never quite recovered from its sudden toppling . . . I took the seat opposite him and sat with my hands folded demurely in my lap. Aidan Matthews might want me back, but I was going to make him work for it. 'So, here I am.'

'Here you are . . .' His lazy smile sashayed its way

across his tanned features and I shifted a little to halt the forward route march of the butterflies in my stomach. Then he straightened and cleared his throat, the act so suddenly vulnerable that I had to fight the urge to leap across his desk and snog him for all I was worth.

'Nell, there's something I have to tell you. I've known since yesterday, and I have to say it came as somewhat of a shock to me. I honestly couldn't have predicted this.'

You're not the only one . . . 'Really?'

His eyes were intent on me. 'Really. I just – Nell, I don't know how to say this, what words to use . . .'

My heart went out to him. 'Aidan, I know. Just say it.'

A flash of confusion traversed his face. 'You know? H-how do you . . .?'

Full of confidence, I smiled and leaned towards him. 'I just do, Aidan. It's written all over your face. So don't worry about the right words: just say it.'

'Wow.' He looked bewildered but relieved at my invitation. 'You're being incredible about this – you *are* a wonderful woman . . .'

My smile broadened as I cast a quick glance in the direction of the not-so-healthy yucca plant by his desk. *Prepare for another re-potting, plant* . . .

'. . . That's why it's such a tragedy we're going to lose you.'

I don't know what happened then: it was as if what Aidan said was usurped by the words the Aidan Matthews in my mind was at that moment expressing: *I love you, Nell. I can't fight it any more. Will you take me back . . .?*

For a while the two Aidans faced off: one uttering irresistible words of love, the other retorting with – well, whatever it was he *was* saying that I couldn't comprehend.

'Nell? Say something, for heaven's sake.'

I scrabbled my way back to the here and now. 'I just . . . I thought . . . Sorry, *what* did you say?'

Aidan's shoulders dropped and guilt stained his face. 'I didn't want you finding out at the same time as everybody else. Like I said, I only knew for definite yesterday and I almost told you after the briefing meeting. But we've been through so much together, you and I, that I just couldn't bear the thought of you hearing it from anyone other than me. I care about you, you know that . . .'

His mouth was moving, but none of the words made any coherent sense. And then, slowly, like a pinprick of light piercing the darkness of a tunnel, the truth began to dawn.

'You're *sacking* me?'

'I wouldn't have put it like that, but . . .'

'How else would you have put it, Aidan? You're taking my job away!'

'It's not me personally, Nell . . .'

'Well it feels like it.'

'Of course you'll feel that way. But at least it isn't just you, honey . . .'

Rage pulsed through my body. 'Oh *that's* OK then! As long as I get to share the ignominy of redundancy with my colleagues! What kind of stupid, cruel logic is that?'

'Try to keep your voice down, OK? I'm not meant to be telling you this.'

I snorted. 'Well, lucky old me.'

He leapt from his chair and was suddenly beside me, his hands on my shoulders. 'I know this is difficult. Believe me, I didn't sleep last night agonising over how to tell you. But don't you see, Nell? It's out of my hands! I tried to speak up for you, but they're rearranging the entire department. It's come from top level – budget cuts and the recession have forced their hand. There's nothing I can do.'

I bit back tears as I looked into his beautiful blue eyes and hated myself for even caring what he thought of me. 'What am I going to do?' I begged him, my voice disgustingly weak and needy. 'What about my rent? My car? How am I going to find another job that pays like this one? Nobody's hiring at the moment.'

He stroked my cheek with his hand. 'At least you'll have your redundancy pay. They have to acknowledge the service you've given for six years. At least it'll pay the bills for a couple of months . . . Believe me, there are people in a far worse situation than you in this department.'

This news did anything but comfort me. I glared at him. 'Who else?'

'Beg your pardon?'

'Who else is being sacked, Aidan?'

He swallowed hard and I hated the shame I saw in his face. 'Almost everyone. Nick will stay on as Chief Planning Officer, I'll remain as Head of Department and Connie will be asked to become office manager for Parks and Recreation as well as Planning.'

I let out a hollow laugh. So all of Connie's sucking up

to management over the years hadn't gone unnoticed . . . 'Right. I'm going now.'

He wobbled backwards as I stood, and I suddenly realised how pathetic he looked, stripped of his work-related bravado.

'Please don't say anything to anyone. We're calling them all into the meeting room in half an hour.'

Part of me wanted to grab the ailing yucca and ram it down his traitorous throat, but despite my fury I walked steadily out of Aidan's office and back to my desk, where for the next thirty minutes I hid behind my computer screen, feeling like the biggest traitor in the world as the regular banter of my colleagues tore my heart to shreds.

I am losing my job . . .

The words felt alien, cold, jagged. No matter how many times I repeated them in my head I couldn't reconcile them to my life. I had *never* been made redundant, not in all the years I'd been working. In the three positions I'd held since graduating from university, I'd always been promoted, or resigned when a better job came along. The carefully mapped-out schedule for my life hadn't accounted space for a 'redundant' block. My home, my car, my career – and even my secret future dream of running my own business – were all nothing without money, without stability.

I stared at my reflection in the dark screen of my computer monitor and saw pure, hollow-eyed fear glaring back at me.

I'm losing my job. What am I going to do?

CHAPTER TWO

So long, farewell . . .

Processing the news was a surreal experience. I felt as if I was floating just above a room filled with rotating knives, knowing my descent was inevitable. How dare Aidan drop this on me? How could he think this was a better option than learning about it with the rest of the team? At least if I'd heard it at the same time as them we could have reacted as a team, united by a common experience. Now I was in limbo – not in with Aidan and the lucky few who would walk out of the office today knowing they had a job to come back to, and not with my workmates who were about to learn their fate. I hated it; and I hated Aidan more for once again demonstrating how little he really knew me. I wanted to tell Vicky but she had disappeared to the canteen to grab a bacon sandwich. Feeling completely helpless, I wished the seconds away until the inevitable meeting.

Thirty minutes later, we filed into the meeting room like sheep into an abattoir, my colleagues completely unprepared for the lightning bolt about to fire at them. Aidan and two of his superiors calmly handed out letters to all of us, detailing the consequences of the Council's 'programme of restructuring'. Vicky and two of my other female colleagues began to sob quietly, while my male friends stared in gut-wrenched silence, eyes not blinking as the awful reality set in. Some idiot from HR who nobody knew then stood up and explained how *committed* the Council was to ensuring our personal development – a ridiculous stance to take considering it was happily sacking fifteen people. When he asked for any questions he was met by uniform, wordless hatred.

I could feel Aidan's eyes on me, but I refused to look back, focusing instead on the impersonal general letter in my hand:

We regret to inform you . . . This is not a personal reflection on your considerable contribution to the Department, rather a necessary measure to protect the financial integrity of the Council . . .

No longer required.

Out of a job.

Unemployed . . .

However I looked at the words I couldn't help but take them personally. This couldn't be happening to me! Only that morning I'd wished for something to change . . .

And then, it hit me.

Something *had* changed. Admittedly not in a good way, but my secret wish had been granted. From this moment on, my life would never be the same again. Nell Sullivan, Assistant Planning Officer, was no more. That chapter of my life had been brought to a sudden end and now . . .

Well, *now* what?

The prat from HR was handing out tissues and wittering on about a hastily arranged consultation with a local recruitment agency to follow the end of the meeting. But it was as if I had become cocooned in a bubble, separated from the devastated expressions of my colleagues by a million new thoughts that sparkled and spun around my eyes. I hadn't planned for this, hadn't even considered its possibility in my carefully ordered life. And yet, here it was, together with the promise of three months' wages in one go . . .

At the end of the meeting, I followed my colleagues out, my heart inexplicably light despite the devastation that surrounded me. Vicky grabbed my arm and pulled me from the line of zombie-like shufflers heading down the corridor to the room set aside for 'career repositioning advice'.

'Can you believe they've just done that?' she demanded, trails of blue-black mascara running down her cheeks. 'Bastards! I've just taken out a new mortgage on the house – how on earth am I going to pay for it now?'

'I don't know, hun.'

'And Greg's had his hours cut at the factory, too . . . This is such a mess.'

'You're telling me,' the bulky, middle-aged hulk of our colleague Terry appeared beside us. 'Can't believe I chose this bloody week to give up smoking. Either of you have any fags?'

We shook our heads and watched him lumber away.

'I think I might take up smoking,' Vicky said, staring blankly after Terry. 'Look at me: I'm shaking, Nell.' She held out her hand and I could see the light from the strip-lights overhead undulating gently over her newly manicured nails. 'I'm going to have to phone Greg and tell him. So much for our wedding plans next year.'

'The agency might have something for you, Vix,' I suggested, immediately hating myself for sounding like Aidan's henchwoman. As I considered it, the thought that had begun in the meeting room grew. I didn't want to be a victim of this. I wanted to do something else . . .

'. . . Of course the Disney World trip Greg wanted to take me and Ruby on is out of the window. I might have to ask Mum to look after Ruby for an extra day because there'll be no way I can justify paying nursery fees five days a week now. And *then* I'll have to endure her endless diatribes on how reckless Greg and I were to have Ruby before we were fully settled. I swear if we have to move back to his parents' house in Brentwood I will go *insane* . . .'

Vicky was listing all the things she now couldn't afford and I had to force myself away from the burgeoning idea to give her my full attention. 'Vix, hun, try not to think the worst. I know you're still in shock – we all are – but we don't know what the situation is yet. You and Greg have been through worse and look at how happy you guys are. Ruby's gorgeous and loves you both to bits and you know Greg is a great dad and partner. You'll work through this.'

She sniffed. 'You think so?'

'If anyone can get through this, you guys can.'

'Thanks, babe. And you will, too. At least you and Aidan patched things up and worst-case scenario you could always move into that big house of his . . .'

I averted my eyes and she stopped.

'You *did* get back together, didn't you?'

I let out a long sigh. She wasn't going to like it, but I couldn't lie to her. 'No, we didn't.'

'I don't understand. Why call you into his office if he wasn't going to . . .?' Her eyes widened as the truth dawned. 'Oh my life. You *knew* . . .'

'He asked me not to say anything . . .'

Her expression darkened. 'You knew, Nell! You came out of his office and you sat at your desk like nothing had changed, and all the time you knew?'

'What was I supposed to do? I wasn't going to be the one who broke everyone's hearts!'

Vicky shook her head and instantly the room temperature seemed to drop. Deliberately, she turned her back on me and followed the others down the corridor.

What on earth was I supposed to say to her? I knew she was just angry and hitting out at the nearest person, but I felt frustration gnawing at me that she hadn't afforded me the chance to reply.

'Probably best to let her go.' A hand appeared on my shoulder and I turned to see the pinched, triumphant expression of the office secretary. 'She's upset: it's understandable . . .'

Angrily, I shrugged my shoulder free. 'Get lost, Connie.'

I didn't accompany my colleagues to the recruitment agency meeting, instead returning to the office to fetch my bag and coat. I needed to get out for a while, the atmosphere in the office sucking the life from my body and the whirling thoughts in my head making me dizzy.

'Shall we grab some fresh air?' It was Aidan, standing a few feet away, his eyes full of concern as he wrung his hands. 'I don't know about you, but I need a coffee after that.'

'No thank you.' I struggled into my coat and swung my bag over my shoulder.

'Nell – I know this is hard. But I can look after you. Having to give you that news today made me realise how I feel about you. We've been tiptoeing round the subject for months now. Maybe this could be the making of us? I have that big house all to myself, after all. Let's stop pretending: we're meant to be together . . .'

Incredulously, I turned to look at him. 'Seriously? You're declaring your love for me *now*?'

He mistook my tone for surprise, his confident grin widening as he stepped towards me. 'Yes, baby. Let me look after you. You have to admit this is what we both want . . .'

I couldn't believe what I was hearing. Was Aidan Matthews so deluded that he thought news of my imminent unemployment was a suitable precursor to renewing our relationship?

'Go away, Aidan. I don't think we have anything more to discuss.'

He was staring after me like a dumb animal as I swept out of the office.

I didn't go far: just for a walk around the periphery of the Council office complex, its landscaped grounds curving around the multi-million-pound building that had been the cause of much controversy when it had been built eight years ago. The flat grey sky cast a subdued light over everything and a lack of breeze made the space seem ominously quiet.

This had not been the way I expected today to pan out. In the space of four hours I had assumed I was getting back with Aidan, discovered I was losing my job, unintentionally offended my best friend and then been propositioned by the man who had just sacked me. Not bad going for a Thursday morning. And now, everything hung precariously like question marks suspended in my mind. How did I really feel about this? What was going to happen with my room in the rented house-share? Without a steady income, things didn't look promising. How long could I exist on my redundancy pay?

As I walked around the car park, the idea that had occurred to me before my run-in with Vicky returned – and with it, a sense of injustice that grew the more I considered it. Why *should* I have to obediently sit and wait until I found another job? It might take months to find something else. I only had to watch the news to see how hopeless the jobs situation was right now . . .

I deserve more than this.

I thought about the figure that had been typed on my redundancy letter. As an indication of how much my soon-to-be former employer thought of my contribution to them, it was an insult. But, as an unexpected lump sum, it could be seen as a bit of a windfall. Perhaps it was a sign that my carefully planned life wasn't the best way to live. Perhaps it was an opportunity to do something different . . .

What do you want, Nell Sullivan?

The question presented itself suddenly, stopping me in my tracks. I was hurt and angry and dreading the prospect of being unemployed. I *didn't* want this to be my life for the next however many months it would take to find another job. I wanted something positive, something that would build me up, not drag me down.

I want to do something just for me . . .

And then, it hit me. I could go somewhere – far away from my former job and uncertain future. My trip to New York with Vicky two years ago had been the last time I'd had a proper holiday – the sort that involved plane tickets and duty free, anyway. This could be something just for me. I didn't just want a break from everyday life: I needed an adventure. And while my measly redundancy settlement wouldn't go far to pay my bills, it would make a nice little nest-egg to invest in a trip . . .

It was *brilliant*. I didn't know where I wanted to go, only that I needed to do it – and soon.

The devastated visages of my colleagues brought me heavily back to earth when I returned to the office. Terry's face was grey – although this might have had more to do with the half packet of cigarettes he had just coughed his way through. Dave and Sid, Planning Officers for twenty years each, were sitting like deflated balloon bookends on the edges of Terry's desk. Nick was trying his best to look sympathetic for everyone while clearly relieved he was still employed. Vicky was slumped in her office chair, systematically peeling the layers of French polish from her nails. She didn't look up when I arrived.

'She's back, then,' Terry said. 'We thought you'd legged it.'

'I just needed to get out for a while.'

'Fair enough.'

'Couldn't face seeing the people she sold out,' Vicky muttered, still not looking at me.

'Now *hang on* a minute . . .' I began, but Dave held up his hand.

'It's OK, Sully. She's just upset. We all are.' His smile bore the weight of the world. 'We know Matthews put you in a position.'

'Thank you.'

'You probably shouldn't be standing around chatting.' Connie's expression was one of pure, spiteful delight. 'Management want you out in ten minutes.'

'Who told you that?' Vicky demanded.

'Mr Matthews. While you were in the recruitment agency meeting.' Her grin was about as sincere as a politician's promise. 'There are cardboard boxes in the meeting room. You might want to use them.'

I could feel the resigned despair of my colleagues as we collected the empty copier paper boxes and began to clear the contents of our desks. Packing my box alongside them, I felt a bit of a fraud: yes, it was horrible and scary, but since my revelation I couldn't escape a tiny thrill of excitement dancing around within me. The sensible part of me, which had been in charge for most of my life, was uncharacteristically quiet and for the first time in many years I felt as if the constraints of my life had been removed by this curveball of sudden redundancy.

Out on the street we gathered, a box-toting band of newly unemployed people, not ready to walk away from each other yet secretly not wanting to prolong the agony. After a few mumbled words of solidarity and promises to meet soon for a drink, we dispersed. Vicky sniffed and walked over to me.

'I'm sorry, Nell. I shouldn't have said what I did.'

Relief flooded through me as I hugged her. 'It's OK. You were upset and angry.'

'And also a bitch. But thanks for understanding.' She sighed and looked at the sickly cactus that was poking out from her box of belongings. 'I think I'm going to go straight home. Are you coming to the tube station?'

'No, not yet.' I wanted to pursue the thought in my mind while it still burned, before cold reality had a chance to dawn and spoil the party. 'I just need to – you know . . .' I tilted my head in the direction of the shops in the distance.

Vicky clearly thought I was referring to the pub at the end of the street. 'Don't blame you. Call me tonight when you get home, OK?'

I watched her slumping frame shuffle away and finally allowed myself to feel the excitement that had been steadily building within me. Taking a deep breath, I turned and walked purposefully down the street, my resolve building with each step.

This is it, Nell Sullivan: this is your *time.*

A few blocks down from the Council building, I stopped outside a small travel agency. Its windows were filled with cards promising exciting destinations and deals. It was as if I was staring at a gallery of possibilities, each smiling model asking me the same question:

Where are you going, Nell Sullivan?

A young male sales advisor with startlingly lustrous black hair smiled as I entered, his friendly expression flickering a little when I put my cardboard box on his desk. The bushy fronds of my desk plant spilled over the edge of the box, while my stolen office stapler – one final act of defiance against my now former employer – caught the light from his computer monitor.

'How can I help?' he managed, scrabbling to reconstruct his professionalism. His name badge read: *Hi, I'm Josh*.

'I want to know where I can go for –' I pulled the folded redundancy notice from my jacket pocket and handed it to him to show him the sum my former employer was willing to pay to be rid of me '– *this* much.'

'Um, well, *lots* of places,' Josh stammered, his travel agent training clearly not having covered crazy customers with pot plants and cardboard boxes. 'Where would you like to go?'

I hadn't considered this far ahead in my plan. 'I'm not sure. I want to do something exciting, something just for me. I've just been made redundant, you see.'

'Wow. I'm sorry to hear that. When?'

'About three hours ago.'

'Heck, that's awful. So you definitely deserve a treat.' He smiled and heaved a huge stack of brochures onto his desk. 'OK, let's start with the kind of things you fancy doing on holiday. Beach?'

'No, I don't think so. I want to move about more, I think.'

'No problem.' He pulled out four brochures and dropped them onto the floor by the side of his desk. 'Ski holiday? Watersports?'

'No. I don't mind activities but I don't want to just focus on that.'

'Excellent.' Two more brochures were eliminated from the pile. 'How about a trek? Some kind of adventure trip?'

'Maybe.' I tried to picture myself hiking across the Gobi Desert, or climbing the Great Wall of China. Even with the most optimistic version of myself this seemed a little extreme. 'Actually, no.'

Another brochure was dropped to the brown carpet. 'Good. We're making progress.' After several more questions, Josh's slightly russet features worked into a smile and he held up a thick brochure. 'How about the USA?'

On its cover were Rocky Mountains, Las Vegas signs, bustling cities, New England autumn trees and the majestic sweep of the Grand Canyon. '*America – where anything can happen*' was emblazoned across the images and instantly I felt my heart racing.

'Yes! That looks amazing.'

'Excellent.' Josh nodded and began to flick through the glossy pages. 'So – America pretty much has something for everyone. What do you want to do? Cities? Beach? Fly-drive?'

My mind was racing. 'I – I don't know. Where would you suggest?'

'Personally, I love Vegas. But Florida is great if you want beaches and theme parks. If history's your thing there's New England or Philadelphia. Or how about one of the cities? New York? Chicago? San Francisco . . .?'

'That's it!' I yelled, making Josh jump and a middle-aged female customer at the next desk frown at me. Giggling, I lowered my voice. 'Sorry. My cousin Lizzie lives in San

Francisco. I don't know why I didn't think about it before. I could visit her.'

'Well, it would certainly keep your costs down if you could arrange some of your accommodation.'

'It would.' A thought occurred to me. 'Actually, would you mind if I just made a phone call?'

'Um, sure. Be my guest.' From Josh's expression it was clear this latest development couldn't make his current customer any odder in his eyes.

I checked my watch, mentally calculating the current time in San Francisco. Seven hours behind GMT – so Lizzie would be just getting up. Or at least that was what I hoped. I dialled her number, willing her to pick up. After more rings than were comfortable, the call connected and a sleepy voice spoke.

'Hello . . .?'

'Lizzie, it's Nell. Did I wake you?'

'Who . . .? Oh *Nellie*! Hi! Sorry, I've not had my coffee yet. How are you? Why on earth are you calling me at seven fifteen in the morning? Is everything alright?'

I giggled. 'I'm fine. Well, apart from losing my job today. It's so good to speak to you!'

'You lost your job? Oh Nell, that's terrible! I'm so sorry . . .'

'It's OK, honestly. But I have a bit of a favour to ask – and please say no if it's going to be an imposition . . .'

'Ask away.' I could hear the whirr of a coffee machine in the background and tried to imagine my cousin's apartment in the colourful Haight-Ashbury district of the city that I'd seen from the photos she'd sent with her annual Christmas letter to me.

'I'm going to get some redundancy money and I've decided I want to do something different for a few weeks. How would you feel if I came to visit you?'

The squeal from my cousin reverberated around the travel agency, eliciting another disdainful glance from the disgruntled customer next to me.

'That would be amazing! How long do you want to come for?'

Everything was progressing with such speed that I hadn't even considered how long my adventure was going to last. Plucking a number from thin air, I replied, 'Six weeks?'

'Great. Or why not make it eight?'

'Lizzie, would that be OK?'

'Of course! It'll give you a chance to sightsee and really get a feel for the place. And I can show you around – you can meet my friends and be an honorary San Franciscan!'

Five minutes later, I ended the call. It was happening so fast, but it felt right. My mind was made up – there was no time to waste. 'Right. I'd like to go to San Francisco next week. For two months, please!'

Two months in a brand new city. Two months to experience everything San Francisco had to offer me. Two months to throw caution to the wind and be somebody different to dutiful Nell Sullivan, former Assistant Planning Officer. It was *perfect* . . .

CHAPTER THREE

Pack up your troubles

'You're doing *what*?'

My housemates – Charlotte, Sarah and Tom – were staring at me as if I'd just dyed my hair green. Already suspicious when I'd called a house meeting, they were now sitting like the Three Wise (and Grumpy) Monkeys on the faded IKEA sofa in the living room of our shared house in Woodford. I couldn't blame them for their suspicion: the last time we'd had a house meeting was six years ago to find out which of us knew the slightly odd man who had been sleeping on our sofa since a house party the week before. (It turned out, none of us did – and we had, in fact, been feeding and housing a random bloke who'd wandered in from the street while the party was in full flow . . .)

'I lost my job yesterday. So I'm going to San Francisco for eight weeks,' I repeated, hoping this time they would understand.

They didn't.

'Excuse me?' Sarah crossed her long legs and looked at me like the headmistress she was working hard to become. Her teacher's tone, when inflicted, could reduce a grown man to tears. I had seen this happen on several occasions, more often than not the man in question being her boyfriend Tom, who now appeared to be cowering on my behalf. 'Have you even thought this through? What are you going to do for money once your redundancy payment runs out? And what about your room, Nell? We can't afford to carry *two* people on the dole.'

She shot an accusing look at Tom, who visibly winced. It was common knowledge that Sarah had been supporting him financially since he was laid off from a London advertising agency. Tom's experience of unemployment was another reason why I didn't want to stay in the UK wallowing. He might have been content to spend the last six months in his pyjamas playing X-Box and watching *The Real Housewives of Atlanta*, but it was my idea of hell.

'I am *trying* to get a job,' he protested, sounding more like a whining three-year-old than a tragic victim of the recession. 'It's tough out there. For what it's worth, Nell, I think you've got the right idea. Get out while you can.'

'*Tom . . .*' Sarah growled through gritted teeth, 'you're *not* helping.' She turned back to me. 'If you don't mind me saying, Nell, I think you're being completely irresponsible.'

Charlotte, who up until now had remained silent, folded her arms and nodded in agreement. In all the time we'd shared a house, I hadn't managed to click with her. My latest bombshell was unlikely to change this.

'Well, that's your opinion,' I replied. They had never shown much interest in my life to this point, beyond when rent was due or if I'd been baking. I could hardly expect them to start now. 'But I want to do this. And if it backfires horribly, I'm happy to bear the consequences.'

As if I didn't exist, Charlotte turned to Sarah, flicking her too-straight blonde hair – which, apart from her eyes that seemed to stare directly through your skull, was her only truly remarkable feature. 'Dave could move in.'

'Could he?' Sarah's mood lifted from annoyed to mildly ruffled.

'I think so. He has a *good job* –' she aimed the emphasis directly at me, but I was impervious to it '– he's reliable and he'd make a great housemate.'

'Um, Nell's still here?' Tom said, but Sarah wasn't listening. Clearly Charlotte's suggestion appealed to her. Knowing how much like immature schoolgirls they could be I guessed she was probably already imagining the two couples playing house and co-ordinating a double wedding . . .

Sarah beamed. 'It's *perfect*. When are you moving out, Nell?'

I didn't mind her reaction, or the blatant glee with which Charlotte and Sarah helped me to clear out my room later that day. Of course, Charlotte and Sarah made polite small talk as we worked but I knew we wouldn't miss each other. We had never really bonded anyway – the house-share was nothing more than a sensible choice until I could afford a place of my own. The fact was we only really interacted when we passed in the hallway or occasionally met up when bills needed paying. If we'd been close friends I imagined it could have been harder to leave: as it was, they were surprisingly easy to walk away from.

'Will you miss Woodford?' Dad asked as we drove his packed Volvo through London traffic towards my parents' home in Richmond.

'Not really.'

'Don't blame you, Nelliegirl. Bloody awful place. Besides, your great American adventure awaits!'

I smiled back, loving my dad today even more than usual. When I had told him and Mum yesterday about my San Francisco plans, his first reaction was to congratulate me: 'Splendid! Don't let the Council scum grind you down, darling . . .' Initially I'd wondered how they would take the news that their daughter who'd flown the nest was now creeping back into it, but neither of them batted an eyelid.

Mum fussed around me for the next few days, insisting on washing all of the clothes I planned to take with me and cooking all my favourite meals. It felt good to be surrounded by my parents, even if the sudden lack of personal space was more than a little challenging at first.

Aidan made repeated attempts to contact me, at first leaving voicemail messages, then switching to text messages and finally resorting to missed calls, all of which stacked up on my mobile screen – and all of which I resolutely ignored. I was still angry with him, not least for choosing the day I'd been made redundant to try to make a move on me. I was determined not to think about him while I was away. This was my chance to focus on myself and I wasn't likely to waste it agonising over

Aidan. He'd commandeered far too much of my time already.

As the days passed, I allowed myself to be caught up in the practicalities of my planned trip, worried that if I paused for too long I might end up reconsidering. I was doing this for me, I reminded myself whenever butterflies appeared; this was a good thing.

The day before I was due to leave, I arranged to meet Vicky. She was agog with the news of my sudden decision and concerned that this signalled the beginning of a nervous breakdown or onset of a very early mid-life crisis.

'It can't be a mid-life crisis,' I laughed. 'I'm only thirty-two.'

'It's possible, Nell,' she insisted. 'I was reading in *Cosmo* last week about women who reach thirty and completely change their lives. And there was that incident where you suddenly dyed your hair black last year, remember? Even you had to admit it was a daft decision. Now, I know we've had a setback with losing our jobs, but don't you think this is a little – *extreme* – especially for you? I mean, you're always the one I used to rely on to get us home after a wild night out. You *are* Ms Sensible. I'm a bit worried about this change of direction.'

'I'm just going on holiday,' I replied, handing her a fresh gin and tonic. 'I'm not trying to "find myself" or anything contrived like that. But I've played it safe for six years and never really done anything just for me. I'm not running away. I'm just taking a break.'

Vicky had been almost convinced by this, on one condition: 'Promise you will email me, *every* week. I want to make sure you're OK. More than that, I want to know that you're not squandering this opportunity. So I expect you to squeeze every bit of joy out of the next two months. And I expect *details*, missy. As often as you can.'

I happily agreed, yet again grateful that I had such an amazing support circle around me.

As I lay in bed that night, too excited to sleep, I wondered what the next eight weeks might hold in store for me.

This is it, Nell Sullivan, I told myself. *Tomorrow my adventure begins.*

CHAPTER FOUR

Good morning, San Francisco

'Ladies and gentlemen, we will shortly be approaching San Francisco International airport. Local time is eleven thirty a.m. It's sunny, with a light westerly breeze and the temperature on the ground is a very pleasant twenty-two degrees Celsius. Please fasten your seat belts and place your seats and trays in the upright position . . .'

'Almost home,' smiled the tanned woman in the seat beside me. During the eleven-hour flight from my connection at Paris Charles de Gaulle airport, I had learned that her name was Patti, she was returning to San Francisco after a business trip to Paris and was something big in electronic security systems. When she discovered this was my first time in her city, she had launched into an enthusiastic commentary on all the places I *simply had* to visit: from Alcatraz to the Museum of Modern Art, Macy's to a particular Latino-jazz bar she often frequented in the Mission District. After several waking hours of her tour suggestions, part of me felt as if I knew the city already. 'You're going to have *the best* time, honey. There's nowhere on earth like it.'

I gazed out of the window as the aircraft began a slow, stomach-flipping descent through the white, wispy cloud-bank. The week since my momentous decision in the small Islington travel agency had passed in a blur: giving notice to my startled housemates, moving back in with my even more startled parents, applying for a visa, buying a new suitcase and clothes for my two-month American adventure and avoiding calls from Aidan, who didn't seem to have received the message that I wanted nothing more to do with him. When I'd checked my mobile in Paris waiting for my connecting flight, the number of missed calls from him had been heading towards twenty. I had no intention of speaking to him yet. The next eight weeks of my life were a clean sheet, a chance to start afresh. Once this time was over I would start to think of what was next for me. But right now, Nell Sullivan was about to arrive in San Francisco with no agenda, no plan and no restrictions.

I had been so engrossed in the details and logistics of my brilliant plan that it was only when the plane landed at San Francisco International airport that reality actually hit me. As the plane made its slow taxi along the runways towards the terminals, the sensible side of me (which had been so noticeably absent in my decision-making over the last seven days) made a magnificent return with a hissy fit to end them all.

What am I doing? Why am I blowing all my money on this?

I was going to a place I'd never visited before, to

spend eight weeks with a cousin I hadn't seen for years. Yes, we had been virtually inseparable during our teens, but that was a long time ago. Lizzie had undoubtedly changed and so had I. I hadn't given her much option, calling from the travel agency and more or less holding a gun to her head. What if she had only suggested eight weeks because she felt it was the right thing to do? One thing I knew about my cousin was that she was officially the sweetest being on the planet. Growing up, she would always tie herself in knots rather than offend someone.

In the stuffy confines of the pressurised air cabin, my nerves tipped further on edge as I lurched towards a full-blown panic attack. After we'd brought each other up to speed on our respective lives, what would we talk about then? I realised that for the last couple of years my life had more or less revolved around my job and whether Aidan and I were together or not. Even my beloved baking had taken a back seat, especially given the dubious state of the kitchen in my former house-share. Not only was I leaving all of that behind, but I also had to figure out what would fit in their place. Questions about my future waited at home to be dealt with later, but questions of the next two months of my life lay in wait for me in San Francisco. What if Lizzie wasn't ready to welcome someone who knew so little about herself?

Once my nerves had run themselves sufficiently ragged and we were nearing the terminal building, I began to feel decidedly more positive. Everything would be *fine*, I reassured myself. There was nothing I could do about any of this now – I would have to discover the answers in San Francisco.

Besides, I'd promised Vicky that I would make the most of my time here. Knowing that she was at home facing the horrors of unemployment unsettled me, but she'd insisted I was doing the right thing.

'Don't you worry about me. You need this, Nell. And I need every gorgeous, gory detail you can chuck my way. I'm counting on you to entertain me, OK?'

Standing in the seemingly never-moving line for Immigration at San Francisco airport, I smiled to myself. Only Vicky could make that kind of demand sound like fun.

'First time in San Francisco, Ma'am?' the huge Immigration officer asked, his politeness at odds with the fact that he looked as if he could quite easily snap my neck like a pencil if he wanted to.

'Yes it is.'

He held up my passport, dark eyes beneath his thickset brow flicking between my face and my totally embarrassing passport photo. Just as the scrutiny was beginning to verge on uncomfortable, he handed it back. 'Thank you. Enjoy your trip.'

As heartfelt sentiments go, this wasn't a contender for welcome of the year, but I smiled my thanks and scurried away in case the neck-snapping option began to appeal to him.

Even though I was surrounded by my fellow passengers from England and France, the moment I walked into the baggage hall I knew I was in America. The noise in the cavernous hangar was distinctive in tone, the phrases on the overhead signs a little dissimilar to those at Heathrow or Paris Charles de Gaulle – even the atmosphere of the admittedly impersonal surroundings seemed different.

Emerging from the long tunnel-like walkway into the blast of noise, light and activity, I struggled momentarily to gain my bearings. Scanning along the selection of name signs being held by the barriers, I spotted Lizzie, grinning like a Cheshire Cat on happy gas and brandishing a sheet of card framed in what looked like a cerise feather boa, my name artfully spelled out in multicoloured glitter-glue and sequins. I was struck by how beautifully relaxed she looked. Her wavy blonde hair was loosely pinned up, her sunglasses tucked into it at the crown of her head, and her tanned skin glowed against the loose white blouse and pale blue shorts she wore.

'Nellie!' she yelled, ducking underneath the stretched elastic barrier, shedding bright pink feathers as she went. 'Hi!'

I was hit with the full force of my cousin's embrace as she nearly rugby-tackled me to the shiny-tiled airport floor.

'I'm so glad you're here! How are you? How was the flight? Are you hungry? I bet you're hungry. Well we're catching a cab home so we can pretty much stop anywhere. You just tell me what you fancy and we'll find it. This is San Francisco, after all. *Coffee!* I bet you need coffee. Your first shot of American Joe is always special, trust me . . .' She paused long enough to draw breath and gave me a rueful smile. 'I'm talking too much, aren't I?'

I had to laugh. 'Um . . .'

'Oh I'm sorry. I couldn't sleep last night because I was so excited, so I had my first coffee at five a.m. Consequently, I'm buzzing a bit. So – welcome to San Francisco!'

I laughed. 'Thank you. Nice sign, by the way.'

'It's a bit showbiz, isn't it?' Lizzie giggled and shook the sign, sending a small cloud of glitter and stray feathers fluttering to the floor. 'I told the kids at the after-school club I run about you and they wanted to help. I'll have you know this is a unique, one-of-a-kind welcome sign.'

'Well, I'm honoured.'

'You'll have to come and meet the kids while you're here. They're so excited to meet "another English". You'll feel like a celebrity.' Lizzie took my suitcase and we walked through the terminal building towards the exit. 'Now, we can do whatever you like. I'd recommend not sleeping yet, to lessen the chance of jetlag beating you up. That flight used to slay me every time.'

I was tired – the kind of weariness you feel aching in the very marrow of your bones – but I was also suddenly ravenously hungry. And, like a kid in the early hours of Christmas morning, I was determined not to miss a second of the day that lay ahead. Sleep could wait: I had a brand new city to meet.

Our cab driver, a portly Greek man in his early fifties, introduced himself as Apollo as we pulled away from the airport terminal and joined the lines of traffic heading onto the freeway.

'Your first time in San Fran? You'll love it, lady! I been here sixteen years this fall, and it's the best place I ever lived. Bar none. I make my home here, I meet my wife here, I raise my kids here. It's a special place.'

His dark eyes twinkled as he looked in the rear view mirror at Lizzie and I in the back seat. I smiled back, overwhelmed by the feeling of being at home, despite being a thousand miles away from it.

Warm Californian sun flooded into the car and even though my sudden entry into the middle of the morning in a brand new country had left my brain a little befuddled, the scenery whizzing past the windows was enough to grab my attention. Tall hills rose in the far distance, blue skies arced overhead and everything seemed to catch the sun.

'I can't believe you're here,' Lizzie said, linking her arm through mine. 'It's just so good to see you.'

'You too. It's been too long.'

'It has. But we have eight whole weeks to make up for lost time, so let's make the most of it. Now, I've taken a week off from my piano students, so I can show you around.'

'That's really kind – but are you sure? I know holidays are like gold dust over here.'

My cousin dismissed my concern. 'It will be my pleasure.' Her smile faded a little and she took both my hands in hers. 'Now, honestly, tell me how you are. Losing your job must have been dreadful.'

'I don't know how I am,' I answered truthfully. 'It hurt me that they didn't want me any more but I think I channelled my anger into action to get here. It's going to take some time for me to work through it.'

'Take all the time you need, it's a huge thing to deal

with.' Lizzie squeezed my hands. 'Have you thought about what you want to do while you're here?'

'A little. But I'm up for almost anything. Any suggestions will be gratefully received.'

Lizzie observed me, a sly grin appearing. 'That is not the Nell Sullivan I knew. You were always Miss Five-Year Plan, even when we were growing up. What's changed?'

'My five-year plan has. Which had actually become a six-year plan, without me realising. And then became a *defunct* plan. Up until last week I let it guide my decisions, but now it's been taken away I don't have to stick to the programme any longer. I just want to know what it feels like to have *no* plan – to step out into my life and see what happens.'

'Amazing.' Lizzie stared at me as if seeing her cousin for the first time. 'And what happens if it isn't what you want?'

I shrugged, loving the rush of positivity I felt. 'Then two months isn't a long time to stick it out before I go home and pick up where I left off.'

'You go for it, *glikia mu*,' Apollo interjected. 'You only get one chance to live your life. What's the worst that can happen, eh?'

'Thanks, Apollo,' I replied, as Lizzie buried her face in her neck-scarf to stifle her giggles. 'I'll remember that.'

'All's part of the service.' His super-white smile rivalled the Californian sun for brightness as it flashed at me in the rear view mirror.

Then, suddenly, the glittering cityscape of San Francisco appeared on the horizon and I lost my breath.

'Oh *wow* . . .'

Lizzie smiled and squeezed my shoulder as I sat upright, drinking in the sight. 'There she is. Gorgeous, eh?'

'It's beautiful. I had no idea.'

'I told you it's a special place,' Apollo grinned over his shoulder, before launching into his own commentary on the sights passing by. The pride he had in his adopted city was infectious and soon Lizzie and I were both nodding along to everything he told us as we began to pass through downtown San Francisco streets that appeared to have come straight out of a film.

We turned a corner into a wide street lined with kooky Victorian houses beneath which were a variety of businesses. The street was lined with trees and every shop sign was hand-painted. Elaborately chalked A-boards promised everything from t-shirts, ice cream and herbal teas to vintage records and books, while bright awnings hung over gaudily coloured shop window displays filled with vintage clothing, hand-crafted items and candles, next to restaurants and bars that spilled out onto the broad sidewalk.

'Welcome to Haight-Ashbury,' Lizzie grinned. 'Your home for the next eight weeks!'

The taxi came to a halt outside a three-storey building with two floors of hexagonal-shaped windows above a New Age clothing and music store, which wrapped around the corner of Haight Street and Cole Street. At one side was an enormous rainbow mosaic, which covered the wall to the next shop further up Cole Street, and a large tree on the sidewalk shaded the entrance to the shop. In the far end of the rainbow mosaic was a door covered in a hand-painted mural to look like acacia blossoms climbing over a dark green brick wall.

Lizzie turned and smiled at me. 'Here we are.'

We paid Apollo and I thanked him as he unloaded my suitcase from the boot.

'You have a great time,' he grinned.

'I will, thank you.'

Lizzie laughed as we walked up two flights of stairs to her apartment on the top floor. 'You'll certainly meet a lot of characters like Apollo while you're here.' She opened her front door and ushered me inside. 'Here it is – home sweet home.'

Her apartment was light and airy, the walls painted white to reflect the sunlight streaming in from the hexagonal bay window. Huge abstract art canvases and vintage posters for San Francisco were displayed on the walls and two enormous spherical paper lampshades hung from decorative plaster roses in the ceiling. In the centre of the main living area was a collection of armchairs and a large squashy couch, all draped in patchwork throws made of tiny pieces of printed Indian fabric. A small table and two chairs were nestled in the window bay and a kitchen area was separated from the main room by a teak breakfast bar. An odd collection of ornaments filled the room – the most noteworthy being a rooster on a motorcycle made out of scrap metal and a life-sized cut-out of Wonder Woman. The aroma of roses was everywhere: from bunches of dried blooms suspended from the edges of paintings and rosebud-studded hearts that hung on every door.

Depositing my suitcase by the front door, Lizzie turned

to me. 'Now, I suppose before I show you around, I should tell you about the man in my life.'

This was news to me. 'You have a *man*?'

'Yes, I do. And it's important the two of you get on because you're going to be spending a lot of time together.'

'Lizzie Sullivan, you dark horse! Is he here now?' I peered into the apartment half-expecting her beau to appear.

'He is, as a matter of fact.' She walked over to a vintage sideboard and patted the lid of a blue glass tank, where a small goldfish was swimming.

'Nell, I'd like to introduce you to Pablo.'

I suppressed a giggle. 'Pablo?'

She nodded with mock seriousness. 'Pablo the Goldfish. Sharer of my space, confidant of my secrets, more-or-less-constant companion. In Pablo I have found all the qualities I could want from a man. Apart from – you know – the *obvious* . . .'

'Ugh! That's a mental picture I don't need.'

Her face flushed red. 'No! I mean he can't put out the trash. Or mow the lawn. Not that I have a lawn yet, but . . . OK, I think I've taken that analogy far enough.'

'I think you have. Seriously though, are there any blokes on the scene?'

She shrugged. 'A few dates. Nothing major. How about you? Is that Aidan chap still hanging around?'

'He's the one who told me I was losing my job.'

'Ooh, nasty. And not exactly conducive to romance.'

'Nope.' The memory of Aidan was sharper than I expected. 'He tried calling me before I came out here but I don't think we've anything more to say to each other.'

'Are you sure about that?'

I hoped my answer was believable. 'I think so. But it's fine. It's been a long time coming, really.'

Lizzie hugged me. 'Well I think you're worth more, anyhow. And you're here to have fun, so that's all that matters. Right, let me give you the guided tour of Apartment 24B Cole Street. Which should last approximately thirty seconds. So – this is the kitchen area. I'm hoping for lots of your amazing baking creations to be inspired here. But no pressure! That's the dining area over there and main living room – feel free to sit wherever you like, I don't have a favourite chair. Then the first door on the right is my bedroom, the middle door is the bathroom, which is, thankfully, much bigger than you think it's going to be. And then the last door is your room. It's actually my office but I prefer to work at the table anyway so don't go worrying that you're inconveniencing me. I've put a futon in there, which is really comfy, and I've cleared the closet so you can hang your stuff up. Everything is yours for the next eight weeks, so if you want to watch TV or make yourself some food or coffee, even if it's in the middle of the night, you're welcome to help yourself.'

It was homely and kooky and completely Lizzie – and, considering I had been awake for over twenty-four hours and was now standing in an apartment I had never been in before, I felt surprisingly at home. Seeing my cousin so excited about me spending two months with her went a long way to making me feel like that, but there was also something distinctly familiar about Haight-Ashbury, even from the small amount I had seen during our taxi ride and arriving in Lizzie's neighbourhood. I had a feeling I was going to enjoy living here for the next eight weeks.

'Now sit down and I'll pop the kettle on,' Lizzie said, hurrying into the kitchen. 'We'll go and grab something to eat if you like, but first you need a decent cuppa.' She reached into an overhead cupboard and produced a box of English breakfast tea like it was the most precious gem in the world. 'Mum sends me these,' she said, popping two teabags into a brightly painted teapot. 'I've been able to cope with most changes living in America but decent tea is something I refuse to compromise on.'

'I like your teapot. Did you paint it yourself?'

'No – although I did take a pottery class when I first got here. You know me, always a bit crafty. I made those vases on the bookcase – not bad for a beginner. I bought this in Brighton when I last came home, actually. One of Mum's friends Guin owns a fab pottery studio in Shoreham-by-Sea and I bought this when I met her. Had to smuggle it home in my hand luggage – I think airport security thought I was mad.' She grinned as she filled the teapot and brought it over. 'And now I have three things in my house from England: the tea, the teapot and you.'

Growing up together on the Kent coast before my parents moved to Richmond, Lizzie and I had always been close. I envied her artiness and creativity – she was always making something, learning a new instrument or baking. Where I had swimming lessons and occasionally went horse riding at the local stables, Lizzie's calendar of clubs, groups and lessons for the week was dizzying. Art club, chess club, ballet, jazz dance, drama club, photography class and singing lessons . . . By the time my family moved to Richmond, however, Lizzie's attention had been claimed by two loves: playing piano and baking. While I didn't possess a single musical bone in my body, I did love to bake and that became the activity that bound us together, even when we only saw each other during school holidays. When Lizzie emigrated to the States eight years ago, recipes became our primary form of communication, both of us emailing each other with links to new recipes and photos of our most recent culinary endeavours.

Lizzie now worked as a piano teacher, going into Bay Area schools to teach music classes and tutoring some private students in the neighbourhood. She also ran an after-school baking and crafts club at an elementary school in the Mission District, which had become so successful that three other schools in the city had adopted Lizzie's programme. Because of this she had been asked to advise on after-school programmes for the California Department of Education.

'What's great about it all is that everything I'm doing now happened by chance,' she grinned. 'I offered to do a one-off after-school session at the school in Mission and it all stemmed from that. It isn't what I thought I'd spend my life doing but I can't imagine doing anything else now.'

As she told me about the recent developments of her

life I was immensely proud of my cousin. I remembered how nervous she had been when she first booked her gap year trip to the States; how, nine days into her adventure, she had reverse-charge called me in tears, insisting that she'd made the biggest mistake of her life, was almost broke already and wanted to come home. But then she had a chance meeting with a travelling music and theatre company who were visiting a school in the town where she was staying. When they heard her play they invited her to join them. The wealthy organisation funding the company arranged Lizzie's Green Card and within a year she was a fully-fledged American citizen. She had settled in San Francisco after falling in love with the city while on tour – and looking at her now I honestly couldn't imagine her living anywhere else.

'This is a bit weird, catching up on large amounts of our lives, isn't it?' she asked. 'I mean, it's great, but it's only when we talk about it that I realise how many years it's been since we last did this.'

'I like what I'm discovering, though. You've done so well.'

'Aw, thanks hun. And so have you.'

I stared at her. 'Hardly. I've just lost my job – thanks to my ex who I had mistakenly assumed I was about to get back together with. I've moved back with my parents and when I get home I have to start looking for a new job at a time when so many people are unemployed.' When I said it out loud, I realised I didn't really have much to show for the last six years of my life. 'That's why it feels good to be here. Like I'm doing something positive.'

Lizzie put her arm around me. 'You *are* doing something positive. You can take your life in whatever direction you can from this point on. I think it's exciting.'

'It is. And terrifying not to know what's coming next. But I'm lucky to have my lovely family to support me. Thanks Lizzie.'

'My pleasure! So how do you feel about living back with your mum and dad?' Groaning, she slapped her hand against her forehead. 'Forgive me. What a daft thing to ask.'

'Don't apologise, it's a valid question. Actually, I think I'm fine. It was a bit difficult losing my personal space and all that, such as it was – but they've been brilliant.'

Lizzie offered to refill my mug but I declined. 'And how did your housemates take the news?'

I grimaced. It hadn't been the easiest conversation I'd ever had but that was more to do with the fact they were going to be a quarter down on the bills than without someone they had shared a home with for five years.

'They were a bit annoyed, obviously. And I think Sarah thought I was mad. But I don't think they'll miss me. They're all nice people but it was more like being in university halls than living with great friends.'

During the flight to San Francisco, I'd had time to reflect a little on my life. So much had changed since the day I lost my job but one thing I had realised was how little life I had actually lived before then. Everything had been a means to an end, an 'I'll-be-happy-*when*' existence, as if I was holding on until the good stuff arrived. I had always been the sensible one, the girl who could answer the 'where do you see yourself in five years' time' question at job interviews without stopping to think about it.

So I'd moved into the dreary house-share in Woodford with people I had nothing in common with other than a shared kitchen and desire to live near a tube station, because it was the sensible choice, allowing me to save for a place of my own while I rented. I had taken a job in the well-respected London Borough Council and had remained there for six years, waiting for the next opportunity to arise. It made sense to stay there until I found something else. Or until Aidan and I decided to be together permanently, when two wages coming in each month might offer a little leeway for something else.

Even though I had a secret dream career that bore no resemblance to planning law or development permissions, I hadn't allowed myself to consider it because it was risky and had serious potential to fail. *When* I'd saved enough . . . *when* I was in a better position to make the leap . . . *when* I felt ready . . . then I might allow myself to pursue it.

But losing my job had thrown everything into question: it had removed my sensible living arrangements, challenged my savings and absolutely, definitely, ruled out any future with Aidan Matthews. I was already in a risky situation with no guarantee of anything other than unemployment and two months to do whatever I wanted to. Given this, the playing field was open wide and *anything* was now possible . . .

Lizzie squeezed my arm. 'I'm going to make sure you have the best time here. And we'll start by getting you something to eat.'

If my grumbling stomach could have whooped for joy it would have done so with gusto at that moment. 'That's a fantastic idea. Where are we going?'

Lizzie's broad smile seemed to illuminate the room. 'Only the *best* place in the neighbourhood! I'm taking you to Annie's.'

CHAPTER FIVE

Welcome to the neighbourhood

There are times in your life when you find yourself in exactly the right place. It might not make sense at the time, but deep down inside you feel it: you were always meant to be there, on that date, at that time. Walking into Annie's diner on my first day in San Francisco felt like one of those moments.

Annie's was everything I'd hoped a true American diner would be. Nestled on the corner of Haight and Clayton Streets, it was a neighbourhood hub that had been feeding the good people of The Haight for nearly forty years. From the outside it was unremarkable, save for the pink and blue neon signs hung in its wide windows, which wrapped around the corner that joined the two streets. The wood panelled frontage was painted the colour of very milky coffee and bore the scars and scrapes of years of weather, traffic and city air. Had it been in England, it would probably have been dismissed as a 'greasy spoon' café and avoided. But here in San Francisco, its time-earned war wounds of standing proud in the city merely added to its charm. I could imagine a scene from a US cop drama set here – where the hard-bitten detective would arrange a secret rendezvous with one of his illicit moles, dishing the dirt on a crime gang over huge stacks of pancakes and coffee so strong it could melt spoons . . .

Lizzie laughed when she saw me taking in all the details of Annie's exterior. 'Your face – anyone would think I'd taken you to Disney World for the first time. It's *just* a diner. A great diner, mind you, but still a regular, Stateside eatery.'

Now it was my turn to giggle. 'You said *eatery* . . . You're such a Yank now!'

But Lizzie was wrong. Annie's was so much more than just a diner. I was later to learn what an institution it was in the community and how even people who had moved out of The Haight faithfully made the pilgrimage back here every weekend for brunch. The whole building smelled of coffee, sugar, vanilla, the delicious aroma of pancakes and frying steak, which wrapped around our nostrils. We approached the polished chrome counter, where customers were hunched on bottle-green leather bar stools over enormous cups of black coffee and gargantuan portions of food that made your eyes water as much as your mouth. Faded black and white photographs of past customers and staff peppered the red-painted walls, the smiling faces and bulging brunch plates in them no different from those filling the diner today. It was as if history hung heavily around the current customers, the eyes of the past bestowing their blessings on the faces of the present.

'I've been coming here since my first weekend in San Francisco,' Lizzie said. 'You have to try the French toast – it's pretty much legendary in The Haight.'

'Hey Lizzie! You on a loyalty bonus from Annie now?' shouted a broad-backed, balding man from the far edge of the counter.

Sat next to him, a man of similar build with an impressive bushy beard but less hair chuckled. 'Yeah – she's on a short-stack bonus. One more customer introduced and she finally makes the three-stack!'

'You wish,' my cousin called back, as several other diners raised their heads in greeting. 'Marty, Frankie, this is my cousin Nell from England. She's here for a couple of months so you'd better get used to another Brit in the joint.'

Marty – the one *sans* beard – raised his hand in greeting. 'Well hello, Nell-from-England. This your first time here?'

'It is, yes.'

'You gotta be gentle with her, Marty,' Frankie said, wiping ketchup from his beard with a paper napkin. 'Annie'll skin ya alive if you spook any more customers outta here. Nell, nice to meet ya. Don't you listen to a word Marty says and you'll fit right in.'

I laughed. 'I'll remember that, thanks.'

A couple moved from a table near the counter and Lizzie grabbed it quickly. 'Marty and Frankie are cab drivers,' she informed me, holding a menu up to her face to shield her words, 'and our resident philosophers. Anything you want an opinion on, they're your men.'

I looked at the considerable array of options on the

laminated menu card, which wouldn't have looked out of place on the tables of Al's Diner in *Happy Days*. 'Wow, when you said French toast was big here you weren't kidding. *Seventeen* varieties?'

'Oh yes. And every one of them *awesome*.' Lizzie's expression reminded me of years before when our families would meet for Pancake Day tea. Out of the two of us, Lizzie had always possessed the sweet tooth, which made her extremely easy to buy birthday and Christmas presents for. I never saw her happier than when she was about to consume obscene amounts of sugar. 'You should try all of them, of course, but my favourite is Banana Maple Walnut. Unbelievable. Some nights I actually wake myself up dreaming of it.'

'I'll give that a go then. And a cup of coffee, please.'

'Oh don't worry about that. You get coffee here even if you haven't ordered it.' She righted the upturned mugs on our table. 'And coffee here is the best.' She looked up as a young waitress approached us. 'Hey Laverne. This is my cousin Nell from England.'

Laverne stuffed her order pad into the waistband of her apron and shook my hand. 'Hi! Lizzie's told me so much about you!'

'She has?' Her enthusiastic welcome took me a little by surprise.

'I was telling Laverne about that amazing chocolate orange cheesecake you used to make when we were teenagers, do you remember?'

It had been a long time since I had last thought of that, but instantly memories of consolation cheesecake afternoons at my house after inevitable teenage breakups rushed back. 'Yes, I do. We ate a lot of cheesecake after all our disastrous relationships.'

Laverne smiled. 'I'm, like, a total baking fan. You have to give me the recipe before you go back to England.'

'No problem. If I can remember it, that is. I haven't baked in a while.'

'Thank you so much! So, what can I get you guys?'

'One Banana Maple Walnut, one Nutella Pomegranate please.' Watching Lizzie ordering struck me how utterly San Franciscan my cousin had become. The inflection of her voice now had a characteristic West Coast upward flick and she was relaxed and happy.

'Sure thing. I'll go grab the coffee pot for you guys. And hey, I'll tell Annie you're here. She'll bust a gut to meet you!'

When she left us, I leaned closer to Lizzie. 'Annie? Is that *the* Annie?'

'The very same. Founded this place thirty-seven years ago and still going strong. You'll love her.'

'I'm looking forward to it already.'

Lizzie folded her hands on the checkerboard tabletop. 'So what's this about you not baking, Nellie? You baked all the time when we were kids.'

I relaxed back into the squashy booth seat. 'Recently I just haven't done it. Not since Aidan and I – since the last time we were together.'

My cousin frowned. 'But you didn't just bake for him. It's always been your thing, hasn't it?'

It made me uncomfortable to be thinking about Aidan, especially as I had tried so hard *not* to think about him over the last week. 'I think after the last attempt between us failed I shelved everything that reminded me of him. I wanted to be someone different, I suppose. I was sick of the merry-go-round of our relationship.'

'I can understand that. But, you know, my kitchen is your kitchen while you're here. So if you get the urge to bake again you're more than welcome.'

I laughed as her veneer of innocence completely failed to cover the ulterior motive. 'Oh and I suppose it wouldn't be too much of an imposition if you had to eat whatever I made?'

Busted, she giggled. 'Maybe it wouldn't be the *worst* thing . . .'

Laverne returned with a jug of freshly brewed coffee and filled our huge coffee cups. 'Here you go. Annie's house coffee, Golden Grain.'

Puzzled, I looked at Lizzie. 'But coffee isn't made from grain.'

Laverne giggled. 'You know that and I know that. It's one of the mysteries about this place. Enjoy,' she chirped as she left us.

My first cup of American coffee smelled good and tasted like heaven, although it was considerably stronger than the filter coffee I was used to in the Planning Department – even when caffeine-fan Terry was making it. The memory of my former colleagues brought a glimmer of sadness to the pit of my stomach. I wondered how they were all doing. I made a mental note to ask Lizzie if I could email Vicky when we returned to her apartment.

'So I hear the Brit invasion is happening?'

I looked up from my two-pint coffee mug to see the

half-smile of a diminutive woman of uncertain years. Her hair was dyed the colour of a new penny and her white smile glowed against the warm caramel of her skin. She had a red pencil behind one ear and several gold chains were arranged about her neck. Dressed in a black polo shirt several sizes too large for her that had *Annie's* emblazoned in red embroidery on the front, black skin-tight jeans and leopard print pumps, she possessed a presence so all-encompassing that it was as if the sunlight streaming in from the diner windows dimmed a little in reverence.

'Hey. I'm Annie Legado. I own this place.'

'Hi. I'm Nell.' I wasn't sure whether I should curtsey or bow in her presence. Instead I extended my hand and she shook it, her grip surprisingly strong for her slight frame.

'You look like Lizzie. How long you here for?'

'Two months.'

She nodded, the strange almost-smile still in place. 'Two months is good.'

'So that means we have two months to turn my cousin into a fully-fledged San Franciscan, Annie,' Lizzie grinned.

Annie drew in a breath through her teeth, like the sound a mechanic makes just before he tells you how much your car repairs will cost. 'Tall order. But I guess we'll try.' She slapped the back of my seat. 'You ladies have a good day.' And with that, she was gone.

I stared at Lizzie. 'She is one scary woman.'

'Wait till you get to know her. I think the term you'll choose then is *indomitable*. You can see why her business has survived as long as it has. Nobody would dare to take it away from her.'

The buzz in Annie's was incredible, with several conversations crossing the room. A young couple dressed entirely in black with pale faces and matching Goth make-up at one end of the counter were happily conversing with Marty and Frankie at the other, comments occasionally moving to the opposite side of the diner where a woman with three small children was seated. Annie stalked the room like a stealthy lioness, dipping her head into conversations at every table as she went, nodding with her trademark half-smile before moving on.

Lizzie nudged me. 'So, do you like Annie's?'

I knew that I was grinning although I couldn't tell whether this was due to a chronic lack of sleep, the power of turbo-caffeine racing through my body or simply the thrill of being here. 'It's wonderful,' I replied. 'Surreal, but wonderful. Two weeks ago I was losing my job and now I'm in San Francisco in a real-life American neighbourhood diner. For the first time in my life I don't have a clue what will happen next. And it feels good.'

'O-K, we got one Banana Maple Walnut, one Nutella Pomegranate.' Laverne handed us oval plates so big that two of them barely fit on the table. '*En-joy.*'

A gargantuan mountain of buttery toast triangles nestling between a blanket of banana slices, dusted in icing sugar and swimming in a glistening pool of maple syrup gazed oozily up at me. It was truly a sight to behold.

'Are all the varieties of French toast here *this* big?' I asked, staring at my plate.

'Yup. Actually, compared to some other diners I've been to that's a small portion.'

I wondered if my arteries were going to hate me for dragging them across the Pond to be assaulted by this amount of fat. But as this was the first day of my American odyssey, I reasoned it was only right I made an effort. Although, if the food was going to be this amazing for the next eight weeks, I realised I would have to make sure I upped my exercise while I was here to stop me returning to the UK looking like Jabba the Hutt after a slave binge.

An hour later, Lizzie and I struggled out onto the sidewalk in the bright sunshine. My stomach felt as if it had dropped several inches and was now snoozing somewhere around my knees.

Lizzie gave a loud groan. 'I was going to suggest we catch the Muni home, but given the amount of food we just ate, I think a walk might be good.'

'A walk would definitely be good.'

We crossed the street and walked for several blocks, passing a church and multicoloured wooden buildings. The sound of the traffic mingled with birdsong from the trees lining the pavements and at one corner we could hear the enthusiastic rhythms of a drummer practising in his apartment. Walking further still, we reached a grand stone staircase leading up into a park.

'It's a bit of a scramble up here, but I promise you, the views are worth it,' Lizzie puffed, as the after-effects of our enormous brunch laboured our breathing. 'This is Buena Vista Park. I didn't even know it existed for the first two years I lived here. But then quite a few of the people who help out at my after-school club are San Francisco natives and they didn't know about it either.'

The park was more of a wooded hill, with pathways disappearing off into the trees around us. We passed a couple of people walking dogs and a tramp asleep on a bench, but besides them the park was largely empty. It seemed surprising to find this in the middle of a city and as soon as the trees overhead blocked the view down to the road I could have believed I was out in the wilds. Birdsong surrounded us and the wind rustled through swaying branches and these became the only sounds, spoiled a little by the puffing and groaning from two overfed women struggling up the hill.

When we reached the summit we flopped down to catch our breath, Lizzie flinging herself dramatically back onto the sun-baked grass in the clearing.

'You'd think, after so long living here, that my stomach would know its limits,' she said, patting her belly, which made the long glass bead necklaces around her neck tinkle together. 'But no. One trip to Annie's and my resolve disintegrates.'

'That French toast is amazing. How on earth do you manage not to be the size of a house?'

'I walk. A lot. And with the schools work, my music lessons and all the other things I don't tend to sit down for very long most days.'

'You look amazing. So West Coast.'

My cousin giggled. 'Why, thank you, Ma'am. You look great too, Nellie. Happier. It's a good look on you. Now,' she struggled back to her feet and took my hand to drag me up, too, 'you need to see the real reason we came up here. Just look at *that* . . .'

I followed her pointing finger and my breath caught.

Out beyond the sprawl of the city far below us, an expanse of azure blue water curved beneath a distinctive, vivid red structure spanning its width.

'It's the Golden Gate Bridge!'

It was beautiful – a scene so familiar from TV programmes and films but breathtaking in real life.

'And the most beautiful bay in the world.' Lizzie linked her arm through mine. 'I promise you, these eight weeks are going to be the making of you.'

Standing there, with the beautiful San Francisco Bay glistening in the midday sun, I couldn't do anything but agree. This was going to be the holiday of a lifetime . . .

CHAPTER SIX

Down and out in San Francisco

Jetlag is a strange and curious animal. After going to bed just before seven p.m. when my drooping eyelids refused to allow me to stay up any longer, I awoke bolt upright at five a.m. and couldn't go back to sleep. For the next four hours I drifted around Lizzie's apartment like an aching spectre, lurching between weariness and heart-pounding alertness. I knew I should be sleeping but my body wouldn't allow me to, my mind too alive with thoughts racing unceasing circuits.

I made myself a cup of tea and logged onto Lizzie's computer in my makeshift bedroom. As I hoped, I'd received an email from Vicky. It was sitting on top of five unopened emails from Aidan, the subject line identical on all of them:

Nell – please read this

If I'd thought ignoring his calls and texts would be enough to stop him contacting me I was wrong. The cursor hovered over his name on the screen. Maybe I would open them when my body felt less like a zoned-out punch-bag . . . For now, I needed something positive from home.

From: vickster1981@me-mail.com
To: nell.sullygirl@gmail.com
Subject: ARE YOU THERE YET?

Hey Nell

Well, are you? I tried to work out the time difference but gave up when I realised my brain wasn't playing ball. Is it possible to still have pregnancy brain two and a half years after giving birth? Greg thinks I've lost the plot worrying about you. He says you'll be fine. I know he's right but I still need to hear from you.

EMAIL me, woman!

Big love

Vix xxx

Smiling, I typed a reply:

From: nell.sullygirl@gmail.com
To: vickster1981@me-mail.com
Subject: Stop worrying – I'm here!

Hi Vix

Stop worrying – I made it!

I still can't believe I'm here. Lizzie's place is really cool. It's in Haight-Ashbury – which everybody calls 'The Haight' – and it's where the hippies were in the Summer of Love. There's still the odd hippy about and the shops are all little bit alternative and quirky. I like it: it reminds me a little of Camden, although people smile more.

I've also made my first trip to a real-life American diner. Lizzie took me to Annie's – and seriously, Vix, it's like something out of a movie. The food is phenomenal and it has a fantastic atmosphere. It really brought the spirit of the city home to me today and even though I've not yet been here twenty-four hours, I know I was right to come to San Francisco. If nothing else, I'll have happy memories to look back on when I start job-hunting again.

Talking of job-hunting, how's it going? Any luck on that front? And have you heard from any of the others? Really hope things are looking brighter for you, hun. At least you have Greg and gorgeous little Ruby to make you smile. I'm keeping everything crossed for you.

Better go. I'll email again tomorrow.

Love ya

Nell xxx

It felt strange to think that my friend was so far away – along with everything else in my life. Thinking about home made my stomach tighten. I had eight weeks to figure out what I was going to do and all of a sudden that felt like an inordinately long time to be away. I was just beginning to panic when a new email flashed onto the screen:

From: vickster1981@me-mail.com
To: nell.sullygirl@gmail.com
Subject: Re: Stop worrying – I'm here!

Woo-hoo!

I am so glad you made it safely! I've been driving Greg mad since you left, listening to the news in case there were any reports of air crashes or earthquakes. You know me: always cautious. The thing is, I need you to have a good time but most importantly I NEED YOU TO COME HOME IN EIGHT WEEKS. Being unemployed is doing my head in and I need our chats.

I have an appointment with a careers advisor tomorrow. A careers advisor, Nell! At 32! It's like being 16 again and I'm dreading it. I feel like such a failure. Even though I could've been Britain's best planning officer and it wouldn't have made any difference to me losing my job. Apart from Brown-Nosed Connie, I don't think any of us could have done it differently. And I wasn't willing to get carpet burns on my knees to secure my career prospects, if you get what I mean . . . ☺

I need updates as often as you can send

them. And for heaven's sake, have FUN. Then at least one of us will be and I'll have something to read other than my mother's discarded copies of *Star* magazine. I'd rather obsess over your trip than whether or not Kerry Katona's had Botox.

Love ya lots
Vix xxx

It was so good to hear from my friend and the joy of reading her words coupled with my current fragile state brought tears to my eyes.

'Hey early-bird.' Lizzie's smiling face appeared around the door. 'I thought you'd still be dead to the world.'

I wiped my eyes quickly. 'I probably should be. But my body had other ideas. I was checking my emails – hope that's OK?'

'Of course it is. So, ready for your first day exploring San Francisco?'

I nodded. 'Absolutely!'

The sun bathed Haight-Ashbury, making every colour brighter and giving the streets a carnival atmosphere. As we wandered along the streets and in and out of the shops, people stopped to greet us – Lizzie providing the introductions:

'This is Anya – I teach her daughter piano . . . Marcella was one of my first students when I started teaching here . . . Stanley's son Karl is my star pupil . . .'

'Have you taught everyone in Haight-Ashbury?' I giggled when the fifth person had stopped us to say hello.

Lizzie blushed. 'It looks like it, doesn't it? This is a very close neighbourhood and I've had a lot of recommendations over the years. I've been very lucky.'

'They're certainly friendly,' I said, still coming to terms with the very tactile welcomes of complete strangers. I had been hugged by four of the five people we had met that morning and was feeling a little out of my depth.

'Ah yes, I forgot to warn you about that. It took me a while to feel comfortable with the hugs. People here have a different understanding of personal space than they do in London. Don't worry, though, you get used to it.'

I wasn't convinced. Having my personal space invaded by random people was a shock to the system. Even the homeless guys – who were present on almost every corner and street crossing – would step into our path and say hello. The homeless issue was a surprise to me, largely because nobody had told me how overt it was in San Francisco. Mostly men, they were polite and not threatening but there were so many of them for such a relatively small area. Already today we had encountered four men shaking paper cups on the street and I found it unsettling when Lizzie advised me to walk past them. In London I would always stop to buy a *Big Issue*, but the sellers there were far less willing to follow you down the street than the homeless guys were here. After a couple of hours I ducked my head whenever I heard a cup shaking, feeling awful for doing so.

I think Lizzie must have sensed my unease because she grabbed my arm when we had completed a large loop of the neighbourhood and were walking back towards her apartment.

'Right. I'm taking you somewhere where you won't be hugged, hounded or stalked. Come with me.'

She had stopped outside the ebony-black frontage of a coffee shop, its windows dressed in swathes of purple velvet with the name *Java's Crypt* painted in spidery silver letters above.

I stared at it. 'It looks like a funeral parlour.'

'Appearances can be deceptive. You'll love it.'

Java's Crypt was the kind of place you would run for the hills to avoid in the UK, but here in San Francisco its presence on Haight Street made perfect sense, despite being slightly scary to walk into at first. I could imagine Edgar Allan Poe feeling right at home in its black and purple interior, sipping his iced Java latte beneath silver spider's web lampshades in booths bedecked with purple velvet and black lace. The coffee shop (or 'caffeine lair' as Lizzie told me its owner preferred) was buzzing with a diverse mix of clientele, from members of the Goth community to loudly dressed American tourists, Chinese families and kookily attired locals. It was a surprise to see so many people who ordinarily would avoid each other sitting together in apparent harmony.

We approached the black ash serving counter and I jumped as a tall, black-haired man with a deathly pale face and all-black clothes rose from behind it, looming ominously over us. I was about to turn and run when his black-lined eyes wrinkled and a broad smile spread across his purple stained lips.

'Yo Lizzie! Haven't seen you in a while.'

'Hey Ced.' To my surprise – and amusement – my cousin and the happy Goth greeted one another with a respectful fist-bump. 'I thought I should introduce my cousin to the delights of your establishment.'

His pale blue eyes flicked to me. 'Hey, Lizzie's cousin.'

'Hi – I'm Nell.'

He held out his fist, the black leather and silver bangles wobbling around his slim wrist. Following Lizzie's example I offered a tentative fist-bump. It certainly made a refreshing change from the over-friendly hugs I'd been receiving.

'Good to meet you. I'm Ced. Welcome to Java's Crypt. What can I get you?'

'We'll have two of your Peruvian filter coffees please,' Lizzie smiled.

'Cool. Listen, find a booth and I'll bring it over.'

'Come here often?' I whispered to Lizzie when we were sitting down. 'I didn't have you pegged as a Goth.'

She laughed. 'I'm not – as most of the customers in here aren't. Ced's wife Autumn is one of my piano students. And they're good friends.'

Five minutes later, Ced arrived with our coffee, together with a huge slice of white and dark chocolate-swirled baked cheesecake. 'From Autumn,' he explained, sitting next to Lizzie. 'She said she'd been telling you about it?'

Lizzie's expression was one of pure joy and I had to laugh despite my slight unease in Ced's company. 'She did! We spent most of last week's lesson talking about this amazing recipe.'

'Your weapons of choice, ladies.' Ced produced two forks and presented them to us. 'So, Nell, how long are you visiting for?'

'Eight weeks.'

He seemed impressed by this. 'Big US adventure, huh?'

I took a forkful of delicious cheesecake and nodded. 'Something like that.'

'Nell just lost her job in the UK, so she's come out here to have fun,' Lizzie offered, which surprised me. I must have been staring at her because her smile suddenly vanished. 'Sorry hun. But that is why you're here.'

'It's fine, I'm just –' I looked at Ced. 'Forgive me. I'm still getting used to how forward everyone is here.'

The Goth smiled. 'It's cool. And hey, good call. I'm in this city because I lost my job, actually.'

'You are?'

He nodded. 'Ten years ago this July. Believe it or not I used to be a lawyer in New York City.'

The thought of Ced as a suited lawyer was incredible, given his appearance. 'Wow.'

He waved a pale hand. 'It's OK, Nell, you have my permission to laugh. I find it hilarious myself. Hard to believe I was the golden boy of Jefferson Jones and Associates on Wall Street for two years. Golden in more ways than one, actually. This,' he wound a strand of jet-black hair around his fingers, 'is, unsurprisingly, not my natural colour.'

His dry sense of humour made me smile and I began to relax a little. 'I like it,' I replied. 'How come you ended up in San Francisco?'

'I got fired. For nothing more than the fact that one of the partners decided to hate me. And that was it for law and me. I walked around Central Park for hours, thinking about how much of my life I'd given to my career – and how fruitless it had proved to be. So, I made a decision. I quit my apartment, trashed my business suits and moved to the West Coast with one suitcase and my guitar. I busked around for a while, met Autumn at a beach gig in Santa Monica, we settled here and within two years I'd opened Java's Crypt.'

I was amazed by his story but also encouraged that he had achieved so much from such inauspicious beginnings. If it had happened for Ced, could it happen for me? 'That's really good to hear.'

'This town is a place for adventurers, Nell. There ain't nothing you can't do here if you work hard at it.'

As we were speaking one of the homeless men Lizzie and I had encountered that morning entered the coffee shop. I felt every muscle tense in my shoulders: in London this situation usually was a precursor to an ugly scene. Calmly, Ced left our table and walked over to greet the man.

'Hey brother, what can I do for ya?'

'You got any coffee on hold?' the man asked, his voice gruff and low.

'Sure, man. Come over to the bar.'

I watched as the man accompanied Ced to the counter, where the coffee shop owner made him a large coffee. Thanking Ced, the man shuffled out, tipping his baseball cap to us as he went. I turned to Lizzie, confused by what I'd seen.

'What just happened?'

Lizzie smiled. 'That happens a lot here. People buy a coffee to take out and one "suspended". It then means that when the homeless guys come in they have a drink already paid for. It doesn't happen everywhere, but it's something Ced has always done since he opened this place.'

I was quickly learning that this was a city that made no bones about itself. Everything was presented just as it was – good and bad, beautiful and not-so-attractive. It was brash and bold and would definitely take some getting used to.

By the time we returned to Lizzie's apartment I felt as if I'd gone eight rounds with a heavyweight boxer. Succumbing to the jetlag still pummelling my body, I slept for another couple of hours and when I woke I checked my emails, the familiar task comforting. And then I don't know why, but I clicked on the latest email from Aidan. Despite my best efforts earlier that day to convince myself I didn't want to hear from him, the temptation to know what he had to say was too great. As soon as I opened it, however, I wished I hadn't:

From: a.matthews@me-mail.com
To: nell.sullygirl@gmail.com
Subject: Nell – please read this

Nell

I feel terrible. I wish we could talk so I could tell you all this in person. But you won't return my calls and seem to have disappeared off the face of the planet, so this is the best I can do.

I hated giving you the news about your job and I hated even more that you left before I had a chance to explain.

I fought for you, honestly I did. I tried everything I could to save your job. But I couldn't change their minds. And now the office is like a morgue and you're not here. And I miss you.

I know I was an idiot to say what I said about us. But it's still true. Being without you for the past week has only strengthened how I feel. I love you, Nell. I'm going to email you every day until I get an answer. Because I know you feel it too.

You're angry now – I get that. But look in your heart. Can you honestly say you don't want us to be together?

We've been through too much for this not to happen. I'm not giving up on us.

I love you.

Aidan xx

Angrily, I logged out. I didn't want to know that Aidan was hurting too and I certainly didn't want to feel the glimmer of hope it gave me. Suddenly I was stuck in limbo between the newness of San Francisco that I didn't yet feel a part of and the aspects of my old life I was trying to leave. I decided to ignore the other messages waiting unread in my inbox. Reading any more of Aidan's words while I was here wouldn't solve anything, only leave me with more questions. I was still angry with him for making me redundant and then trying to get back with me. Besides, I wanted to use the time I had here to think about the future and how I fitted into it. Whether

Aidan could – or should – ever be a part of my life again was something I wasn't ready to consider yet.

While I had been sleeping, Lizzie had been busy. Keen to make me feel more a part of her city she had invited her friend Eric to join us for dinner.

'You'll love him,' she promised me, dashing around her tiny kitchen as she prepared food. 'If anyone can cheer you up, Eric can.'

Eric Walker was a six-foot bundle of pure energy, from the cheeky grin playing on his face to his ever-moving hands which he used to accentuate every word. Even sitting at Lizzie's dining table he didn't keep still, animatedly jumping from anecdote to anecdote. Originally from Dagenham in Essex, Eric had come to San Francisco for a year and ended up with a lucrative job entertaining visitors at Pier 39 with his unique blend of British humour, circus skills and crazy unicycle riding – which he was still doing fifteen years later. It was wonderful to meet him and especially lovely to talk to another British person, even if his accent had adopted a noticeable West Coast twang.

'If I'd stayed in the UK I'd be an accountant by now,' he told me, after reducing me to tears of laughter by juggling various ornaments from Lizzie's living room. 'That's what my dad wanted me to be. Instead I'm in San Francisco, where juggling swords while balancing on a unicycle is perfectly acceptable. I make a good wage from the daily shows and teach circus skills to private students – most of which are accountants, lawyers and bankers. Can you imagine me doing that for a living in Dagenham?'

Watching Lizzie's friend performing his impromptu

routine I found it hard to imagine Eric wading through tax returns in an office.

'So Lizzie tells me you've had a tough day?' he asked, when Lizzie was in the kitchen dishing up dessert.

'Not really. I've just felt a bit out of place. Everything's different here: crossing the road, ordering a cup of coffee, even buying things in shops.'

Eric laughed. 'Don't worry, we all go through it. Listen, have you been to Fisherman's Wharf yet?'

'No, I only arrived yesterday. But it's on my list of places to visit.'

'Excellent!' He grabbed a handful of cutlery and began to juggle it, making me laugh again. 'Why don't you two come and see my show tomorrow? You'll love Pier 39. It reminds me of summer holidays in Southend and Bournemouth when I was a kid.' He added a pepper grinder to the collection of tumbling knives and forks – chuckling when a cloud of pepper dust covered his lap. 'Trust me, it's impossible to feel out of place there. Lizzie, what do you reckon?'

Lizzie returned to the table with enormous bowls of ice cream sprinkled with tiny Oreo cookies. 'I think it's a great idea, but this is Nell's trip.'

By now I was laughing so hard I had to struggle to catch my breath, feeling so much better already. Eric's suggestion sounded like the perfect choice.

'Yes – let's do it!'

CHAPTER SEVEN

Cable cars and seaside jazz

Next morning we made our way down to Fisherman's Wharf. Eric had recommended a great place for lunch and suggested it was worth spending time wandering along the Bayside streets to soak in the atmosphere before we visited his afternoon show.

'I really like Eric,' I said to Lizzie as we walked past the numbered piers stretching out into the San Francisco Bay. 'How did you come to meet him?'

'He was teaching circus skills in one of the schools I teach piano at. My friend Tyler introduced us – he's the principal of Sacred Heart Elementary where my after-school kids' club meets. I think his exact words to me were, "we have another crazy Brit here you should meet". Of course, he expected me to know Eric simply by virtue of the fact we both hailed from the same country. You'll notice Americans think that *a lot*. As it turned out, we got on instantly and he became a really good friend. Actually, it was because of Eric's work with the children that I was inspired to start the club, so I have a lot to thank him for.'

Restaurants and food stalls selling fresh crab, clam chowder, hot dogs and seafood lined the seafront, the scent of cooking food surrounding us as we walked past gift shops (stacked with jokey t-shirts, souvenirs and cheap sunglasses), brightly painted coffee stalls, bicycle hire companies and electrical goods stores. I breathed it all in, feeling decidedly more positive than I had yesterday, the innate sense of fun making me grin like a big kid.

On every street corner, we passed buskers playing. Their music styles were as varied as the food stalls they were often performing beside: reggae by the clam chowder stands, classic rock by the coffee and pretzel stand, jazz by the Italian pizzeria unwisely named 'Pompeii's Grotto', funk by the twenty-four-hour breakfast diner and even classical opera next to an Asian-Japanese restaurant. It was my first introduction to the two major things that seemed to underpin everything in San Francisco: music and food.

'The restaurant Eric recommended is over there,' Lizzie said, putting a dollar in the bucket of a reggae-playing dreadlocked busker who appeared to be working his way through the *Bob Marley Songbook* on a battered synthesiser. She pointed towards a cluster of wooden tables beside a fish restaurant.

We ordered steaming clam chowder served in bowls made of hollowed-out bread loaves and settled down for a great lunch.

'I read one of Aidan's emails yesterday,' I confessed, blowing on a hot, sweet spoonful of buttery chowder.

'You did?' She made no attempt to disguise her reaction. 'And what did he have to say for himself?'

'That he's sorry. And he loves me. He said the experience of making me redundant made him realise how much he wants me in his life.'

'He actually said that?' Lizzie shook her head. 'Oh well, how nice for him. How do you feel?'

'I don't know. I mean, when he called me into his office I thought he was going to ask us to get back together, so in one way knowing that's how he feels confirms what I'd been thinking for a while. But that was my life before and losing my job has called everything into question. And I'm still angry with him. He said he tried to save my job, but that's easy to say after the event, isn't it? When I thought about it this morning I came to the conclusion that I'm just not ready to go down that road again yet. Not until I work out which direction I want to go in.' I stirred another handful of crunchy oyster crackers into my chowder. 'Does that make sense at all?'

'Yes, absolutely. This trip should be about you, not about Aidan's guilt.' She held up her hand. 'Not that I'm saying he doesn't love you. I'm sure he does. But you need to focus on yourself, not him. It's like when I first moved here. I got involved with a bloke a couple of years ago who was enthusiastic one minute then cold as ice the next. I'd been battling to keep the relationship going for six months when Eric pointed out that the guy was demanding so much time from me that I never had any for myself. I argued with him about it for a couple of weeks, but he had totally summed up where I was. I pulled back and the guy disappeared.'

It was so good to find that Lizzie understood what I was feeling and also to share in more details about her life. I was intrigued by the fact that Eric had been the one to dissuade her from her previous relationship. Seeing how close they had been last night made me wonder if their friendship was a precursor to more. 'Eric seems like a good friend.'

'He is.' Her expression gave nothing away.

'And you have Ced and his wife, too. And who was the principal guy you mentioned? Tom?'

Lizzie gave a self-conscious giggle. 'Tyler.'

This was too good an opportunity to miss. 'What's that giggle for? I think you need to tell me about Tyler.'

She shot me a look but her smile was as bright as the seaside sunshine. 'Nothing to tell, thank you very much. I've known him about four years. He's thirty-five, one of the youngest principals in the area and he's a great friend. I asked for his help with the cross-city education programme I've been writing and he's been amazing with it. And *that* is all.' She looked down at her watch to signal the subject was closed. 'Right, we'd better head to Pier 39.'

We made our way along the seafront past the multi-coloured vintage trams of the F-Line system, the crowds of tourists with their cameras and matching anoraks and the lines of bicycles waiting for hire towards Pier 39. We reached the entrance, flanked by colourful flags flapping in the Bay breeze and a giant sculpture of a crab made from iron and clad in growing plants.

'Where does Eric perform?' I asked Lizzie.

'Right in the middle of the pier's boardwalk. But we'll hear him before we see him.'

'What does that mean?'

My cousin smiled. 'You'll see. We're a little bit early but I reckon we should just head straight there.'

We walked onto the dark wooden boardwalk and as we rounded a corner a familiar Essex voice called out above the hum of the crowd.

'Ladies and gentlemen, roll up, roll up! Fifteen minutes to the show of the decade, a plethora of pluck, a phantasmagoria of feats! You do not want to miss this, people! Come and see me by the carousel at two p.m. sharp!'

I turned to Lizzie. 'Eric?'

'That's him.'

We followed the sound of his voice until we saw Eric, dressed in black t-shirt and baggy red streetdance trousers, wheeling around amused tourists on a unicycle. When he saw us, he raised his hand and pedalled over.

'You came!' He wobbled between us, planting a kiss on my cheek then Lizzie's. 'Are you having a better day, Nell? Was I right about this place or what?'

I smiled back – but then with Eric around it was impossible not to. 'My day is much better, thank you. And I love your office.'

He chuckled and spread his arms wide. 'Beats a stuffy accountancy firm, eh?'

'Can I get you anything before your show?' Lizzie asked. 'Do you have water?'

Eric's eyes shone. 'Darlin', you read my mind. I'm good for water but I could murder a coffee. I didn't get the chance for one this morning. Would you mind?'

'Not at all.' My cousin opened her bag and searched around its considerable depths to find her purse.

'Why don't I get them?' I offered. I was enjoying the atmosphere and wanted to say thank you to Lizzie and Eric. 'What can I get you?'

With their coffee orders, I made my way back through the crowds to the boardwalk entrance where I'd seen a coffee kiosk. The friendly lady behind the counter asked where in England I was from and wished me a pleasant stay in the city as she handed over cups of steaming coffee. Popping plastic lids on the paper cups, I fitted them into a cardboard carrier and turned to leave the kiosk – just as somebody's elbow caught under mine and sent the carrier and three cups flying into the air. Shocked, I jumped out of the way to escape the hot liquid's rapid return to earth and turned to confront the person who had knocked into me.

And that was the first time I saw him.

His eyes were shaded behind sunglasses and his dark wavy hair was being blown about his tanned face by the chilly breeze gusting in from the Bay. He was dressed in a black t-shirt and jeans with a khaki jacket – and he looked utterly horrified.

'Man, I'm so sorry,' he said, his voice deep and pure West Coast. 'I wasn't looking where I was going.'

'No you weren't. That coffee was hot – it could've hurt someone.'

He reached out and touched my arm. 'I'm sorry, are you OK?'

I took a breath. 'I'm fine. Are you?'

He took off his sunglasses to reveal dove-grey eyes filled with concern. 'I'm good. Hey, please let me replace your drinks. It's the least I can do.'

I was still ruffled but the gorgeous stranger's earnest apology and kind offer were some compensation for my embarrassment. I couldn't tell whether my sudden rise in temperature was due to the after-effects of our very public collision or the handsome man now offering to make amends for it. I agreed and watched as he quickly joined the queue, eager to resolve the problem he had unwittingly caused.

'Here,' he said, handing me fresh drinks. 'Again, my humble apologies.'

'That's very kind of you, thanks.'

His smile was warm and wide. 'You're English?'

'Yes, I am.'

'Cool.' As if remembering something important he held his hand out. 'I'm Max.'

When I shook it, his hand was as warm as his smile. 'Nell. Thanks for these.'

'No problem.' His eyes held mine for a moment. 'So – great to meet you, Nell.'

I was struck by a strong urge to stay where I was, enjoying the unexpected pleasure of his company. But I was aware that Lizzie and Eric were waiting for me and that the circus performer would appreciate caffeine before his show. So, kicking myself for failing to think of anything more inventive, I smiled back. 'Nice to meet you too, Max. I'd better . . .'

'Sure. Um – bye.'

My heart was racing as I turned and hurried back along the boardwalk. Maybe it was my imagination but I could have *sworn* he was watching me until I disappeared from view . . .

'You are an *angel*,' Eric grinned, accepting a cup.

'Sorry it took so long. I had a bit of a mishap.'

Lizzie took her cup from the carrier. 'What happened?'

'Someone bumped into me and sent everything flying. But he replaced them and was really sweet about it.'

'Nell Sullivan, you're blushing!'

I giggled. 'Well, he was quite easy on the eye.'

My cousin laughed. 'Wow, Nellie, this is a turnaround. Yesterday you said you felt out of place, but now you're fraternising with the locals. I'm proud of you.'

'OK, lovely ladies,' Eric said, picking up three long clubs and clambering back onto his unicycle. 'Showtime!'

Eric's colleague was gathering a crowd in the large central piazza of the pier, shouting his encouragement through a squeaky loudhailer.

'Our amazing, one-of-a-kind show is about to start,' he yelled. 'Trust me, people, miss this and you'll regret it for the rest of your life! Come closer, please, gather in. Plenty of room for you all!'

As we watched the intrigued onlookers shuffling into place, Lizzie told me that Eric had regular visitors who would come often to watch his shows. And it was certainly a spectacle. Within minutes of welcoming his audience, Eric was balanced on a unicycle, with flaming clubs in his hands.

'Now I may or may not have done this before and it may or may not have worked in the past,' he grinned, causing the people at the front of his audience to shriek and step back as he wobbled towards them. 'So if this all goes wrong, at least I'll be able to say I went out in a blaze of glory . . .'

The crowd gasped as he appeared to almost topple off the unicycle before regaining his balance and perfectly juggling the firebrands, eliciting another cheer and enthusiastic applause from his rapt audience. His colleague then took over the commentating duties as they launched into a well-practised banter about their supposedly dubious juggling skills, moving on to carving knives and watermelons, then axes. Clearly loving the eager applause, Eric hopped off the unicycle and sprinted up the steps to the Pier's first-floor level, where he hopped over the banister to mount a unicycle with a seat that extended almost two metres above the wheel.

Lizzie and I laughed, gasped and applauded along with the crowd, watching the consummate professionals at work. As they neared their big finale, I looked up at the clearing sky and noticed the man from the coffee kiosk leaning on the first-floor balcony where Eric had climbed onto the unicycle. He was smiling as he watched the show, and once I saw him I couldn't stop staring. With the benefit of distance I was able to take in his appearance fully. He didn't look like a tourist, nor did he appear to work at the Pier, yet he seemed entirely at home standing there, laughing at Eric's antics. It was only when he half-turned his head and looked straight at me that I averted my eyes. His smile widened in recognition and he raised his hand in a little salute. Blushing, I turned back to Eric's show – and I was just about to tell Lizzie to look when I realised he had gone.

Meeting him had been the most random of happenings, but for some unknown reason it completely caught my attention. The memory of his smile was still dancing in my mind when Eric's show ended with a thunderous round of applause and the audience began to noisily disperse to Pier 39's other attractions.

Taking his final bow, Eric bounded over, wiping his brow with a towel.

'Did you enjoy the show?'

'It was incredible,' I replied. 'How on earth do you ride that thing *and* juggle?'

'I'll let you into a secret,' he beamed, leaning closer in case any of his audience heard his confession. 'For about twelve months I couldn't. Not that it stopped me trying. Thankfully the punters thought it was part of the comedy show. Good job Chad and me are such convincing comedians, eh?'

Eric's performance partner appeared and handed him a bottle of water. 'Hey ladies. Eric said he had a rent-a-crowd coming down today. Good show?' His accent was pure mid-West, a laid-back, lazy drawl that perfectly fitted his surroundings.

Lizzie nodded. 'Amazing as always, Chad. Although I think you almost gave that lady in the front of the crowd a coronary with your axe-juggling.'

'Ha, I saw that. What can I say? I have that effect on women.'

Lizzie promised Eric another dinner invitation soon and we left them to prepare for their next show, for which the audience was already gathering. We walked away from Pier 39 towards Aquatic Park and Ghirardelli Square. The shroud of mist over the Bay had cleared to just a thin layer on the horizon, making the distant blue hills appear to be floating over the deep blue-green stretch of water. Tourist boats buzzed towards the red span of the Golden Gate Bridge and around the ghostly ruins of Alcatraz Island, enjoying the freedom to explore the Bay that many of the infamous island prison's inmates literally would have died for.

When we reached the Powell Street terminal of San Francisco's iconic cable cars, my cousin nudged my arm.

'I reckon we should brave the queue and have a cable car ride. You can't come here and not try it out.'

The queue was considerable, wrapping around the manual turntable and back up the street, but the warm afternoon sun was shining and the atmosphere amongst the waiting tourists was affable. We joined the back of the line, Lizzie amused by the touristy thing we were doing.

'You know, it's strange but it's been years since I last rode in a cable car. When I arrived I did a bit of sightseeing but pretty soon I was living here and life just kind of took over.'

'In that case, we're absolutely doing the right thing.'

'I concur, dear cousin. And I'm still keeping my eye out for your handsome stranger. I can't believe you saw him again and didn't tell me.'

'I tried to, but he'd gone before I had a chance.'

'Yeah, yeah, I know. Keeping all the gorgeous ones for yourself,' Lizzie joked.

As we neared the front of the queue, several wooden cable cars rumbled down towards the turntable, the drivers and brakemen hopping off and trading loud, good-natured banter with each other as they pulled and pushed the cars around to turn them. I was very amused when the drivers took a break by the tiny wooden hut beside the turntable and passed around a large plastic tub of red liquorice. One lady, who was later revealed to be a visitor from New York, protested loudly when she saw this, insinuating that their break was tantamount to treason for the tourists waiting to travel. But a brakeman caused a ripple of laughter to move through the rest of the queue when he replied, 'Lady, if we don't get our liquorice you don't get our help hauling your ass up Powell. Any questions?'

By the time Lizzie and I climbed inside the wooden cable car, my face was aching from smiling so much. There was a great deal about Fisherman's Wharf that proved the neighbourhood didn't take itself too seriously and didn't expect its visitors to either. Riding the cable car was the perfect way to end the day's sightseeing and was exciting beyond words. Lizzie and I sat on bench seats, holding on and giggling as the burgundy and gold cable car clunked and bumped in wooden splendour, warm wind blowing through its open windows as it sped up and down the steep streets.

When we finally swapped the cable car for a slightly more sedate Muni trolleybus, Lizzie grinned at me.

'Good day?'

'*Great* day. Thank you.'

'Oh it's my pleasure. I feel like I'm rediscovering the city. So, where to tomorrow?'

I pulled my guidebook from my bag and consulted its folded-edge pages. How on earth could I choose when everywhere I'd read about sounded so amazing? 'I don't know. Where would you recommend?'

Lizzie shook her head. 'Nope, this is *your* trip. I know – close your eyes.'

'Do what?'

'Don't argue, Nellie, just do it.'

I did as I was told. 'OK. Now what?'

'Open the guidebook anywhere.'

'That's daft . . .'

'No it's not! Come on, Nell, live dangerously! You're meant to be having an adventure, remember?'

Laughing, I flicked through the guidebook pages and stopped at one.

'Brilliant!' Lizzie said. 'So – where are we going tomorrow?'

I opened my eyes and looked at the page, a large grin spreading across my already aching face when I saw the location. It was perfect and already I couldn't wait to see it.

'*Here.*'

CHAPTER EIGHT

Famous names

We started our next day of sightseeing with a visit to Annie's for breakfast. Today I decided to try the 'S-B-K Crêpes' – two light and crispy crêpes stuffed with fresh strawberries, banana and kiwi fruit, served with warm maple syrup. With several mugs of Annie's signature house coffee it was the most delicious way to start the day. We were just finishing our breakfast when Laverne appeared at our table, along with an elderly man and woman.

'Nell, I have two very special Annie's regulars who want to meet you. This is Mr and Mrs Alfaro.'

'Pleased to meet Lizzie's family,' Mr Alfaro smiled, his eyes almost disappearing behind the thick lenses of his glasses. 'We are very fond of your cousin.'

I shook his hand. 'Lovely to meet you, sir.'

'Enough with the "sir" or we'll never drag him away from you,' Mrs Alfaro chuckled. 'Saul Alfaro doesn't often get attention from young ladies these days.'

'Like *you* know . . .' Mr Alfaro muttered back, still grinning at me.

'Oh, I *know*. I've been married to you for fifty-nine years. Nell, it's a pleasure to meet you. You should both come to tea with us.'

'That's very kind, Mrs A, but we couldn't impose on you,' Lizzie replied, immediately silenced by a disgruntled sweep of the old lady's hand.

'Nonsense. Your cousin is new in this city, so you must both come for tea. Tomorrow afternoon is good for us. Saul, make them say yes.'

Saul Alfaro stared at his wife of fifty-nine years. 'And how am I meant to do that?' He turned to Lizzie and me. 'Girls, please say you'll come for tea. It would please my wife. And it would make my day a whole lot easier.'

Esther tutted and muttered something indecipherable under her breath. Keen to rescue Mr Alfaro and placate his wife, Lizzie jumped in.

'Of course. We'd love to.'

The relief on the old man's face was immense. 'Wonderful news. You ladies have a great day,' Mr Alfaro said with a wink.

Lizzie smiled at him. 'We will, thanks Saul.'

Mrs Alfaro linked arms with her husband and they began to shuffle away. 'And now you're winking at the ladies? Since when did you ever wink at ladies?'

'Maybe I've always winked at the ladies,' I heard Mr Alfaro retort. 'Maybe I just don't wink at *you* . . .'

'I hope you realise you've just met royalty,' Lizzie said, twenty minutes later, as we walked to the Muni trolleybus stop enjoying the warm sunshine. 'The Alfaros have been coming to Annie's since opening day. I don't think they've missed a week since. You're in for a treat tomorrow afternoon.'

I was looking forward to it already.

I had read so much about Union Square but arriving in it was something else. A wide stone piazza with a tall Corinthian column topped with a statue of Victoria (the Goddess of Victory) at its heart, it was surrounded on all sides by famous stores whose names I instantly recognised: Macy's, Saks Fifth Avenue, Tiffany, Neiman Marcus, Barney's and Bloomingdale's. The endless hum of city traffic mingled in the air with the low moan of fire truck sirens and the quaint tinkling of cable car bells running up Powell Street. In truth, I'd been looking forward to visiting the department stores with little thought to what the Square itself might look like, but now I was here the spectacle of it was so enticing I could have stayed there all day, just watching the world go by. However, I was on a special mission for my best friend: Vicky had long been obsessed with Macy's since we visited it on our shopping trip to New York two years ago and had begged me to buy her something from the iconic department store.

'Even if it's just a *carrier bag*,' she had urged me before I left for San Francisco. 'I didn't buy anything when we went to the New York one. Then at least I can pretend I shop there regularly.'

Walking around the brightly lit, shiny interior of Macy's, it was hard to believe I was still in the same city as the gaudy brashness of Fisherman's Wharf from yesterday. Here everything was polished, impeccably placed and elegantly laid out, much like the piazza around which the stores were positioned. Lizzie and I spent hours walking around the floors of the department stores, feeling like we were starring in an episode of a glamorous US drama. I was tempted to add to the scary total on my credit card – especially when I saw all the wonderful designer clothes and shoes on offer – but I decided to be sensible, knowing that the next seven and a half weeks would see my credit hammered enough. Lizzie, however, found a beautiful pair of shoes reduced to half price and succumbed to their charms. While she kept chastising herself for such uncharacteristic decadence, I could see how happy she was with her purchase.

'Now all you need is a special occasion to wear them,' I said, as we ate lunch in The Cheesecake Factory at the top of Macy's on an elegant glass-edged terrace overlooking Union Square.

'I'll wear them for Pablo.'

'You can't just wear them around your apartment, Lizzie! Clearly we need to find you a man to take you on a fabulous date so that you can wear them.'

My cousin groaned. 'Good luck with that one. I think I'm safer having a stay-at-home date with my goldfish.'

'But you said you'd had some dates?'

'Sure, I've dated.' She twisted her wine glass and stared into it. 'But dating here is just agreeing to dinner or a drink with someone. It rarely leads anywhere. Most people are just out to socialise.'

I considered this and decided to push the topic. 'What about Eric? He seemed really pleased to see you yesterday and he was incredibly attentive when he came over for dinner. He's good looking and fun to be with . . .'

Lizzie laughed. 'Now you can stop right there. Eric's a great friend and he's one of those people who always gives you his full attention. He's *also* incredibly in love with Xiu Min, his gorgeous Chinese girlfriend – who happens to be a good friend of mine as well.'

'Ah.'

'Exactly. Anyway, enough about me. If we're match-making anyone it should be you. Especially after your *brief encounter* yesterday.'

I knew Lizzie was deliberately changing the subject, but I didn't object. Instead, it was my turn to dismiss a question. 'Oh no, the last thing I need is a holiday fling . . .'

'But Californian men meet with your approval?' Her expression was pure wicked delight.

I had to laugh. 'Yes, OK, they're rather easy on the eye. I suppose a *little* window-shopping is acceptable while I'm here?'

'Completely acceptable. In fact, I think you should definitely make it a feature of your stay.'

From: nell.sullygirl@gmail.com
To: vickster1981@me-mail.com
Subject: Shopping!

Hi Vix

Please see attached photo of the bag I'm going to send you from Macy's! There's a little gift in it as well, but I'm saving that as a surprise . . .

Macy's is enormous – one whole side of Union Square – and I reckon you would have to move in for a week to see everything!

Hope things are looking brighter on the jobs front for you. Keeping everything crossed for a fantastic job to turn up really soon. Don't give up. In just over seven weeks I'll be home and probably straight into the dole queue . . .

Love ya

Nell xxx

From: vickster1981@me-mail.com
To: nell.sullygirl@gmail.com
Subject: Re: Shopping!

NELL SULLIVAN I LOVE YOU!!!

Honestly, the bag alone is wonderful but I'm so excited about the surprise gift! I will be stalking the postman until it arrives . . .

Job-wise, it's bleak, Nellie. BLEAK. There's nothing out there. Even the eleven-year-old careers advisor I saw said it 'might be best to go back to college for a year to retrain' because the jobs market is 'stagnant'. To be honest, I was quite impressed he knew such a big word. But that's the reality, hun. Greg has managed to get some night shifts at Sainsbury's shelf-stacking. It's great but makes me feel even more useless because

I'm here doing nothing. Actually, I'm wondering if CBeebies would pay me for ongoing viewer research. I'm watching so many hours of it with Ruby at the moment I'm sure it qualifies me as an expert. Maybe I'll email them.

Have a fantastic time. And keep sending pictures. !

Big loves,

Vix xxx

Inside the Macy's bag I put a cute bracelet in Vicky's favourite colours of pink and lilac, a sweet little notebook with the Tiffany logo and two postcards of Union Square I'd bought that afternoon. I popped down to EarthSong, the New Age shop underneath Lizzie's apartment, and Rosita the friendly Mexican owner picked out a lovely batik card for me, embroidered with the words 'Believe in Best' in delicate gold thread.

I sent the parcel, hoping that it would be the first of many positive things for Vicky. I couldn't do much to help my friend while I was here, but if surprise parcels and emails with photos provided welcome distraction from her job and money worries it was an easy thing to offer. I kept thinking about her – and the rest of my former work colleagues – biding time until they found another job. Part of me felt guilty for escaping the horrors of redundancy, strolling in late afternoon sun in California while they were stuck at home. I was only delaying the inevitable, but a large part of me was glad I'd chosen to do this.

'Beautiful afternoon,' a man with almost more piercings than skin said as he passed me.

'It is,' I smiled.

'Make the most of it,' called his companion, a tall, slender lady with long silver hair whose full Indian cotton skirt embroidered with tiny bells tinkled as she moved.

I loved the sense of acceptance that seemed to characterise The Haight. It was all part of the crazy, wonderful mix of the neighbourhood I was growing to love already – where a newly unemployed Assistant Planning Officer from Richmond via Woodford could happily coexist with hippies, Goths, geeks and the man who lived in The Panhandle who talked to trees. Anywhere else in the world this wouldn't have been possible. Here, it was. And as to the manifold delights of this most accepting of cities, I had so many more to discover . . .

CHAPTER NINE

Fortune cookies and fate

The old Chinese man playing his *huquin* on the corner of Grant Avenue and Sacramento Street next day was the perfect picture of Chinatown authenticity – until I realised he was energetically bowing his way through 'Smells Like Teen Spirit'. A delighted crowd of Canadian students had gathered around him, the Canadian flags stitched to their backpacks bopping in time to the unexpected Nirvana tribute. Pleased with their rapturous applause, he then launched into 'Clementine' and 'Happy Birthday to You'.

'I can't help thinking he played his ace too soon there,' Lizzie chuckled as we carried on walking down Grant Avenue, the traditional frontages of the Chinatown shops at odds with the glimpses of the Financial District we saw down the hill at each road junction.

'We should have bought one of his CDs. Vicky will never believe me when I tell her.'

Red lanterns for Chinese New Year were strung from

one side of the street to the other, their colour matching the lucky red of so many of Grant Avenue's shop frontages and signs. The scent of incense and tea was in the air, punctuated at intervals by the spicy umami of roasting meat, soy noodles and ginger from the noodle bars and dim sum stands. Had it not been for the enormous American cars, trolleybuses and ever-impatient white and yellow taxicabs rumbling down the road, I could have imagined I was strolling in the streets of a Chinese town.

After a visit to the Golden Gate Fortune Cookie factory in Ross Alley – which turned out to be a tiny room that stretched back into dimness with five ladies moulding hot dough around small slips of paper and depositing the finished fortune cookies into bamboo baskets – we found a bench overlooking a kids' play area in Portsmouth Square. Next to us a group of Chinese men played *mahjong* on a concrete bench, each man engaged in conversation with the rest without pausing to listen, yet apparently understanding everything being said by everyone. A group of women at the next bench along cast disapproving glances in their direction, shaking their heads and tutting loudly. Children were playing on the playground, being watched by mothers and grandmothers, while smartly dressed men and women in suits ate lunch from bento boxes – indicating how close the square was to the sleek, high-rise buildings of the Financial District. The Transamerica Pyramid loomed large on the skyline over the multicultural, multigenerational mix playing out before us.

'Well, the Fortune Cookie factory was an experience,' I laughed.

'Don't be so quick to mock,' Lizzie warned, brandishing

the carrier bag of cookies. 'Hidden in the sugar and polythene of this bag may lie our very fortunes.'

'Oh well, when you put it like *that* . . .'

She snapped a sweet cookie open and pulled out the paper fortune. 'Listen to this: "Soon you will see what your destiny holds" . . . Spooky, Nell.'

I cracked open another cookie. 'Ooh, Lizzie, here's a good one for you: "An unexpected visitor may delight you" . . . I bet that isn't Pablo.'

'Sounds promising.' She opened another cookie and her smile faded. 'Ah. This isn't such good news: "Solitude is a path you must walk for a season". Rats!'

I smiled at her, enjoying our game. 'You know, I'm so glad we bought these, or else we would never know what our lives had in store.'

My cousin laughed. 'True. Although I have a feeling you'll leave San Francisco with more of an idea than you arrived with.'

The *mahjong* game came to a triumphant end beside us, with one man jumping up and performing a delighted dance, while his fellow players loudly disputed his win.

'I hope so, Liz. Either that or I'll just go home happier, heavier and poorer . . .'

'. . . But with a *fabulous* tan . . .'

'And ending all of my sentences with a West Coast question mark?'

'. . . while carrying a whole suitcase of spookily accurate fortune cookies!'

Breathless from giggling, I smiled at my cousin. 'Sounds perfect to me.'

'Good. Hey, we'd better get back. We have a date with Haight royalty, remember?'

An hour later, Lizzie and I stood outside a coffee-coloured wooden house in Broderick Street.

'Here we are,' she grinned. 'Ready for tea with the Alfaros?'

She led the way down a path at the side to a ground-level front door and rang the doorbell. We could see Mr Alfaro's shuffling figure approaching down the hallway through the frosted glass door for a long time before he reached us.

'I swear that hallway gets longer every day,' he apologised when he eventually opened the door, ushering us into his home.

Inside smelled of super-strength floral air freshener and bleach. Across the walls on either side of the entrance lobby neatly hung lines of family photos told the story of the elderly couple and showcased some of their many grandchildren and great-grandchildren. Mr Alfaro made a point of introducing us to each one, almost as if the people were actually standing in a receiving line down the hallway.

'That's my brother Caleb, my sister Miryam and my youngest brother Zaccai . . . Esther's father Benny – was he ever terrifying! My mother, God rest her . . . And these are our sons Daniel, Micah and Clint . . .' Seeing our amusement, he gave a shrug. 'So my wife is a *Dirty Harry* fanatic, what can I tell you?'

Esther was in the couple's small kitchen, her best blue dress and neatly starched white apron standing out from the brown and beige colour scheme of the rest of the apartment. Seeing us, she bustled into the hall, shooing Saul away to make drinks.

'Now, I can't say our tea will be as accomplished as those you have in England,' she conceded, clearly believing every English person enjoyed tea at the Ritz every day as she led us into their living room, 'but I have been baking this morning, which I hope you will like, Nell.'

'You didn't have to go to so much trouble,' I said.

'Ah, this is nothing. If we invite you for dinner you won't eat again for days,' she smiled. 'Now sit, please, and my husband and I will attend to you.'

As they hurried around us delivering glasses of iced peach tea and plate after plate of delicious-looking pastries and biscuits, I stole glances around. The walls of the living room were clad in varnished wood, with panels covered in heavily patterned brown and cream wallpaper. Every flat surface boasted a crowd of photographs, displayed in frames of all shapes and sizes. As we sat at the Alfaros' mahogany dining table it was as if we were surrounded by a black and white, sepia and Kodak-Color-hued audience, which made the small apartment feel a great deal fuller than it actually was.

'Try one of these,' Esther Alfaro urged, passing a plate of crescent-shaped pastries filled with chocolate and cinnamon. 'They're called *rugelach*. My mother always made them when we had guests. This is her recipe.'

'First time I tasted them, I almost married her mother,' Saul grinned, ducking his wife's hand as it swung around towards him. 'Do you like them, ladies?'

It was difficult to answer with faces stuffed with rich pastry, but we did our best.

'And so, Nell, what are your plans for your time here?' Mrs Alfaro asked.

'Sightseeing to begin with, and then I don't know, really. It's going to be fun discovering the city and especially spending time with Lizzie.'

'I've taken the week off from my students so I can be Nell's guide,' Lizzie grinned, reaching for another delicious pastry as Mrs Alfaro looked on with unfettered pride. 'I'm looking forward to taking her to my favourite places.'

'This is a beautiful city,' Mr Alfaro agreed. 'I grew up here, we raised our boys here and I will be laid out here, too. Of all the many places I've visited in my life, San Francisco is the best. You should take Nell to Alamo Square, Lizzie. Beautiful views over the whole city. I always said to my wife if I ever became a millionaire we'd live there.'

Mrs Alfaro harrumphed. 'And you can see how much of a millionaire he became.'

'You have a lovely home, Mrs A,' Lizzie replied, seeing the crestfallen look Saul Alfaro was now wearing.

'I do. But it isn't Alamo Square.'

'Sure, you may not have the millionaire house, but look at what you got for a husband,' Saul said, the twinkle returning. 'Admit it, Esther: you hit the jackpot when you got me.'

Esther Alfaro tutted but her eyes were smiling when they met ours. 'You'd think he was the only boy in San Francisco I could have chosen.'

'How did you two meet?' Lizzie asked. 'I don't think you've told me before.'

'I fell from heaven, straight into her arms,' Mr Alfaro joked. 'OK, I'm kidding. Actually, I hung around her parents' house like a sick puppy for weeks until she agreed to take a walk with me.' He gazed over at his wife. 'Esther Miechowicz was the most beautiful girl I ever saw. First day her family moved into my neighbourhood, I told my friends, "That's the girl I'm gonna marry." And it took five years, but it happened.'

'Aw, Mr A, how romantic,' Lizzie grinned.

'He can be when he puts his mind to it,' Mrs Alfaro replied, giving her husband a playful cuff. 'You have a young man in your life, Nell?'

I coughed and took a quick swig of iced tea. 'Not at the moment.' Seeing her expectant smile I knew I wouldn't be let off the hook with such a short answer. 'There was someone, back in England. But it didn't work out.'

'Boy must be a *schmuck*,' Mrs Alfaro concluded. 'Well, don't you worry. I believe love has a way of finding you, especially when you least expect it. Take me and my husband: love had its work cut out when it brought us together and yet, here we are.' Satisfied, she patted the tablecloth and furnished us all with a matronly smile. 'Well, this is wonderful: new friends and old, all together around our table.' She refilled our glasses with iced tea and lifted hers. 'Nell, welcome to our city. May it exceed your wildest dreams.'

That evening, as Lizzie and I prepared pasta with roasted vegetables bought from the market across the road on our way home from the Alfaros', I was suddenly aware of how peaceful I felt – and how different this was to the day I'd lost my job. That day felt like a lifetime ago and I liked the way my life was changing.

'This is good,' I said, drizzling olive oil over crushed garlic, sliced beef tomatoes and huge pieces of red, yellow and green peppers.

'You look happier,' my cousin observed. 'And very at home in my kitchen.'

'I feel very at home,' I replied, thinking how much I'd missed cooking. But with all the amazing food we had enjoyed over the last few days it was impossible not to be inspired. I thought about my dream of a diner and wondered if one day I might be preparing food for more people than just my cousin. Should I share it with Lizzie, or would she think it was a folly inspired by holiday enthusiasm? I was about to say something when she started to tell me an anecdote about Eric. Taking this as a fortuitous sign, I smiled and kept my silence.

Next morning we were about to leave the apartment when Lizzie's mobile rang.

'Hi, Lizzie speaking . . . What? Wait . . . Margaretha, slow down . . . OK, now tell me . . .' She looked at me then raised her eyes heavenwards. 'Stop panicking! You've put in the hours, you know your pieces, you'll be *fine* . . .'

I could hear the frantic voice of the caller and saw Lizzie's face tense.

'I know that, honey, but I have my cousin with me and I promised I'd spend this week with her . . .' She mouthed an apology at me.

I waved my hand to catch her attention. 'Don't worry if there's something you have to do . . .' I whispered.

'OK, OK, hold on a minute . . .' She cupped her hand over the phone. 'Nell, I'm so sorry. One of my piano students has an exam at noon and she's having a meltdown with nerves. Would you mind if I popped out to sit with her while she takes it? I'll be about a couple of hours?'

'It's no problem at all.' After all the sightseeing we had done this week the prospect of a quieter day was surprisingly appealing.

Relief spread across my cousin's face. 'Thank you! OK, Margaretha? I'm coming over. Yes, I'll be there in about thirty minutes. Just keep practising the pieces, OK?'

Lizzie gave me a spare key and fussed around making sure I knew where everything was, until I had to almost bundle her out of the door. Once alone, I made myself a cup of tea and settled down on the squashy sofa by the window to read a book I'd bought at Heathrow while waiting for my flight.

Thirty minutes later, the beautiful late morning sunshine dappled by the leaves of the tree outside was too lovely to ignore, so I took my book, bag and Lizzie's spare keys and headed out into Haight-Ashbury on my own. It was strange how familiar the neighbourhood felt already and I was buoyed by the freedom I felt. After spending some time in Booksmith, reading the quotes from famous books chalked on blackboards above the tall bookshelves and the quirkily opinionated handwritten review cards displayed everywhere, I wandered along Haight Street, peering into shop windows. Wandering into one of the clothing boutiques, I bought a vintage rock t-shirt and a long cotton scarf, enjoying the buzz that the little bit of shopping gave me. When I reached the corner of Haight and Clayton, the neon signs of Annie's came into view.

'Why not?' I said out loud, crossing the road to the diner.

I didn't recognise the server behind the counter but he seemed to know me when I approached.

'Hey, you're Lizzie's cousin, right? I'm PJ – I work the afternoon shift here. Laverne's told me all about ya. Grab a seat by the counter and I'll be straight over.'

Slightly unnerved by my surprise celebrity, I sat up at the counter and cast a glance around the diner. It was quieter than I'd seen it during the morning rush, but then I knew from what Lizzie and Laverne had told me that breakfast and brunch were the busiest times here. There was always at least an hour wait from seven a.m. onwards at weekends and the queues were as much a part of the Annie's experience as the huge list of French toast options on the menu.

'You having a good day?' PJ asked, placing a full coffee mug beside me without waiting for me to ask for it.

'Great thanks. Lizzie's helping a piano student with an exam so I'm having fun being out on my own.'

'Lizzie's great. My nephew goes to her after-school club and he loves her. She's all he ever talks about, especially the music zone she runs at the club.'

I loved hearing about the amount of respect people had for my cousin and it brought home to me just how much a part of the community she had become.

'Now, what can I get ya? We've a special on blueberry pie today.'

I couldn't tell whether I was hungry or not – a phenomenon I'd encountered since arriving in San Francisco – but I decided this qualified as a plausible manifestation of my intention to sample American culture: and what could be more American than blueberry pie?

When it arrived – large and glossy, dredged in powdered sugar and swimming in cream and ice cream – I took my book from my bag and began my onslaught on the mountain of sweetness. All around me, American and Latin American voices chattered. Clanks and hisses of steam drifted through from the kitchen and the siren of a police car wailed past the window. George Benson crooned from the diner's sound system and occasionally a laugh from a particularly loud customer at a nearby table broke through it all. I felt happy and at peace in my new surroundings, enjoying the sensation of being relaxed after all the stress of losing my job. After a while, I wasn't really reading, my eyes remaining on the same page as I let the sounds of Annie's diner wash over me.

'Nell.'

I jumped as Mrs Alfaro's bony hand on my shoulder brought me out of my reverie. 'Oh hi, Mrs Alfaro.'

'Forgive me, I didn't mean to startle you. Are you enjoying your pie?'

Slightly dazed, I nodded. 'Yes – it's very good.'

'I'm glad. I saw you ordering the pie and I said to my husband, "She's ordered the pie." And he said, "The pie is good, she'll like it." And I agreed. And you do like it. So. There you go.' She grinned at me.

I wasn't quite sure how to respond, as she seemed to be waiting for an answer. 'I'm enjoying it, thanks.'

'I'm glad. It was wonderful to have you over this week. I hope it won't be your last visit. I would like to hear all about your England. Lizzie tells us you live in London?'

'I do. In Richmond at the moment, with my parents.'

This appeared to please Mrs Alfaro, who gave me an appreciative nod as she folded her hands in front of her. 'And how proud they must be of you. Our sons don't live so close. They have their own lives, of course, but as a mother I miss them. But that's life.' She paused, her expectant smile still in place, and appeared to be deciding what to say next. Was there something she wanted to ask me but didn't know how? After a rather theatrical look around her, she launched into her small talk again. 'And you're here by yourself, I see?'

'Only for a couple of hours. Lizzie had to see a piano student. But I'm enjoying being out on my own.'

'This is a friendly neighbourhood, Nell. You'll be safe here by yourself. I still feel safe even though I'm old.' She smiled again. 'Actually, there is someone I think you should meet, if you don't mind the introduction?'

This was a surprise, but I was touched that Esther Alfaro wanted to introduce me to someone in the neighbourhood. 'Of course, that would be lovely.'

Her eyes twinkled and for a moment I was concerned about what I might just have agreed to. 'Good.' She lifted a bony hand and waved back towards the busy tables of the diner. 'My husband is bringing him over here now.'

Before I could reply, Saul Alfaro appeared, beckoning behind him.

'Is he coming?' his wife demanded.

'He is. He's on his way.'

'Well, where is he?'

'Give the boy a chance, Esther! We don't need him sprinting . . .'

'It's OK, Mrs A, I'm here.' A new voice behind me spoke. It was deep and soft in tone and inexplicably made me smile before I twisted to see its owner. When I turned, my breath caught in the back of my throat.

His wavy dark hair was pushed back behind his ears, his sunglasses were hooked into the collar of his purple t-shirt and his dove-grey eyes shone against his tanned skin. As he neared me I saw surprise colour his expression – and I knew I was staring as Max from Pier 39 offered his hand.

'Wow – um – hello again,' he smiled.

'Hi.' His hand was unbelievably warm when I shook it.

'Don't worry, I'm staying a safe distance away from your coffee today,' he joked, the mischief in his eyes causing my stomach to flutter a little. 'You'll have to forgive the intrusion. My friends the Alfaros are kinda persuasive when they want to be.'

'I know that already.' I was glad of the green leather stool supporting my weight: I suspected my legs might at that moment have failed had the task been assigned to them.

'You two know each other? Excellent! *Talk,*' Mrs Alfaro urged us. 'Be friends now.' Pleased with a mission successfully completed, she hooked her arm through her husband's and they hurried back to their table.

'May I?' Max asked. I nodded and he took the vacant

stool next to mine. 'Well, this is a surprise. I guess I'm the last person you expected to see today?'

That was an understatement. 'You could say that. How do you know the Alfaros?'

He smiled. 'They're benefactors of the art collective I'm a part of. Over the years they've become good friends, too. But I didn't realise they knew you.' He gave a self-conscious laugh and brushed stray sugar crystals from the counter-top as PJ placed a mug of coffee beside him. 'Man, this is such a set-up. I hope you don't think I engineered this?'

'No – at least, I don't think so.' I shared a grin with him and was surprised by the sudden change in the air between us.

Max laughed. 'I swear this is as much a surprise to me as to you. Believe it or not I don't generally make a habit of destroying beautiful women's coffee orders.' He pulled a face. 'Man, now *that* was a line I'm not proud of . . .'

His self-deprecating humour was endearing. 'As lines go, that was a cheesy one.'

'My apologies. I'm a little rusty. Quick, help me out before I confirm your suspicions that I'm a total loser.'

It felt a little odd to be bantering with a man I'd barely met but I was enjoying the experience. 'OK. What brings you to The Haight?'

'I live here. You?'

'I'm staying with my cousin for a couple of months.'

His smile was as delicious as it had been at Pier 39. 'This is good. I feel we're steering into safer waters here.' He took a sip of coffee and gazed out to Haight Street.

'But at the risk of undoing our hard work, do you mind if I say something?'

I folded my arms and pretended to be concerned. 'We-ell, I don't know . . .'

Max placed his hand on his heart. 'Just one thing, I promise. If you don't like it you can tell me to leave?'

'Fair enough. Please do.'

He leaned in slightly, but not so much as to make me uncomfortable and lowered his voice. 'OK, here it is: I'm glad I bumped into you this week. And it's good to meet you again.' The faintest hint of colour appeared underneath his cheekbones and he sat back again.

Maybe it was the considerable caffeine content of Annie's house blend, but my head was spinning. Taken aback, I struggled to reply, hoping my smile was enough.

'That said . . .' Clearly keen to change the subject now his dangerous admission had been aired, Max dug in the pocket of his dark grey chinos and handed me a delightfully warm and slightly creased business card. 'My art collective has an exhibition in two weeks. I'd love it if you could come. Bring your cousin, too, of course.'

MAX ROSSI
Haight Urban Art Collective

So, your name is Max Rossi . . . I read the card, which listed the various art disciplines represented by the group. 'That sounds interesting. I'd love to come and see what you do. Which one of these are you?'

'Pardon me?' He tipped his head to one side to read the card and his finger brushed the back of my hand as he pointed. 'Oh. I'm a sculptor. Mostly. I tend to use whatever medium feels appropriate – I don't like to be restricted. Although I tried a bit of improv last season with our theatre team and, let's just say, I won't be filming *Inside The Actor's Studio* any time soon.'

'I see.' My heart had begun to thump embarrassingly loudly and I was convinced everyone in Annie's could hear it. I was aware of the time and that Lizzie would probably be back at home wondering where I was. Besides, if I stayed here much longer I might lose my nerve altogether and so far I'd managed to hold my own in the conversation quite well.

Max seemed to sense that it was time to leave. 'I'd better go. I have an art class in an hour and, trust me, I do not want to face their wrath if I'm late.'

'Sounds scary! So, I suppose I'll see you around?'

He smiled as he hopped down from the stool. 'Given our recent history I'd say that's a given.' With a wave back at the Alfaros he gave me another half-salute. 'Great to see you, Nell.'

'You too, Max.'

And with that, he left Annie's, striding along Clayton Street until he disappeared from view. Heart still racing, I stared back at my pie, which was still three-quarters uneaten. I stared at it for a long time, my thoughts only returning to the present when I realised PJ was attempting to refill my coffee mug.

'No – no more coffee thanks, PJ. I think I've had enough.'

PJ surveyed me with the kind of suspicion normally reserved for people who say they think large lizard men are about to invade earth. 'You sure about that? We have decaf – if I can sneak it past Annie.'

'No thanks. I'd better get back.'

'Suit yourself. You want this wrapped to go?'

'Er – yes. Please.'

'Okie dokie.'

My thoughts were all over the place. *What just happened?* After our brief meeting at the start of the week I'd assumed Max would become a lovely memory of San Francisco, a cheeky anecdote I could entertain Vicky with and pull out now and again when I wanted to remind myself that men other than Aidan could make my pulse race. But now I'd met him again – unwittingly reintroduced by the well-meaning Alfaros. And he was *gorgeous*. Funny, attentive, intelligent – and interested in me?

Walking back along Haight Street towards Lizzie's, clutching the box of considerable remains of my pie (which I'd now inexplicably lost all appetite for), I mentally turned the events of the past hour over and over. He was just being polite, surely. He'd simply found himself hijacked by two nonagenarian matchmakers and didn't want to embarrass me by leaving. Which made him both considerate and a gentleman . . .

. . . But was it my imagination or had chemistry fizzed between us as we'd spoken? Did he really mean it when he said he was pleased to see me? Or was that just wishful thinking on my part?

Whatever the truth, I was excited. It made no sense and I wasn't expecting it, but somehow the handsome guy from my brief meeting in Fisherman's Wharf had strolled magnificently into my new neighbourhood diner. And invited me to his exhibition. And if that wasn't a welcome opportunity San Francisco was offering me then I didn't know what was.

When I was almost at Cole Street, Aidan's face suddenly drifted into my mind. The chemistry I always experienced when we were together hadn't changed, but it was good to know I could feel that way with someone else, even if it was just a fleeting attraction. Aidan had always assumed I would be waiting for him whenever we broke up: well, it showed how much he knew.

Meeting Max Rossi might be nothing more than a brief flirtation, but it had proved to me that my life had possibilities without Aidan Matthews. For now, that was all I needed to know. And that was enough to sit back and enjoy the ride . . .

CHAPTER TEN

Eat your heart out, Tony Bennett

From: nell.sullygirl@gmail.com
To: vickster1981@me-mail.com
Subject: Food!

Hey Vix

This week I've discovered food trucks – and I know you would love them!

Not far from Lizzie's there is a street where a group of food trucks turn up and it's like a world banquet on wheels. There's even one dedicated to Belgian waffles. I could imagine you and Lizzie hijacking it and moving in! We went there this afternoon and the choice was so amazing I felt like I used to when Mum took me to the sweet shop at the end of our road and said I could choose anything. It took a full twenty minutes for me to decide. I went for a

Vietnamese Banh Mi, which is like a sub roll stuffed with spicy pork and kimchee, a mix of fermented veg. Gorgeous!

I'm almost at the end of my sightseeing week with Lizzie. From next Monday, I'll be on my own during the day. I've already found some places I know I'm going to go back and revisit – and some I haven't seen yet. It's exciting and a little terrifying, but I know I can do it.

Will let you know how I get on. Hope all is good with you, hun.

Love ya

Nell xxx

From: vickster1981@me-mail.com
To: nell.sullygirl@gmail.com
Subject: Re: Food!

It sounds amazing! And now I'm ravenously hungry, thank you very much.

Is there a bloke working in the Belgian waffle truck who looks like Ryan Gosling? PLEASE tell me there is and then my personal fantasy will be complete ;o)

I need PHOTOS, girl! Especially if RG is serving waffles. In fact, if he is, just kidnap him, fold him into that new suitcase of yours and BRING HIM HOME TO MOMMA.

That is all.

Vix xxx

I didn't tell Vicky about Max Rossi. Not yet. I would, of course, if anything happened. But I wasn't sure I would even see him again, let alone . . . well, anything else. I also hadn't told Lizzie. This had the potential to be problematic, but when I'd arrived back at her apartment yesterday I didn't have the opportunity to say anything. My cousin quickly became too engrossed in the demolition of the remainder of the blueberry pie to hear anything other than the contented sound of her own munching. My cousin, the Nemesis of All Desserts . . .

I *would* tell her – but for now it was actually fun to keep my conversation with Max to myself.

'Two Bacon Peanut Butter waffles?'

'Yes, over here.'

The decidedly un-Ryan-Gosling waffle truck guy handed over our order with about as much enthusiasm as I have for filing tax returns. I giggled as I handed Lizzie her waffle.

'What's amusing?'

'Vicky wants that bloke to look like Ryan Gosling.'

Lizzie grimaced. 'Blimey. If he did I'd eat here every day. You'd better not take a photo of him. It'd break her heart.'

Although clouds blocked the sun this afternoon, it was still warm on the outskirts of Golden Gate Park and quite a few people had ventured out onto the grass in their lunch breaks, enjoying delights from the small group of food trucks parked up under the trees on Martin Luther King Jr. Drive.

'Last day of our sightseeing, eh?'

'I know.' My cousin wriggled her toes in the cool grass. 'Are you going to be alright without me, hun?'

'I'll be fine. I know which buses to take, Ced's lectured me on all the areas I should avoid and I'm feeling really at home here. Stop worrying, Liz. This is what I came here for.'

After we'd been defeated by crazy savoury Belgian treats we walked back through Haight and along The Panhandle park towards one of San Francisco's most famous sights. Following Mrs Alfaro's impassioned description of the houses she one day longed to reside in, it would have been rude not to visit The Painted Ladies – a row of historic, pastel-hued wooden houses in Alamo Square.

'I wonder which one Esther Alfaro was coveting?' I asked Lizzie as we moved through the crowds of tourists standing on the green hill focusing their cameras towards the famous buildings.

'Whichever one she could, I imagine,' Lizzie replied, pulling me alongside her and lifting her phone up to frame a photo of us together with the houses behind.

'One for the tourist album,' she grinned.

All around Alamo Square colourful dwellings housed families and children and dogs: real life carrying on alongside the sightseeing tour buses, flashing cameras and swarms of overseas visitors. A group of Japanese tourists buzzed onto the grass beside us and posed with 'V for Victory' hand gestures. One of the men then grabbed his wife and waltzed her around the grass, singing a very loud, very sharp rendition of the Tony Bennett classic 'I Left My Heart in San Francisco' as another of his party enthusiastically filmed them on an iPad. In the past week I must have heard that song twenty times, yet this version was something new and definitely an experience. When he finished to loud applause from the tour party, he bowed at Lizzie and me.

'I am Yuuto, Tony Bennett long-lost Kyoto cousin. Crooner till I die!'

'One of the houses is for sale,' Lizzie observed. 'Fancy living in Postcard Row?'

'Wow, can you imagine?' I let myself consider the dream for a moment. 'They look like something out of a fairytale. Mind you, I'm not sure that what's left of my redundancy money would cover it. And I bet crowds of strangers peering into your house every day is a little annoying.'

Lizzie giggled. 'Can you imagine my mum living here, with her infamous random aversion to seeing into people's windows?'

The thought of Auntie Sue rushing around hanging thick net curtains at every window in the Alamo Square house was hilarious. My parents, in contrast, often forgot to close curtains even late at night, the house in Richmond a blazing beacon of visibility most evenings. When Auntie Sue and Uncle Dave came to visit, Dad used to chide her for 'twitching' when she could see the streetlights on outside and the curtains hadn't been closed.

After a week of being in the city, I was surprised to find how easily I could imagine myself living in it. I could see myself jogging in its parks, visiting Annie's for brunch at weekends, hanging out with friends at gigs, bars, book readings and exhibitions. *Especially* exhibitions . . . I couldn't conceal my smile as Max's face appeared in my mind. I didn't know when or if I might bump into him again but at least I had a firm invitation to visit his exhibition in a fortnight's time. And if the Alfaros had anything to do with it, I might even see him sooner . . .

Today, however, I had more pressing things to think about. All week an idea had been brewing about how I could thank Lizzie for showing me around San Francisco, not to mention putting me up rent-free for two months. Now it was time to put my plan into action.

After my cousin's mention of it the other day, I'd decided to recreate the baked chocolate orange cheesecake that Lizzie had loved so much during our teens. First thing this morning I had snuck out to Annie's to pick up takeaway coffee and French toast for breakfast while Lizzie was still asleep. While waiting for my order to be cooked, I'd enlisted the help of Laverne (in return for a handwritten recipe) to source all the ingredients I needed and drop them off with Rosita, the nice Mexican lady who ran the New Age shop below Lizzie's apartment. All day when we were out, I had been secretly going over the recipe in my mind, buzzing with the thrill of surprising my cousin.

When we returned to Lizzie's, she headed out for an hour to meet a prospective piano student. I waited until she left before jumping into action. Dashing downstairs I collected the bag of goodies from Rosita, promising her I'd save her a slice, and returned to the apartment. It took a while to find the cake tin and utensils I needed in Lizzie's odd kitchen cupboard organisational system (cake tin under packets of rice and noodles, mixing bowl randomly stashed in a drawer with tea towels, wooden spoon in the pocket of an apron hanging beside the refrigerator . . .), but when everything was together I worked as quickly as possible, keeping a constant eye on the time. I had suggested we meet at Java's Crypt for coffee at five o'clock, which I hoped would give her surprise dessert long enough to chill in the fridge before I presented it to her.

It felt so wonderful to be baking again and it was only when my face began to ache that I realised how broadly I'd been smiling while doing it. For as long as I could remember I had always loved baking for other people the most, the mixture of pride in my ability to create delicious food and the irresistible allure of a planned surprise giving me a huge sense of fulfilment. I loved watching other people enjoying my food. I can't explain it any more than to say it was the time when I felt most like the person I wanted to be. Being surrounded by so much food here had made me want to cook again, bringing back that urge to create food that I'd been ignoring for the last few years.

The cheesecake baked like a dream, putting my concerns about baking in an unfamiliar oven to rest. As a final flourish, I melted some local Ghirardelli bitter orange dark chocolate, made a piping bag out of baking parchment and drizzled thin lines across the surface of the cheesecake, before stashing it safely in the fridge to chill.

'I heard about your covert baking,' Ced grinned when I hurried into Java's Crypt, only to find my cousin hadn't yet arrived.

I stared at him. 'How did you hear?'

'Laverne. She stopped by after making the drop at Rosita's place.' He laughed when he saw my incredulity at the speed the news had travelled. 'We're like a network of ninja spies here, dude. *Nothing* gets past The Haight-vine.' He reached behind the ancient Victorian till (painted black, of course) and handed me a flyer. 'On that subject – sorta – we have a band here Tuesday. Be great if you could come.'

The advertised band appeared to be heavily made-up middle-aged men posing Gene-Simmonds-like with guitars in bad eighties' wigs.

'"Bayfinger"?'

'Yeah,' Ced nodded solemnly. 'They're America's leading Hellfinger tribute band – that weird, cult English rock band from the eighties? It's my uncle's band. They're pretty good – even if you don't know the songs.'

After that glowing recommendation, I didn't dare refuse. 'I'll mention it to Lizzie. It could be fun.' Knowing my cousin I was pretty sure she would find a really good reason to give it a miss, but I didn't want to hurt Ced's feelings.

'Sweet. Grab a booth and I'll bring your poison over.'

Ah Ced, such a way with words . . .

When Lizzie hurried in, profusely apologising, twenty minutes later, I could hardly contain my excitement as we drank our coffee, dying to see the look on her face when the cheesecake was revealed. By the time we walked back into her apartment I was at bursting point.

'OK, I have a surprise for you,' I blurted, incapable of keeping the secret a moment longer.

'You do? Oh Nellie, you didn't need to.'

'Yes, I did. You've given me a fabulous first week and if it weren't for you this whole trip would have been impossible. I just wanted to do something to thank you, so –' I stepped to one side so that she was facing the kitchen '– open your fridge.'

Casting me a look of suspicion, Lizzie walked to the large refrigerator, gingerly opening the door as if it might be booby-trapped. When the interior light illuminated her features, she let out a shriek so loud I thought the lady in the apartment below us might call 911 fearing the worst for her neighbour.

'*Cheesecake!* Oh Nellie! Oh – cheesecake!' She hugged me with all her might and jumped around the kitchen with me, turning the small area into a mosh-pit of dessert-related dancing. When she eventually calmed down enough to take a slice, the delight on her face was exactly how I'd hoped it would be. I felt on top of the world. I still had it: I could still make people smile with my food.

Several large slices later, Lizzie collapsed beside me on the sofa. 'It's perfect, Nell! *This* is perfect! We are going to have the best time while you're here.'

Feeling fulfilled and utterly at peace with the world, I beamed back. 'I already am.'

CHAPTER ELEVEN

A spoonful of sugar

My dreams that night were filled with images of food I had enjoyed making in the past, culinary possibilities I could perhaps revisit in Lizzie's compact kitchen. The baking bug was magnificently back and in my slumber I revelled in its re-emergence in my life. After the best night's sleep in months, I woke refreshed and energised by the experience.

'I have a confession to make,' my cousin said as I joined her in the living room. 'I sneaked to the fridge in the middle of the night to have another slice of that phenomenal cheesecake.'

I pretended to be shocked by this sheepish early morning revelation. 'Lizzie Sullivan, what are you like?'

'It was just too good to resist. You don't know how long my fridge has been crying out for awesome home-made desserts to nestle in it! Actually, it got me thinking.' She handed me a plate of buttered toast and we sat at the dining table together. 'How would you fancy doing some baking with the kids at my after-school club? They're excited to meet you and I know they'd love to learn some of your recipes.'

It was a great idea and I marvelled again at the opportunities San Francisco was offering me. 'We could bake Stained Glass Biscuits,' I suggested, remembering summer holiday baking days with Lizzie, Auntie Sue and my mum – flour-covered, messy and giggling in Sue's large farmhouse kitchen by the sea.

Delighted, Lizzie clapped her hands. 'Yes! Blimey, it's been years since I had one of those!'

'That's a plan then. When's the club?'

'This afternoon. We usually do Wednesdays but there was a school Baking Bee this week so we're doing a one-off Friday special.'

'OK. I'll start making a list of ingredients and you need to tell me how many kids you think are likely to want to bake. Then we'd better do some shopping.'

After breakfast we headed out in search of ingredients, choosing fruit-flavoured Life Saver candies to create the coloured sugar glass. Shopping for ingredients made me remember how much I'd missed dreaming up recipes. When I had first moved into the house-share in Woodford I had baked almost every weekend – my new housemates enamoured with the cakes, cookies and pies I baked even if they weren't as bothered about me. Then, when Aidan and I were together, my baking had moved to his house on Sunday mornings, rising early to make sweet pastries while he was still sleeping. I wondered what he would make of me now, the once sensible girl he had known (who never did anything without copious amounts of planning first) being replaced by someone who was daring to be different. Part of me wondered if he would like the change, although when I found myself thinking this, I quickly pushed it away. Right now I was doing this for me, and nobody else.

Back at Lizzie's apartment we measured the ingredients for each child, separating the boiled sweets into piles of single colours and smashing them up (something that hadn't lost any of its fun factor in the many years since we'd last done it). Then we bagged everything up ready for the after-school session, caught the Muni bus to Mission and walked one block to the school.

Sacred Heart Elementary looked more like a college building than a primary school, although Lizzie assured me it was one of the smaller schools in the area. Parents were waiting outside as we approached and several greeted Lizzie like old friends.

'It's a real community school,' Lizzie explained as we walked up the paved path to the smooth stone steps at its entrance. 'They encourage the parents to get involved and there are always fundraisers going on during the year. Out of all the schools I work with in San Francisco this is my favourite.'

Entering the building, we walked down a long, tiled corridor with doors leading to classrooms on both sides. Banks of dark grey lockers lined the walls, covered in stickers, hand-drawn name signs and pictures. The space smelled slightly of disinfectant and the corridor echoed with the muted chatter of small voices from behind the classroom doors.

'How old are the children in the after-school club?' I asked.

'The youngest is six, but most of our kids are between seven and ten. Not all the children come every week, but with some parents working till six we tend to have a core group of around twenty that are always here. You'll love them – they're a great bunch of kids.'

At the end of the corridor, we turned right and were just about to enter the school's main hall when a voice behind us made Lizzie stop and look back.

'Hey Lizzie!'

I turned to see first my cousin's broad grin and then the equally smiling face of a good-looking man who was walking quickly towards us. He wore a blue and white checked shirt, navy-blue slacks and a navy-blue tie and reminded me a little of Jamie Foxx. It was difficult to tell how old he was as he wore his hair closely cropped, but his sparkly chocolate-brown eyes and easy gait made me instantly like him.

'Hi Tyler,' Lizzie replied and I noticed her face flush a little.

'I was hoping I'd catch you. The PTA has given us the go-ahead for our summer art camp. So we should get together soon to begin planning.'

'Sure.' Lizzie moved her blonde hair behind her ear and nodded happily. Tyler smiled back and put his hands in his trouser pockets. And I was suddenly aware of a rather large part of my cousin's life that I knew nothing about.

Tyler caught my eye and stepped forward. 'Forgive me. I haven't greeted your friend. Hi, I'm Tyler Palmer – principal of Sacred Heart.'

I shook his hand, which dwarfed mine. 'Nell Sullivan. I'm Lizzie's cousin.'

'Oh sure, Lizzie told me you would be visiting us. Welcome to my school.'

'Nell's a baking wizard,' Lizzie said, lifting the large grocery bags she carried to show him. 'She's making biscuits with the kids today.'

'Well if there are cookies being made maybe I should hang around.'

'You're welcome to join us, Ty.'

A bell rang and Tyler checked his watch. 'Uh-oh, you'd better hurry and hide, before we're overrun. Nell, great to meet you. Lizzie, I'll – call you?'

'Yes. Speak to you later.'

As children began to spill out of the classrooms, their excited voices filling the space with energy, Lizzie and I ducked into the relative stillness of the school hall.

I fixed my cousin with a stare. 'So *that's* your friend Tyler, is it? Would I be correct in assuming Pablo the Goldfish isn't the only man in your life?'

She blushed and stacked the grocery bags on a table by the wall. 'You know very well I could never be unfaithful to Pablo.'

'Don't give me that. The chemistry between you two was strong enough to power the Large Hadron Collider.'

Lizzie gave me a look. 'Hardly. Ty's a lovely bloke and yes, I'd be lying if I said I didn't like him. But we've only had one date so it's very early days.'

'*Only* one date? That's more than you admitted to me before. I thought he was just helping you with the after-school club curriculum. Judging by what I just saw, I reckon there are a few other things he'd like to help you with as well.'

'Nell! What a suggestion! But I hope so.' She laughed and I knew after this admission the subject was closed. 'Right, we need to put these tables out around the hall, four chairs to a table. I'll set up a long table here and that's where you can demonstrate making the biscuits.'

'Where do we bake them?'

Lizzie opened a door and showed me into a small room with four cookers. 'This is the school's home ec room.' She stopped in the doorway. 'It really is lovely to have you here, Nell. I don't get to share this with anyone usually.'

'Apart from *Tyler* . . .' I ducked as an apron came flying in my direction.

'Behave. And put that on.'

I picked up the apron from the floor and unfolded it to reveal the club name appliquéd in bright fabrics in the front:

Spoonful of Sugar Club

'Like it?'

I nodded. 'It's perfect.'

At almost four o'clock the sound of voices by the hall's double doors heralded the arrival of the after-school club children. Lizzie and I had set out the hall for various activities in what Lizzie called 'Super Zones' – for music, art, games, stories and baking – and more volunteers had arrived to prepare for the club. Miguel and Poppy Gimenez, a husband and wife team who volunteered in the group each week even though their two sons were now at college; Sam Yip, who had a daughter at the school; and Astrid Vinter, who had three kids at high school and one son at Sacred Heart. I was so impressed by their genuine enthusiasm for supporting the school's activities and their positive attitude to everything. Unlike at home where friends with kids were forever bemoaning attempts by schools to get them involved, the volunteers of the Spoonful of Sugar Club – or 'S-O-S Club' as everybody else called it – told me they looked forward to every session and were eloquent about the value of the club for the children.

'Being a part of the club has really made us feel like we're serving the community,' Poppy said, as we pinned up the Super Zone signs. 'There was nothing like this when I was a kid. Lizzie's brought something special to Sacred Heart and I love that I can make it happen for these children.'

'Plus you spend every session feeling like a celebrity,' Astrid laughed, as she joined us. 'I get more hugs during the hour of S-O-S Club than I get in a year from my own family. The kids are so sweet – and they adore you just for turning up. That's what I call job satisfaction!'

Lizzie smiled at her team. 'Right, I think it's time. Brace yourselves!' She opened the door and a crowd of small children came rushing in, high-fiving the volunteers, flinging coats and school bags on the table by the doors and claiming seats in their favourite areas. In the middle of the chaos, Lizzie walked calmly around, ticking off names on a register. When all the children were seated, she raised her hands and the kids did the same, the noise fading in the hall.

'OK, welcome everybody. Today we have a new friend joining us. Everyone say hi to Nell.'

She pointed at me and I waved back as a chorus of 'Hi Nell' rang out.

'Nell is our baking queen,' Lizzie grinned, 'so, S-O-S bakers, you're in for a treat.'

After the welcome, Miguel led the kids in a warm-up game. I took the opportunity to go into the small kitchen and set the ovens to the right temperature. Surprisingly I felt a little nervous but the prospect of supporting Lizzie far outweighed it. I prepared baking trays and collected bowls, wooden spoons and rolling pins to take back into the hall.

'You're English.'

I looked up to see a young girl standing in the doorway. Her black curly hair was scooped up into a high bun on the top of her head and she was dressed in a denim pinafore dress over a pink-and-white striped long-sleeved top, bright pink leggings and blue baseball boots.

'Hello,' I replied. 'You're right, I am.'

The little girl's chocolate-brown eyes widened. 'You speak like Mary Poppins!'

I laughed. 'Do I?'

'For sure!'

'I'll take that as a compliment, thank you.'

She shrugged. 'You should. I'm Eva.'

I was amused by the confident little girl smiling up at me. 'Hi Eva, I'm Nell. Are you going to do some baking with me today?'

'Just you try stopping me. But I should warn you, I'm *excellent* at baking.'

'You are?'

'Mm-hmm. Been doing it since I was five.'

'Wow. And how old are you now?'

'I'm eight. But I'll be nine soon.'

'Well then, that makes you an expert.'

Eva strolled into the kitchen and began to inspect the stack of baking trays. 'Lizzie said you were coming. We all made you a sign. Did you see?'

I nodded. 'It was very nice.'

'It was too much,' she replied, wrinkling her nose. 'But Maya and LeSean decided to put on all the feathers. In my opinion, glitter would've been enough.'

I smiled. 'Don't you like feathers?'

'They're OK, I guess. For dress-up. But not for *signs*. Maya's my best friend but she made a mistake with the feathers. Sticking them round signs is just dumb. You want these taking to the Bake Zone now?'

'Yes please, if you don't mind.'

Eva carried the baking trays while I took the bowls and utensils back into the hall. Lizzie grinned as she walked across to the baking area.

'I see you've met Eva.'

'I have. We've been talking about the welcome sign.'

'Ah yes. There was a little bit of heated debate over its creation. Eva, can you be Nell's second-in-command today? She'll need a good helper and I know you're great at mixing.'

Eva's eyes lit up. 'Can I?'

I nodded. 'Of course. I'm definitely in need of someone who knows what she's doing.'

'Yay! I'm going to tell Maya. She'll be *so* jealous . . .'

As she hurried away, Lizzie shook her head. 'That's our Eva. Generous to the last.'

'She's fab,' I replied. 'I like her a lot.'

'Eva's a great kid. I mean they're all adorable in their own way, but there are one or two who just shine above the rest. JJ is one of our stars – he's the little Chinese guy in the red baseball cap over there. So cute. And Eva is another. Sometimes I could swear I'm talking to a forty-year-old, the things she comes out with. I think she may just be wiser than everyone else put together.' She looked over her shoulder to see Miguel wrapping up the game. 'Oh, better go. Will you be OK to start baking in a couple of minutes?'

I looked at everything laid out on the table and a small flutter of nerves brushed across my stomach. 'Ready when you are.'

A group of children crowded around the table, sleeves rolled up and excited eyes watching my every move. Eva helped me to hand out the ingredient packs and we went through the recipe step-by-step, the children's smiles, arms and hands gradually becoming more flour-covered as the biscuit dough came together. Maya, almost the exact opposite to Eva with her pale skin and ash-blonde hair, watched my every move with breathless awe. Cutters were shared between them and gradually the baking trays filled with slightly wonky flower shapes, the top sections cut out ready for filling. When I gave each of the children a bag of crushed boiled sweets they looked at me as if I'd lost the plot, but I assured them that the recipe would work if they trusted me. They followed my instructions still unconvinced, with much hilarity when the pieces of boiled sweet stuck to their fingers.

'I'm like a green monster!' JJ shrieked, wiggling his

green sugar-coated fingers in the cutest impression of a scary beast I'd ever seen.

'It's sticky,' Maya giggled. 'And my hands smell like strawberries.'

'How is this ever going to work?' Eva asked, holding up her hands covered in fragments of orange sugar. 'Is this an English thing?'

'You'll see,' I replied, taking the baking trays into the small kitchen and filling the ovens.

While we waited for the biscuits to cook, the kids and I cleared the Bake Zone station, the children's excitement building as the delicious aroma of baking grew stronger.

'Do they bake cookies in England, too?' asked JJ, gazing up at me with chocolate button eyes.

'Yes, we do. Except what we've made today we call biscuits.'

He frowned under his baseball cap. 'They don't look like the biscuits my grandma makes.'

'Are those the ones you have with gravy and collared greens?' Lizzie asked, arriving at our table followed by Astrid. They were carrying a stack of paper bags for the children to decorate before they used them to carry their biscuits home.

JJ nodded. Lizzie smiled at me. 'I should've explained. Biscuits in America refer to savoury baked buns – like scones – and they're eaten with a sausage-filled sauce, which is called gravy but isn't like our gravy. I know, it gets confusing.'

'Only if you're from England,' Astrid laughed. 'We get it just fine!'

Ten minutes later, a bell in the small hen-shaped oven

timer on the table rang out and the children clustered around me.

'OK, kids. Are you ready to see some magic?'

A chorus of little voices answered. 'Yeah!'

I felt a rush of excitement as I took the biscuits out of the oven and brought a tray through to the hall to show the children. The boiled sweets had melted into glossy, glass-like middles, making a multicoloured selection on the tray. I loved how entranced the children were, especially Eva who kept looking from me to the biscuits and back again as if she had never seen anything so wonderful. I asked the children to take their places around the table once more and carefully reunited the biscuits with their mini-bakers. As a final decoration, we dusted the edges of each biscuit with cinnamon sugar.

All too quickly, the after-school club session came to an end and Astrid came over to help me pack the biscuits into the decorated bags for the children to take home.

'Have you had a good time with us?' she asked.

'I have. It's been a lot of fun.'

'Nell, look – I'm drawing you!' Maya said proudly. The drawing looked more like a flower with a face than a person, but I was touched that she had decided to immortalise me in crayon on her cake bag.

'Wow, that is amazing,' I replied. 'You've given me such a big smile.'

'That's because you smile a lot,' Maya said, turning her attention back to her masterpiece.

It was such a small thing, but the fact that a child I'd only just met noticed how happy I was when I was baking meant a great deal. I *had* been happy this afternoon – and sharing my love of baking with the children had given me the biggest buzz.

'It's been good to have you,' Astrid said. 'The kids have been talking about you all through the session. It's weird that they seem so surprised when the leaders have lives outside of S-O-S Club. When I brought my eldest daughter in last term they were amazed I had more kids – they only know my youngest. Plus, they adore Lizzie so it was a given they'd love you.'

'I've been made to feel very welcome. It's a great club.'

Astrid patted my arm. 'It is. I hope we'll see you again while you're here.'

Soon, the parents began to arrive. Eva ran to the hall doors and returned with a beautiful woman in tow.

'Mom – this is Nell from England. She talks like Mary Poppins!'

As soon as the woman smiled, I could see the resemblance between her and her daughter. 'Eva's been so looking forward to meeting you,' she said. 'She's fascinated by England due to that movie. Hi – I'm Shanti.'

I shook her hand as Eva bounced around us, telling her mother about the 'cookies that are called biscuits but not like JJ's grandma's biscuits' and how she thought the 'smashed-up candy' was going to make a mess when it went in the oven. In between responding to her daughter, Shanti told me that Eva's grandmother had given her *Mary Poppins* last Christmas and it had since become her favourite film.

'I'm afraid Eva thinks everyone in England talks like Julie Andrews and wears old-fashioned clothes. I've told her that isn't so.'

'I sometimes wish London was a little more like the film,' I replied. 'It would be great fun if we had more people dancing on rooftops and talking like Dick Van Dyke!'

As they left, I felt a tug on the right leg of my jeans and looked down to see JJ gazing up at me, holding his hands out. Unsure how to respond, I looked at Lizzie who indicated it was fine to give him a hug. I bent down and was almost knocked over as JJ hugged my knees with all of his might. His mother, holding his coat, rucksack and bag of biscuits, laughed.

'Whoa, you've just had a JJ hug. I hope you know what an honour that is.'

'I'm very honoured,' I replied, reaching down to pat his back. As they left I turned to Lizzie. 'How cute is he?'

'He is. I could just munch him up. And his mum is fantastic.' She lowered her voice and stepped closer. 'Amazing family, actually. They lost JJ's dad to cancer last year and pretty much lost everything else – their home, the family business, their security. They spent some time living in an awful apartment block in Tenderloin, in a place that to be honest with you I wouldn't walk through alone in the daylight, and JJ saw his mum attacked by a mugger just before Christmas. No child should have to see something like that – especially an eight-year-old. But Tyler helped them to find accommodation nearer the school and they seem a lot happier now.'

I stared after JJ and his mother, shocked by what they had endured. To look at the pretty lady and her adorable little boy doing giant steps out of the hall, I could never have guessed the horrors they had lived through.

Lizzie saw my reaction and put her hand on my shoulder. 'That's why I consider this club a privilege. We offer an hour of fun for the kids but more than that we offer security, constancy and a precious hour for parents where they know their children are safe. We can't do much to influence their lives outside of this single hour each week, but while they're here we can show them how wonderful they are and give them somewhere positive to have fun and enjoy just being children.'

When all the children had gone, Lizzie, the volunteers and I cleared everything away and gathered together in the middle of the hall. I was exhausted but happy, surprised by how much the children's company had impressed me.

'I hope you'll join us again, Nell?' Miguel asked. 'The kids love seeing new faces.'

I loved the thought of spending more time in the frantically fun environment. 'I'm here for another seven weeks, so if you'll have me back I'd be more than happy to.'

Astrid, Sam, Poppy and Miguel responded with loud affirmations and I caught Lizzie's proud smile as I agreed.

After leaving the school, Lizzie suggested we go to her favourite burrito restaurant, a few blocks away. Over huge burritos stuffed with spicy meat, cheese and rice, smothered in red and green chilli sauces, we chatted about the club, the children and the success of our baking session.

'I'm so happy you enjoyed S-O-S Club,' Lizzie said, in between enormous bites of burrito. 'Most people I know would run a mile if I asked them to take part. The kids are wonderful, but the prospect of all of them bearing down on you at once must be terrifying if you haven't experienced that before.'

I shook my head. 'It wasn't terrifying at all. In fact, I loved it. I didn't think I would, to be honest, but it gave me such a rush to share those biscuits with them. It made me remember all the baking we did as kids, and how magical it was to see something we'd mixed together coming out of the oven as finished items.'

My cousin grinned at me. 'You're a natural, Nell. And the kids adored you. Especially Eva.'

'She's one smart kid.' The thought of the little girl with an attitude far beyond her eight years made me mirror my cousin's grin. 'And how gorgeous is her mum?'

'I know. Shanti Michaelson is one of those women who could look elegant no matter where she was or what she was wearing. You can see where Eva inherited her beautiful features. So, I bet when you decided to come to San Francisco you never thought you'd end up as an after-school club volunteer?'

I didn't. But then I was quickly learning that San Francisco had many surprises waiting for me. Already, my mind was abuzz with possible recipes to share with the children and I realised that, for the first time in a long time, I felt fulfilled. It was a good feeling.

CHAPTER TWELVE

Rare finds in Haight-Ashbury

'Morning, Nell.'

'Morning.'

Rosita, the constantly smiling owner of the New Age store beneath Lizzie's apartment, smiled as I entered her shop. The smell of woody incense and spicy candles curled around my nostrils, infusing everything around me with the aroma. After helping me with Lizzie's surprise, Rosita had invited me to pop down for a cup of herb tea whenever I felt like it and we had struck up a friendship.

I handed her a plate of freshly baked cinnamon and nutmeg sugar cookies I had baked that morning. 'There you go. I tried a new recipe today.'

'Oh, *chiquita*, you are wonderful!' She picked up one of the still-warm cookies and took a bite. 'Girl, these are something else!'

I felt a thrill at the sight of my new friend enjoying my edible gift. 'You think they work?'

'They're so good. You're one talented lady. You know, I have just the tea to accompany these.' She opened a glass-lidded tea chest and produced two bagged teabags. 'Lemongrass green tea – they're new in this week.'

As she made the tea I looked around the shop at the clothes, bags, scarves and stacks of incense and candles as colourful as the rainbow mural on the wall outside. 'So, how's business?'

Rosita shrugged. 'Quiet for now but the tourists don't arrive until lunchtime. Yesterday I sold my entire stock of tie-dyed tees to a Japanese tour party. So, you can celebrate with me.' She handed me a mug emblazoned with a peace sign – a motif I had seen in almost every shop window along Haight Street.

The lemongrass green tea was fragrant and matched the spiciness of the cookies perfectly. 'I might buy some of these teabags,' I said, inhaling the grassy aroma. 'It'll give my system a break from all the great coffee I keep drinking.'

'You can have a box,' Rosita smiled, 'if you promise to test all your recipes on me.'

I clinked my mug against hers. 'Deal. I'm going to do these cookies with the kids this week but I think I might add lemon water icing and maybe pull back on the nutmeg.' I loved the rush that creating recipes gave me.

'Sounds good. So what are your plans today, Miss Sullivan?'

I grinned at the prospect of my intended activity. 'I'm going shopping!'

Not far from Lizzie's apartment were several stores that had quickly become firm favourites of mine. One was Well Beloved, a vintage clothes shop, tucked between a Tibetan goods store and a shop that sold hand-carved pipes, tobacco and – erm – *other products* to smoke. I had first wandered into the clothes store in the middle of my first week here when Lizzie had popped to the food mart to buy supplies, and been blown away by the sheer number of vintage garments filling the small space of the shop. Like all of the stores in this neighbourhood, what the shop lacked in square footage, it more than made up for in height; consequently the racks of clothes soared right up into the ceiling and the owners had constructed an ingenious system of pulleys and long-handled hooks to bring down any garments you wanted to look at.

I wasn't likely to pass up a shopping opportunity, especially as I had already worked my way through the clothes I had brought with me. This, I told myself (as if I needed an excuse), was another part of becoming the new me. I felt like I wanted to look as different on the outside as I was feeling on the inside – so to buy something from my temporarily adopted new neighbourhood was the perfect way to do it.

I spent a while looking through the racks, sorting through sixties tie-dyed t-shirts, fringed tops and Indian-inspired shirts, until I came to a collection of sleeveless mini dresses in delicate, floral fabrics. In the middle of them I found a beautiful cream dress covered in a mass of tiny yellow primrose-like flowers, with pale gold ric-rac braiding around the collar and hem. It was fraying a little in places and in need of a bit of repair but it was perfect. Sunny, kitsch, a little bit eccentric – in fact everything that The Haight was proving to be. I loved it immediately.

'I was wondering who would buy this,' the lady behind the counter said, studying me. 'Have you picked it for you?'

'I couldn't resist it,' I nodded as I handed her a twenty-dollar bill. 'I really like the print.'

'Late sixties,' she said, a hint of wistfulness in her eyes. 'Around '68, '69 I'd guess. The Summer of Love and all was beautiful . . . It's seen better days but with care it could last a lifetime.'

'I was thinking I might customise it,' I said, stroking the faded floral fabric as it lay on the glass counter. 'Bring it back to life again.'

The woman's smile reminded me of Mum and for a brief moment I found myself missing her. Since my arrival I had spoken to her and Dad a number of times and they both seemed thrilled that I was doing something so exciting. Knowing that Mum had been a little concerned about me being in America, I had edited what I'd told her a little – but I would certainly have a lot to tell her when I got home . . .

'I have the perfect thing!' She ducked behind the counter and garments, shoes and boxes started flying in all directions. 'Now where did I . . .? I was certain I'd put it . . . Aha!' She reappeared, a little flushed for her journey and handed me a wooden box with a beaded panel inserted in its lid. 'This arrived months ago with a box of garments. I'd like you to have it.'

Surprised by her gesture, I opened the box to find it stuffed with scraps of fabric, buttons, glass beads and embroidery silks. 'Wow, this is fantastic! But are you sure? I'd be happy to pay for it.'

'Of course I'm sure. I've kept this box waiting for the right customer,' she replied. 'I think you should find something in there to bring beauty back to the dress.'

'I'm sure I will. Thank you.'

She folded the dress, put it with the box into a brown bag with string handles and handed it to me. 'You're welcome. You have a nice day, now.'

'I will. Thanks.'

A blond-dreadlocked man in an Indian shirt, wide denim jeans and sandals held the door open for me as I left the shop and I caught a waft of patchouli scent as I thanked him. Pleased with my purchase, I rounded the corner and began to walk up Masonic Avenue, past bars, shops and cafés.

A sudden burst of sunlight from behind the grey clouds made me look down – and I screeched to a halt.

The pavement beneath my feet appeared to fall away into a deep chasm. Shocked, I half-fell back from the jagged edges of the paving slabs exposing vertical walls of earth tumbling down from my feet. How had a chasm so deep opened up outside the shop? And was the silver streak miles below the shattered pavement a river?

And then, I heard laughter. Breathing heavily, I turned to see a group of middle-aged tourists by my side.

'Clever, huh?' A short, squat man with a very red face and twinkling eyes pointed at the gaping hole in the sidewalk. 'Plain got me first time I saw it.'

'We're from Ohio,' an equally squat woman chimed in. 'They don't have this kinda thing there.'

'Thought I was done for, I did. Almost stopped my heart.'

As my own heart was currently threatening to beat out through my ears, I sympathised with him. 'I thought I was going to fall.'

'It's a chalk painting,' the woman said. 'Took me a while to figure that out. Whoever painted it knows what they're doing . . .'

As she was talking another pedestrian gasped and scrabbled backwards, eliciting more good-hearted guffaws from the group.

'It's OK, it's a painting on the sidewalk.'

'Near stopped my heart it did.'

'We're from Ohio. You don't get anything like it in Ohio . . .'

Now that I knew I wasn't going to plummet to my death, the apparent gap in the pavement fascinated me. When I looked closer I could see the lighted windows of a tiny village clinging to one side of the exposed cliff edge and an eagle's eyrie with three chicks perched on a rock platform on the other. From a couple of angles it was obviously a painting, but with the sun on the right side it was scarily real. So much so that when I crossed the street and bought an iced coffee at a small café to watch, nearly twenty more people were fooled by the illusion.

Why would anyone go to so much trouble, I wondered? And who had created such a painstakingly detailed work of art – especially one that would be destroyed as soon as it rained?

'Can I get you another coffee?' the waiter asked, clearing the table next to me.

'I'd love one, thanks.' A scream brought both of our heads round to face the painted chasm once more. A young woman was being comforted by her considerably taller boyfriend, who looked as if his spine might snap from the effort of bending down to put his arm around her. 'Oh, poor girl. It looks so real when you're about to step on it.'

The waiter laughed. 'The guy is a genius. Gets folks every time.'

'Do you know him?'

'Personally? No. Nobody does. But we see his work here all the time.'

I loved the thought of someone doing this unseen. 'I wonder why he does it?'

'Guy's an artist. Does this kinda thing all over town. I see him working sometimes when I arrive about six thirty a.m. He's always disguised, of course. It's a Haight thing. People wait for his next one.'

'And they're all over The Haight?' I asked. I wanted to discover more of the secret artist's work.

'They're everywhere in the city. If you look for them.' He collected my empty coffee glass and gave the table a quick wipe with the cloth he carried. 'Like I said, the guy's an institution here.'

From: nell.sullygirl@gmail.com
To: vickster1981@me-mail.com
Subject: A Haight mystery

OK, here's something strange.

Last week was my first week walking around SF on my own as Lizzie went back to her teaching and schools' advisory stuff, so I've been trying to get to a different bit of the city every day. And I've discovered these really brilliant pavement paintings. They're painted to give an optical illusion, so you think you're stepping on a river, or that Spiderman is climbing up the side of a building where the kerb is the roof. Apparently the guy who paints them works all over the city but nobody knows who he is. Rosita who works in the shop below Lizzie's apartment is a big fan. She follows him on Twitter and she's been tipping me off about new locations for his work. She thinks he's an older guy because there's been a history of secret art appearing around The Haight for years.

How cool is that?

Nell xxx

From: vickster1981@me-mail.com
To: nell.sullygirl@gmail.com
Subject: Re: A Haight mystery

I can't imagine anyone going to that much bother around here.

I'm stuck applying for jobs I don't think even exist and the highlight of my day is watching *Rastamouse* with Ruby. I'd marry that mouse if I could. Oh and Greg isn't speaking to me now because I placed him third on my list of dream men after Ryan G (number one, of course) and Olly Murs. I like them cheeky, what can I say? But he went off to work in a huff this morning and hasn't replied to my texts. I give up. Why do men ask these questions if they don't want to know the answer?

You should find out who this dude is. For one reason only: HE MIGHT BE FIT. Maybe that's just my desperate vicarious ambition for you but I've said it now. Hunt him down, Sullivan! And send pics!

(And if he's minging, at least you only have six weeks left in the same city as him. I've seen the films – there are lots of places to hide from psychos in San Francisco.)

Do it!

Vix xxxx

As I followed the new painting locations each day I began to discover new places in the city. A painting on the edge of the sidewalk onto the road that transformed the kerbstones into a skyscraper's roof garden with delicate tendrils of ivy cascading down to the street far below led me to a beautiful church in Mission. Another that looked like the top of a Coke can with a glimpse of a Caribbean beach through the hole was outside a gorgeous shop selling jewellery handcrafted by an artist collective in North Beach. And a series of paintings shaped like dinosaur footprints filled with sparkling rock-pools pointed the way to a view of the Golden Gate Bridge from Marina Green, which took my breath away. It became a delightful game: almost as if the artist was leading me to the places he loved the most in his city.

As I followed this colourful trail, I started to hope I might catch a glimpse of the artist at work. It was a delicious mystery and I started taking photographs of each of the pavement paintings when I found them, emailing the evidence back to Vicky, who received each one in her own inimitable fashion:

'He's talented with his hands, Nell. That's all you need to know . . .'

'You've seen what he can do with chalks. Imagine if YOU were the pavement . . .'

'Damn it, Nell. Find him and MARRY HIM. Even if he's in his nineties and looks like Mr Miyagi . . .'

It made me laugh every time she replied but it also felt good to be entertaining her while she was facing a very scary time. Her search for a new job was a premonition of what was waiting for me when I returned and I was intensely thankful to be delaying it for a while. It was as if I had a simultaneous view of two parallel lives: what my life in London could have been had I stayed and what it was becoming after making the decision to come here. I did feel a tiny whisper of guilt that I'd left when my best friend was hurting, but perhaps my being here would prove more helpful than if we were together in London. Neither of us needed to indulge in a pity party and I was sure that would have been the inevitable outcome.

When a chalk painting appeared around the corner from Lizzie's apartment, I took my cousin to see it. She was amazed by the image of a polar bear breaking out of a paving slab ice floe and we spent nearly an hour inspecting the work of art.

'I can't believe I've lived here all this time and never seen these,' she said. 'I thought I'd be the one showing you round San Francisco, not the other way around.' She squeezed my arm. 'I'm really happy that you love it here, you know. I was hoping you would. It's just so wonderful to be able to share it with you.'

Following the work of the unknown artist around the city for nearly two weeks had done more than endear its delights to me. It had made me think about the things I most longed to do with my life that I hadn't shared with anyone. Maybe it was the safety that being thousands of miles away from home afforded me, but somehow I found it easier to think here. When I'd been at the Council I'd packed my dream into storage until 'the right time'. But now I suspected that, had I remained in my comfortable job and focused instead on whether Aidan and I would bite the bullet and get together permanently, the 'right time' might never have happened. Being here, surrounded by positivity, creativity and optimism, I could finally allow myself to dream.

They call America the Land of Dreams – and what it might have lacked in ability for its people to realise those dreams it more than made up for in enthusiasm for trying. Everybody here had something else they were aiming for, something deep within them driving them on. Like Marty and Frankie, the cab drivers at Annie's: Marty planned to retire at fifty; Frankie was saving for a boat to run his own fishing trips out into the Bay. When the time came, I truly believed both of them could see their ambitions come to fruition, simply because of the way they spoke about it:

'Sure, boats cost money,' Frankie told me. 'And I don't have a lot of that. But every week I'm saving dollars and every year that passes I'm getting closer to what I need. I know the boatyard I'll buy her from, the specification I want, even the colour of her hull. I can see it in my mind, like I just took a picture. I might be ninety when I get there, but I'll get there.'

'Yeah,' Marty smirked, 'and then – watch out fish!'

The pavement artist was working out his dream – whatever that was. Could he be aiming for international stardom? Recognition from the art world? Or maybe just the ability to do what he loved, day in, day out, for the rest of his life? Perhaps the chalk paintings *were* his dream. Maybe he had been stuck in lifeless jobs for years dreaming of filling his city with colour and spectacle. And then, one day, he had resigned, bought chalks and embarked on living his dream . . .

And so, I considered my secret ambition that only I knew about; the hidden vision that had brightened many a dull Council Planning Committee meeting when I needed to escape and reconnect with the person I felt I really was. In the warm Californian sunshine, it suddenly didn't seem so unrealistic or out of my reach any more. Was the possibility of running my business even viable? And if so, where would I even start?

As it turned out, the answers to my questions were only a chance remark away . . .

CHAPTER THIRTEEN

Beware the chance remark

'You're good at baking.'

Maya was scrutinising my mixing technique with her impossibly big blue eyes as I led the S-O-S bakers in making fruity flapjacks. I noticed that if I began to stir in the opposite direction, she did the same. I'd never seen so much concentration employed over one bowl of baking mixture before and it was really sweet.

'Thanks Maya. You're very good too.'

She shrugged. 'I know *that*. My mommy tells me all the time.'

It was my third week as a guest volunteer at the club and I was thoroughly enjoying myself. The kids had an inbuilt positivity, so much so that I always felt better for having spent time with them. Maya and JJ were my chief mixture tasters, excitedly offering their ideas on what could make the batters 'even more awesomer'; Declan, a shy boy who had barely spoken two words during my first week, was beginning to respond when I asked for his suggestions about how best to stir the mixtures; while Eva had become my stripy-tights-wearing, sparkly-hair-clipped shadow – wanting to sit with me when we had group time, helping me to set out bowls, utensils and ingredients for each session's baking and always the first to volunteer for clearing up.

'I think you have a little fan club there,' Lizzie said as the children proudly carried their still-warm flapjacks to show their parents and guardians at the end of the session.

I was surprised by how much the children responded to me. Being amongst such characters was incredibly uplifting. Eva amused me particularly, with her opinion on everything and searing wit someone twenty years her senior would be proud of, frequently making me giggle with her remarks.

'Does it hurt to talk like that?'

'Like what?'

'Like you do it.'

'Er, no. Why do you think it hurts?'

'Because when I try to speak British it hurts my throat. I figured it might hurt you too . . .'

Many of the things Eva said had no answer, but that didn't seem to matter to her. She was just excited to be having a conversation and it was a quality I admired. What she loved more than anything was talking about England. She had a lot of questions – most, it has to be said, influenced by a certain Disney film – but I was happy to answer all of them. It made me feel a little nostalgic and brought a piece of home into the hall of Sacred Heart Elementary.

At the end of the third S-O-S Club session, Eva ran up for a goodbye hug and thrust a crumpled sheet of paper at me.

'I did it for you,' she beamed. 'Mom says it's one of my best. I think it is, too.'

She had drawn a picture of the S-O-S Club volunteers, with me in the middle and, oddly, the St Paul's bird woman from *Mary Poppins* (her favourite scene from the film). All around us were small Vs. 'We're all feeding the birds, tuppence a bag,' she explained.

Once Eva had given me a gift, more of the children followed suit. Soon, I had a sweet collection of pictures pinned to the wall of my makeshift bedroom at Lizzie's: a car collage made of scraps of magazine pages from Declan; a crayon drawing of the Golden Gate Bridge with me holding a biscuit that was bigger than I was from Maya; and two portraits of JJ that he gave me 'so you don't forget me when we're not at S-O-S'.

'You know, I'm loving S-O-S Club,' I admitted to Lizzie one evening, as we tucked into takeaway quesadillas and red and green chilli from Comida Hermosa, a fab little Latin American restaurant not far from Lizzie's apartment. 'It's great to support you too.'

'You know, when I first suggested the club to Tyler he wasn't sure it would last past one term.'

'Really?'

'Mm-hmm. Looking back I can see why: I mean, I was completely unprepared for the amount of work needed, not just to run it but also to promote it, secure funding for it and come up with a challenging programme of activities that would be suited to the mix of children it would attract. It's been a pretty steep learning curve but I'm proud of what we've achieved.'

I took a bite of quesadilla and enjoyed the spices tingling on my lips and tongue. 'So, come on, what's the deal with you and Tyler?'

Lizzie grinned. 'He's gorgeous and we get on really well. But even though I'd like there to be more, I don't get the feeling that he's willing to go there yet. I think he values our working relationship and doesn't want to jeopardise it.'

'Have you told him how you feel?'

A look of horror passed over her face. 'Are you mad? Of course I haven't! The moment you even mention the possibility it changes everything.'

'But you'd like it to change, wouldn't you?'

'Yes, but – it's complicated, Nellie. Ty isn't just a great friend, he's an important ally. Many of the doors that have opened for me here wouldn't have done so had it not been for his intervention. He's really respected within the education system and his recommendation counts for a lot. The moment we get involved he could be accused of vested interests and it lessens my claim to the changes we want to make. It's difficult.'

'You like him, Liz, and he's clearly interested in you. I think if you took the risk you'd be surprised.'

'Ha, this coming from Miss Play-It-Safe,' she laughed. 'Although I can see you're starting to take some risks of your own, which is good. Like volunteering at S-O-S Club. You're a natural. And the kids adore you. Perhaps you could consider working with children as a possible career change when you go home?'

The thought of the decisions I faced when I returned to the UK brought an uncomfortable tightness to my insides. 'Perhaps. Or maybe I should just stay in San Francisco. Find a Pablo of my own.'

Lizzie topped up my wine glass. 'Have you thought what you'd like to do for your next career move?'

I considered her question and decided now was the time to share my dream career with my cousin. 'There is one thing – but you'll probably laugh.'

My cousin fixed me with a stare. 'Hardly. I live in The Haight – nothing can be more preposterous than what I see here every day.'

I took a breath. Even in my closest moments with Aidan I'd never felt the urge to share my secret career dream for fear of jinxing it. But maybe this was the right time and place – thousands of miles from home.

'OK, here it is: I would love to open a diner – a real American diner like Annie's – but in London. It's an idea that's been building for a few years since Vicky and I visited New York and it's become a bit of a secret daydream for me. The thing is, I think I could do it. I'm never happier than when I'm baking and the thought of creating somewhere that could become a real hub of the community thrills the heck out of me. Of course, I could just be fooling myself. I mean, it's hardly the best time to start out on my own. I don't know how I could raise the capital to buy somewhere, or even rent, and I have no idea about how to run a restaurant. But I keep coming back to a mental picture of me being there, serving customers in my own business.'

I couldn't work out what Lizzie was thinking. Her expression was thoughtful, but other than that gave little away. 'So come on, tell me. Is it a completely daft idea?'

She slowly shook her head. 'I don't think so. You aren't the kind of person who would embark on something like that without really considering all the options. It might be a struggle financially to get established, but after that I don't doubt you have the tenacity to make it succeed.'

I had fully expected Lizzie to dismiss my dream; but to hear her support for it meant the world to me. Surprised, I suddenly burst into tears, laughing as they ran down my face. San Francisco was definitely bringing me more in touch with my emotions . . . 'Look at me – I'm a wuss! But that's wonderful, Liz.'

Lizzie handed me a tissue as she gave me a hug. 'This really means a lot to you, doesn't it? Why didn't you say something before?'

'I thought it was just a pipe dream – you know, something you think about on Monday mornings when work's dragging? I thought I was kidding myself.'

'Well, stop thinking like that. The very fact that you're here shows what trusting your gut instinct can do.' She stopped, waving her hands as if suddenly beset by a swarm of invisible flies. 'Wait a minute – that's it!'

'What?'

'You could ask Annie! Come on, Nell, it's a brilliant idea! There is nothing about running a diner business that Annie Legado doesn't know. She's made her diner a success for thirty-seven years and even branched out to establish one in New York, which her cousin runs. She's an entrepreneur, a visionary and, apart from being slightly scary, is the most driven person I know.'

The thought of consulting Annie Legado for business advice terrified me more than I'd admit, but Lizzie was right. If anyone could tell me whether I had the potential to succeed, Annie could. 'Lizzie, that's a great idea! I'll go and ask her tomorrow.'

Lizzie held her hands out. 'Why wait until tomorrow? We could call her now!'

'Pardon?'

She leapt off the sofa and grabbed her telephone. 'I have her number.'

Panic hit me. I'd only just been brave enough to tell Lizzie what I wanted to do. I hadn't prepared any questions or thought through what I wanted to know . . .

'No, Lizzie! Not now . . . I-I need to think about this.'

She held the phone at arm's length from me. 'What is there to think about?'

'*Everything!* Please, just wait a minute . . .'

'Too late – I'm dialling. Hi Annie? It's Lizzie. I'm good thanks. Listen, I was wondering if you fancied popping over this evening? I have wine.' She laughed, giving me an enthusiastic thumbs-up, which did nothing to assuage my jangling nerves. 'That's brilliant! See you soon.' She hung up and whooped loudly. 'Success!'

I dropped my head into my hands as my thoughts turned cartwheels. 'What am I going to say? She'll laugh me out of the room.'

'No, she won't. I think there was a reason you told me this evening. It's too good an opportunity to miss.' Her smile was kind as she hurried into the kitchen to fetch wine and another glass. 'You were the one advising me to take risks five minutes ago. It's going to be fine – trust me!'

By the time Annie arrived I was a nervous wreck, with a barely legible list of questions I'd scribbled down that suddenly seemed nonsensical.

'Hi Annie,' Lizzie chirped, sending my list speedily into my back pocket as I stood. 'So glad you could come.'

'You have wine, I have a night off. What's not to like about this?' Her face crinkled into a smile when she saw me. 'Hey, Nell. I hear from Laverne your cheesecake recipe rocks.'

'You can find that out for yourself,' my cousin replied quickly, lifting up the plate of cheesecake. 'Care for a slice?'

Annie lifted her glasses from the chain around her neck to peer at my creation. 'Good work, lady. Good structure, great presentation. Smells good too. Make mine a large one, Lizzie.'

Watching The Haight catering legend eating my cheesecake I knew exactly how the contestants felt watching Mary Berry and Paul Hollywood testing cakes on *The Great British Bake Off*. Minutes seemed to slow to months and I felt every inch of me tensing in anticipation of her verdict. She closed her eyes as she savoured the bite. Was that a good sign? After an agonising wait, she opened her eyes.

'This,' she said, tapping the plate with the prongs of her fork, 'is very, very good.'

I let out the breath I'd been holding in and just about stopped myself from bursting into tears of relief. 'Is it? Thank you.'

'Nell wants to open a diner,' Lizzie rushed, not missing a trick. 'And she wants your advice.'

Annie's hazel eyes squinted over the rim of her glasses. 'For real?'

I nodded. So did Lizzie. Annie looked from me to my cousin and, unexpectedly, let out a mighty laugh that sent Pablo the Goldfish scurrying for the safety of the stone castle ornament in his tank.

'I'm looking at a pair of Brit nodding dogs. Let me tell you this, Nell, you clearly have the baking skill. But running a diner – or any restaurant – requires more than skill. It can take over your life. In fact, it has to become your life, in the early years at least. I didn't take a day off in my first three years, save for Christmas and Thanksgiving, and I didn't draw a decent wage for almost four. It's hard work, it breaks your heart every day and often you get no thanks. Now you tell me, are you ready for that kinda commitment?'

Slightly terrified by the prospect, I took a deep breath. 'If I had the opportunity to make it happen, I believe I would give it everything.'

Annie considered me for a long time, taking another leisurely bite of cheesecake. With a side-glance at Lizzie, she nodded – her trademark half-smile appearing. 'Then I'll give you an opportunity.'

'How do you mean?' I stared at her, then at Lizzie, who smiled her surprise back.

'Come work for me. Work the breakfast-brunch crowd.

Best way to learn the business is from within it. How many weeks you have left now?'

'Five weeks.'

'So. Five weeks, say four days a week: that's a good base for figuring out if you're ready yet.'

Lizzie clapped her hands. 'That's perfect, isn't it, Nell?'

'Wait a moment . . .' This was happening too quickly. I needed to jump out of the speeding traffic for a moment, to consider Annie's suggestion properly. It was a fantastic offer but I was in America on a visitor visa – so working of any kind was not permitted. I knew that much from the careful study of the paperwork I'd made before I left England.

Then, a thought struck me. In my final year working for the Planning department, the Council had adopted a new scheme for interns – unpaid volunteers who would work with the Planning Officers for up to three months at a time, gaining valuable first-hand experience of working in the career they hoped to enter. Could that work for me here?

'I can't work on my visa,' I explained, seeing Lizzie's crestfallen expression over Annie's shoulder. 'But I have a proposition for you: take me on as your unpaid intern for five weeks. I'll work four mornings a week and you can show me all the aspects of running the diner – and if anyone asks, we can call it extended work experience. What do you think?'

Annie's half-smile widened to at least three-quarters. 'I like you, kid. You've got *chutzpah*. If you're happy with it, so am I. How about starting tomorrow morning, at six?'

Heart beating faster than the crazy African drum player on the corner of Haight and Cole, I smiled at Annie and Lizzie. 'I'll be there!'

From: nell.sullygirl@gmail.com
To: vickster1981@me-mail.com
Subject: Big news!

Hi Vix

You'll never guess what – I'm an intern!

I know, thirty-two is a little old to do work experience, but I have an opportunity to work at an American diner. Annie's – remember the place I told you about two weeks ago? We arranged it tonight. I'm doing four shifts a week for the rest of my stay. I start tomorrow. And I'm so excited about it!

The thing is – and I probably should have told you this before – but I've harboured a dream to one day open a diner ever since we went on that shopping trip to New York. Do you remember O'Hare's Diner in West Village? While this isn't running my own place, it'll help me to decide if it's just a daydream or if it's something I could realistically aim for.

I'm practising my 'Have a nice day' and

refilling coffee cups even before they're empty. Can you imagine that?

Hope all is good with you.

Love ya,

Nell xx

From: vickster1981@me-mail.com
To: nell.sullygirl@gmail.com
Subject: Re: Big news!

That is hilarious!

I'm picturing you in one of those cute diner waitress outfits like the ones they wear in my favourite ice cream shop in Brighton. And rollerboots! Tell me there's a drive-in and my joy will be complete!

Seriously, Nell, I could see you running your own place. Those cakes you used to bring into work were amazing and part of the reason I was hoping you and Aidan would get back together was that you might start baking again. It's a brilliant idea and I know you're going to rock at it!

Not so bad here. Went for another pointless interview with an agency where I swear I was ten years older than any of the staff. Their idea of an aptitude test was me saying which character from *The Only Way is Essex* I most identified with. They're basing personality types on reality TV now! But at least it amused me. Some good news, though – Terry's just got a job. His nephew works for a property developer so Tel's advising them on planning law. Nice to see the gang slowly getting back on their feet.

But go you, diner intern! (That's my best attempt at being American. Greg says I'm watching far too much *Glee* at the mo, but I've told him it's either that or Jeremy Kyle . . .)

Remember, I need details! Good luck, lovely!

Vix xx

CHAPTER FOURTEEN

Carpe diem

Next morning I struggled out of bed, after a brief disagreement with my alarm clock, not believing the time it was telling me. When I'd agreed to work the breakfast and brunch shift last night it didn't really sink in that Annie's opened for breakfast at four thirty a.m. Annie suggested I start at six, which meant getting up at five.

The smell of toast wafted through to my room and when I walked into the kitchen I found my cousin, bleary-eyed and swathed in a bathrobe that dwarfed her, preparing tea in her Brighton teapot.

'Morning,' she said sleepily.

'Morning. You didn't have to do this, Liz.'

'Yes, I did. You have a long morning ahead of you. It's going to be demanding and you need to eat something to keep you going. Also, while I love Annie and revere everything on her menu, her tea is awful and you need a decent brew.' She handed me a mug of tea.

'You're a star. Thank you.'

Lizzie picked up a plate of toast and her own mug and shuffled through to the living room behind me. 'Are you excited?'

'I am. I hardly slept last night.' I looked out of the bay window. Haight Street was still dark and empty, save for a few lazily moving cars and a light coming from Java's Crypt, where Ced had arrived to open up. People began their days early in this city.

Lizzie grinned. 'Might be worth getting an early night tonight then. What time do you finish?'

'One o'clock. I think I might try and catch a couple of hours' sleep afterwards.'

'We'll have a quiet night then. I'll be home around five p.m. and we'll order pizza.'

'Sounds amazing.' I checked my watch. 'Right, I'd better get going.' Panic suddenly took hold of me and I stared at my cousin. 'What if I can't do this, Lizzie? What if I get there and discover that running a diner is the last thing I should be doing?'

My cousin hugged me. 'Stop worrying. It's just work experience, after all. I know you're going to have a fantastic time. I'm so proud of you, Nellie!'

I hadn't expected to find many customers at Annie's, having seen only two other people on my short walk there. But the diner was three-quarters full, Laverne already running around taking orders from the busy tables.

'Hey Nell, welcome to the team,' she grinned. 'This is so cool!'

'And here's the new recruit!' Annie clapped her hands and hurried to the front of the counter.

Marty and Frankie turned from their triple stack pancakes. 'You hired the Brit?'

'Technically, no. She's my intern. Who knew this place would get an intern, huh?'

Frankie sniggered. 'Move over Donald Trump.'

'If you think you're getting staff discount, think again,' Marty warned me. 'I've been eating here thirty years and I never so much as got a bagel on the house.'

Annie gave his ear a swift cuff and Marty almost fell off his stool laughing. 'That's because you don't work for me.'

'So hire me already.'

'If I did we'd go out of business in a week, Marty.' Annie rolled her eyes as she handed me my staff t-shirt. 'Did I mention some of our clientele are knuckleheads?'

I smiled. 'I expected as much.'

'Good. You'll fit right in. Come through to the kitchen and we'll get started. Laverne, you good to hold the fort?'

'I'm on it,' Laverne replied.

The long, narrow galley kitchen ran the length of the diner and connected to front of house with a small hatch where plates of Annie's delicious culinary delights would appear. To see behind the scenes was a real treat and inevitably turned my thoughts to what a diner of my own would look like some day. The stainless steel work surfaces were spotless, lined with rows of steel containers stuffed with ingredients – huge slices of beef tomato, freshly cut lettuce, stacks of square American and Swiss cheese slices, onion rings, blueberries in deep purple syrup, large pickled gherkins, soured cream, a bank of mayonnaises and sauces, and a whole vat of maple syrup. As I watched, Dominic and Karin, the chefs, effortlessly assembled orders, moving seamlessly between the preparation area and the large 'flat-top' grill, where thick pancakes studded with peanut butter chips, blueberries and banana slices were cooking.

'Karin, Dom, you know Nell?'

They looked up briefly, never missing a beat with their deftly choreographed routine. 'Hey, Nell.'

'These guys have been with me ten years,' Annie said. 'This place wouldn't work without them.'

'Does that mean we get a raise, Annie?' Karin smiled, flipping six pancakes in quick succession on the flat-top grill.

'Sure. When I get one.' She winked at me. 'You can change into your staff t-shirt in the staff restroom over there. I'll get you an apron and we'll begin.'

For the next thirty minutes, I had the privilege of a personal Annie Legado tour of her diner. Every piece of equipment, every method and every custom of the neighbourhood diner was patiently described and I tried my best to make mental notes of everything she said. Seeing that I was becoming overwhelmed by all the new information, Annie stopped and half-smiled at me.

'Hey, don't sweat it, kid. It all makes sense eventually.'

After the tour, it was time to make my debut behind the counter. My first job was filling the ingenious orange juicing machine with fresh, sweet Californian navel oranges from a crate. Tipped into the top of the clear, box-like machine, the oranges passed between rotating plastic cogs – peel and all – and the juice was collected in large jugs underneath. Almost every customer ordered the orange juice and I already knew from my previous visits to Annie's how delicious it was. What it meant for the diner staff, however, was that refilling the orange squeezing machine was a regular part of the day's tasks. As was my next job – the coffee refill round.

Annie's instruction for this was straightforward: 'If it's empty, fill it. If it's not empty, top it up. Don't ask permission and don't be offended if they refuse. Bottom line, there's always coffee.'

A great thing about the coffee refill round was that it gave me the opportunity to meet all the customers. Marty and Frankie were very complimentary on my newly acquired 'top-up technique'.

'It looks like she was born to do this, eh Frankie?'

'She sure was, Marty. Good job, Nell. One thing you gotta know about Annie's – as long as you keep the coffee coming, the customers will love you.'

An eclectic mix of customers had ventured to Annie's at this early hour. City workers in sharp suits relaxed over Eggs Benedict with sides of crispy American bacon; the bookstore owner and his assistant manager were tucking into enormous slices of pillowy Cinnamon-Walnut French toast before work; while a group of clocking-off security guards chowed down on spicy Mexican breakfast *huevos rancheros*, trading banter as they ate.

'So you're from England?'

I smiled at the man sitting at table twenty, who looked as if he'd moved into Haight during the Summer of Love and never left, his crocheted waistcoat, embroidered Indian shirt and long, straggly hair the unmistakable signs of a hippy uniform. 'Yes, I'm from London.'

'I went to London once,' he grinned, revealing an impressive set of gold teeth. 'Carnaby Street and Covent Garden blew my mind. You live near there?'

'Not far.'

'Man, those were some good times. Your Underground system is *intense*.'

Not knowing how else to respond, I accepted the compliment on behalf of my home city, hoping Boris Johnson wouldn't mind the impertinence.

Being constantly busy meant that the time passed quickly and before I knew it the nine-thirty breakfast queue was waiting out of the door and onto the street outside.

'This is where the fun really starts,' Laverne grinned at me as we narrowly avoided a collision delivering meals to customers. 'You ready for it?'

I was exhausted already and the prospect of the mammoth line was daunting to say the least. But I wanted to know if I could manage during one of Annie's busiest times. Feeling a rush of adrenalin, I nodded. 'I'm ready.'

Within minutes it was as if a switch had been flicked and everything went into hyper-drive. Suddenly, every customer wanted something and nobody was willing to wait.

'Hey, can I get more coffee here?' a gruff-faced woman barked at me.

'No problem. I'll be with you as soon as I can.'

A harassed-looking mother with three small kids grabbed my elbow as I hurried back to the counter, nearly causing me to lose my balance. 'Miss? Could we order another side of bacon?'

'Of course.'

Bacon – table eight . . . Refill – table four . . .

'Can I get three more English muffins and a refill?'

'I'll be right with you.'

Bacon – table eight . . . Refill – table four . . . English muffins times three and more coffee – table . . . table . . . Crap, which table asked me for that?

Panicking as the requests stacked up in my head, I ducked behind the counter, avoiding the irate couple who felt their wait in the breakfast queue was unacceptably long and were consequently hijacking any member of staff who passed close enough to air their grievances.

'Nell, the juice machine needs refilling,' Annie called over her shoulder, not looking up from her order pad as she served the customer at the front of the queue.

'OK.' I grabbed the crate of oranges from the kitchen and tipped them into the hopper at the top of the machine.

'Short stack, three eggs over easy, table fifteen, order up!' Dom shouted, sliding a plate into the hatch. Beginning to panic I tipped the orange crate at a steeper angle sending oranges bouncing off the top of the machine and skidding across the floor.

'Orange stampede!' Marty yelled as Frankie guffawed loudly.

'Nell – watch the angle!' Annie shouted back, kicking a stray orange out of the way as she collected the food order from the hatch to deliver it herself.

Feeling like an idiot, I stammered, 'Sorry!'

'Deep breath, Ms Brit!' Frankie called out. 'This ain't the busiest this place gets.'

'Give her a break, Frankie,' Annie growled as she headed back behind the counter. 'Kid's new.'

'I give her a week,' Marty grinned. 'No offence, Nell.'

Laverne appeared by my side. 'Hey Nell, did you take the order for table twelve already?'

Flustered, exhausted and my brain now flailing, I stared at her. 'I – er – Oh heck, I'm not sure.'

I must have looked incredibly pathetic because she burst out laughing. 'OK, welcome to first day panic! Table twelve is the one with the three fat tourists – in the middle there?' She pointed into the heaving interior of the diner.

'Did they ask for English muffins?'

'Yes.'

Relief flooded through me. 'Great. Yes, I took their order and yes I'm sorting it now.'

Laverne patted my shoulder. 'Good job. Just remember to *breathe*, OK? This next hour is as crazy as it gets. Your feet will hurt, your body will start to ache more than it ever has and all you'll want to do is curl up and sleep somewhere. But you just have to push through it. Get through this and then you'll be coasting to shift-end.'

'Thank you.'

'You're welcome.'

The adrenalin was astonishing as we reached Annie's peak business hour. There was no time to think, my actions and reactions becoming almost automatic as I moved from one order to the next. After my bumbling attempts I followed Laverne's lead and for the last twenty minutes found a rhythm of sorts.

'Hey lady, this ain't what I ordered,' yelled an overfed man with a scowl no amount of Botox could fix as I passed by his table.

Panicking a little, I checked my order pad. 'I'm terribly sorry, sir. What was it you ordered?'

He stared at me like I'd just sprouted wings. 'You're *British*? They're hiring foreigners here now? Sheesh, this place has gone down the pan.' He raised his voice louder, enunciating each word as though I couldn't understand him at normal speed. 'I – ordered – two – eggs – *over-easy*. These – ain't – over-easy.'

The sour-faced woman sitting opposite him sucked the air between her teeth. 'Is she stupid or something?'

'Yeah. Stupid *and* British . . .'

Their rudeness took me by surprise and I stared back impotently, torn between telling them where to go and remaining professionally polite. Tears threatened my eyes and I blinked them back, determined not to give the abusive customers the pleasure.

'And dumb,' the man continued. 'What? You ain't got nothing to say?'

'Is there a problem here?'

I turned to see Annie beside me, her eyes fixed on the angry guy.

'You're too right there's a problem. *She* got the order wrong.'

Her face giving nothing away, Annie turned to me. 'What was the order, kid?'

I handed her my order pad, where I had written the customer's order exactly as he'd given it. Annie nodded and gave it back.

'Your order is correct, sir.'

'Are you kidding me? These ain't over-easy.' His raised voice had attracted the attention of customers at the nearby tables, who were now watching the unfolding spectacle with interest.

Annie's voice remained quiet but firm. 'I would respectfully ask you to keep your voice down, sir. You're disturbing the other customers.'

'Like I give a crap about that . . .'

'Clearly. But if you continue to be abusive to me and my staff I will have to take the matter further.'

'Your food stinks. I want a refund!'

'You appear to have eaten most of it, so maybe it doesn't stink as much as you say.' There was a growing threat in her tone even though her expression didn't change. It was like hearing the rumble of approaching thunder and several of Annie's regulars began to smirk as if they knew what was coming,

'This is unbelievable! You send a foreigner to serve us, she stuffs up and *we're* in the wrong? This ain't customer service, lady, this is a joke!'

And then, I witnessed the reason Annie Legado's customers held her in such high regard. In a flash she had the man's collar in her hand and was marching him bodily towards the door as his wife screamed abuse in their wake. Seeing the tiny Puerto Rican lady frog-marching a man almost twice her height and several times her width was truly a sight to behold.

'I don't need your attitude in my restaurant,' Annie growled, ejecting the onerous individual onto the street. 'Don't you ever come here again, you hear?'

The man's wife rushed over to confront Annie, but clearly thought better of it when she saw her expression. Once the abusive couple were out of the building, Annie slammed the door and walked calmly back through the diner as several of the regulars cheered. She patted my shoulder as she passed me.

'You did great, kid, don't let numbskulls like that upset you. Now, the orange juice machine needs filling again. You good to handle it?'

A little shaken but relieved by what I'd just seen, I smiled at her. 'I think I can manage it. Thank you.'

'You're welcome.'

For the next twenty minutes service continued at pace and I quickly forgot the incident as I raced around fulfilling orders and topping up coffee mugs. Just when I thought the busy period would never end, the queue to the street became a queue to the door and eventually dwindled to four people waiting to be seated. I felt proud of myself for surviving, but the reality of day-to-day work in a diner was hitting home hard. When I had daydreamed about running my own place, I'd seen myself serenely floating around the tables, taking orders and laughing with customers in slow motion – no pressure, no demands. Now, in the relative calm after the breakfast rush, I reflected on how different the reality of it was. My feet hurt, my brain hurt and I ached all over. And this was just being a waitress: the fleeting glimpses I'd had of Annie Legado during the craziness had revealed how hard she worked. She never stopped: serving at the counter, doing the refill rounds, bringing out new boxes of ingredients from the cold store, mixing batters and slicing mountains of fresh fruit in the prep area. All the time she knew exactly where everybody was, often calling out to us without looking up from her tasks. And she was always steady – calm, collected, in control. Of course, this was the benefit of thirty-seven years of diner management, but it was still impressive.

If I decided to pursue my diner dream, this would be my reality. Not to mention all the other work that happened unseen out of business hours. Accounts, stock ordering, wages, menu plans, staff rotas . . . It would be a complete life change, overhauling my understanding of the word 'work' and quite possibly taking over my life. Was I ready for that kind of commitment and sacrifice?

At eleven o'clock Annie tapped me on the shoulder. 'Hey kid, you did good. Take thirty and get something to eat. Dom'll prepare whatever you like.'

I ordered a breakfast crêpe with ham, onions, cheese and green bell peppers and found a seat by the window to take my break. Laverne brought me a large mug of coffee and a glass of orange juice and it was only when I started to drink them that I realised how thirsty I was. My head was beginning to throb and I kicked my shoes off under the table to rest my burning bare feet on the soothing coolness of the tiled floor.

'Mind if I sit here?'

Keen to enjoy my precious thirty minutes, I was about to say no when I saw the owner of the voice. 'Oh, hello. Please do.'

Max Rossi slid onto the bench seat opposite me, looking as lovely as he had the last time we'd met in Annie's. 'Breakfast by yourself?'

'Just taking a break. It's my first day.'

Max frowned until I pinched out the fabric of my t-shirt to indicate the Annie's logo. 'Oh, I see. When were you hired?'

'Last night. And technically *not* hired. Annie's invited me to be her intern during the rest of my stay.'

'Wait – let me get this straight – you're on holiday but you *volunteered* to work? Are you out of things to do here so quickly?'

I laughed. 'Not at all. But Annie found out that I'd love to open a diner one day and she suggested I get some work experience here.'

'Wow. So you're working every day?'

'Nope. Just Mondays to Thursdays, six a.m. till one p.m. The rest of the time I'll be sightseeing and making the most of my stay.'

'Or sleeping.' The sparkle in his eyes was irresistible.

'Yes, definitely sleeping. Especially after today.' I wondered if I looked as tired as I felt inside.

'I don't doubt it. So, I hope you enjoy working your butt off for zero pay.'

I smiled happily. 'I am and I will.'

He seemed amused by this. 'Crazy Brit. Well, I'll see you around.'

'Aren't you having breakfast?' I asked, kicking myself afterwards for sounding so obviously disappointed.

'I am, but to go. Laverne's making up my order. The theatre group at the art collective had a bust-up last night and I'm providing breakfast to smooth over the cracks.' He shook his head. 'Artistic temperaments, they're a killer. Put a bunch of them together in a confined space and it's like *Apocalypse Now*. You have a good day.'

'I will. You too.'

I watched him walk back to the counter, where Laverne was waiting with several brown paper bags and a cardboard tray of takeaway coffee cups. Was I giddy from the post-breakfast rush or the extra-strong coffee, or something else . . .?

CHAPTER FIFTEEN

Interesting developments

I was so exhausted when I walked out of Annie's at lunchtime that I went straight back to Lizzie's and curled up in bed. I slept for five hours straight, finally waking when my amused cousin brought me a welcome cup of tea.

'You survived then, sleeping beauty?'

I blinked the sleep from my eyes and sipped the hot tea, which tasted as close to heaven as it was possible to be. 'I did.'

Lizzie perched on the edge of the futon. 'And how was it?'

'Scary at first. And completely overwhelming when the breakfast rush kicked in. Annie chucked out some obnoxious customers who had been hassling me – no, it was fine, don't worry – and it was incredible to watch. But I loved it, Lizzie! I'm so knackered I can hardly think straight but it's a *good* tired, if you know what I mean.'

'I get that. Maybe it's because you've been doing what you're meant to do. And I don't mean waitressing. Apart from the people Annie ejected, did the rest of the customers behave for you?'

I instantly thought of Max and the way his cheeky smile had made me feel. 'They were very kind. Marty and Frankie were on form. There were a couple of people queuing during the rush who complained a bit but I didn't take it personally.'

'Good.' She gave me a quizzical look. 'OK, what aren't you telling me?'

'Sorry?' Had my cousin worked me out so quickly?

'I felt like you were going to add something else there.'

I couldn't stop the forward progress of my smile. 'Maybe . . .'

Lizzie shrieked and bounced on the futon, almost showering me with tea. 'I *knew* it! What's his name?'

'Who says it's a bloke?'

'Your face!'

I put my tea on Lizzie's desk to keep it safe from her bouncing. 'Fine. You remember the guy who bumped into me when we went to see Eric's show?'

'The sexy coffee bloke?'

'The very same. Well it turns out he lives in The Haight and knows the Alfaros.'

Lizzie's eyes were as wide as dinner plates. 'No!'

'Yep. In fact, Mrs Alfaro introduced him to me last week and he came in again today.'

'*And?*'

'And we had a nice chat.'

'You are not leaving it there, Nellie! I need details.'

So I told her about Max Rossi, his lovely dove-grey eyes and cheeky smile that made me lose all sense of time.

'Nell Sullivan, you sly woman! Why didn't you tell me this last week?'

I blushed. 'I don't know, I think I just wanted time to process it. You're not offended are you?'

'Don't be daft. If he's as gorgeous as you say I think I'd want to keep him to myself, too. Wow, so he lives here? How spooky is that!'

'Do you know him?'

'Max Rossi, did you say his name was? His name sounds familiar but I can't picture him. From your description I'm sure I would remember if I'd seen him. Oh Nell, how exciting! Are you going to see him again?'

'I'm not seeing him, Lizzie.'

'Not *yet*. But there's time. Well, good for you. I hope he comes in every day and makes you smile. It's about time you had a bit of fun. You should ask him out for coffee after your shift.'

'*Lizzie . . .*'

'No, I'm just saying. It could be nice to get to know him.'

'I'm not sure about that. Plus, if he is coming into Annie's every day he'll be swimming in coffee.'

She swiped at me. 'Tea, then. Or one of Ced's iced Chai latte things. Or water. The beverage isn't important.'

I thought about our first conversation at Annie's and the art collective's business card tucked safely in my purse. 'Actually, he did mention he's having an exhibition next week. I suppose we could pop down there?'

Lizzie's eyes were wide as a bushbaby's. 'Too right we could! That's perfect, Nellie. You can see him again and I can check him out. It's a definite date!'

Once I'd told Lizzie, it was clearly time to share the news with a certain someone else too . . .

From: vickster1981@me-mail.com
To: nell.sullygirl@gmail.com
Subject: Re: A bit of a confession

Nell Sullivan, you HUSSY!

Seriously, I am proud of you. Firstly for finding a hottie on your doorstep and secondly (but most importantly) for it not being Aidan. You've been mooning over that man for far too long. It's time you did a bit of window-shopping and, if the opportunity arises, indulge in something tasty!

I'm so jealous! He sounds gorgeous too. Like Johnny Depp in *Chocolat* – and you know JD is my third reserve after RG, OM and of course Greg (we're still on shaky ground after the Top Three conversation, so I have to put that in case he's checking my emails). If you get the chance, snog him. For me? Consider it your contribution to maintaining the mental stability of your best friend. Because if I don't get a job soon, I'll be one of those stories you read in *Take a Break* about a woman losing the plot in ASDA and running amok with her trolley.

Do it for me, Nell!
Big love
Vix xxx

'You be the prince and I'll be Cinderella.'

JJ observed Maya with distrust. 'Are you gonna kiss me again?'

Maya heaved an enormous sigh and put her hands on her hips. 'You *have* to kiss me if you're the prince. It's what princes *do*.'

'Oh if only it were that easy,' I whispered to Lizzie who was watching the unfolding scene as we put toffee popcorn cupcakes into individual boxes for the children to take home.

My cousin smiled. 'Maybe you should try Maya's theory out on Max.'

'Maybe *you* should with Tyler,' I returned, laughing when she slapped my arm and shushed me as the handsome teacher approached us.

'So, what's happening here?' Tyler asked, strolling up to the Bake Zone table.

'JJ won't be the prince because he doesn't like kissing,' Maya complained, staring up at her school principal.

'Ah, I see,' he winked at Lizzie and I. 'Well maybe you guys should play something else that doesn't involve kissing. How about Goldilocks and the Three Bears?'

JJ's face beamed. 'I can be a bear. Bears don't have to kiss anybody.' He pointed at Maya. 'And you can be Goldilocks because you have yellow hair and you eat stuff.'

Placated, the pair joined hands and headed towards the dressing-up area.

Tyler laughed and turned to us. 'And the moral of the story is, if you don't like kissing be a bear instead.' Amusement lit his expression. 'I think we've all learned something important today. So, how'd the baking go?'

I held up a cupcake. 'Pretty good. We've baked *and* frosted today.'

'They look amazing, Nell. Please tell me there are leftovers.'

'Of course, Lizzie has them,' I replied innocently, enjoying the look of muted protest my cousin shot back.

'Then Lizzie is my official new best friend,' Tyler smiled, his dark eyes catching the sparkle of the lights in the hall ceiling. I smiled as he and Lizzie walked into the kitchen in search of cupcakes.

'Nell . . .' The voice beside me was so quiet that I almost didn't hear it over the noise of the S-O-S Club children in the hall. I looked down to see Declan's shy smile and crouched down until I was at eye-level with him.

'Hey Declan. What can I do for you?'

'Read me a story?' he asked, his fingers covering his mouth.

'Of course I can.' I held out my hand and he took it, pulling me towards the Story Zone. As I sat down with him on one of the large floor cushions he snuggled onto my lap, resting his head against me. I opened the book and began to tell the story, but was suddenly struck by a rush of emotion at the trust the small child had placed in me. To be accepted so completely – especially by a child renowned in the club for his shyness – was a powerful endorsement. When his mother arrived to collect him, the pleasant surprise on her face was all the reward I could have asked for.

'Thank you,' she said, shaking my hand. 'Declan has a mild form of autism and he finds social situations threatening. It takes a great deal for my son to trust someone. What do you say to Nell, Declan?'

Declan's smile was so fleeting I could have easily missed it. 'Thank you for my story.'

I can't explain why the simple act of reading a shy child a story meant so much to me, but it did. Next day when I arrived for work at Annie's it was still making me glow inside. I felt better here, too: I was beginning to find my feet, learning how to retain orders when I was doing other tasks and keep a cool head when customers lost theirs. My confidence must have been showing because the regulars at Annie's were beginning to notice.

'I gotta hand it to ya, Nell,' Marty said as I refilled his coffee mug, 'I didn't think you'd last a week here. But you proved me wrong.'

'Aw, thanks Marty. Anyone would think you were impressed.'

Marty looked flustered and muttered something about me knowing nothing as Frankie laughed.

'Ha, Marty, she got you with the compliment! Nice move, kid.'

After the breakfast rush, Annie appeared by my side. 'Hey Nell, I got you breakfast. Come and sit with me.'

We sat at the table nearest the door and tucked into Dom's speciality cinnamon iced buns.

'I just wanted to say thank you,' Annie said. 'You're doing good, girl.'

'Thanks Annie. I feel more confident now and at least I haven't repeated my attempt at the orange rolling world record.'

Annie held up her hand. 'I'm serious. And I know this is more than a holiday adventure for you. I know this is your dream. So, I wanted to give you this.'

She handed me one of the diner's handled brown paper takeaway bags. Surprised, I reached inside and lifted out a black leather notebook. When I opened it I found page after page covered in Annie's elongated handwriting.

'I've been writing this for you the last few days,' she said. 'I know what it's like to have a dream and not know how to make it happen. When I opened this place I was as green as they come. Everything I learned about business I learned the hard way. But I don't want you to have to find out like that. These days nobody has time to learn. You have to hit the ground running and be a success or you lose your chance. And I thought –' she raised her head and for the first time I saw vulnerability there '– if I'd had a daughter, I would have wanted her to be passionate about what she wanted to do with her life. I'd have helped her, any way I could.'

I knew I was staring at her, but I couldn't help it. Annie Legado – hard-bitten, no-nonsense doyenne of Haight-Ashbury's iconic diner – was showing me a side to her that I suspected few others were privileged to see. 'I don't know what to say . . .' I began, emotion stealing the words from me.

'You're welcome. I wrote down everything I think you need to know. But keep that notebook with you, in case you want to add more. See, I believe in you, kid. I think you can make a success of your diner if you're willing to take the leap. And while you're in this city I want you to know I'll do everything I can to help.'

Her gift – and the meaning behind it – was the most precious thing I had received and meant so much more than I could tell her right then. I resisted the urge to hug her, reasoning that this might be a step too far, hugging the notebook to me instead. 'Thank you.'

'Good.' Her half-smile was back, the brief glimpse behind the Legado curtain gone. 'Now, drink your coffee.'

CHAPTER SIXTEEN

Serendipity strikes again

My first week at Annie's was so steep a learning curve it was almost a vertical climb. One of the things that amused me was Annie's love of acronyms to describe the items on her menu. S-B-K crêpes were strawberry, kiwi and banana. N-B-P-B waffles were smothered in Nutella, sliced banana and peanut butter chips. C-A-B-Ps were Cinnamon Almond Butter Pancakes, and the 'P-M-Double-E Scramble' stood for scrambled eggs with 'pretty much everything else'.

'And what's an "O-M-G"?' I asked, looking at the list of abbreviations taped to the counter by the cash register. 'Orange, mango and . . .? What do we have beginning with G? Grapes?'

Laverne grinned. 'That's the Belgian waffle with Nutella, marshmallow fluff, toasted almonds, banana and chocolate syrup. It's called the OMG because that's usually what customers say when they see it.'

Annie was proving to be a great mentor, taking the

time every day to point out aspects of her business that she thought were important for me. I scribbled notes in the leather notebook that I kept safely in the front pocket of my apron, its existence our shared secret that made both of us smile.

'Remember that great service is a given but the ethos you present to your staff is your primary concern. Demonstrate to them how you'd like to operate and they'll provide it to your customers . . . Never promise anything you can't fulfil right there and then . . . We're here to serve, but don't be afraid to call the shots when necessary. It's your business so be prepared to fight to defend it if you have to . . . Don't stop innovating. People might like the constants on your menu but they're looking for the new too . . . Your specials board is your secret weapon. Even the most habitual customer will venture there once in awhile . . . Always offer refills. I know it amuses you, but trust me, kid, coffee for free makes people feel at home. Nobody ever got offended by free coffee . . .'

In the evenings, Lizzie and I talked in great detail about the potential business I could run – possible locations, names, menu items and more. It was a game more than anything, but it fanned the flames of ambition within me, strengthening my belief. Vicky provided long-distance cheerleading from home, too, urging me to pursue my diner dream, 'because, let's face it, you've more chance of getting a job working for yourself at the moment'.

I didn't see Max for the rest of my first week at Annie's but, while it would have been lovely if he had wandered in, it didn't really worry me. I was consumed by all the new things I was learning in my internship and loving discovering the ambition inside that had lain so dormant for so long. Seeing Max Rossi would have been the icing on the cake.

In my afternoons off I headed out into the city again, discovering more of its delights. One place I found by myself was Crissy Field, a strip of beachside park running from Marina Park to West Bluff at the feet of the Golden Gate Bridge. Here local people came to run, walk their dogs, fly kites with their kids and enjoy barbecues with friends and family, admiring the stunning view of the San Francisco Bay with the city in the far distance. At weekends a flotilla of small, white-sailed yachts studded the deep blue of the Bay, sailing out from Fisherman's Wharf and Sausalito, navigating past Alcatraz Island and out towards the Golden Gate Bridge.

I think I fell in love with this strip of San Francisco because I didn't feel like a tourist here. As far as my fellow walkers, joggers, kite-flyers, dog-walkers and barbecue revellers were concerned, if you were there you were one of them. It was a wonderful place to take a book, relax and watch the world go by. And with such stunning scenery, there was always something to catch my attention. I met some fantastic people there and had some wonderful, serendipitous conversations. Like the lady from Baltimore who told me how she'd tracked down her birth mother to San Francisco after thirty years of searching and had just celebrated her seventieth birthday with her, surrounded by a family she'd never known existed. Or the man taking a break from his afternoon run who turned out to be an ex-pat from

Birmingham who had emigrated here to open a beachside diner and spent almost an hour giving me fantastic advice about my own diner dream.

'Don't wait for it to make sense,' he told me, 'because on paper it never will. I've never worked so hard, but I've never been happier.'

The Warming Hut, a large cream painted wooden building on the westernmost edge of Crissy Field, became one of my favourite places to buy takeaway coffee. Brenda, the friendly cashier, quickly learned my name and always had questions for me about 'merry old England' whenever I visited. She was a big fan of the Royal Family and was over the moon when I told her my mum had met the Queen once at a garden party.

'How wonderful! And now I can say I know someone who's related to someone who has shaken hands with the Queen of England!'

After a busy breakfast and brunch shift at Annie's, sitting here and breathing in the fresh sea air became my favourite place to dream about what I could achieve when I went back to England. I made pages of plans in Annie's notebook, inspired by the constant positivity around me, and slowly the diner I'd daydreamed about for years started to dig foundations, appearing brick by brick on the pages of my notebook.

It was while travelling back from a visit to Crissy Field on the second Monday I'd worked at Annie's that serendipity struck again. I was sitting on the Muni trolleybus, my thoughts a thousand miles away, when a familiar voice said my name.

'Hey Nell.'

Max Rossi was hovering by the empty seat next to me, waiting for an invitation. How hadn't I seen him walk onto the bus? It had been over a week since I'd last seen him but my reaction was exactly the same: heart rate increasing, everything around me suddenly undulating a little. Remembering my manners I signalled for him to sit.

'Sorry, I was miles away.'

'Pardon me?'

'Nothing. So what brings you on this bus today?'

He smiled. 'How very polite of you to ask. My workplace is one block north of here – the art collective? I finished early because the exhibition starts tomorrow. I hope you and your cousin will visit? It runs till Saturday evening.'

'I think we're aiming to see it on Thursday night,' I replied, loving the reaction this elicited from him.

'Great.' He stared ahead for a moment, his smile straining a little as he considered what to say next.

I hid my smile and looked out of the window to take the pressure off him. Maybe I should speak first?

'So—' we both started together.

I laughed and motioned for him to go ahead. 'I'm sorry. After you.'

'OK, I'm just going to say it.' He turned to face me. 'We keep meeting. And I like that we do. So how about . . . is it possible you might like to have dinner with me? Or a cup of coffee? Or . . .?'

My smile could be restrained no longer. 'Or a journey on a Muni bus?'

He laughed, a delightful vulnerability chiming within it. 'Or even that. The thing is, I think it could be fun.'

Had this happened even a month ago I might have felt cornered and shied away from making a decision, but here on the bumpy Number 43 trolleybus ascending Masonic Avenue I found that I didn't need time to consider my answer.

'Yes. I'd love to.'

'Wonderful.' Max Rossi's smile made my toes tingle.

I smiled back and San Francisco smiled with us.

After a few seconds, the merest indication of confusion passed across his face. 'Just to clarify, which of the options did you just agree to?'

How sweet was that?

'Well, we're already doing the Muni thing successfully, I'm happy to do coffee as long as it's decaf and I wouldn't say no to dinner either.'

'I see. That's good. How about coffee at Java's Crypt after your shift tomorrow?'

'Perfect.'

'It's a date.'

Satisfied, we sat back in our seats and watched the city pass by in amiable silence. I was thrilled, not only by Max's suggestion but also by my own spontaneity. I knew nothing about him – other than the sketchy details he'd already shared – but I was looking forward to finding out more. How far I'd come in three weeks: from suddenly redundant Assistant Planning Officer to international traveller, San Franciscan diner intern and now soon-to-be dater of a handsome local.

Nice work, Nell Sullivan . . .

CHAPTER SEVENTEEN

It's only coffee . . .

'*Aaaaaaarrrrrgggggghhhhhh!*'

Lizzie's scream made my eardrums ring and before I could protest I was being waltzed at high speed around her living room.

'It's just coffee . . .'

'It's a *date*! You have your first date in San Francisco! I'm so happy for you, Nellie!'

I wasn't aware that securing my first date here was some kind of rite of passage, but from my cousin's reaction anyone would think I'd just reached a significant milestone in my San Franciscan experience. 'I'm happy that you're happy but can we stop dancing now please? You're making me dizzy.'

Laughing too loudly at her own reaction, my cousin let go of me and collapsed on the sofa. 'I'm sorry, hun. You know you could be dizzy from *love* for this wonderful man who is taking you for *coffee* . . .' She clasped a hand to her heart and descended into another bout of giggles.

I stared at her. 'No, it's definitely the dancing. You really need to get out more, Liz. Or finally admit you're not just seeing Tyler.'

Lizzie pulled a face. 'Don't you turn this on me. This is your moment of glory.'

'It's *just* a coffee.'

'But he said it was a date.'

'Yes, as in "a date in the diary" not "a date with destiny".'

'But you're excited about it?'

'Of course I am. But I'm also *realistic*. I don't want to plan this. I just want to enjoy coffee with Max tomorrow and see where it goes. He said he wants to spend some time with me and I said I'd like that.'

'But *think* where it might lead . . .'

'Lizzie, seriously, let's stop this. I don't want to live out an entire relationship before I've even been on one date. However excited my barmy cousin might be.'

Lizzie held up her hands in surrender. 'Consider the subject moot. I'm going to jump in the shower and then how do you fancy Mongolian barbecue tonight? There's a great place near Telegraph Hill you'll love. And we'll talk about everything *but* Max Rossi.'

Seeing how happy Lizzie was I suspected that she couldn't avoid the subject of Max all night, but Mongolian food sounded intriguing and I was hungry, so I was willing to take the risk. 'Sounds great.'

From: nell.sullygirl@gmail.com
To: vickster1981@me-mail.com
Subject: I have a date ☺

. . . but it's **just for coffee**.

I'm telling you this purely in the interests of your ongoing entertainment and not because I'm declaring any kind of potential relationship status. Max asked me to have coffee with him tomorrow after work and I agreed. That is all.

Lizzie is doing her best not to marry us off and have us riding into the sunset in a Disney-style finale. Meanwhile, I'm quietly chuffed about it.

So now you know.

Big love

Nell xxx

From: vickster1981@me-mail.com
To: nell.sullygirl@gmail.com
Subject: Re: I have a date ☺

. . . BUT it's a date with a hot Johnny Depp lookalike!! This is progress!

Good work Sullivan. SNOG HIM. And report back.

So proud!

Vix xxx

p.s. Please let him have a brother who looks like RG. *Please.* ☺ ☺

Annie's was as busy as ever and I was glad of the distraction. Despite my fervent protests about not wanting to think too much about Max, fluttering nerves had commenced their siege to my insides since nine a.m., just as the breakfast rush began. I focused as hard as I could on clearing tables, seating customers, refilling coffee and taking orders. I made polite conversation, bantered with the regulars and had a bit of a giggle with the Alfaros.

'My wife says I need a haircut,' Mr Alfaro informed me as I handed them their breakfast waffles. He lifted his plaid trilby and pointed at the thin covering of hair over his balding head. 'Is she serious? At my age I want to hang on to what hair I still have.'

'You can afford to lose a quarter inch, Saul,' Mrs Alfaro countered. 'Don't you agree, Nell?'

Not wanting to offend either of them, I kept to safer ground. 'Haircuts can be tricky things to judge. It's all about personal choice, I think.'

Mrs Alfaro clapped her hands. 'Exactly! You see? Nell agrees with me.'

Saul Alfaro raised his eyes heavenwards. 'How was what she just said agreeing with you? She said it's personal choice.'

'And what if it's *my* personal choice for you to have a haircut, hmm?'

Blinking in disbelief, Saul turned to me. '*This* is what I've endured for years, Nell. Promise me when you get a husband you'll allow him power of attorney over his own hair at least?'

I chuckled. 'If I ever have a husband, I promise I'll let him decide.'

'It won't be an "if" but a "when", young lady,' Mrs Alfaro replied. 'And *when* it happens, you'll see why it's important to keep an eye on his grooming habits. Talking of which, be sure to remember us to Max Rossi – if you happen to see him.'

'*Esther* . . .' Mr Alfaro scowled at his wife. 'Leave the poor kid be.'

Esther Alfaro was the picture of wronged innocence. 'What? All I said is *if* she sees him. We like Max. We haven't seen him much lately. It was just an observation.'

'I'll pass the message on. *If* I see him,' I smiled. As I left them, I could hear Saul chastising his wife.

'You shouldn't interfere.'

'Who said I was interfering? Kids these days need a little . . . *push*, that's all.'

'Oh they could write a book about all you know about pushing, Esther Alfaro . . .'

Trying not to read too much into Mrs Alfaro's mention of Max, I took more notes from Annie, chatted with Laverne about the counselling course she was taking at evening school and shared a little of my own career ambitions with her in return. But even with all this effort, the prospect of time in the company of a handsome man with gorgeous eyes and a smile that could make the hardest-hearted person melt like butter over a hot stack of pancakes was never far from my thoughts.

At one p.m. Annie patted me on the back. 'Great work today, kid. You have a good day, now.'

Changing in the cramped staff loo into the vintage floral mini dress I'd bought a few weeks ago – newly embroidered with the addition of cotton daisies and tiny gold beads from the box of trimmings the shop owner had given me – I realised my hands were shaking. *This is ridiculous*, I scolded myself. *It's* just *a coffee . . .*

But as I neared Java's Crypt and the mist overhead began to clear, I hoped it might be more. I liked Max. He intrigued me and his easy manner invited me to spend more time with him. I was on holiday and had limited time in this city: why not make the most of it while I was here? Stopping short of admitting what I hoped might happen, I smiled at my reflection in the coffee shop's window and stepped inside.

Ced was deep in conversation with Max, leaning on the edge of the booth and nodding gravely at whatever point Max was making. They were so engrossed that I had to pretend to cough before they realised I was standing beside them.

'Nell – hi.' Ced's pale face and bruised purple lips broke into a non-Goth smile. 'Great outfit. You make it yourself?'

'I bought it from Well Beloved but customised it myself.'

'Sweet. Loving your work. I'll let you settle in – shout when you're ready to order, yeah?'

'Hi.' Max half-stood to greet me, which was considerably problematic considering the table between the padded booth seats didn't allow much room for such a movement.

'Hi.' I sat opposite him, my heart thumping in time with the heavy metal being pumped at a respectable volume into the coffee shop. Java's Crypt might be true to its roots but it was nothing if not inclusive . . .

'You look great.' He pulled a face. 'Man, how lame

was that for an opener? I'll start again. Nell, it's good to see you.'

I giggled. 'Good to see you, too. How's it going with your exhibition? Everything ready for opening night?'

'I think so. I was at our building from six this morning. We had circuits blowing, an installation collapse and half the artists threaten to leave – you know, the usual hitches. But when I left everyone was playing nice. So . . .' he held up the black leather-bound menu, 'shall we order?'

Ced brought coffee for Max and peppermint iced tea for me, with two of his signature Caesar's Blood Wraps – which thankfully were sundried tomato tortillas wrapped around a creamy chicken Caesar filling with iceberg lettuce, and not the gory horror the name suggested. 'Enjoy,' he said, giving Max a blokey shoulder punch before he left us.

Max coughed awkwardly and smiled at me. 'Ced's a true original. So how was your diner internship today?'

'Busy. Mrs Alfaro asked to be remembered to you "if I happened" to see you.'

'Ah.'

'You didn't by any chance mention we were meeting today, did you?'

He shrugged. 'Not intentionally. The Alfaros are my neighbours and I often see them when I come home from work. I did talk to them yesterday but I'm pretty sure I didn't mention it.'

'Knowing how fast word spreads around here you probably didn't need to,' I smiled.

He studied me. 'Would it matter if people knew?'

'Not at all.'

'Good.'

There was a pause as we both bit self-consciously into our wraps, the iceberg lettuce suddenly becoming the loudest salad vegetable known to man. Every bite seemed to echo ominously around Java's Crypt, louder even than the music on the sound system. Swallowing was worse. After a couple of bites, I gave up. My appetite had vanished anyway and the peppermint iced tea looked like a much safer option.

And then, Max laughed. 'Pardon me for mentioning this, but how loud is this lettuce?'

His remark blew away the awkwardness between us and I felt myself relaxing at last. 'I know! I'm sorry. I know this is just a coffee date but it's been a while since I've been on one.'

'Hey, don't sweat it. It's been a while for me too. You leave someone behind in England?'

I didn't mind his direct question. 'No. I had an on-off thing with one guy for a few years but that's over now. Hence the first date rustiness.'

'I see. Me too, as a matter of fact. It's been ten years since my last first date. I thought I'd forgotten how to do this – start from the beginning, that is. But I'm glad I did. I'd like to get to know you. And I was wondering if you'd consider spending some time with me?'

How perfect was this? 'I'd really like that, Max.'

'Excellent. I'm glad.'

We talked about where we grew up, what our families were like, what we'd wanted to do with our lives when we were kids. Max explained how he fell in love with sculpture at school and how his doting mother and grandfather had created a tiny studio for him in the back of the family garage, his grandpa fetching off-cuts of roof joists from a local builder for his first forays into what would become his profession. 'I started with wood, moved to stone when I was at college and into other mediums as soon as I had any money. But there'll always be something special about working with wood – it's where I began.'

I told him about my former career in Planning and how, at the age of sixteen, I'd almost enrolled on a catering course at the local college until a careers advisor talked me out of it. He'd felt I should be pursuing a 'higher profession' and that I would soon tire of 'just cooking'.

'And now you're planning your own restaurant,' Max said. 'Life has a way of bringing you back to the important stuff.'

'It does. Although I'm a long way off from actually opening my own business,' I said. 'But knowing the direction I'm going in is a big leap forward.'

'I believe that.'

Before I realised it, over an hour had passed. Talking to Max was so easy, his attentiveness and genuine interest in me both flattering and very attractive. And what was strange was how safe I felt in his company. There was no agenda, no sense of hidden ambushes lying in wait for me – just an honest, authentic interest in who I was. With Max I had no sense of caution – perhaps because I knew this couldn't become anything other than a lovely holiday fling. I wasn't pinning my hopes on Max Rossi being the love of my life, so the usual pressure of expectation simply wasn't there. It felt good – and it made me want to get to know him even more.

When we stood in the street outside Java's Crypt to say goodbye, the sun had finally broken through the cloud layer, making the whole of Haight Street sparkle. Max stepped forward and planted the softest of kisses on my cheek, lingering there a moment longer which caused every nerve in my spine to tingle.

'Thank you. I had fun today.'

'Me too.'

He pushed his hands into the pockets of his navy-blue jeans and squinted up at the sky. 'So what do you think about doing this again?'

'I think it's a great idea.'

'Me too. The question is, when?'

My head was buzzing and I wasn't certain I was capable of planning another date given my current giddiness. 'Lizzie and I are coming to your exhibition on Thursday – perhaps we can discuss it then?'

'Good idea. I'll see you soon, Miss Sullivan.'

'You certainly will, Mr Rossi.'

We parted with shy smiles and I didn't turn back as I walked towards Lizzie's apartment, but my feet barely touched the ground. When I'd come to San Francisco, I hadn't planned on a holiday romance. But then, I hadn't planned on Max Rossi walking into my life . . .

CHAPTER EIGHTEEN

Getting to know you

'Are we overdressed?' Lizzie asked on Thursday evening, as the taxi dropped us on the sidewalk outside what looked like an old redbrick factory building down a side road off Divisadero Street. She indicated her turquoise dress, my little black dress and our high heels.

I had to admit that on first impressions this building was no MOMA and goosebumps prickled up my bare arms as I rapidly reached the same conclusion as Lizzie. 'It didn't say anything on the flyer about casual dress.'

'It didn't mention formal dress either.' She shivered in the cool early evening breeze, taking off her wide silk scarf and wrapping it around her shoulders like a shawl.

'Think it'll be warmer inside?' I asked, giggling more from cold than design.

'It'd better be. I know you like this guy but I have my limits.'

Entering through an unremarkable steel door, what waited for us inside couldn't have been further removed from the building's drab exterior. The upper floors of the former warehouse had been removed and the entire interior painted bright white, lit by spotlights, creating an impressive art space. At one side a low black stage had been erected, where a group of people dressed in white jumpsuits and brandishing pots of paint were apparently engaged in a competition to see how many coloured spots they could paint on each other. A darkened area at one end of the art space was filled with a curved wall of flat-screen TV monitors in a video installation. Huge canvases hung on the white walls, a riot of colour and texture. Invited guests milled around, served champagne by smiling young servers dressed in white t-shirts printed with the exhibition's flyer artwork. We accepted our glasses and joined the groups of onlookers floating slowly from one exhibit to another.

The bump of a palm against a microphone summoned our attention and we turned to the stage area. Max was standing there, looking amazing in a black shirt, trousers and shoes, the collar open at his neck and a single red rose resting in his shirt pocket. I know my intake of breath was louder than I'd intended because Lizzie giggled and jabbed me in the ribs with her elbow.

'Ladies and gentlemen, on behalf of Haight Urban Art Collective I want to welcome you to our fifth annual art exhibition. The works you see have been created as part of a citywide art initiative this year and I'm grateful to the Mayor's office and Department of Arts for their generous support in supporting our efforts to bring art to the diverse communities of this great city.'

Polite applause rippled through the guests. Max

continued, thanking a list of community groups and benefactors who had helped to create the works of art on show. But I didn't really take it in: I was just watching the movements he made with his hands, the way his mouth moved when he spoke and the delight in his eyes whenever he had to pause to receive his audience's applause . . .

'So, I would like to invite you to enjoy this exhibition. If you would be interested in purchasing any of the works on display, please approach one of the artists – including myself.'

He stepped down to applause as technicians dressed in black buzzed about, resetting the stage for the theatre group's imminent performance. People in the crowd of guests came up to him, shaking his hand, offering their congratulations. In the middle of a group of well-wishers he raised his head and waved when he saw me, his smile widening as he made his way towards us.

'You made it!' He kissed my cheek, whispering, 'You look wonderful,' close to my ear, his warm breath tickling my skin. Pulling back, he turned to greet Lizzie.

'And you must be Nell's cousin. I'm Max.'

'Lizzie. It's good to finally meet you.'

'You're both welcome.' He held my gaze for a moment. 'I should get back to my hosting duties. Enjoy the exhibition and I'll catch up with you later, OK?'

Lizzie only just managed to contain her delight as Max left. 'My *life*, Nellie, when you said he was good looking you didn't say he looked like *that*.'

I beamed back. 'He's gorgeous, isn't he?'

'Is he ever! Please tell me you're going to see him again

if he asks you. I want you to be able to enjoy *that view* as much as possible before you have to go home.'

'Lizzie!'

We pretended to consider one of the enormous painted canvases as a group of exhibition guests walked slowly by.

'Gorgeous,' Lizzie smirked, waving her half-empty champagne flute in the general direction of the painting.

'Indeed.'

'Personally, I could gaze at *that* for hours . . .' She winked in Max's direction.

'Isn't it wonderful?' one of the guests commented, impressed by our apparent art appreciation. 'The craftsmanship is remarkable, don't you think?'

Lizzie gave a solemn nod. 'Stunning.'

The woman leaned towards us. 'You know, that would look *awesome* in my bedroom?' Smiling conspiratorially, she wandered away.

Lizzie snorted, pretending to sneeze when several of the other visitors turned. 'I bet you were just thinking the same thing, Nell . . .'

'Behave, you. We're meant to be appreciating art here.'

'I thought we were.'

An hour later canapés were served and the artists, performers and technical staff were introduced to warm applause, moving to mingle with the visitors. Max wove through the bodies towards me and I noticed Lizzie discreetly move away to look at a large bronze sculpture. I loved her for giving us a moment together.

'What do you think?'

'It's really good, Max. I wish I knew more about art but I like what I've seen.'

'That's what counts,' he replied, pleased with my response. 'Art should be something you feel *here*.' He rested his hand just below the scarlet-red rose in his shirt pocket. 'Your gut response is all that matters. I find if a piece resonates with me, it stays with me. I don't subscribe to the theory that you should battle with it. If it provokes human response, it's valid for the person responding.' He laughed. 'And *now* I sound like an art professor. Forgive me.'

'Don't apologise. I like hearing you talk about your work.'

'Thank you.' He placed his hand lightly at the small of my back and steered me a little way from the crowd. I was surprised by the intimacy of such a small gesture. 'I have to say, it's great you're here. Could I see you on Saturday some time?'

'Of course. Any time, actually, I don't work at Annie's at weekends. But won't you need to rest before the exhibition's last night? You'll be exhausted by then.'

'I'll be fine. And I want to spend some time with you. Meet me at the 43 Muni stop on Haight, Saturday morning at ten.'

'OK.'

'And bring a jacket. It may be a little cold.'

Saturday morning was bright as I walked to the Muni trolleybus stop. With no sign of Max I walked a little way up the street to look at the new window display at 4:13 Dream, the strange clothes boutique. I wouldn't be brave enough to wear the kind of clothing they sold, but their window displays were incredible. Papier mâché skulls covered in roses and stars surrounded what looked like a waterfall and river made from the shop's trademark skull-and-rose print shirts. The top half of a shop window dummy rose from the centre of the shirt river, her body sprayed silver and covered in stick-on crystals, blood-red ribbons tied in her jet-black hair and at her neck.

'Thinking of buying something?' I turned to see Ced's deathly pale face, noticing that his hair had been cut into a long shaggy bob, a new fringe framing his eyes.

'I don't have the guts to. But I adore their windows.'

'You could work their style,' he said thoughtfully. 'Your hair's a good colour, pale English skin, great green eyes.'

'Wow, um, thank you.'

'Welcome.'

After such a surprising compliment I felt I should return the favour. 'I like your new hairdo by the way.'

'Hair *what*?'

I laughed as the translation issue caused Ced to stare at me in case I'd just insulted him in another language. 'Sorry – your haircut is nice.'

'Oh. Thanks. Autumn did it last night. I'm not sure yet – it's a bit Jon Bon Jovi right now. Not really the undead look I was going for.'

'It suits you. Makes the colour of your eyes stand out.' This was the least I could say, given his sudden assessment of my own features.

'OK.' We stood awkwardly on Haight Street for a moment, both finding ourselves in unfamiliar territory.

'Hey, I meant to say,' Ced rushed, as if the words would escape him if he didn't utter them immediately. 'I heard about you wanting to open your own food place? I think it's cool. And, you know, I've been in the business a few years. If you need advice, you know where I am.'

I was touched by his offer. 'That's very kind, thank you. I'll definitely take you up on that. When would be a good time to talk?'

'Tuesdays after two p.m. are quiet most weeks. Or just drop in whenever.'

'That would be great. Thanks Ced.'

'You're welcome. I'd – uh – better get back.' He knocked on the shop window with his knuckle. 'You should think about that stuff. You'd rock it.'

As he walked away I was amused by the revelation of Ced as a fashion guru. Haight-Ashbury was certainly full of surprises. Looking towards the bus stop I saw the unmistakable saunter of my date. *My date* – it was going to take a while to get used to that . . .

'Hey,' he smiled when I reached him. He was wearing his black leather jacket, a white t-shirt beneath with faded black jeans and he smelled of green tea and lemongrass as he leaned in to kiss my cheek. 'So are you ready for our more-than-coffee-or-an-art-exhibition date?'

'I think so.' I noticed he had a rucksack slung over one shoulder. 'Are we hiking?'

'Maybe. Maybe not.' He looked down at my trainers. 'But good choice of footwear.'

'Thank you. I thought if we were catching the Muni then there would probably be walking involved.'

Max laughed. 'I have a regular Miss Marple here. There will be walking involved, yes. But that's all I'm saying – the rest is a surprise.'

True to his word, Max gave no more clues as to where

we were going as we travelled through San Francisco, the pastel-hued houses passing us by claiming his attention.

'You see that yellow house there – one back from the corner? That was the first place I rented when I moved here from Oakland. There were four of us living there, two artists and two city workers. We cooked for them because we were in all day and they paid for the wine. It was the perfect arrangement.'

'Did you always know you wanted to live here?' I asked, amused that I already accepted these street views as normal, instead of wanting to photograph every painted house like I had during my first week.

'Growing up in Oakland you could always see San Francisco across the Bay. I wouldn't say it called to me, but it felt like home whenever I visited. I guess it was a safe place to branch away from my family without leaving them behind altogether. That kind of thing is not so important when you're a teenager but when you get older it's nice to have your people nearby, you know?'

I did know. If it hadn't been for my family I'd be homeless now. 'I've just moved back with my parents.'

He pulled a face. 'Wow. How are you finding that?'

'Oh it's fine. Mum was fussing around me a little at first but then that's Mum. I actually like being back there. My housemates at my previous address weren't exactly my best friends. Anyway, why the face? I thought you said it was important to have your family near you.'

'*Near* me, sure, but at a safe distance, like roughly the distance between San Francisco and the furthest end of the Bay Bridge!' He laughed. 'Don't get me wrong, I love my folks, but I'm a big believer that when you move out, you move out for good.'

That was funny: I'd always felt that way until I lost my job. But then it's very easy to believe in a principle like that while your bills are being paid. 'Well, I didn't have a choice in the circumstances.'

Max's face fell. 'Oh gosh, I didn't mean . . . Of course in your situation having your family around you must have been comforting.'

'No offence taken. It isn't perfect, but I had to make the best of a bad lot.'

The bus rounded a corner and began a steep descent down one of the city's many hills.

'I'm curious: what made you decide to come to San Francisco? Was it because Lizzie lives here?'

'Not initially, no. Although when San Francisco was mentioned I called Lizzie straight away. To begin with, I just knew I didn't want my whole life to be defined by this thing that had happened to me, which I had no control over. I didn't want to become a victim of it, so I decided to do something positive. Of course I'll be completely broke when I go home, but out here I feel like I've taken back some control of my life, you know? Even if it turns out to be an unwise choice, at least I'll have had two months of fun.'

Max was looking straight at me now, his hand millimetres away from mine on the seat between us. 'I love that you think that way, Nell. It's bold and courageous. And I think life rewards those who take chances.'

'Thank you.' I was struck by an overwhelming urge to bridge the gap between our fingers and take hold of his hand. Suddenly aware of how close our faces were to each other I sat back and looked out of the window to steady myself. 'So are we nearly there yet?'

He reached across me and yanked the metal cord that ran the length of the trolleybus to alert the driver to stop. 'This is us now.'

I had quickly learned that Muni trolleybus drivers stopped sharply and now waited until the bus had braked before I even attempted to stand. We stepped off in a suburban street unremarkable from countless others we had passed on our journey.

'Where are we?'

Max began to walk away. 'You'll see. Come on.'

At the end of the street I could see a line of trees, leading to a park gate with a main road winding its way into the park.

'Is this The Presidio?' I asked.

'Part of it. Have you been here yet?'

'I've been to the bottom edge of it, where the Palace of Fine Arts is.'

We passed whitewashed wooden buildings that wouldn't have looked out of place in a movie set at the turn of the nineteenth century, with neatly clipped gardens and beautifully pristine pathways. As we walked through a deserted strip of car park, Max suddenly grabbed my hand.

'Nell – look . . .' he whispered.

It was a while until I realised what he was asking me to do, due to the shock of him holding my hand – and how natural it felt. When I pulled myself together I followed the direction of his arm until I could see something buzzing about the flowers in the bushes that edged the car park. At first I thought it was a large moth or a dragonfly. It was larger than a bumblebee but no bigger than my thumb. It was moving quickly, hovering for a moment on a flower, then flitting across to another. I took off my sunglasses and squinted a little – instantly reminding me of Vicky's reading technique, which made me smile. And then, I recognised it.

'Oh goodness, it's a hummingbird!'

I had seen hummingbirds before on television wildlife programmes (of which Dad was an avid fan) but never in real life. This creature was much tinier than I'd imagined and far more beautiful. The miniature bird had a shock of vivid green on its head and back, which was the only thing I could focus on as the rest of its body moved at such high speed. I was mesmerised as we watched the hummingbird collecting nectar from the yellow flowers of the bush.

'They're awesome, aren't they?' Max's hushed question was close to my ear and I felt his hand squeeze mine.

'I can't believe how beautiful they are – or how tiny.'

I was acutely aware of his breath, of his closeness to me. It was exciting and yet somehow comforting. I didn't fight it, keeping my eyes on the tiny birds.

Max was still holding my hand, only letting go when we began to walk again. I was aware of a stab of disappointment when he did. He laughed nervously and so did I.

Being with Max was like being fifteen all over again. I remembered those first, excruciating dates in my teens when I felt like a fish out of water and everything I did seemed to have been scripted by Buster Keaton. Tripping over my words, blurting out exactly the wrong thing at exactly the wrong time, falling over myself to try to impress boys who clearly weren't interested and, on more than one occasion, *actually* falling over. My left knee still bears the scar of my ill-fated attempt to woo Ross Andrews, fourteen-year-old heart-throb of Year Nine, by nicking my next-door neighbour's skateboard and sailing past him straight into a brick wall at the edge of our local skate park . . .

Now, at thirty-two years old, it seemed I was no better at avoiding awkwardness on a first date. Although technically this was our second – or third, if I counted visiting his exhibition last night. Being with Max Rossi – especially being *alone* with Max Rossi – was something that left me both thrilled and terrified: thrilled because of the effect he had on me and terrified because of how much I already felt for him . . .

After a sudden steep climb we emerged in another car park – and I suddenly realised where we were. Ahead of us, rising tall into the cloudless blue sky and reflecting in the waters of the San Francisco Bay, was the Golden Gate Bridge. It was beautiful, and from the viewing point I could see the sweep of the Bay to the right, over the tops of the dark green cedar trees at the edge of Crissy Field towards the rise of San Francisco and Oakland beyond.

'It's gorgeous, Max,' I breathed, feeling the sting of cooler air at the back of my throat.

'That's where we're going,' he replied, his eyes alive with the success of his surprise. 'We're going to walk the Golden Gate Bridge.'

Since arriving in San Francisco, I had of course seen the enormous red metal and steel cabled structure many times: on the horizon from Fisherman's Wharf and Aquatic Park, its towers usually shrouded in mist; closer by at West Bluff and Crissy Field; and in the far distance from between the cedar and palm trees on the brow of Alamo Square Park – but this was going to be a new experience.

Tourists and sightseers clustered at the small viewing point, posing for the 'must-have' shot of the bridge, and a few local people exercising their dogs were kept busy taking photos for them. They didn't seem to mind at all, being thoroughly proud of their local landmark. An older man with a very sweet spaniel offered to take a picture of us and I was about to refuse when Max thanked him and slung his arm around my shoulders, grinning from ear to ear.

'Aw, you two look so happy. Smile now!' Job done, he handed the camera back to Max and beamed at us. 'So how long are the two of you in San Francisco?'

'I live here,' Max replied, 'but Nell's visiting for a while.'

The local nodded sagely. 'Ah, I see. *Holiday romance*. How sweet. And what a great day for you it is.'

I knew I was blushing, but maintained my smile as Max agreed with him.

'Isn't it? I was just about to tell Nell how lucky we are to have a clear view.'

'First clear morning we've had for weeks,' the man said. 'Usually the fog stays until early afternoon. My wife and I take it as a sign that something good is going to happen if we can see the whole bridge. I hope that's the case for the both of you.'

When he had walked on, I gave Max a nudge. 'So we're having a holiday romance now, are we?'

His expression was pure cheekiness. 'It would appear so.' He held out his hand. 'I'd like to think we might.'

'Me too.'

His hand was warm and soft when I accepted it, a thrill dancing through me as his fingers laced lazily through mine, as if they should have been there all along. The new contact was welcome but I was very aware of it as we set off, almost as if every sightseer would see it and rush for their cameras to take evidence of the remarkable event. It felt as if we had passed some unseen milestone. Did Max feel the same way? I couldn't tell. But he seemed completely relaxed and at peace, which put me at ease.

Walking alongside groups of other people I could feel a tangible sense of excitement building as the towers of the bridge loomed ahead. So many of my experiences in this city were like mental snapshots I knew I would pore over when I was back at home and as we stepped onto the walkway of the famous bridge, holding hands, I knew this would be one I would come back to time and again. It was a palette of blues: the perfect blue sky over us, the deep blue waters of the Bay below us, the dusky blue hills of Marin County ahead of us, cut through with a vivid splash of red in the metalwork, cables, railings and supports of the bridge. Although the side looking along the Bay towards Alcatraz Island and the city was protected with wire fencing, it didn't lessen the impact of the view and all along it visitors were pressed close with their cameras focused through the holes in the fencing to the beautiful landscape beyond.

'You know, it was years before I actually walked across this bridge,' Max said. 'I'd lived in the city a long time and seen so much of what people all over the world come here to witness. Then a friend came to visit from Baltimore so I decided it would be a good thing to do with him. And he wasn't impressed, as I recall. But I, on the other hand, walked across like an open-mouthed kid seeing Santa for the first time.' He squeezed my hand. 'So, what do you think?'

'It's magnificent.'

He laughed and raised my hand with his to kiss the back of it. 'That's such a British word. Bless you.'

'I'm glad it amuses you.'

'I'm glad you're here . . .' he said, suddenly. 'With me.'

I looked up then, his words reverberating in my mind. What I was feeling – the peace in his presence at odds with every nerve within me standing to attention – did he feel it too? I saw my reflection in his sunglasses begin to grow larger as he leaned closer, his warm breath beating the cold Bay wind to blow softly across my lips. I closed my eyes and willed Max closer still . . .

'Excuse me!'

We pulled apart as a family of large American tourists hurried past on 'Bike the Bridge' hire bicycles and it was only then that I realised we had stopped walking and had been facing each other in the middle of the bridge walkway. A little flushed and embarrassed, we succumbed to teenage giggles as we resumed our walk – and the moment passed . . .

From: nell.sullygirl@gmail.com
To: vickster1981@me-mail.com
Subject: I almost kissed him

Honestly, it nearly happened. The setting couldn't have been more perfect – walking across the Golden Gate Bridge in the sunshine, on a gorgeous clear day. He was holding my hand (and seriously, Vix, the agonies I went through trying to get my head around *that* development were just ridiculous) and we were talking and then suddenly, we weren't talking any more and he was leaning in . . . And I almost kissed him.

If it hadn't been for a group of overfed Yanks on bikes (you had to be there) I would actually have done it. But once they charged between us it kind of killed the moment. The rest of the date was lovely, but no more near-kiss experiences, although he seems to like holding my hand. When we got back home he had a phone call from a friend and had to leave the Muni bus two stops before mine. He kissed me on the cheek – I've had quite a few of those – but nothing more.

The thing is, I really wanted him to kiss me. I've thought of little else since. But I'm not sure I want to be this fixated on someone while I'm here. This trip is meant to be about me, not finding a man. Does that make sense? Or is it just me panicking?

I really did want to kiss him, though.

Off to boil my head or something . . . Will keep you updated.

Big love

Nell xxx

From: vickster1981@me-mail.com
To: nell.sullygirl@gmail.com
Subject: Re: I almost kissed him

Aaargh, Nell!!

Your email was as frustrating as when the *EastEnders* drums kick in at a crucial moment.

Why didn't you wait till the fat bikers had gone and jump him? WHY? I've just Googled the Golden Gate Bridge and it's 1.7 miles from end to end. That's 1.7 miles for you to grab that gorgeous man and snog his face right off. And that's only if you walked one way, which I presume you didn't. In which case that would have been 3.4 miles of possible snog mileage – and you HELD HANDS instead?

Honestly, I'm disappointed in you. After all that waiting and hoping you did before Aidan kissed you for the first time, I expected more. Do you remember that? You mooned about for weeks with the 'maybe it's me, maybe he doesn't like me' routine. If you learned anything from dating him it should be that you have to seize the day – or more to the point, seize the MAN – when you get the chance.

I know this isn't what you expected. I know it's not what you were looking for in SF. But I think you need to see it as another opportunity to try something out. Like volunteering at the diner. Like jumping on a plane there in the first place. You don't have long before you have to come back to all the lifeless crap of being unemployed. MAKE THE MOST OF IT!

Consider yourself told, woman!

Love you tons

Vix xxx

CHAPTER NINETEEN

The sweetest thing

Lizzie, it transpired, had been a little busy herself while I was out with Max. When I walked into her apartment she was wearing a sheepish smile, which I quickly discovered was directly linked to a certain handsome principal of Sacred Heart Elementary – a fact confirmed when he strolled into the living room wearing only a towel. The shock on his face, coupled with my cousin's sudden fit of nervous coughing was too funny for words. I burst out laughing, which in turn broke the otherwise awkward moment and resulted in a surreal hour of polite conversation over tea (thankfully with Tyler fully clothed).

When he had gone, my cousin turned to me. 'I'm sorry, hun. I thought you and Max might be out later than you were.'

'Don't apologise. When you told me you had lesson planning to do, I didn't realise you meant *those* kind of lessons.'

Lizzie's cheeks matched her rose-pink t-shirt. 'Stop it!

I didn't plan on it happening. Tyler just offered to help me with a proposal I have to put together for the School Board. We met at Java's Crypt and ended up coming back here for lunch. And then . . . I honestly don't know how it happened, Nell. We were talking about the proposal and then we were kissing.'

'About time too! It was obvious you both wanted more than friendship. I'm just happy you finally did something about it.'

'So am I.' She handed me a cold bottle of orange juice from the fridge. 'He surprised me. The couple of dates we'd had before had been lovely, but Ty was always polite and restrained. This afternoon – he was anything but.'

'But you're happy?'

She paused for a moment but the sparkles in her eyes gave the game away. 'I'm over the moon! He's perfect, Nell – and he feels the same about me. I haven't felt this way for ages. But how was your date?'

Now it was my turn to shine. 'Amazing. We almost kissed . . .'

'No! Really?'

'Yes. And next time I think it will happen.'

'I love this, Nellie! I feel like it's all coming together for both of us.'

The change in my cousin was remarkable. For the rest of the weekend she was constantly upbeat, finding joy in the smallest observations or details.

The following day, I woke early and checked my emails on Lizzie's Mac.

From: vickster1981@me-mail.com
To: nell.sullygirl@gmail.com
Subject: Happy Birthday! (I hope)

Happy Birthday!

OK, confession time: I still can't work out this stupid time difference between London and San Francisco, so this email might be perfectly timed (in which case YAY, many happy returns, etc) or not (in which case I'm either getting in early or helping you extend the birthday celebrations . . .).

I wish I could see you to celebrate properly but I know you're going to have the best time out there. So I just want you to know that right now, in honour of your birthday, Ryan Gosling is feeding me Aldi's finest Merlot. WITH HIS FACE!* ☺ ☺ ☺

(*That would be a wine glass I found on Etsy etched with RG's face! Wine and The Gosling, my two favourite things combined: nirvana achieved!)

Have a fab one, Sully!

Big loves

Vix xxx

'Surprise!' Lizzie burst in and dog-piled onto my bed. 'Happy birthday lovely cousin!'

I struggled to push her off, giggling. 'Are you sure you're thirty-four?'

'Yep. And *you*, my fabulous temporary flatmate, are

thirty-three today! Can you believe it, Nell? I could swear it was only yesterday we were in our teens and fighting over who was going to marry Harry from McFly.'

'That was always going to be me,' I grinned, thinking how different my life had turned out compared to what I'd imagined when I was a teenager. But spending my thirty-third birthday in San Francisco with Lizzie was better than anything I could have planned.

'You wish! Anyway, it's Sunday, neither of us has to work and I have a whole day of birthday fun organised for you! So get up and we're going to start the day with a birthday breakfast.'

Ordinarily being taken to my workplace wouldn't have classified as a birthday treat, but here I couldn't think of anywhere better. Everyone at Annie's was in on my birthday surprise and I walked in to find a table near the counter decked out in pink and blue balloons and streamers. Karin brought a chef's hat through from the kitchen (decorated with three cocktail umbrellas) and made me wear it. Dom cooked an enormous stack of birthday pancakes, smothered in whipped cream, chocolate and toffee sauce, sliced banana, peanut butter chips, miniature Hershey's Kisses and caramelised pecans. He'd even piped 'Happy Birthday Server Three' in coffee icing around the edge of the platter.

Annie came over to give her good wishes and refused money from Lizzie when she asked for the bill. 'This one's on the house,' she insisted. 'It's a special day for our valued member of staff.'

Laverne gave me a birthday card signed by all the staff and regulars and Frankie presented himself as my personal chauffeur for the day.

'You win me until three p.m.,' he announced, scowling at Marty who almost fell off his counter stool laughing.

'Yeah. But second prize is Frankie for a week!'

Lizzie was incredibly proud of herself and all the way through breakfast was beaming like a lighthouse in the middle of Annie's. When I had eaten as much as I could of my birthday pancake stack (which was less than half of it), she handed me an envelope. Inside was a strip of paper, which read:

Welcome to your San Francisco Birthday
Treasure Trail!
We begin where money and journeys meet,
in a nook where a fun guy awaits.

'What is that supposed to mean?'

'You'll find out.' Lizzie clicked her fingers. 'Mr Chauffeur, are you ready to go?'

Frankie jumped to attention, saluting us. 'Ready when you are, ladies.'

Sitting in the generously proportioned back seat of Frankie's cab I tried to extract more clues to our first destination but neither he nor Lizzie would crack. We were definitely driving downtown, that much I could tell, and when we pulled onto North Point Street beside the vintage F-Line trams overlooking the San Francisco Bay, I thought I'd guessed it.

'We're going to Pier 39, where tourists spend their money. And the fun guy waiting for us is Eric!'

'I like your reasoning, but you're wrong.' My cousin was obviously enjoying this and while I pretended to be frustrated by her cryptic clue, I was touched that she had gone to so much trouble to create an elaborate birthday surprise for me.

After passing more historic piers we continued driving on The Embarcadero and soon the skyscrapers of the Financial District loomed into view.

'Is the Financial District the money bit of the clue?'

'Clever girl,' Frankie said over his shoulder. 'OK Lizzie, I'm gonna drop you both as close to the entrance as I can get and drive a loop until you're good to go.'

We came to a halt outside the famous San Francisco Ferry Building, a long pale grey building with an elegant clock tower rising from its centre.

'Money and journeys – Financial District and the Ferry Building!' I exclaimed. 'Brilliant Lizzie! But where's the fun guy?'

We got out of Frankie's cab on the wide sidewalk by the historic building and Lizzie linked arms with me. 'We'll find him inside.'

The interior of the Ferry Building had been transformed into an arcade of restaurants, cafés and speciality food market stalls. Just about every kind of foodstuff was represented here: fresh herbs, meat, olive oil, pickles, handmade chocolates and cakes – and an entire stall devoted to mushrooms.

I started to laugh as soon as I saw the stall and Lizzie led me towards the display of mushroom growing kits, rare and exotic mushrooms and mushroom-related gifts. 'Fun guy – fungi. Lizzie, that's *dreadful*.'

'One of the S-O-S Club mums owns it,' she explained. 'It was the only clue I could think of.' She smiled as a petite, blonde lady in a mushroom-brown apron approached us and I recognised her as Kennedy Syms-Bannerman, Maya's mother.

'Hey Lizzie. Nell, good to see you and happy birthday!'

'Thank you.'

'So, I have a gift for you.' She handed me a tiny pot shaped like a mushroom, with sparkly string tied around it. 'It's a little something to remind you of my stall – and to thank you for inspiring my daughter. And here is your next clue.'

'Thanks for doing this, Kenni,' Lizzie said.

'It's my pleasure. Nell's toffee popcorn cupcakes have turned my kids into baking nuts. Have a lovely day, Nell.'

'I will. Thank you.'

Leaving the stall I was about to head for the front doors when Lizzie stopped me. 'Actually, while we're here you need to experience a San Francisco original.'

Five minutes later, armed with very smoky house coffee from Peet's – a local coffee chain – we climbed back into Frankie's taxi.

'Next stop?' he asked, accepting a coffee from my cousin.

'Next stop,' Lizzie confirmed. She took my takeout coffee cup as I opened the next clue.

**Next stop is a place where the bell tolls
and ancient rail runners rest at 1201.**

'Is it the church in Mission? Although what the "rail runners" are I don't know . . .' As I considered the conundrum, Frankie paused to let a vintage tram pass by, its bell ringing angrily at the taxi driver ahead of us who hadn't been as courteous. 'Oh hang on – it's a tram!'

'Almost,' Frankie said. 'Think about another thing that runs on rails in this city.'

'Cable cars? Is the next clue on one of the cable cars?'

I saw Frankie grin at Lizzie in the rear view mirror. 'I think that's close enough.'

We drove along streets away from the Bay until Frankie parked the taxi by the side of a redbrick building that housed the San Francisco Cable Car Museum. Above the glass entrance the number '1201' was painted in large gold letters.

'Welcome to 1201 Mason Street,' Lizzie said.

Leaving Frankie reading his newspaper in the sun outside, Lizzie and I wandered into the museum. We spent almost an hour looking at the gorgeous old cable cars, fascinated by the simple system of cables and pulleys that kept the iconic cars transporting people up and down the steep streets of the city. In the gift shop Lizzie bought me a miniature cable car bell and handed me my next envelope.

Stop three on your birthday odyssey
is a shape that a smoothie painted
in the shadow of a famous name.

'OK, I have no idea about this one,' I admitted, after scrutinising the clue for several minutes. 'You might have to help me.'

'It's easy,' Frankie said. 'Think about a shape you associate with San Francisco.'

'Pyramid! It's the Transamerica Pyramid.'

Lizzie shook her head. 'Think a little more *romantic* than that.'

'Romantic? Oh, is it a heart? OK, "a heart a smoothie painted" – well I've kept seeing the painted hearts everywhere, but a "smoothie"? Ah, I think I've got it – it's the heart sculpture that Tony Bennett painted in Union Square . . . and the "shadow of a famous name" is Saks!'

The palm trees in Union Square were moving in the breeze when Frankie dropped us off by the red heart painted by Tony Bennett with a landscape image of the Golden Gate Bridge. Lizzie asked a friendly tourist to take our photo and we posed by the heart with cheesy grins and jazz-hands, reminding me of the sightseeing we used to do in London during the holidays, the photographic evidence of which was stuck to our bedroom walls for most of our teens. Giggling, she handed me the next clue and it was lovely to see her so thrilled at her own plans.

To reach the fourth stop you must brave hairpins and step into the movies at the Hillards' home.

'Right,' I said, as I worked out the first half of the clue, 'I think "hairpins" must refer to the hairpin bends on Lombard Street. "Hillards' home" – why do I know that name?' Suddenly, it hit me: my favourite film from my childhood that at one point I could quote verbatim. 'The Hillard House from *Mrs Doubtfire*!'

Lizzie applauded me. 'And the address?'

'I don't know where it is. I know the address Sally Field mentions in the film, but . . .'

'So say that . . .'

'2640 Steiner Street – but that's only in the film.'

We clambered back into Frankie's cab. Lizzie mentioned the two addresses to him and turned to me. 'They used the actual address in the film. Well done for remembering, though. I had to look it up.'

Driving down the famous steep section of Lombard Street with its eight hairpin bends was definitely an experience – even if it was done very slowly, due to the large number of cars, taxis and sightseeing tour buses that were making a snail-like procession down its stomach-flipping curves. From there, Frankie drove us to Steiner Street and Lizzie and I stood outside the pale yellow house I had seen countless times in the film since I was a kid. Like so many places in this city, it felt surreal to be standing somewhere I had never been before, but which felt so familiar.

'OK. Last clue,' Lizzie said, handing me the final envelope.

Meet at the dark table of friendly undead
to commemorate years past and years ahead.

I didn't even have to think about that one. Laughing, we got back into the cab and I leaned forward to tap Frankie's shoulder.

'Take us to Java's Crypt, please!'

In the darkened interior of our local coffee house – sitting in the aptly named Zombie Booth – were several of my new friends and a huge, three-layer birthday cake decorated with pink and white icing (looking a little out of place against its dark surroundings). Tyler rested his arm around Lizzie's shoulders while Rosita from EarthSong presented me with a small tea caddy like the one I had often admired in her shop.

'I filled it with a selection of the teas you liked,' she said. 'I hope you enjoy them.'

'I will, thank you so much!'

'Oh and when you've opened your presents I have a little more gossip on the chalk artist. My friend Ricardo thinks it could be his uncle. We have much to talk about, *chica*.'

'I can't stay long, but I made you this,' Laverne said, handing me a gorgeous patchwork bag, embellished with beads and embroidered flowers.

'It's lovely, Laverne. I can't believe you made this. Thank you.'

'My darling Nell,' Eric grinned, reaching behind my ear to produce a small package beautifully wrapped in tissue paper and ribbon. 'A small gift to inspire *certain* people to get their act together.' He winked at Lizzie and I groaned. There was no point keeping anything about Max and I a secret when my cousin was happily informing her friends of every detail. When I opened the box I found a beautiful necklace with a pair of silver lips and two heart charms. Laughing, I hugged him and waggled a warning finger at my cousin.

Ced's wife Autumn gave me a parcel wrapped in black tissue with silver stars. 'Ced assures me this was the right thing to get you,' she smiled, her red curls dancing about her pale powdered face as she kissed my cheek. Inside I found one of the skull and rose t-shirts from 4:13 Dream and laughed as I held it up against my chest.

'You see?' Ced said. 'I told you you'd rock it.'

'I love it,' I replied, completely overwhelmed by everybody's generosity.

Ced handed out cranberry and champagne cocktails and the party toasted my good health amid laughter and cheers. As I relaxed in the middle of the convivial conversation, I felt completely at home. So much about my life now was different from what I'd imagined it to be, but thinking about my diner dream – and the burgeoning friendship with a certain handsome art director – I sensed the best was yet to come.

CHAPTER TWENTY

Take me out

'Hey Nell! Can you serve table eleven?' Annie yelled over the noise of the diner as I finished refilling the coffee filters.

'On my way,' I called back, grabbing a new order pad from the counter and winding through the packed seating area towards the row of tables nearest the window looking out onto Haight Street. As I neared the table, my heart performed a perfect somersault.

'Morning, beautiful,' Max grinned, his eyes twinkling from beneath a dark blue Kangol cap. 'Sorry for the conspiracy to get you over here but I wanted to ask you a question.'

'Oh?'

'Why didn't you tell me it was your birthday?'

A little embarrassed, I shuffled my feet on the tiled diner floor. 'I didn't think to. After all, we've only just met.'

'Hey, I'm not offended. Laverne mentioned it yesterday

and I felt bad I'd missed it. So I'd like to make amends. What are you doing this afternoon?'

'Nothing. But don't you have to be at work?'

'I work with artists, which means all time is relative.' He smiled at my puzzled frown. 'We operate evening sessions on Tuesdays and Thursdays and I don't work afternoons on those days. So, what do you say? Let me take you on a belated birthday date.'

If Max Rossi was trying to endear himself to me, it was working. 'Yes, OK. I'd love that.'

Trying to eat slippery Fettuccine Alfredo while remaining attractive and elegant was something I quickly discovered was impossible. Thankfully, Max was learning this too – and as our eyes met across the table in the small *trattoria* in North Beach the sight of our struggles was too funny for words. His laugh was deep and infectious and the couple at the next table joined in, not really knowing why they were laughing, which made our mirth double.

'OK, so lesson learned: don't take your date for pasta if you want to look cool,' he noted. 'Should have remembered that one.'

'At least it wasn't spaghetti and meatballs,' I offered. 'Otherwise I might have worried you were going to push a meatball towards me with your nose, like in *Lady and the Tramp*!'

'I'd have given it a damn good try.'

'Aw, Max. I'm touched.'

'You're welcome. So how am I doing?'

I looked at him, not really sure what he was asking. 'Sorry?'

His smile was warm and welcoming. 'Today. Last week at Ced's place and the Golden Gate . . . Are you enjoying our dates?'

I blushed. 'Yes, very much.'

'Good. I had to check.' He leaned towards me, reaching across the table to take my hand. 'I think you're wonderful, Nell.' His thumb moved in slow circles across the back of my hand, sending electrically charged shivers travelling across my skin. 'Forgive me if that's forward.'

My breath quickened as I gazed into the dove-grey depths of his eyes. 'You're not being forward. I like you, too.'

He smiled again and I found myself wanting to be in his arms then and there. The urge was so strong that I had to look away, my half-empty wine glass a much safer option than maintaining eye contact.

Our conversation moved easily to more general territory as dessert and then coffee arrived, the chemistry between us deepened somewhat by our mutual confession. When we were finished, Max paid the waiter and we emerged into the warm June afternoon. His hand found mine as he hailed a taxi.

'Feel like a walk to work off lunch?' he asked. 'I know a great place but it's a little steep to get there.'

My stomach was complaining at the amount of food it had consumed, so a walk would be the perfect remedy. 'Sounds great.'

I recognised Telegraph Hill from my guidebooks as soon as we left the taxi, the notable white landmark of Coit Tower at its steep summit. We climbed up Filbert Street, the effort matching the exhilaration I felt walking beside Max. While the climb was steep and challenging, we rose quickly, the view of San Francisco below becoming more impressive the higher we climbed. At the base of Coit Tower we paused to catch our breath, looking out at the city, which was shrouded in a layer of fog making me feel as if we were standing above the clouds.

Max rested his hands on his knees and looked across at me. 'Ready to head up there?' He nodded at the tower. 'The view is worth the effort.'

I gazed up at the tower, my heart still thudding hard. 'We've come this far. Why not?'

When we reached the viewing deck at the top the views over San Francisco were wonderful. The fog had begun to clear over the Bay and from our vantage point we could see tiny white yachts skimming over the shimmering water.

'Beautiful, huh?' I was aware of Max's arm sliding gently around my waist as he joined me to look at the view. The closeness of the contact was amazing and I settled back against the firmness of his warm body. It felt completely right – as if we had been designed to fit together. Comfortable in his half-embrace and confident in his feelings for me I turned my head and my lips found his. Our first kiss was as natural as breathing, deepening as his arm pulled my body closer to him. Feelings I'd held at bay broke free, drawing me into him. In that moment I was completely surrounded by Max Rossi, wanting to be lost there for a lifetime.

When our kiss ended, Max laughed and buried his face in my neck. 'I have been wanting that to happen since we met.'

I felt as if I was floating on air, two hundred metres up above Telegraph Hill. 'So have I.'

From: nell.sullygirl@gmail.com
To: vickster1981@me-mail.com
Subject: Mission accomplished

I kissed him. And it was WONDERFUL!
N xxx

From: vickster1981@me-mail.com
To: nell.sullygirl@gmail.com
Subject: Re: Mission accomplished

GOOD GIRL!!!
Now I need details! When, where, how good was it, how long did it last? My vicarious happiness depends on these answers.
So proud of ya
Vix xxxxxxxxxxxx

From: nell.sullygirl@gmail.com
To: vickster1981@me-mail.com
Subject: Re: Re: Mission accomplished

Where: At the top of Coit Tower looking out at gorgeous San Francisco. (Then again on the steps on the way down, outside the tower, going back down Filbert Street, waiting for a taxi, in the taxi and outside Lizzie's apartment where we said goodbye . . . Yes, I'm a hussy and no, I don't care ☺)

How long: The first kiss seemed to last forever and I didn't want it to end.

How good: I'll leave that to your imagination!

Big loves
Nell xxx

Lizzie was beside herself when I shared the events of my day.

'Oh Nellie, that's fabulous!' she squealed. 'He's a lovely guy and completely into you! When are you seeing him again?'

'Thursday,' I said, the reality of the sudden surge forward in events still making me dizzy. 'I can't wait.'

As it turned out, neither could Max. On Wednesday night I was watching a film with Lizzie when the door intercom buzzed. Lizzie answered and I was thrilled to hear Max's voice.

'Hey Lizzie, can you send Nell down to meet me?'

Not even worrying about the fact that I was in my PJs, I hurried down the stairs to the street entrance and was in his arms kissing him before he could speak. It was all I had thought of all day and to be back there was the best feeling in the world. When we finally broke apart, Max laughed, his face flushed pink.

'Now *that's* what I call a welcome! Hello you.'

'Hi. Want to come up?'

'I can't. I have to be somewhere. But I wanted to give you these.' He handed me a posy of bright Ranunculus blooms, their tightly curled heads a confection of pink, yellow, orange, purple and red.

'They're beautiful, thank you.'

'So are you. Yes, it's cheesy but I didn't want to wait until tomorrow to see you again.'

'Then I'm glad you didn't.'

He kissed me again, groaning as he pulled away. 'I got to go, I'm sorry. I'm meeting a prospective investor for the art collective. But I'll see you tomorrow at Annie's, OK?'

Hugging my flowers, I watched him stroll away. Handsome, thoughtful, sexy and surprising – what else had Max Rossi got up his sleeve for me?

I couldn't hide my smile next day at Annie's and nothing was able to remove it: not the relentless busyness that didn't let up from the start of my shift till the end; not when the orange juicing machine stuck and I had to reach in and dig out the orange skin, getting my arm covered in sticky mess which took several minutes to wash off; and not even when an irate customer in the breakfast queue accused me of being 'an arrogant English' and was almost tackled in a fist-fight by Marty who came over all chivalrous and had to be held back by Annie.

'What's happened to you?' Laverne asked as she passed me with a precariously balanced stack of plates.

'Nothing. I'm just happy, that's all.'

'*Bull*. You finally got it on with Max, didn't you?'

I feigned shock. 'Laverne!' Seeing this didn't wash with

her, I laughed. 'OK, things are good with us. I really like him.'

Laverne whooped loudly, almost letting go of the crockery in her arms. 'That is *so cool*! I could tell you guys were into each other but I'm so happy you're doing something about it. Go girl!'

'Did something happen with Max already?' Mr Alfaro grinned up at me and I realised he and his wife were waiting at the table beside us and had heard it all.

'Maybe,' I replied, the diner suddenly stifling hot.

'You see? I told you it would,' he said to Mrs Alfaro.

Esther Alfaro sucked air between her teeth. 'Was that ever in doubt, Saul? We introduced them, remember? It was bound to work out.'

'All the same, it's a wonderful thing. Young love is a delicate flower.'

'A delicate flower? Who made you a poet?'

Saul winked at his wife. 'It was ever thus. Don't pretend my way with words wasn't what won you over, Esther. I wooed you with my prose.'

'Your words wooed my mother.' Esther's rolled eyes couldn't detract from her smile. 'I just happened to agree with her.'

Mr Alfaro reached up and patted my hand. 'You enjoy it, young lady. Maxim is a wonderful man. You will be happy with him.'

Their interest was touching but it did feel a little like I was dating Max by committee. I was still getting used to the ease with which everyone at Annie's assumed advisory roles in my love life. Back at home this was never the case, Vicky being the only person with whom

I ever really discussed my relationship with Aidan. Of course they were happy for me, which meant a great deal, even if I wished they would be a little less *public* about it.

When Max arrived early to meet me Annie greeted him warmly.

'Mr Maxim Rossi! Good to see ya. How's business today?'

He took off his grey trilby and ran a hand through his hair. 'Slow, to be frank. But I have the afternoon free to focus on this lovely lady.'

'Well, isn't that just sweet? Nell, you're good to go.'

I looked up at the chrome and neon clock above the counter, which read twelve forty-five p.m.

'Are you sure? I still have fifteen minutes of my shift and we're really busy.'

Annie let out a great, gravelly guffaw as she virtually pushed us both out of the diner. 'We'll manage. You two have fun. Go, go!'

Outside, Max pulled me to him for a long kiss. Then, smiling at one another, we began to walk down Haight Street.

'Where are we going?' I asked, taking his hand.

'To my favourite place in San Francisco,' he replied. 'The Japanese Tea Garden in Golden Gate Park. I think you'll love it.'

We crossed the road at the end of Haight Street and walked alongside the carriageway around the periphery of Golden Gate Park. Tall trees formed a guard and we followed these through the wooded avenues of Martin Luther King Jr. Drive – offering glimpses of wide, open green spaces surrounded by trees dressed in all shades for autumn. We turned right into Hagiwara Tea Garden Drive, heading towards a golden pagoda at the beautiful entrance to the tea garden.

'My grandma often brought me here,' Max said, gazing up at the pagoda. 'She used to bring a book and sit while I watched the carp in the lake, and then we'd have tea together at the Tea House.'

I loved seeing the wistfulness in his eyes and tried to imagine Max Rossi as a child. He would have been adorable and probably a bit precocious, I decided, with a mass of dark hair and those big grey eyes that probably earned him a free pass out of trouble more often than not.

Bringing myself back to the present, I smiled up at him. 'It already looks amazing. I can't wait to see it.'

The garden was beautiful, each twist in the path revealing new colour and form. As we walked I noticed for the hundredth time that day how handsome Max was; how the sunlight caught the line of stubble around his jaw line and how his soft grey eyes seemed to sparkle like the surface of the waters around us.

We had reached the central lake, where artfully trimmed trees and shrubs spanned a steep embankment like the rainbow colours in the Murano *millefiori* glass paperweight my dad kept on his desk – vivid, pillow-like mounds of green, amber and gold arranged in a delicate living patchwork. On the brow of the hill two dragon-red and shining gold pagodas rose like majestic emperors, casting perfect reflections in the lake below. I took a breath and drank in the view. No wonder Max loved this place so much. It was as if an artist had painstakingly arranged each leaf and blade of grass to create a space unhindered by time.

We walked slowly through the seemingly sacred space, our conversation as easy and flowing as the gentle waters around us. As we talked I took photographs, some of which I intended to email to Vicky who had demanded more pictures (especially of Max).

After an hour, we made our way to the ornate Tea House, where we sat at long benches while Japanese ladies served us nutty-tasting green Genmaicha tea and sweet rice cakes flavoured with green tea, strawberry, lychee and kinako. We shared the tiny space with tourists from across the world and the chatter of excited voices was punctuated by the click and whirr of countless cameras. It was at once intimate and anonymous: a shared experience of the beautiful garden and Japanese refreshments tempered by the huddle of forty strangers in a landmark far from home.

'The diner was crazy today,' Max said, breaking open a rice cake. 'Are you certain you still want to run one?'

'It was definitely the busiest day I've worked through so far,' I agreed. 'But you get into a strange headspace when it's too busy to think. Now I feel more like I know what I'm doing I'm just going with the flow.'

'Have you thought about what you'll do when you get home?' he asked. 'I mean, how does one go about starting a thing like that?'

It was a question I had been considering increasingly during the past couple of weeks, aware of the time passing. 'I'm starting to make a list of the things I need to research. Business courses, funding, advice – there's a lot to consider.'

'And that doesn't scare you?'

'It terrifies me! But I know it's what I want to do. I will look for another job as well. I don't want to be dependent on my parents for too long and it would be good to get some money behind me. But I feel like my goal is set now.'

He gave me a soft kiss. 'I believe you'll do it.'

'Really?'

'Yes really. You're a go-getter, Nell. You're the kind of person who makes things happen. And I like that about you.'

I smiled. Hearing this description of the way Max saw me made me wonder what he would have thought if we'd met before I lost my job. I liked that he knew me now – and could see the changes I knew were happening.

'And how about you? What's your dream?' I asked him.

'Sorry – I don't know what you mean.'

'If you could be doing anything what would it be?'

His smile was steady. 'I would be with you,' he said, pulling me closer until his lips were on my neck. 'Only with less people around. Preferably for a *long* time . . .'

I giggled and pushed him back. 'It's a serious question. Would you like to have your own studio some day? An exhibition in New York or London?'

He laughed and shook his head. 'I don't think about things like that.'

'Why not?'

'Because – I don't believe in planning. Everything good

in my life has happened because I was open to anything. There's no point me setting goals. I like the spontaneity.'

I stared at him over the rim of my teacup as I considered this. 'But you're the one telling me to go for my dream.'

'That's because it hasn't happened for you yet. But you're open to it. Which means the universe will know you're positioned for good things.'

'The *universe*?'

He rolled his eyes. 'Life, destiny, fate – whatever. I wanted to be an artist, and now I'm an artist. Anything else that happens from this point on is a bonus.'

I knew he could see my confusion. It didn't make sense to me: how could someone as talented as Max not want to achieve all he could? 'OK.'

'Nell, just trust me on this. We're in different places. But that's good.' He stroked my hair as he kissed me. 'Now, about that great idea of mine to lose this crowd . . .'

CHAPTER TWENTY-ONE

Tall tales and revelations

'Tell us the story, Nell!'

One thing I quickly learned about Eva was her tenacity. When she wanted something, nothing was going to dissuade her from it. She wasn't a demanding child, but the cheekiness of her expression made me give in to more or less any request she made. Especially when it came to stories.

Over the weeks I'd been volunteering at S-O-S Club, Eva, Maya and JJ had delighted in the stories I told them about England. Maya always begged me to describe the jewels in Queen Elizabeth's crown in the Tower of London. JJ wanted to know about castles and was convinced that we had dragons living beneath them. And Eva believed most English people lived in palaces and were cared for by butlers and nannies. Their vision of my country amused me – frozen in a Hollywood-style time somewhere between the Middle Ages and the Victorian era. Maya didn't believe me when I told her we had roads and cars and malls just like her home city. Eva loved to hear about kings and queens, not minding that most of the stories I told her were completely made up to match her vision of England.

The story she loved the most – and the one to which she was referring today – was the story of the lady on the steps of St Paul's Cathedral who fed the pigeons. Of course, this was a verbal retelling of her favourite scene from *Mary Poppins*, but it didn't matter. Eva liked hearing it and I liked telling it.

She curled up on a cushion in the Story Zone as I told her and the other children about the woman – who I'd named Ethel – who loved the pigeons and was worried that they wouldn't have enough to eat. I described her poor little house and the sacks of bird food that she kept in her coal cellar, and how she rose early each morning to fill small paper bags with the seed to sell at St Paul's so that the people of London could feed her beloved birds.

'You're such a storyteller,' Lizzie grinned as Miguel and Poppy gathered the children in the centre of the hall to play the Rollercoaster Game – which consisted of the kids running themselves ragged in a long line, pretending to climb the hills and race around the curves of a rollercoaster track. 'Although you realise they'll all be thoroughly disappointed if they ever visit London when they grow up.' She laughed as Eva's excited voice drifted over the other children's, singing 'Feed the Birds' as loud as her lungs would allow. 'It's sweet that Eva loves that film so much. I couldn't stand it when I was a kid.'

I couldn't contain my shock at this revelation. 'Lizzie,

I never knew that! I thought everybody loved *Mary Poppins*.'

Lizzie was unrepentant in her near-blasphemous stance. 'Not me. Julie Andrews irritated me. And I was scared of the chimney sweeps.'

'Wow. I thought I knew everything about your life, Lizzie Sullivan. But now it turns out you're an enigma!'

'Hardly,' she laughed. 'Actually Nell, I've been meaning to ask, how would you feel about putting some recipes together for S-O-S Bake Zone that I can use when you go home? I know you still have a couple of weeks here but I thought I'd ask now to give you time to put something together. The Bake Zone has been such a success since you've taken it on. What do you think?'

The mention of the end of my time at S-O-S Club gave me a funny feeling in the pit of my stomach, but I loved the idea of my recipes remaining long after I'd gone. 'I'd love to.'

Next day I rose early, making a strong pot of Saturday morning coffee and settling myself at Lizzie's Mac to begin researching recipes for the club. As I found ideas I made notes, and it occurred to me that I could do this when I got home to begin researching menu items for my diner. I had collected over twenty possible recipes when the door intercom buzzed, making me jump. Rushing through to the kitchen to answer it before it disturbed Lizzie, I was surprised to hear Rosita's panicked voice.

'*Chica*, I need to see you.'

'Rosita, what is it?'

'The sidewalk artist guy – he's down there now!'

'Down where?'

'By the Stanyan Street entrance to Golden Gate Park. My cousin Seve saw him. If you hurry you may catch him!'

I got dressed at high speed, grabbed my front door key and ran down Haight Street as fast as I could. Reaching the end of the street the road crossing turned to red just as I got there, but between the speeding cars and trucks I could just make out a figure hunched over the pavement, working colour into the concrete with wide, flamboyant strokes. He was wearing layers of clothes and an old orange puffer jacket, parts of the stuffing exposed where the fabric had ripped around the sleeves.

It seemed to take forever for the lights to change and I kept my eyes on him, praying I could get there before he left. Finally the red hand disappeared, replaced by the walk sign and I sprinted across the road just in time to see the man stand, pick up his chalks and begin to walk away.

'Wait!' I shouted.

He half-turned and I could see his woollen beanie hat pulled low over the sunglasses shading his eyes and a Paisley print scarf tied around his face to mask his features. His steps quickened and I had to sprint to catch up.

'Please, stop for a minute?'

'I can't.' His deep voice was muffled by the scarf around his mouth.

As I neared him I reached out, my fingers brushing the shiny orange fabric of his jacket sleeve.

'I don't want to know who you are,' I gulped between gasps for air. 'I just want to say thank you.'

He stopped and slowly faced me, his breathing pronounced beneath the layers of clothes. 'Yeah?'

'Yes. I'm here on holiday and your paintings introduced me to this city when I first arrived. I would never have visited as much of it as I have if it weren't for them. So – um – thanks . . .'

He said nothing, but didn't turn to leave either. In all the time I'd spent searching for the artist, I hadn't considered what I would actually say to him if I happened to find him. Now I had, my self-conscious Britishness took over and all other words deserted me. With nothing else to say, I smiled dumbly, feeling a complete idiot. Just as I was concocting a plausible exit strategy, he grabbed my hand with chalk-stained fingers.

Now *this* was unexpected. Considering I knew nothing about this person save for the artwork he decorated San Franciscan streets with, the new development set my nerves on edge. What if he was a crazed mass-murderer who liked to paint sidewalks in his spare time? What if he was in the habit of mugging unsuspecting admirers when they eventually tracked him down? What if . . .?

As the progressively more hysterical eventualities raced around my brain, the street artist holding my hand looked cautiously around and began to pull me towards the gates at the entrance of Golden Gate Park. Now I was really panicking, clamping my hand over his in an attempt to prise his fingers away.

'Let go of me!'

'Calm down,' he urged, but I wasn't listening. What

was I thinking, stalking someone I didn't know? What did I really expect to happen? There was obviously a reason he wished to remain anonymous – how was I to know what that was?

'I'll give you money – if that's what you want? But please don't hurt me.' I was still cursing my naivety when he spoke again, stopping me in my tracks.

'Please calm down, Nell.'

Eh?

He was still pulling my arm but this time I let him lead me away from the road, the mention of my name knocking me off-guard. When we rounded the gate, he took a step towards me and removed his sunglasses and scarf.

My chin virtually hit the floor. '*Max?*'

'You *have* to promise to keep my secret,' he said, anxiety in his eyes. 'Swear it, Nell!'

Max Rossi was San Francisco's answer to Banksy? I could hardly take it in. Why hadn't he said anything before? Especially after all the personal things we had talked about – and all of ourselves I thought we'd openly shared. But this new development intrigued rather than annoyed me. His paintings were beautiful: and knowing a little of the beautiful character Max Rossi clearly was, it now all made sense. 'You did all those amazing paintings?'

'Yes.'

'But you said you were a sculptor.'

'I did and I am. But I'm an artist first and foremost and this – it's just something I do.'

'They're wonderful. You should tell everyone.'

'I'm serious. You have to promise to keep this secret.'

'Of course I won't say anything. But I don't understand why you want to remain anonymous. Your work is . . . inspirational.'

'I like people not knowing who I am. It makes the work speak for itself. If they knew it was me they'd compare my street art to the regular work I do and devalue it. Nobody knows, Nell. Not my family, not my friends.'

'So why tell me?'

He flushed the merest hint of pink. 'Because it's you. And because you sought me out.' He stroked my cheek. 'I kinda like that you did that.'

'A man in demand, eh?'

'Sure. Who doesn't want to be tracked down by a beautiful British woman?'

I folded my arms, pretending I wasn't loving the situation I'd unwittingly uncovered. 'Except of course, that I didn't know it was you.'

'Hey, it's the thought that counts.'

'I only loved the street artist for his work, you know.'

'Loved? Interesting choice of words . . .'

Now it was my turn to blush. 'I was talking about the work.'

'I know.'

We shared equally self-satisfied smiles.

'So now you've unmasked me, how about coffee?'

'Coffee to buy my silence?'

He laughed. 'No. Coffee to buy me some time with you.'

I took his hand when he offered it, my heart pulsing

in time with the traffic thundering along Stanyan Street beside us. 'Well in that case, how can I refuse?'

The more time I spent with Max, the more I began to realise how hard it was going to be to leave him when it was time to go home. I hadn't anticipated meeting anyone when I arrived in San Francisco and when I agreed to date Max I never thought it would be anything other than a holiday fling. But gazing into his lovely grey eyes as we sat in a Java's Crypt booth I knew this had the potential to be so much more. Truth was, he fascinated me: his unconventional logic, the way he saw the world, his relentless positivity. His personality was as colourful as the painted buildings gracing The Haight's streets, his regard for me as warm as the Californian sun. When I was with Max, it was as if the world opened up a little and the tiniest possibilities stretched into being, just out of reach. Whenever I told him about my dream of running my own diner, Max was the one encouraging me to dream wilder, to hope for more. When he spoke about the way he saw the world, I wanted to wander in it. This was so much more than a holiday romance. This had the potential to be life-changing . . . but how could I tell him that without scaring him away?

Lizzie picked up on my quandary immediately, thank goodness. We were enjoying spicy dim sum in Chinatown when she pushed away her bowl and fixed me with a stare.

'Right, Sullivan. What's up?'

'Nothing.'

This was never going to dissuade my cousin, whose

perception was so sharp it required a health and safety directive. 'Rubbish. You've been wearing that strange half-frown of yours all week. Tyler even noticed it last night when he came over for dinner and that kind of thing normally passes him by. Spill.'

'I think I might be falling for Max.'

Entirely nonplussed, Lizzie shrugged. 'No newsflash there. So?'

'No, I mean *really* falling for him, Liz.'

'Again, why is that a problem, exactly?'

'It's absolutely a problem! I didn't come here to get involved in another complicated relationship scenario. I've had more than my fair share of that with Aidan. I came to San Francisco to get away from all of that. I came to . . .'

Lizzie groaned. 'You came here because you wanted to have some fun. Much-deserved fun, in my opinion. And have you or have you not been having fun with Max?'

'Of course I've been having fun, but . . .'

'But nothing, Nell! You are spending time with an incredibly good-looking bloke who is clearly besotted with you. Don't throw that away just because you're scared.'

I stared into my steaming bowl of shrimp dumplings, sticky rice and spicy baozi bun. 'I'm not scared. I'm just . . .'

'You feel out of control because you didn't pencil this into your list of things to do in San Francisco. Just relax. Leave the agonising for next week when you guys have to work out the next step.'

'What if there is no next step for us?'

My cousin smiled that quietly confident smile of hers and infuriatingly I felt better. How dare she successfully placate me at a time like this?

'Deal with that when you get there. At least then you won't have wasted the rest of your time here worrying.'

CHAPTER TWENTY-TWO

Three little words

During the next two weeks I spent more time with Max, trying to take Lizzie's advice and enjoy every moment without worrying what came next. We visited his favourite places in San Francisco – small art galleries, hidden restaurants, kitsch tourist attractions and streets where he had been inspired. Snuggled up on the futon at Lizzie's we spoke long into the night about his passion for art and the many anonymous chalk artworks he had left around the city. I loved to hear him talk about his work. His eyes came alive and his words tumbled over themselves in his eagerness to explain why art was the lifeblood of who he was.

My feelings for Max were deepening with every day we spent together. And other people were noticing it, too.

'Max Rossi tells me you two have been spending a lot of time together,' Mrs Alfaro said, beaming brightly as we ate lox and cream cheese blinis around their dining table.

Lizzie hid her smile as I did my best to appear nonchalant. 'We have. He's lovely and I like him very much.'

'I'm not so sure about the "like". I think it's obvious you *love* the boy.'

Taken aback, I fought to reply. 'Well, I—'

Mrs Alfaro reached across and patted my hand. 'Now, don't you get embarrassed. Being in love is a beautiful thing.'

'Like you say *that* to me every day,' Mr Alfaro muttered into his forkful of stuffed blini.

His wife's head snapped round. 'I'm not talking about *you*. Was I talking about you? Since when was this conversation about you?' She looked back at me. 'Love is a beautiful thing, Nell. Look at your cousin and that handsome school principal of hers – both so young and caught up in love for each other . . .'

Now it was Lizzie's turn to blush.

Unaware of this, Mrs Alfaro carried on. '. . . And when you fall in love, you know. It might *take you months* to say it,' she shot an accusatory look at her husband, 'but when you do, it's beautiful.'

'I don't have months to say anything,' I replied, instantly regretting it when I saw the Alfaros' eyes lighting up. They could clearly see how I was feeling – but it couldn't be love yet, could it? 'I'm only here for just over another week.'

Mrs Alfaro winked at me. 'That's more than enough time to fall in love.'

Mr Alfaro shook his head. 'What my wife is referring to is that it took me almost a year to pluck up courage to say those three little words. She knew, of course, but she never let on.'

'*This* again,' Mrs Alfaro tutted, but the apples of her cheeks turned pink. 'Always with the *story*.'

'Well maybe I like stories, Esther. And maybe you do, too. Not that you'll ever admit it, woman.'

'Admit what? That I fell for a *schmuck*? I admit that every day.'

He groaned and shrugged at me. 'You see what happens when you say you love somebody? Years of *this* . . .'

'Don't pretend you don't love it, Saul Alfaro.'

Undeterred, Mr Alfaro leaned against the creaky back of his chair. 'Do you know, Nellie, this woman made me sweat it out for months? Until one evening, after dinner at Friedrich's – our favourite restaurant in Mission – when my time came to say it. I saw the candlelight illuminating Esther Miechowicz's beautiful face and I just blurted it out. And do you know what she said to me, after all that agonising? "*Finally*, you tell me." As matter-of-fact as you like! We were eating *Wiener Schnitzel* at the time and since then whenever I tell her I love her she says to me, "I think I smell *Wiener Schnitzel*."'

For a moment, Esther Alfaro completely forgot her exasperation with her husband of fifty-nine years, and exchanged smiles with him instead. It was nothing more than a fleeting gesture, but in that moment I understood why they had spent so many years together. All the bickering, the long sighs and the rolled eyes were revealed as nothing more than ripples on the surface of the ocean, the calm depths of their love far beneath being the real reason for the longevity of their marriage.

I watched the sun glinting through the cream net curtains in the Alfaros' apartment and asked myself the question. Was I in love? It was impossible to tell. What I felt for Max was completely different from how I'd felt with Aidan. Love with Aidan Matthews was comfortable and familiar, sometimes exciting when we fought or reunited after one of our many breaks. With Max I felt more confident in myself, as if we were more equally matched. But was that just because I was far from home, on an extended holiday where the cares of ordinary life were on hold? Soon I would be returning to the city where Aidan was waiting and I still had to decide how I felt about him. Would I feel the same about Max when he was thousands of miles away and my former flame was back in my life?

At the beginning of my final week in San Francisco, Max took me to the dockside beside the Ferry Building on The Embarcadero as darkness was settling across the city. At night it was transformed into an illuminated landscape, the lights from the city skyscrapers in the Financial District painting trails into the inky black Bay waters. It was breathtaking – vibrant, alive and beautiful.

'I wanted to show you this,' Max said, taking my hand and leading me to the back of the Ferry Building, where a row of benches overlooked the Bay Bridge. When I saw it I lost my breath momentarily: the entire expanse of the Bay Bridge had been covered in millions of moving LED lights, painting its cables and towers with rippling, undulating movement that reflected in the water below. It was mesmerising.

'Wow . . .'

A cluster of people stood with us, a hushed awe falling on the dock as we watched the beautiful light show.

Max's arm moved around my shoulders. 'Come on.'

We walked away from the other onlookers into the darkness of the dock jetty further out into the Bay. Finding a bench, we sat down and kissed, the chill of evening air contrasting with the heat of each other's mouths. Max pulled away to look at me, his fingers warm against my face and his eyes suddenly earnest and still.

'I love you, Nell.'

Stunned, I opened my mouth to reply, but his fingers fell across it.

'Don't say anything. Just hear me: I love you. I don't know what that means for us but it's how I feel.'

A million thoughts raced through my mind at once, but I couldn't have spoken even if I'd tried. I wanted to tell him how I felt, but strangely now was not the time. There was so much to think about with my days left in the city now down to single figures and passing faster than I wanted them to. If I was going to say something back, I had to think it through. I owed Max that much. Telling him I loved him meant questioning if we could ever make this work beyond my last day, with the challenge of the prohibitive distance between us and everything else it entailed.

I thought about what he had said to me as I worked my final shifts at Annie's. A deep sadness had already begun to tinge every task I performed, knowing that it was one less before I had to go home. I hated that all the things I loved about the temporary life I'd built in

Haight-Ashbury now seemed to have countdown clocks attached to them. And I couldn't think about Max without one appearing above the image of his lovely face, either. This time next week, I would be thousands of miles from him – from everything. It didn't seem real.

On my last day at the diner, Annie arranged for all the regular customers to gather together for goodbye drinks. Marty and Frankie were quite emotional as they drank to my future success, Marty blaming it on smoke from the kitchen.

'That's what you get for sitting too close to the hatch. I have smoke in my eyes.'

'If that's smoke in your eyes, Marty Mulhern, I'm George Clooney,' Frankie chuckled, giving me a bristly hug so strong that it squeezed the breath out of my lungs. 'Be happy, kid. It's been an honour to know you.'

'Friend me on Facebook,' Laverne made me promise. 'I want more of your recipes.'

'Of course I will.'

'Me too,' Annie said, making Laverne and I collapse with laughter at the thought of the tough, life-hardened diner owner maintaining an online profile. 'What? So I'm partial to social media. Sue me.' She invited me to embrace her, which felt decidedly odd but was a lovely gesture. As we parted, she put her hand against my cheek. 'Now you remember where I am if you need anything, you hear?'

I smiled. 'I will. Thank you.'

Mr and Mrs Alfaro shuffled over to say goodbye. 'Nell,

it has been a pleasure,' Mr Alfaro smiled. 'I wish you every blessing.'

'I think maybe this city stole your heart?' Mrs Alfaro asked, her pale blue eyes conveying understanding beyond her words.

'It has.'

She took my hand between both of hers. 'Then trust it to make all things possible. Love – love is the greatest mystery. When it's around, anything can happen. Consider this: if Saul Alfaro can tell me he loves me and still be saying it occasionally after fifty-nine years, *anything* is possible.'

'What's with the "occasionally"? I tell you all the time, woman!'

'If you do, I don't hear it.'

'Then you should buy a hearing aid. I love you. There. Heard that well enough, didn't you?' He grinned at me. 'Love will solve the puzzles and straighten the knots, Nell. Just you remember that.'

At the end of my shift I handed my apron and diner t-shirt to Annie, failing to keep my tears under control. She pushed them back at me.

'You keep them, kid. Use them in that diner of yours, OK?'

All too soon, my penultimate day in San Francisco arrived. Max had to attend a meeting about a prospective commission during the day, but he had promised we would spend our final night together.

'I have somewhere really special for our last date,' he promised. 'I want to make the most of my last night with you.'

Lizzie had cancelled her morning piano lessons to spend the time with me. We headed to the boutiques of Ghirardelli Square so that I could buy gifts for my parents and Vicky. Going gift shopping reminded me that I was just one of the many tourists visiting San Francisco, bringing me back to earth.

At lunchtime we returned to Lizzie's apartment, preparing the bags of ingredients for my last S-O-S Club session.

'Feels weird to be doing this for the last time.'

Lizzie sighed. 'I know. Thank you for everything you've done for the kids, hun. They're all going to miss you terribly.'

'I'll miss them too. I've had such an incredible time getting to know them all.'

As we travelled along now familiar streets on my final journey to Mission, I thought about my last date with Max tonight. It was crazy to be even considering it, but I had decided to say something. He might say no – and who would blame him if he did? Long distance relationships rarely worked, especially those formed from holiday romances. It wasn't realistic but then when was anything in love?

'I'm going to tell Max I love him tonight,' I told Lizzie quickly, before I had time to think better of it.

My cousin's mouth dropped open. 'Oh Nell – are you sure?'

I laughed at the ridiculousness of the situation. 'Not at all. But it's my last night here and if I don't tell him now I might never get the chance again.'

'How would it work? You're not going to be able to

afford a flight out here again for some time and I don't think Max will find it easy to travel to you. Do you really think it has the potential to be more?'

I was amazed by how much I did. 'This isn't what I thought would happen and it won't affect my plans for my own business. But I need to tell him what I feel is far beyond a holiday romance. I love him. And he needs to know that.'

Tyler was waiting for us when we arrived at Sacred Heart Elementary, a gift-wrapped hooded sweatshirt with the school logo on it as a present from the school.

'We'll miss you,' he said. 'Thanks for everything you've done.'

'It's been my pleasure,' I replied, accepting his strong hug. 'Promise me you'll take good care of my cousin.'

An enormous smile broke across Tyler's face. 'Now that will be *my* pleasure, Nell.' Having seen them together over the last few weeks and how much in love they seemed to be, I had no doubt that Lizzie and Tyler had much happiness ahead of them.

Lizzie helped me set up the Bake Zone for the last time. Each wooden spoon, bowl and bag of ingredients I put out around the table I took time to place, picturing the faces of the children who would be using them. Maya, JJ, Bonita, LeSean, Tommy, Madison, Declan, Eva . . . Children who, minutes later, burst into the hall in a blur of flung coats, loud screams and scurrying feet as S-O-S Club roared into life again.

Watching their games, I knew I was going to miss them so much. The thought of it brought a rush of tears and I had to duck into the kitchen until they subsided.

'I'm gonna miss you, Nell.'

I wiped my eyes quickly on my shirtsleeve and turned back to see the mournful faces of Eva and Maya, which set me off again. I took their hands as we walked back into the school hall. 'Oh poppets, I'll miss you both too.'

'Why do you have to go back to England?' Maya asked.

'Because it's where I live.'

Eva gazed up at me. 'Why can't you live *here*? Lizzie's from England and she lives here now.'

Tears glistened in Eva's eyes as she looked up at me. 'It's like when Mary Poppins says goodbye to Jane and Michael. I hate that part.'

I smiled at her but my heart was breaking. 'But they're happy, aren't they? Because she's fixed everything with their dad so they can be a family. And another family needs her.'

She sniffed. 'I guess. But it still sucks.'

All too soon, the session came to an end and the children solemnly made a line to say goodbye to me as their parents began to arrive. I tried not to cry but it was a futile attempt. The gifts the children brought for me, including a good luck card they had all signed (complete with feathers which I guessed were stuck on at Maya's insistence), almost destroyed me. Saying goodbye to little JJ, shy Declan, confident LeSean and sweet Maya was hard, especially because I was trying so hard to smile with each parting. With every hug I shared the ache grew and by the time Eva reached me I was a mess. Scooping her into a huge hug I felt her little frame shaking in my arms as she sobbed loudly.

'Don't cry, lovely. You're my superstar. I need you to help Lizzie and make sure my baking class know what they're doing, OK?'

'OK.' She accepted the tissue I offered her and dabbed her nose. 'Will you come and say bye to Mom?'

I smiled. 'Of course I will.'

Lizzie gave me a sympathetic look as I took Eva's hand and walked towards the group of parents gathering at the door.

'This your last time, Nell?' JJ's mum asked as we walked past.

'It is.'

'Good luck to ya. And thanks for making JJ enthusiastic about baking.'

'My pleasure.'

A few more of the parents came over to wish me the best and it was all I could do not to start crying again. As they left, Eva suddenly let go of my hand.

'Daddy!'

She ran off into the crowd as Declan's mother approached and I stopped to receive her thanks, keeping my eye on the direction in which Eva had gone. When Declan's mother moved away, I hurried after Eva. A group of parents in front of me parted and I could see the little girl being spun around by a tall man. I'd assumed that her father was at work as it was always Shanti who picked her up from S-O-S Club. I hovered at a distance, enjoying the sight of my young friend so excited to see her father.

He set her down and she pulled his arm, yanking him

around. 'Come meet my teacher, Dad. She talks like Mary Poppins . . .'

I laughed at her description of me and stepped forward as Eva's father lifted his head . . .

. . . and my heart shattered.

CHAPTER TWENTY-THREE

Secrets and lies

Max's expression was pure horror as his eyes met mine.

Eva was still tugging his hand towards me, her little face a picture of pride.

'Nell! This is my daddy!'

Aware that the other parents and children surrounded us, I forced a smile onto my face, feeling sick. 'Oh? Hello.'

'Hi.' His eyes were searching mine, a thousand unspoken words that would never be said in his stare.

'Nell has to go home to England tomorrow. But we had fun today, didn't we?'

'Yes, we did.' My smile was hurting my face as memories of Max's words tumbled like a hurricane with the facts now emerging. He said he had been with his last partner for ten years, but had he ever said they were over? I'd never asked the question outright: why hadn't I asked him if he was single? I'd taken everything on trust, assuming his interest in me indicated he wasn't seeing anyone else. Just how stupid had I been?

Max is Eva's father. Shanti is his partner. They've been together for ten years . . .

'Why did you come to get me, Daddy?' Eva was standing between us, oblivious to the silent battle raging above her head. 'Mom always does it.'

He cleared his throat. 'Mom had to go and see Grandma. She had a fall so . . .' apology washed across his face, his head slowly shaking '. . . so I came instead.'

'Is Grandma OK?'

'She went to the hospital and they're fixing her leg. Mommy says . . . Your mom says she's good.'

'Eva! Don't forget your cookies . . . Oh.' Lizzie screeched to a halt beside me. 'Max, this is a surprise. I didn't think we were going to see you until later.'

'Do you know my daddy, Lizzie? This is *so* cool!'

'Max is Eva's father,' I said quietly. 'Shanti had to take Eva's grandmother to hospital.'

Confusion painted my cousin's face. 'Oh, I see.'

Max lowered his voice. 'Lizzie, could you – would you mind watching Eva for five minutes? I need to talk to Nell.'

'No, I don't think that's a good idea,' I shot back, but Lizzie was already taking Eva's hand.

'I think it is, Nellie. Eva, can you come and help me make sure I ticked everyone's names on the register today? I know you have a good memory and I think I might have missed something.'

Eva shrugged. 'Sure. I remember *everybody* who came today.' Happy to be asked for her help, Eva trotted off with Lizzie, leaving Max and I facing one another.

'Please Nell? I have to explain.'

'Don't.'

He looked around at the other parents. 'Then just come with me outside – this shouldn't happen here.'

This shouldn't be happening anywhere, I screamed in my head, nausea balling up in my stomach as I followed him into the corridor and out to the schoolyard. I wanted to yell at him, pummel my fists against his chest and demand to know why he'd lied to me. But then I realised it wasn't the first time he hadn't told me something. The pavement art had been a secret too, hadn't it? And while at the time I'd found it a charming discovery, in the light of what I now knew it became another lie Max had willingly told me.

The wind had picked up outside, whipping the branches of the trees lining the yard. Max yanked the hat from his head, stuffing it into his jacket pocket as he faced me.

'I am so sorry. I didn't want you to find out this way.'

'Obviously.'

'I didn't mean for this to happen, Nell. You have to believe that.'

I felt as if the world was caving in around me. 'You're Eva's father.' The words bit like razors on my tongue.

'Yes.'

'And all the time we spent together it didn't occur to you to mention it?'

He kicked at a stone on the concrete schoolyard. 'No, because . . .'

'Why? Because you didn't want me to know?'

'No, Nell.'

'Then why?'

'Because saying "Hey, I have a kid" is not something that you just say.'

'But saying "I love you" is?' The wind blew my hair into my eyes and I angrily pulled it back.

'That's completely different and you know it.'

'I told you *everything* about me. I held nothing back. I thought you'd done the same.'

'It's . . . complicated.'

'No it isn't, Max. I told you the truth. You lied to me!'

Our voices were rising in volume to be heard over the howl of the wind and the lashing tree branches above us.

'I didn't – I didn't *mean* to. You have to believe that. Please, just let me explain.'

'Please don't.' I didn't want to hear it. I didn't want to stand there while he tried to dig himself out of this. Max had lied to me twice already: I couldn't trust him again. 'I just have one question.'

He was breathing heavily, his grey eyes wide and full of regret. 'Ask me anything and I'll tell you the truth.'

'Eva's mother – do you love her?'

He appeared to be stunned by the question, staring at me for a moment before he replied. 'Shanti is the mother of my kid – of course I love her . . .'

That was all I needed to hear. Whatever I thought was happening with Max Rossi ended now. Without replying, I turned and hurried back inside.

I knew he was following me but I didn't look back. Pushing the door into the hall I walked up to Lizzie and Eva, my emotions held at bay by the finest of threads.

'Give me a hug, you.' I knelt down and hugged Eva

for the last time. Stroking her face I willed my tears to hold back until she had gone. 'I'll keep asking Lizzie how you're getting on,' I promised. 'I'm so glad to have met you.'

'Will you do something for me when you get back to England?' she asked.

I could see Max moving through the parents towards us. I didn't want to curtail my time with Eva but I couldn't face another showdown. 'Of course I will, darling. What do you want me to do?'

Eva's mournful expression was almost too much to bear. 'Will you feed the birds? Like the bird lady does?'

'Yes, I will.'

She frowned. 'Promise?'

'I promise.' I stood as Max reached us. 'And now you'd better go with your dad. Goodbye, Eva.'

'Bye, Mary Poppins.'

I had to look away as they left, aware of my cousin's concerned expression in my peripheral vision.

'Nell – I'm so, so sorry. I had no idea . . .'

'Can we just go, please?'

Lizzie nodded. 'Of course we can. Let's get our stuff.'

Poppy, Miguel, Sam and Astrid took my tears as parting sadness, patting my back and wishing me well as Lizzie led me quickly out of the school hall. Instead of waiting for the Muni bus she flagged down a taxi, which sped us back to The Haight.

I remember very little about the journey – I was too hurt, angry and upset to be aware of anything else. Lizzie helped me up the stairs and into her apartment, leaving me dazed and completely numb on the sofa as she hurried into the kitchen to make a pot of tea. I closed my eyes and rested my head against the back of the sofa.

Lizzie's hand on my shoulder made me look up. 'Nell honey, I've brought you tea – I know that's really lame but I had to do something.'

I accepted the mug. 'Thanks.'

My cousin sat next to me. 'I don't know what to say. I've worked with Eva and Shanti for three years but I honestly had no idea Max was her father. He's never visited before. It's only ever been Shanti or her mother. Oh Nell, if I'd realised . . .'

'It's OK. You couldn't have known. I just can't believe he lied to me about something so important.'

Lizzie squeezed my shoulder. 'He didn't lie to you exactly. I know it feels like he did, but having a child – it can be a difficult thing to talk about at the start of a relationship. I know a lot of the S-O-S Club parents have said that to me . . .'

'He said he loves Shanti.'

'Oh.'

'Precisely.' I nodded. 'So that's it.'

'What about your date with him tonight?'

I gave a hollow laugh. 'I think my "date" might be busy looking after his daughter because his partner's mother is in hospital.'

Lizzie observed me for a while, selecting her words with great care. 'Nell, I'm so sorry. And it's your last night, too. Life has really awful timing sometimes.'

My whole body ached. I was angry that I'd wasted so much of my precious San Francisco time on someone it turned out I didn't know at all.

'Let's stay in tonight, Liz – just me and you. We haven't spent enough time together recently and tomorrow I'm going home. Let's order pizza and talk rubbish and remember the embarrassing things we used to get up to as kids. And let's not talk any more about Max. That holiday fling is officially over.'

Lizzie's smile was strangely sad. 'Of course we can stay in. We'll make your last night a great one.'

From: nell.sullygirl@gmail.com
To: vickster1981@me-mail.com
Subject: I'm coming home

Hey Vix

It's my last night in San Francisco. My eight weeks are done and I fly home tomorrow. It seems like a long time since I left and I'm looking forward to seeing you. I'm going to bore you to death with photos, I hope you know, so brace yourself.

I'll be sad to leave this place, especially The Haight. My emotions are all over the place and I'm really torn about coming home. I can't go into details yet, but Max isn't in the picture anymore. I'll explain when I get back but something happened today that ended it and that's all I'm going to say. I'm fine, just feeling a bit of a fool for thinking it could be something more than it was.

My plane arrives back at Heathrow in the

early hours of Saturday morning. I'll probably need a couple of days to get over the jetlag but I'll call you as soon as I can.

I'm going to spend my last night with Lizzie and a large pizza. I'll miss her so much! We're watching a Ryan Gosling film in your honour. (Lizzie's a bit of a fan too.)

Don't worry about replying. By the time you get to read this I'll probably be thirty-seven thousand feet above the Atlantic heading home. I'll see you soon!

Love ya

Nell xxx

'Email sent?' Lizzie asked as I rejoined her in the living room.

'Yep. Last one. In a couple of days I'll be chatting with Vix and emailing you.' Emotion gripped my throat. 'I'm really going to miss you.'

Lizzie hugged me. 'Oh gosh, don't start that or you'll set me off again. I'll miss you too. But we'll email and call. And I'm planning to come back in December for Christmas so I'll see you then.'

On this late June evening, December seemed an awfully long way off. 'You make sure you do.'

'Just think, you might even be running your own diner by then!'

My cousin's faith in me was touching, even if fatally unrealistic. 'Maybe.'

'Oh, that reminds me – Annie said she might drop in this evening to say goodbye. She called while you were emailing Vicky. I think she's going to miss having an intern.'

After a pizza that defeated both our valiant attempts to vanquish it, Lizzie opened a bottle of red wine. Just as we were getting into *The Ides of March*, the door entry intercom buzzed and a minute later, Lizzie welcomed Annie in.

'I hope you'll forgive the intrusion,' she said, nodding at the TV. 'I couldn't say everything I wanted to at the diner this morning. I wanted to thank you for all your hard work and make sure you know I'm only a phone call away.'

'Glass of wine?' Lizzie offered.

'I won't say no. So, what are your plans when you're home, Nell?'

'I'm not sure. I'm going to look into starting my own business, maybe take a business course or just test the waters and see what might be possible. Thank you so much for letting me be a part of your business. It's been a real privilege.'

Annie clinked her wine glass against mine. 'Mutual, kid. You're a natural. Place won't be the same without you.'

'That's very kind, but all I did was . . .'

'No. I mean it. Watching you has made me remember all that passion I had for the business when I started out.' She took a long, slow sip of wine. 'Gave me some perspective and I appreciate that. So, when do you fly?'

'Tomorrow morning at eleven,' I replied. 'I'm not looking forward to leaving to be honest with you.'

'Maybe you'll come back for a visit,' Lizzie offered.

'You know you're always welcome. And everything will be waiting here for you, just as you remember it – apart from . . .'

I lifted my hand to stop her before she started to worry about what she had said. 'I know.'

'Apart from Annie's.'

Lizzie and I stared at Annie. 'Sorry?'

Annie shrugged. 'Like I said, I've gotten perspective lately. I love my work, but it's work for a young woman. I'm sixty-two years old, I've been working my whole life in that place. And I think now it's time for a change.'

I looked at Lizzie and back at Annie. She couldn't be serious, could she? Annie Legado *was* her diner. She was the lifeblood of the place.

'What kind of change?' Lizzie asked.

'Maybe I'll sell.'

Sell . . . The word hung ominously in the air between us.

'But what about your customers?' Lizzie asked. 'Where will they go?'

Annie chuckled. 'They'll find somewhere. When I first started there was one diner between here and Alamo Square. Today every corner has somewhere to eat. It's a young person's game now and everybody thinks they want a slice of the pie – present company excepted, naturally. My sister's boy Mario has been keen to buy the place for years now. I think maybe it's time.'

This was hard to take in, but the peace in Annie's expression made me remember that this was her decision, not ours. 'And what will you do, Annie?'

'I'll begin by getting up at eight a.m. instead of four. Maybe I'll read a paper, maybe I'll stroll along Haight

Street to get a cup of coffee from Ced. I might take a vacation. And then, who knows?' She stared at the dwindling liquid in her glass. 'I want to enjoy my life before I'm too old. You made me realise that, kid. I see the passion in you, that determination to make the most of your life. You'll succeed because you want it so much. This time I want to succeed at something new.'

'Wow. I can't imagine The Haight without you,' Lizzie said.

Annie gave a throaty laugh and held out her glass for more wine. 'Relax, kid, it's not like I'm dying. It'll be months before anything happens, trust me. My family's love of litigation means Mario will want every detail checked before he agrees to anything. It just gives me time to plan. And I won't be leaving The Haight. I grew up here, this is my home. Hey, maybe I'll finally get around to those piano lessons we talked about.'

'I'd love to teach you.'

'Maybe you will. Although I should warn you I'm not the easiest student.' She smiled at us both. 'Lose the long faces, please! Now remember, Nell, I want to hear everything you do when you get home. I think the future has a lot of good things for both of us.'

When Annie had gone, Lizzie and I sat silently, taking it in. And I realised something: that all this week I had been expecting the city to remain as I'd experienced it, unchanging, frozen in time to make me feel better about leaving it. But San Francisco was a city that needed to change, evolve, move on – and my selfish need for nostalgia couldn't prevent it. And I'd changed. I'd rediscovered my dream and was leaving the city determined to make it happen – however long it took.

A loud buzz from the door intercom startled both of us and Lizzie went to answer it.

'Hello?'

A too-familiar voice crackled through the intercom speaker. 'Lizzie, it's Max. I need to talk to Nell.'

Lizzie turned to me but I was shaking my head violently. 'I don't think that's a good idea, Max. She's very upset.'

A sigh cut through the static. 'I know she's hurt. I know I'm to blame. But if she could just listen I can explain it all . . .'

I didn't want to hear anything more from him. Even the sound of his voice tore at my heart. Slowly, fighting tears that threatened to overwhelm me, I stood and walked over to Lizzie's side. Confused, she stepped back as I pressed my finger to the intercom speaker button.

'Max . . .'

'Nell . . .' I could hear the hope in his voice and I hated it.

'I don't want to see you again.'

'Please, Nell – please come down and talk to me.'

'There's no point, Max. Go home.'

'Not until I see you.'

Lizzie touched my arm. 'I'll go down and speak to him.' Without waiting for my reply, she went out of the door.

I stared at the intercom, my hand hovering over the button. There were so many things I wanted to say, so many answers I needed. But I was tired, bruised and desperate to hold on to my few remaining hours in San Francisco. Max didn't deserve to demand anything. He had lied to me and that cancelled everything that had gone before it. I didn't want to spend my final hours in the city that had claimed my heart engaging in a pointless battle with a man who had no right to it. Heart decimated, my hand dropped away from the intercom and I let go of my final chance to speak to Max Rossi.

CHAPTER TWENTY-FOUR

Time to go home

All too soon, morning arrived. I'd slept in fits and starts, the crushing remembrance of Max and the nearness of my impending departure tumbling upon me, moments after waking. I had been so confident of what lay ahead of me but now as I prepared to leave the reality scared me. I was going home to no money, no job and the unresolved mess with Aidan – how was I going to deal with it all? Even the dream of my own business now loomed up like a towering mountain. There was so much to do and I didn't feel ready to tackle any of it. After discovering such certainty during the last eight weeks, the uncertainty of the future seemed too much to deal with.

Lizzie made breakfast while I packed, but neither of us were hungry.

'It didn't occur to me how hard this was going to be,' she said, tears falling as she reached for the Kleenex box. 'I think I should bring this – we're both going to need it!'

There were tears in my eyes too – for more than one

reason. 'Look at us: we're pathetic. We'll see each other again in a couple of months.'

'We will. Of course we will.'

I gazed around the familiar surroundings of my San Francisco home. 'I just don't want to leave.'

'I don't want you to go either. But you have the next great chapter of your life about to start, Nell Sullivan. And I'm going to be cheering you with every new page you write.'

The Departures hall of Terminal 2 at San Francisco International airport was far more impressive than the Arrivals gate had been. A multi-arched steel framed ceiling studded with a line of purple glass arced overhead, row upon row of deserted grey check-in desks standing sentry-like beneath. Now that I was wheeling my suitcase back across the glossy tiled floor it seemed no time since I'd arrived. From the large window I could see the blue hills in the distance, willing me to return to Haight and Lizzie and everything that had been part of my life.

Lizzie's eyes were puffed red as I checked in my suitcase.

'Do you have everything you need for your flight?'

'I think so. Except for you and the whole of San Francisco.'

My cousin gave a loud sob and buried her face in a new tissue from the box in her bag. 'I'm sorry, Nell. I'm such a wuss.' She sniffed and grinned through her tears. 'You'll let me know when you're home safely, won't you?'

'Of course I will. I've had the best time, Liz. Honestly, everything about this trip has been amazing.'

'Even Max?'

It hurt to hear his name. 'Even that. I wouldn't have chosen the way it ended but I thought about it a lot last night and I think it's a good thing it did.'

Lizzie wasn't convinced. 'You do?'

'Yes,' I replied firmly. 'Look at it realistically, what chance did we have? I think I got carried away with the romance of being far from home. I'm glad I didn't tell him I loved him because now I'm wondering if I did. It was good for what it was – a holiday fling. But now I know he lied to me – well, that will stop me feeling like I've left him behind.'

Lizzie hugged me. 'Right. I'm going to go before I flood the place.'

'Probably a good idea. Thank you – for everything.'

'You know you're always welcome back, Nell. And I'll call you next week, OK?'

With over two hours until my flight was due to depart I browsed the stores, trying to keep my mind occupied. I bought a book for the journey although I felt so wrung out I suspected I might just sleep most of the way home. A rack of postcards caused my heart to contract: bright sunny views of the city I'd fallen in love with. In the middle of the rack was a photo of Haight-Ashbury, taken a few feet away from Annie's. Feeling like I was staring at a picture of home, I bought it and a beautiful image of the Golden Gate Bridge with the Marin County Hills behind, tucking them safely into the pages of my book.

When the time finally came for me to board my flight I took one last look through the wide window by the flight gate out at the blue hills sparkling in the sun beyond the airport tarmac. The next time I was on the ground would be five thousand miles away . . .

Now that I was on my way home, I wanted to focus on what lay ahead. I was looking forward to seeing Vicky again, especially as our frequent email exchanges had made her very much a part of everything I had experienced during the last eight weeks. And I had Annie's notebook full of ideas, advice, sketches and to-do lists to consider. I was returning home determined to pursue my dream – and I had San Francisco to thank for it.

Ten and a half hours later, at Paris Charles de Gaulle airport, I received a text message that brought a smile despite my weariness:

Looking forward to seeing you Nelliegirl!
Call us from Paris – don't worry about the
time. Lots of love Dad xx

I quickly called home.

'Hello, weary traveller!' Dad exclaimed, and tears filled my eyes at the familiarity of his voice. 'What time do you get in?'

'My flight arrives at Heathrow at five thirty. I'll catch the tube home.'

'Nonsense, we're coming to get you. Your mum's just warming up the Volvo.'

I smiled into my mobile. 'That would be lovely.'

'Our pleasure, sweetheart. *Bon voyage* and don't let the Froggies get you down!'

It was so good to see the identical grins of my parents when I finally landed at Heathrow two hours later. When I had almost reached them, Mum dashed forward, scooping me into an enormous, enthusiastic hug, as Dad strolled over laughing at her public display of affection.

'It's wonderful to have you home, Nellie! Let me look at you – look at the colour of you! You're a genuine little Californian now! And you've lost weight – hasn't she lost weight, Doug?'

'She didn't need to lose any weight,' Dad retorted, hugging me. 'But you look marvellous, Nelliegirl.'

'Now, how about a proper cup of tea before we tackle the M25, eh? I expect you've been bereft without decent tea for two months.'

I didn't bother trying to explain about Lizzie's secret stash of English breakfast tea, happy just to be back with my family again. The last forty-eight hours had been emotional enough and I was exhausted, so I let myself be carried along by their enthusiasm. More than anything, it was good to be home.

I slept for fourteen hours straight, waking the next day feeling woolly-headed but brighter than when I'd arrived at Heathrow. After lunch with Mum (who was convinced I hadn't eaten anything while I'd been away), I caught the Overground train at Richmond Station to Harlesden, walking the ten minutes from the station to Vicky's terraced house. It was strange to be travelling on British trains and walking very English streets again and I was surprised at how out of place I felt – exactly as I'd done during my first few days in San Francisco.

Vicky flung open the front door and launched herself at me, almost knocking me backwards off the doorstep. 'It's so good to see you! Come in, you sickeningly tanned thing!'

I stepped carefully over the toys strewn across the hallway into Vicky's kitchen-diner as she collected Ruby from her playpen. I noticed how much she had changed in the two months I'd been away as she leaned towards me from her mother's arms for a sticky hug. 'Well hello, big girl! She's gorgeous as ever, Vicky.'

Ruby chuckled and offered me the sucked remains of a breadstick.

'Oh charming – there you go, Nell, I bet when you stepped off the plane yesterday you were desperate for a half-liquidised bread product.'

'Ruby knows me too well.'

Vicky made coffee and I gave her the gifts I'd brought back from San Francisco. Then, with Ruby snoozing beside us on the sofa, we settled down to discuss my trip. Inevitably, the subject of Max reared itself.

Vicky was shocked at the turn of events. 'I can't believe he didn't tell you about Eva. What kind of father doesn't talk about his kid?'

'We'd only been seeing each other for a couple of weeks. In a way I suppose I can't blame him for protecting his family. What hurt was that I assumed if he was pursuing me he must be free. But now I know he's in love with Eva's mother it makes all the things I'd been thinking about him – about us – completely pointless.'

'I think you had a lucky escape,' Vicky said. 'Imagine if you hadn't found out before you came home. You'd be here thinking you had a relationship while he was out there with his family. It doesn't even bear thinking about.'

'I know. At least when I was with Aidan I never worried he had a secret family stashed somewhere.'

Vicky grimaced a little and I wondered if she still blamed Aidan for us losing our jobs. 'Talking of which,' she lowered her voice, even though there was no likelihood of snoozing Ruby broadcasting whatever it was her mother was about to tell me, 'I don't suppose you've heard the latest?'

'I've successfully avoided reading most of the emails he sent me, if that's what you're referring to.'

'No, I mean about him being given the old heave-ho as well.'

This was a surprise. I'd assumed that in return for letting us go, Aidan had negotiated a safe position for himself. 'Seriously? When?'

'Three weeks ago. They made him sack all of us and then they got rid of him. Bastards. Getting him to do their dirty work and then disposing of their messenger.'

'That's horrible. How did you find this out?'

Vicky cleared her throat, fiddling with the hem of a sofa cushion. 'I – *might* have seen him last week.'

This was news to me. In one way I was glad that Vicky didn't consider him Satan's henchman any more but a part of me wondered why she hadn't mentioned it in her emails. 'And how did that go?'

'It was good, actually. I felt better for it. Not that he'd lost his job, obviously, even if it did have a ring of justice to it. But the guy was mortified and very apologetic about what happened with all of us. He asked about you, of course.'

'What did you tell him?'

'That you were having a great time. That you were happy.'

I folded my arms. 'That I was seeing someone?'

'Possibly.' Vicky grinned guiltily. 'Anyway, he asked me to say hi to you from him. I think he said he's working with his dad now. What? You didn't want me to stay angry with him forever, did you?'

'Of course not. So, how's the job-hunting with you?'

Her expression brightened. 'Actually, I have an interview on Wednesday.'

It was so good to hear positive news. 'Where?'

'Architect firm in Islington. They're looking for a policy advisor on planning law.'

'Awesome! Congratulations, Vix!'

'Get you with your West Coast Americanisms,' she laughed, clearly touched by my congratulations. 'I'm not getting my hopes up. But, you know, it feels like a step forward.'

Travelling home on the train the news that my friend was seeing progress in her search for employment was a great tonic. The news about Aidan, on the other hand, intrigued me more than it should have. When the train ground to a halt and the driver informed us of a slight signal delay, I took the opportunity to open his most recent email to me, sent a few days before I left San Francisco:

From: a.matthews@me-mail.com
To: nell.sullygirl@gmail.com
Subject: (no subject)

Hi Nell

I've stopped wondering whether you're reading my emails, but it's been quite cathartic writing regularly to the cyber void, so I'm going to continue.

I met with Vicky today, did she tell you? There's been too much crap between us since the day you lost your jobs and I thought it was time to clear the air. It was good, actually. Better than I expected. I haven't seen anyone since that meeting and I felt a bit out of it. Not that I blame them, I'd have done the same. She said you're having a good time and volunteering in a diner? I'm trying to picture you waiting tables and I hope they haven't given you one of those cheesy diner waitress outfits to wear. I bet it's fun, though. More fun than being here, anyway.

I know you'll be home soon and I just wanted to say that it would be nice to see you if you wanted to meet. No pressure, just a chat. I feel awful about how things ended with us and now I suppose you know about my situation, maybe it won't be so difficult. Anyway, you have my number. Use it if you want to – it would be great to see you.

Take care

A x

The train jolted and I looked up to see that we were moving again. It was good to know that Aidan had made amends with Vicky, but was I ready to let him do the same with me?

CHAPTER TWENTY-FIVE

Time for action

Now that I was home, I set about arranging interviews with temping agencies. My first priority had to be replenishing the severely depleted funds in my bank account so that I could start to build a foundation for the future. I hated the idea of office temping but given the current state of the economy and my deep desire not to be living with my parents forever, it seemed the obvious choice.

But two weeks later, after signing up with four agencies, I had only received three days of work and my plan to secure regular work seemed doomed to failure. When I called one of the agencies they finally admitted that I was 'vastly overqualified' for any of their assignments and that employers were wary of employing me because they assumed I would leave the moment something better came along.

'Don't worry about it, Nelliegirl,' Dad said when I explained the situation to him. 'It's tough out there. Tell you what, I'll ask some of my friends if they have odd bits of office stuff they need doing – paperwork and correspondence, that sort of thing. Not exactly riveting but every little helps, eh?'

Around the few bits of work I managed to get, I turned my attention to my diner dream, taking the opportunity of my increased free time to research the possibility of setting up my own business. Even if the reality might be years away, it felt good to be thinking about it now.

I arranged an appointment with a business advisor at the local Chamber of Commerce. Dusting off my former work suit and collecting together my research and plans, I arrived early for my appointment, nerves jangling as I waited in the reception area beside a sad selection of plastic pot plants.

'Nell Sullivan?' A portly man was looking around reception, clipboard in hand, as if addressing a large crowd, when in reality I was the only one waiting.

'Hi, that's me.'

The man chuckled. 'I like to do that, pretend we've a full house. Makes the person waiting feel important.' He offered his pillowy palm and I shook it. 'Bill Jones, Chief Business Advisor. Step into my office.' He pulled back one of the blue padded room dividers at the edge of the waiting area to reveal two chairs and a desk, with more pot plants on a shelf behind. 'Like to do that too. Makes *me* feel important. Take a seat, Miss Sullivan.'

Instantly liking Bill, despite his questionable stand-up comedy skills, I sat down as he dragged the divider back into place.

'There we go. Door shut, sitting comfortably. I'd offer you a cuppa but my flask only holds one cup.' His face broke into another huge smile. 'Joking again. If you wanted a beverage we have a Maxpax machine in the corridor, but I wouldn't recommend it. Not unless "dusty plastic" tea is your favourite blend. That wasn't a joke, by the way. Tea really is that bad here. So –' he rubbed his hands together, 'what can we do for you this fine day?'

'I want to start my own business and I don't really know if my idea is good, or how to go about making it happen.'

'Oo, now wait – let me guess – mobile hairdresser's?'

'Er, no.'

'Oh.' Bill frowned. 'Gas fitter? Architect? Childminder?'

'None of those. I'd like to—'

'Wait! Don't tell me yet. I quite like the fun of guessing. Leave it with me. It'll come to me as I'm talking to you. Basically, you've come to the right place. We offer all sorts of help, advice and training . . .' He screwed his eyes up. 'Tattooist?'

I had to laugh at that guess. 'No. I'm not a massive fan of needles.'

'Good point. *Point!* Sorry. But there you go, good advice before you start out in business can help you avoid costly mistakes.' He appeared highly amused by his own joke. 'Moving on. So when were you thinking of commencing trading?'

'Oh. I don't have a date.'

'Not a problem. I think you're going to have to tell me what your business will be because I'm trying my psychic powers and nothing's coming through.'

I smiled at him, my initial nerves dispersed by his strange but effective approach to customer care. 'I want to open my own restaurant. An authentic, American-style diner.'

Bill's eyes lit up. 'I'm hungry already. Do you have any experience with this kind of food?'

'I've just returned from a long holiday in San Francisco and I volunteered for five weeks' work experience at a diner there. I learned a great deal and I'm convinced it's something I can do.'

Bill leaned back in his chair, hands folded contentedly over his round belly. 'Impressive. So, do you have a business plan, any funding secured, idea of premises?'

I stared blankly at him. 'No – none of those.'

'Not to worry, pet. That's what we're here for. And also for impromptu taste testing when it comes to planning your menu,' he winked. 'Now, there's a four-week business start-up course we run in conjunction with a couple of the local colleges. The next one starts a week on Thursday. It's forty pounds for the whole course and there are two sessions a week. I can sign you up now, if you'd like that?'

I signed up there and then, encouraged by Bill's reaction to my plans and relieved to find the training I wanted at such a reasonable price.

Bill also gave me some contact numbers for grant-awarding trusts I might approach about funding. At no point did he suggest my dream of running a diner was ridiculous, which I took to be a good sign.

The grant-awarding bodies turned out to be a dead-end road. I was too old for a Prince's Trust Award and several other organisations required evidence of a hefty chunk of investment before they would even consider me. The trainers on the business course were very helpful and suggested other things I could do while trying to secure funding. In the twice-weekly sessions I put together a business plan and gathered a thick file of contacts and suppliers.

In the tiny box-room bedroom at Mum and Dad's two

weeks later, I spread out all of my plans across the bed and enjoyed the thrill of possibility as the pieces slowly came together. Could I really do this? My eyes drifted to the postcard of Haight-Ashbury pinned to the cork notice board on the wall. I wondered which customers might be in Annie's now. It would be just after the main breakfast rush, so Laverne would be taking her break, probably batting her eyelashes at Dom to make her a huge omelette with blueberries and maple syrup that she called her 'guilty pleasure'. The Alfaros might have arrived for their morning Danish and coffee, bickering as always. And would Max be there? Pushing the thought away, I wondered who might come into my diner – what kind of people would become my regular customers? Annie had built a strong community by serving excellent food and coffee. Maybe I could, too?

The following week, I took my notebook from Annie to a coffee shop in Richmond High Street. I had developed a need for decent coffee first thing in the morning, San Francisco still exerting its influence over me. The house coffee wasn't as smoky or as strong, but it was pleasant and gave me an excuse to be out of my parents' house at least. Settled in a comfortable armchair, I began to go through my notes from Annie's.

A good supplier is worth more than you know. Get the ingredients right and the food will sell itself. Speak to people. You only find out what they do if you speak to them. Pay attention to your customers – it'll pay dividends. I have a little word with new people and more often than not we keep chatting, they keep coming back and we find something they have that might benefit the diner . . .

I smiled as I read Annie Legado's pearls of wisdom,

each scribbled note reminding me of the particular conversation and where it had occurred. Even today, sitting in the coffee shop, the smell of roasted coffee sent me right back to performing the refill round at Annie's. It would be a long time until I got over my San Francisco experience . . .

'Um, hi.'

I raised my head. To my surprise, I came face to face with Aidan standing by my table, a nervous half-smile playing on his lips. 'Oh,' I said. 'Hello.'

He was holding a takeaway coffee cup, fiddling with the lid. 'I was just visiting one of Dad's properties up the road. I didn't know you came here.'

'I don't. I just decided to come in today.' There was a long pause as both of us thought of what to say. Finally, I broke the ice. 'Do you want to join me?'

He hesitated for a moment, before sitting on the armchair beside me. 'It's good to see you. I mean, it's a shock, but it's good.'

'Thanks . . . I think.'

He laughed and I noticed his shoulders relax. 'I'm sorry. I wasn't sure you'd want to see me – you know, after the emails and everything.'

'I wasn't sure I wanted to see you either. But I'm glad we met.' I smiled at him. 'So, how's things?'

'Getting better. I don't know if you've spoken to Vicky yet?'

'I have.'

'So you know about my job?'

I nodded. 'I'm sorry you had to go through that. I wouldn't wish it on anyone.'

'No, well you know how it feels.' His eyes were earnest in their survey of me.

There were so many things I thought I would say when I saw Aidan and yet none of them seemed appropriate now. I had been so angry with him for the way things had happened when I lost my job and while I had been in San Francisco it had been easy to paint him as the bad guy. Now he was sitting with me I found that I was inexplicably pleased to see him.

'Vicky said you're working for your dad now?'

'Yep. Me and the old man, who'd have thought it?' He took the lid off his coffee cup and emptied two packets of sugar into it. 'I'm helping him manage his property portfolio. Working with tenants, dealing with leaseholds, that kind of thing. Dad's been banging on about me joining the business for years, so he's happy. At least it's a job.' He looked down at my notes spread across the table. 'So, what's this?'

'Plans.'

'Plans for what?'

I wasn't sure I wanted to share this with him, especially as on paper my diner was still a very long way from becoming reality. But he was here, he was interested and I was tired of avoiding him. 'I'm thinking of starting my own business,' I said, stopping as I remembered the words of Clare, the business trainer who led my course. 'Sorry. I *am* starting my own business. Eventually. This is part of the planning. I'm taking a business course and I did five weeks of unpaid work experience at a diner when I was in San Francisco.'

'Blimey. That's quite a change, Nell.'

'Well, it's time I did something I really wanted to do. I've been working in Planning for too long.'

He stared at me as if seeing someone he didn't quite recognise. 'You'd be great doing that. I still remember the cakes you used to make for me on Sunday mornings . . .' Checking himself, he looked down at his coffee cup. 'So have you found premises yet?'

'What? Oh no, that's not going to happen for a long time yet. I have to secure investment first – and that's proving to be a headache. I'm either too old or too broke or too new to the industry. But I'll work it out.'

'I believe you will.' He stood up. 'Look, I have to go, but it's been really good to see you.'

'You too, Aidan. I'm glad things are working out for you.'

He hesitated, unwilling to leave yet. 'Look, Nell, I don't suppose you'd like to do this again some time? I'd like to hear about your trip and – well, I've missed us hanging out. We could do lunch, say, Saturday?'

His eagerness made my stomach flip but I wasn't sure I was ready for a great emotional showdown. 'I don't know . . .'

'Coffee, then? I visit this place about the same time most days. If you happened to be here tomorrow we could maybe share a table again?'

The Aidan Matthews charm was still functioning, bringing a smile to my lips without my permission. He was cheeky as hell but I could tell his characteristic confidence had taken a battering lately. I liked this version of him and it would be nice to get back to the easy friendship we had enjoyed, despite whatever else was happening between us.

'Maybe I'll see you tomorrow.'

His familiar grin reappeared. 'Maybe you will.'

'Cheeky git,' Vicky exclaimed, when I called her that afternoon. 'He's got some gall, hasn't he?'

'I'm not saying I'm going tomorrow.'

'You're not saying you're not, either. Don't let him off that easily, Nell. I made him buy me a whole bottle of wine before I accepted his apology, and it was good stuff too. We might be forgiving him for sacking us but we should make him sweat it out a bit.'

'Duly noted. I will punish him sufficiently. The thing is, I think he needs friends, Vix. None of us wanted this situation to happen and it's been tough for everyone.'

'OK, be the voice of reason, damn you. But remember you're talking about the guy who sacked you when you thought he was getting back with you and who pathetically emailed you for eight whole weeks even though you didn't answer him. Bear that in mind, OK?'

I loved Vicky for her forthrightness and her parting shot made me smile all day.

When I was getting ready for bed that night, my phone beeped to signal a new email had arrived. Seeing the name of the sender, I quickly opened it.

From: LizzieS@SF-musictuition.com
To: nell.sullygirl@gmail.com
Subject: Hello!

Hi Nellie!

It's so weird to be emailing you – I'm still getting used to not turning round to tell you something. I hope everything's good back in Blighty and that all your plans are coming together.

Everything here is pretty much as you left it. Tyler is here more often ☺ but I know you'll be pleased to hear that. He makes me happy, Nell, and that's the important thing.

The kids at S-O-S Club have been asking about you, so I thought I might set up a club email address for them to email you, if that's OK? Tyler has asked the Parent–Teacher fundraising committee to fund a computer for us so we can add a Tech Zone for kids like JJ who are surgically attached to their games consoles.

Eva and Maya are missing you terribly. But I guess you knew they would. If you want to send them anything from England, you can always send it via me.

Take care and be happy. I'll email again soon.

Lots of love

Lizzie xxx

Thinking about Eva inevitably led my thoughts to Max. I missed Eva and loved the idea of sending her presents from England, but what if Max found out and saw it as an invitation to contact me? Dismissing the idea as ridiculous I focused on what I could send for all of the children. It would be a nice surprise for them and would make me feel like I was still connected to the S-O-S Club in some way. I would start looking for suitable gifts tomorrow. Climbing into bed, I smiled thinking about Lizzie and Tyler, the kids and Haight-Ashbury. I picked up my notebook and turned to the first page of Annie's hand-written notes:

COFFEE
If it's empty, fill it. If it's not empty, top it up.
Don't ask permission and don't be offended
if they refuse.
Bottom line: there's ALWAYS coffee

In my diner, there will be great coffee, I told myself. *People will come in especially for it.*

I giggled. Talking about the diner I would one day run – even to myself in the box-room bedroom at my parents' house with hardly any money to my name and no financial backing whatsoever – made it feel real. Forget what the grant organisations thought: I was exactly the right age with exactly the right experience and what I lacked in quantifiable investment I more than made up for with sheer determination and willingness to work until I saw it become a reality.

I didn't know how it was going to happen, but I was going to make this work.

CHAPTER TWENTY-SIX

An unexpected offer

Aidan was waiting for me when I arrived in the coffee shop next day, doing his best impression of nonchalance but failing spectacularly. *So much for the casual approach*, I mused as I waited in the queue for my coffee.

'Just happened to be here, did you?' I asked as I joined him.

He shrugged. 'I might have been waiting for a while.'

I smiled. 'I have to say when I got back from San Francisco I didn't expect us to meet. I was determined we wouldn't, as a matter of fact.'

'I'm not surprised. But I'm glad you changed your mind.'

'How's the new job?'

Aidan grimaced. 'Dad's a taskmaster. I never realised how much until I started to work for him. He seems to think I'm at his beck and call every waking hour of the day. At least at the Council they didn't call me in the evenings and expect me to be working . . .' Realising what he'd said, he stopped. 'I'm sorry. You don't need to hear that.'

I was in no mood to fight this morning and was touched by his carefulness. 'Don't apologise. That part of my life is over. There's no point bearing grudges. I'm glad you found another job.'

'Nothing on the horizon yet for you?' he ventured.

'A few days here and there, but nothing of any substance yet.'

'Nell, I'm so sorry about you losing your job.'

'Don't be. I know it wasn't your fault. Anyway, I'm using the time as best I can. I've even gone back to college.'

He seemed genuinely surprised by this. 'To study what?'

'An introductory business course and my health and hygiene certificate – something I'll need for the future.' I put my notebook on the table.

'More planning?'

'Mm-hmm. I want to make sure I'm as prepared as I can be. Even though it could be a long time until I actually get to use any of this.'

He leaned towards me. 'Maybe not.'

I knew I was staring at him now, the half-empty packet of sugar still hovering above my coffee mug. 'What do you mean?'

He took a breath. 'OK, there's a possibility I could help you.'

'Aidan, I don't . . .'

'Just listen to me. After we spoke yesterday I happened to mention it to Dad and he said he has a property he needs a tenant for.'

This was a kind thought, but I was definitely not ready to take on premises. 'I'm not at that stage yet. I wish I was. But until I have sufficient funds to cover all the set-up costs I daren't even think about opening for business.'

Aidan waved his hands. 'I realise that. But the possibility I'm talking about wouldn't require you to.'

I sat back in the armchair and observed him carefully. 'I don't understand.'

'Dad recently bought a café in Acton. It's a bit rough around the edges and the most recent tenant was running it as a greasy spoon. But it has a good customer base, is near a new office complex and has passing trade from the high street. Dad's not looking to sell: he wants someone to run it for him.'

It was a curveball, but would the compromises I would have to make on my dream be worth it for being able to open a restaurant? 'I'm not interested in continuing somebody else's business. Especially not a transport café.'

'But it doesn't have to stay a greasy spoon, don't you see? The whole unit has been badly neglected by the former landlord and needs completely gutting. But we could fit it out exactly as you want – make it into the diner you want to run. The only difference would be that initially you would run it for Dad. He'd pay you a salary plus a percentage of profits, with the option to buy in five years. All Dad cares about is making money from it, but to do that requires someone with the vision and drive to make it happen. I think that person could be you.'

I did not see this coming. At all. It was a fantastic opportunity, but was it right for me? I'd envisaged choosing the location myself, deciding where was best to attract the customers I wanted. On the other hand, an established business would bring a ready-made customer base. Thinking of many of the items on Annie's diner menu, there wasn't much difference between what they offered and what a greasy spoon might serve. Eggs, bacon, cheese, coffee – all of these items could be found in both places, meaning that greasy spoon customers wouldn't find the diner food too much of a jump from what they were used to.

If I waited for the right amount of funding, the right location and the right clientele, I might be waiting a long time. Years, even. But if I'd waited for the perfect time to go to San Francisco – when I had enough money, when I had someone else to go with, or when I felt ready – I would have missed out on everything that had happened. Was this another opportunity life was presenting to me?

'What does your dad think about me running it?'

Surprised and pleased at my question, Aidan replied, 'Actually, it was his idea.'

I thought about it, staring out at the red London buses, black taxis and scurrying pedestrians moving past the coffee shop window. Annie Legado had started her business with practically no money, building it up from scratch in a neighbourhood she only chose because it was cheaper than the expensive store units nearer Union Square. She didn't wait for perfect to come along.

'Could I see it?'

'I can take you there this afternoon.'

Although it was early July, heavy rain hung over the city. The wipers on Aidan's BMW squeaked against the glass as sheets of water flooded across the windscreen. In the passenger seat, I suddenly felt very small. The panic rising within me was the same I'd experienced on the first day of school. The terrified child within me screamed again: *No! Stop! I'm not ready for this yet! I want to go back!*

It's just a viewing, I reminded myself. I hadn't agreed to anything yet. I would probably set one foot across the threshold and immediately hate it. All I was doing was investigating it further so I knew for certain.

'You OK?'

'Yes, I'm good.' I stared at the windscreen wipers as they made their noisy progress through the rain.

'You're very quiet, that's all.'

'I don't mean to be.'

'No, well, of course.' 'Ah, here we are.' Aidan steered the BMW through a narrow gap between two rows of shop units in Acton High Street, parking it by a large blue wheelie bin. 'Now, it's in a bit of a state, so you'll have to use your imagination.'

The café had a large sign taped to the front window, advising local people that it was temporarily closed for refurbishment. Inside it smelled of stale fat, carpet tiles and the mustiness that comes from a building lying empty for a while. A blackened, grease-stained steel multi-burner oven and preparation tables filled the kitchen, and empty metal racks were stacked in the storage area. Several large catering fridges and freezers sat like silent sentries on each side of the kitchen and light flooded in from a long, grubby skylight over the preparation tables. The red vinyl floor was so sticky that parts of it lifted with my shoes when I trod on them and the tiles I suspected were actually white were stained yellow from years of fried food.

It was an unlikely setting for what could one day be my dream business but I had to make myself overlook the problems and focus on the potential. There was no point being here if I wasn't willing to investigate it fully.

Through an archway to the serving area I found a long metal counter, dented and scratched with the name of someone called 'Digsy', a redundant cash register quite literally stuck to its surface. Behind the counter was a strip of vinyl-coated chipboard work surface, bearing the ghostly dust-and-grease outlines of drink machines long since removed, and beyond that a thin, letterbox-style serving hatch. The seating area was filled with simple laminated wood and steel bistro tables and chairs that looked new compared with the other fittings. I counted the chairs. Forty covers: roughly one-third of the amount at Annie's.

'What do you think?' Aidan had been watching my slow survey of the café, maintaining a respectable distance as I took it in.

I tried to look beyond the actual state of the place, remembering Annie's advice that she had given me halfway through my work experience: *When you look at premises, ignore everything apart from walls, ceilings and floors. Space is what counts. Everything else can be altered.*

'It's a good size. The kitchen has potential, although the floor covering definitely needs changing and I wouldn't want to use that oven without it being checked. It seems to be in a good location – on the high street, quite a bit of passing trade . . . I think it could work.'

When I turned to look at Aidan, he was staring at me. 'You really know what you want, don't you?'

'I've been thinking about this for a long time.'

'Did you . . .' He paused, taking a step towards me. 'Did you think about this when we were together?'

His question broke through our carefully laid veneer of friendship, digging deeper than I was sure I was comfortable with yet. 'Aidan—'

'No. Forget I asked. I'm sorry.'

'OK.'

He gave a deep sigh. 'Where do you want to go from here?'

For a moment, I thought he might be referring to us – and I was surprised that the possibility didn't seem as awful as I'd imagined it might be. But I quickly realised this was his attempt at a subject change to bring our conversation back to the café. 'I would be interested in talking to your dad about it.'

Surprised, Aidan pulled his mobile from his pocket. 'I can ask him now, if you like?'

My heart was racing and my palms had begun to moisten. It was too good an opportunity to miss.

'Call him.'

From: nell.sullygirl@gmail.com
To: LizzieS@SF-musictuition.com
Subject: I might have premises!

It's early days yet and I haven't officially agreed to anything, but an opportunity has come about that might just make it possible for me to be running a diner by *this Christmas*!

The funny thing is, the person responsible

for bringing this opportunity to me is Aidan. Get that: Aidan Matthews helping me out! He's been really helpful, actually, and I feel like I'm getting a friend back. He's been amazing and I've been surprised by how easy things are between us.

I went to see the café last week and today I met with John, Aidan's father, to discuss how it might work. Basically, he'll own the place and I'll run it like a manager. It means I'll be paid every month and he will cover bills for heating, lighting, staff and ingredients until we start to turn over a profit. The best part is that he's planning a complete refit, so he's happy for me to take the lead on that.

I have two weeks to decide. John wants to start renovating the last week of September, with a view to a December opening to catch the Christmas trade. What do you think? Am I completely crazy?

I'm scared but so excited!

Lots of love

Nell xxx

From: LizzieS@SF-musictuition.com
To: nell.sullygirl@gmail.com
Subject: GO FOR IT!!

Read the subject line.

I think you already know what you want

to do. You should follow your heart on this, Nellie.

This is *your* dream – go for it!
Very proud of you ☺
Lots and lots of love
L xxxx

I considered the opportunity for a week. It wasn't the way I had envisaged it and there were compromises to be made along the way, but I knew it was the right thing to do.

My mind made up, I phoned Aidan from my parents' living room as they stood next to me – Dad holding a bottle of champagne ready in anticipation of my decision.

'Aidan, I'm in.'

CHAPTER TWENTY-SEVEN

The hard work begins

From the moment I verbally agreed to take on the lease of the former Fryer Tuck-in's café, lists began to rule my life. Lists of quotes from builders, electricians, plasterers, gas-fitters, specialist catering equipment suppliers, tilers, painters and damp-proofing companies filled the notice board in my bedroom at Mum and Dad's, until I ran out of drawing pins and available space and had to buy a file to keep them in.

Dad came to visit the former café with me and was a brilliant help advising me on the best way to tackle the electrical and construction changes that were needed.

'It needs work but it's a good, solid structure,' he beamed. 'If Aidan's father is funding the renovation I reckon this place will come together in no time.' Retracting the steel tape measure in his hand, he strolled over to me and planted a kiss on my head. 'I hope you know how proud of you me and Mum are.'

'Thanks Dad. It means so much to have you both rooting for me.'

'It's our pleasure. We haven't seen you so fired up about something for years. And you know we're going to help in any way that we can.'

I loved my parents' enthusiasm and complete faith in me. It was wonderful to feel so supported, especially when moments of doubt beset me.

My notebook was peppered with lists of tasks I had to oversee, from the initial refit to preparing the diner for business to opening day. Every time I remembered something else that needed my attention I would write it down, arranging and rearranging items into a blueprint for the coming weeks so that everything I needed to do could flow easily.

'You are a *machine*, woman!' Vicky laughed one evening as we sat in a bar in Richmond. We had been talking about a meal Vicky and Greg had enjoyed at a friend's house when I suddenly remembered a key ingredient I hadn't added to the list of suppliers I needed to find. Panicking when I found I hadn't put a notebook or pen in my handbag, I'd begged the very amused barman to give me a pen and some sheets from his order pad to remedy the situation.

'I just need to make sure I can remember everything,' I explained, realising how crazy I sounded as I said it.

'You're running yourself ragged with this, hun.'

'I'm fine. I want to do it right, that's all.'

Vicky's smile was the kind my mum gives me when she's about to challenge something I've done. It was the smile that said, 'I love you, *but* . . .'

'You *will* do it right! Because this is your dream and you know how you want it to be. And it will be perfect because you're throwing your soul into it. But you need to try to rest a little, have fun. When the diner is up and running your time is going to get very precious very quickly. You need to make the most of now, of just being able to come out for a drink without worrying that you'll be too tired tomorrow for working – because very soon you're going to have a demanding *thing* that will claim every spare minute.'

I wondered if she was still talking about my diner or if what she said had more relevance to her own life since becoming a mum. I supposed that in a lesser way, my new business was like a new baby – a life that I was bringing into being, which would require my total commitment. 'Thanks Vix. You're keeping me sane.'

'My pleasure. Anyway, we're celebrating this evening.'

I stuffed the list into my bag. 'We are?'

'Yes, we are. Because things are happening for you. And because, as of next Monday, I will be employed again.'

I stared at her, the news sinking in. 'You got the job?'

'Yes!'

'Oh Vix, that's amazing! So does this mean you and Greg can start planning the wedding again?'

'Oh yes! His ass is *mine*!'

Vicky squealed and I squealed and half of the bar customers stared over at the two grown women dancing around like three-year-olds in a fashion very uncharacteristic for central London.

Lists forgotten, I hugged my friend, delighted by her success. She had waited long enough with the uncertainty and strain on her household's finances: this was the best news she could have received and I was thrilled to share it with her.

'It's going to be strange not working with you,' she said, when we had calmed down and ordered another glass of wine. 'I was saying so to Greg before I came out tonight. It sounds daft but I had it in my head that we'd find jobs together when you got back from San Francisco.'

I never realised she felt this way and didn't know how to respond.

Seeing my expression, she smiled. 'I'm not saying I wish you weren't going in a new direction. I'm immensely proud of you, Sully, and I envy you going for what you want. I just got used to us working together, getting one over on Sourpuss Bagley and heading to the pub with the lads after work. I know we can't go back to that, but it was comfy, wasn't it?'

'You can always come and work for me,' I grinned.

'Er, no thanks. Your idea of happiness might be serving pancakes to grumpy Joe Public but it isn't mine. I'd close you down within a week.'

'What's your dream, Vix?' I had never asked her this question, even though we had talked about every other subject under the sun over the years.

She considered it for a moment, swirling the Chardonnay around in her glass. Then, with a grin so filthy it should have had a health warning, she answered. 'Ryan Gosling, oiled, masculine and naked, in a house with a well-stocked wine cellar and no neighbours for twenty miles.'

As I planned my business from the empty unit on Acton High Street, I began to visualise how running the diner would be. Who would be sitting up at the counter, where Marty and Frank used to sit? Who would choose to be near the window, watching the world go by on Acton's High Street? Would families choose to eat here? Acton was a world apart from Haight-Ashbury but people were people wherever you went and they would always need a nice place to eat, whether it was in California or the London Borough of Ealing.

My parents were wonderful, as supportive of this crazy idea as they were of my snap decision to fly to California when I lost my job. Dad threw himself into the task of getting quotes from builders, liaising with his gardening customers to find recommendations of trustworthy tradesmen. Mum, who surprised us all by being an internet research fiend, identified some great local suppliers who could provide the diner with fresh, organic ingredients. Through my parents I also met Joe, a great cook who had been working in a nearby hotel, who became my first choice for chef at the diner. I intended to do some of the cooking, having been taught a few methods by Karin and Dom, but wanted to focus on baking and working front of house.

I was immensely touched by the way my family and friends were supporting me. But it was Aidan who surprised me the most.

Two weeks into the project he asked to meet me in a pub a few streets away from his Marylebone office. When I arrived he was waiting at a table, looking tired and irritated.

'Is everything OK?' I asked as I sat down.

'I've just come from a meeting with Dad,' he said.

'Those alterations you wanted to the interior plan? He disagreed with them. Apparently he thinks we can do it cheaper by sticking to his original layout. So I've just spent the last two hours fighting for every last change.'

Seeing how tired he looked I feared the worst. 'I take it he didn't budge?'

A slow smile spread across his face. 'He tried not to. But I argued until he agreed to every one of your suggestions.'

I was amazed. When we had been at the Council Aidan had always backed down whenever his superiors queried our decisions. It felt good that he was fighting for me now. 'I don't know what to say . . .'

'Then don't say anything. You were right, Dad was wrong. All I did was make him see that.' He laughed. 'Nell, it's OK. We're in this together. If I think you have the best idea, I'll say it. I'm not afraid of taking the old man on at his own game.'

A few days later, I discovered a mistake with one of the quotes we had accepted from the electrical company John had hired to rewire the unit. My calls to him all went to voicemail and I started to panic that the work would commence without the problem being resolved. I called Aidan and within an hour the mistake was rectified.

'All sorted,' he said when he called me back. 'But I'm so glad you spotted the mistake. I'd completely missed it.'

'Thank you again. I really appreciate it.'

'Then buy me dinner.'

I stared at my mobile for a moment, my pulse quickening. 'I'm not sure that's a good idea.'

'Why? We both need to eat. And I did sort that problem for you.'

Despite my best efforts, I had to smile. Aidan certainly hadn't lost any of his persuasive powers.

We met at my favourite restaurant in Richmond and easily found a table, the venue being less than half-full with weekday diners. Over steaks and salad we talked about the progress on the diner and my developing plans for menus.

'I have to say, I love the idea of savoury crêpes for breakfast,' he smiled. 'Was that a San Francisco thing?'

'It was at Annie's. She was famous for them. But her decision to put them on the menu was more than just a great culinary idea. It makes sense from a cost angle too. Crêpe batter is relatively cheap to produce and can yield a lot of servings. All the fillings are used for burgers, sandwiches and pancakes too, both sweet and savoury, so no menu item requires standalone ingredients.'

Aidan was watching me, intently taking in every word. 'I can't get over the change in you,' he said suddenly. 'It's remarkable.' Seeing my reaction he looked down at his meal. 'I'm sorry. I'm just so impressed by what you're becoming. It's like you're someone different to the Nell I knew. It suits you.'

'You've changed too,' I said, before I had the chance to think better of it. It felt strange to be complimenting him but I wanted him to know.

'How?'

'The way you've fought for my plans – for our plans,' I corrected myself, suddenly shy. 'You wouldn't have done that before.'

Aidan nodded. 'Perhaps we've both changed for the better. Perhaps this is what was meant to happen . . .'

Later that evening as I lay in bed, the memory of our conversation drifted back. What if this *was* meant to happen? What if Aidan and I had to lose our jobs, go our separate ways and experience other things before the diner brought us back together? Realising what I was considering, I quickly dismissed the thought. I was still hurting about what happened with Max: surely these thoughts about Aidan were a rebound reaction? Nevertheless, the echoes of them haunted me for the next few days . . .

As we collaborated on the details of the café's renovation, we spent more time together. Working breakfasts, lunches and late-night takeaways happened naturally, and I found myself enjoying his company again. We laughed together – more than we had done during the whole of last year – and developed a good-natured banter that bounced back and forth as we worked. I liked the easiness of our discussions, the gentle mocking that always amused and never hurt and the sense of mutual respect I felt between us. Even Vicky was impressed when she met us for a pub meal and saw how we were together.

'You two don't realise how chilled you are. You were never like that when you were going out.'

Before I went to San Francisco, this would never have been possible. I was always weighing up every conversation, reading between lines that didn't exist and judging too quickly to be able to relax with him. Consequently, he felt he needed to tiptoe around me. Then, instead of talking about how we felt, we acted on our misjudged preconceptions of each other. Now, I felt I understood his point of view and he appreciated mine. It was a brave new world, but I liked the direction we were headed in.

'Are you falling for him again?' Vicky's question was as pointed as ever.

We were watching Greg pushing Ruby on the baby swing in their back garden on a warm Friday evening, as Vicky and I drank wine and watched the golden sun setting.

'What kind of a question is that?' I retorted, buying myself time to consider her question.

'The kind of question you should be asking yourself. Don't get me wrong, I like the guy now and I can see how much he's doing for you. I just wondered if it might be fanning the old flames?'

'No. Aidan's just a friend.'

'A pretty fit friend,' she added with a wink.

'Vix!'

'Come on, Nell. You've been there before, haven't you? So it isn't entirely unreasonable to assume you might again. Aw, look at the two of them.'

Ruby was gurgling and throwing her little chubby arms into the air as Greg pushed her, a huge fatherly smile revealing unbridled pride in his daughter. For a split second I remembered Eva's delight as Max spun her high above his head that day at S-O-S Club and my heart ached to think of all of those times he'd spent with her and Shanti as a tight family unit, just as Greg and Ruby were with Vicky now.

'Are you OK?' Vicky asked, bringing me back to the scene in her garden.

'I'm fine, just tired. And there really isn't anything between Aidan and me. I'm enjoying being his friend.'

Vicky finished her wine and kissed the etching of Ryan Gosling on the wine glass as she refilled it. 'Shame.'

The second week of September saw the builders moving into the café. Everything was gutted from the interior, the salvageable equipment went into storage and the unit became a tangle of exposed wires, large holes in the walls and brick dust everywhere. Lists ran the show, now on a clipboard that travelled with me so much Vicky renamed it Idris Elba, after my favourite actor. When I questioned why, her answer was simple:

'Because at least now when you take it to bed with you – which I know you do – you're guaranteed better dreams than diners and lists.'

I was getting used to fielding calls from tradesmen as I met with potential suppliers, viewed equipment and discussed furniture requirements. Brushing dust from my hair and clothes before meetings became a daily task and I took to keeping a lint roller in my bag to ensure I didn't arrive looking as if I'd come from a demolition site. I was busier than I had ever been, but I loved it.

Aidan invited me for dinner one evening after a particularly late meeting with the builders at the unit. I was tired and looking forward to an early night, but the prospect of a decent meal was too good to ignore. Walking back into his house was a strange experience after being away from it for so long. For over a year I had more or less lived there, preferring to spend time with Aidan than endure the disinterested company of my Woodford housemates.

Arriving that evening, I was aware of Aidan carefully studying my reaction to the changes he had made to the interior since I had last seen it. Much of the original colour scheme had been changed, the furniture updated to reflect the bachelor who owned it. When I had last lived here it had been a mishmash of styles, inherited and collected furniture from his various former homes and a colour scheme that lurched from magnolia to white to lilac. Now, cool white walls contrasted with dark leather and polished wood, carpets had been replaced with wooden flooring and sisal, and striking silver geometric light fittings formed focal centrepieces in every room.

'Bit different from the last time you saw it, hey?' Aidan smiled, handing me a very welcome glass of wine.

I thought about the last time I had been here: the screaming match which had proved the last straw and resulted in us calling time on our relationship, with me finally leaving in the early hours of the morning after hours of quieter debate, followed by a tearful farewell. At the time neither of us had been ready to make the kind of commitment we both secretly wanted. Seeing how different Aidan's home was now I wondered what else might have changed.

'I'm happy with the diner's progress,' Aidan said when we were eating a speedily prepared beef stir fry with noodles. 'I know there were some teething problems with the builder but I think the worst has passed.'

'I hope so. But I still think your dad needs to double-check the estimate. I'm not convinced they've included everything we asked for and I'd hate there to be extra costs for John when the work's done.'

'Noted. I'll chat to Dad in the morning.' Aidan added this to a list in his notebook. 'The electricians start tomorrow morning, so it might be a good idea to pop over there, just to make sure they know what we want.'

'I'll do that.' I scribbled on my clipboard list. Looking over at Aidan checking his list, the humour of the situation dawned on me and I giggled.

'What?'

'Look at us with our matching lists! We've become slaves to tick-boxes.'

'Man, there's no hope for us,' Aidan smiled and I thought how much happier he seemed to be. His smile was one of the first things I had noticed when I met him and it was still one of the nicest smiles I had seen. 'It's worth it, though. Things are running to schedule and Dad's really pleased. We make a good team.'

'Yes, we do. Tradesmen all across Acton now fear our very presence.'

'I heard how you sorted out that foreman,' Aidan said, referring to a heated discussion I had shared with the builders' foreman that afternoon when he suggested that his lads should knock off early because they felt they had 'done enough' for the week.

'All I did was point out that considering his lads hadn't bothered to arrive until eleven today, I didn't think they deserved to leave early. I don't want your father's money wasted.'

'And that's why you're perfect to be the manager,' he said.

Later, when the dishwasher was filled and we were sitting in the living room with coffee, he suddenly turned to me.

'Listen, I just want to say this: I'm sorry I didn't realise you had this dream when we were together.'

Feeling cornered, I began to protest. 'You don't have to say that . . .'

'Yes, I do. I should have seen it. I should have believed more in you.'

'You couldn't have known. I hadn't told anyone, not even Vicky.'

'All the same, I didn't know how much you wanted this to happen. I'm just glad I can help you now. That's all.'

'Thank you.' I managed a smile, but I wasn't sure I was ready to hear this. Vicky's suggestion that I might be growing closer to Aidan played on my mind and I was aware of so much more behind what he was saying. We were approaching dangerous territory and if I wasn't careful I might end up not wanting to leave tonight . . . 'Well, it's getting late. I should go home.'

'You could always stay . . .'

My heart began hammering in my chest. We had been here so many times over the years and I knew what could so easily happen if I let it.

He quickly qualified his offer. 'I mean, in the spare bedroom. If we're going to check on the electricians tomorrow it would be just as easy to go together from here. Nothing else implied, I promise.'

I breathed out and hoped he didn't hear the utter relief in it. 'It's a really kind offer, but I don't think it's a good idea. I'll call a taxi.'

I walked through to the kitchen to make the call, my heart still thudding. Leaning against the breakfast bar I willed my pulse to calm itself. The old Nell would have given in at that point, would have seen the blatant hope in Aidan's blue eyes and succumbed to the ever-present longing to be with him. She would have accepted with every intention of staying in the spare room but every expectation of ending up in his bed. But I recognised that I was vulnerable right now – still hurting from what had happened with Max – and I didn't need the temptation to give in to Aidan.

When the taxi arrived, Aidan held my coat for me as I put it on, trying not to notice how his hands lingered on my shoulders and the closeness of his body to mine.

'Well, goodnight,' he said, opening the door.

I looked up at him, catching the old familiar look of longing in his eyes and for a moment I considered what it would be like to kiss him again. He bent down and kissed my cheek and I hurried away to the safety of the waiting car.

In the back seat, as the cab sped me away from an important step forward, I felt tired and emotional, but I knew I'd made the right decision. For the diner to work, I needed to focus solely upon it. Complications with Aidan could derail the whole project and I needed his friendship more than anything else – even if that night my dreams were peppered with images of what might have happened . . .

CHAPTER TWENTY-EIGHT

Moving the goalposts

Dear S-O-S Club

Hello from England!

It's our fall here, but we call it autumn. All of the leaves on the trees are changing colour and it looks very pretty. There is a big park near where I live and the leaves have turned from green to gold, red and orange.

Are you still enjoying your baking? I hope so! I'm sending Lizzie lots more recipes to show you. I hope you enjoy them!

I wanted to send you all a present from London, where I live, so Lizzie will give them to you for me.

Take care, have fun at S-O-S Club and I'll write again soon.

Lots of love

Nell xxx

In a shop near Richmond station I found some pencil sharpeners shaped like London black cabs, red Routemaster buses and royal crowns for the S-O-S Club children. But I wanted to get something special for Eva, so I also sent a postcard of St Paul's Cathedral and a tiny snowstorm with Buckingham Palace at its centre. As I packaged them up I thought about Eva – and inevitably Max. The memory of Max stung. I hated that my thoughts of the little girl were now inextricably linked with him. Even when I tried to think about the good things I'd shared with Max, the memory of how it all ended obliterated everything else. I wished that he'd told me about Eva, that he had trusted me enough to share the most important thing in his life with me. But wishing wasn't enough to compensate for what he had done and I knew I had to put it behind me.

I arrived in Acton just after eleven, waiting alone in the freshly plastered shell of the diner and surprised again at how different it was from the old greasy spoon café that had been here before. Just as I was starting to wonder if I'd got the wrong day, I heard the painters' van pull up in the car park behind the unit. At the same time, my mobile buzzed with a text message.

> *Hey Nell, Dad's called me into a meeting about another tenant. Can't get out of it - sorry. Good job you didn't stay last night! ☺ Speak soon, A x*

I was relieved that he was joking about last night. At least that was one less thing to worry about.

Gary, Bill and Adrian muttered their apologies as they entered. Their gaffer, Bill, asked if there was any chance of a cuppa before they started, his question supported by the hopeful nods of his brother and younger apprentice. I suggested they start right away considering they were nearly an hour late but offered to make them tea as they worked, which seemed like an acceptable compromise.

Listen to workmen but don't let them take advantage, Annie had written in a Facebook message to me last week. *Believe me, they'll try to. Get the upper hand and they'll do anything for you. Be kind, be respectful but remember it's your money and it's your business.*

Inspired by her words, I handed out mugs of tea from the old kettle plugged into the single electrical socket still working, and passed around a packet of chocolate Hobnobs. The gesture was warmly received and paved the way to a fruitful conversation about plans for the walls and suitable times for the electricians to come in.

Later, I left them working and walked to the station. It amused me to think that Annie would have loved to see me putting her advice into practice. I hoped she would be proud.

I was on my way to a meeting with John Matthews, trying to ignore the butterflies attacking my stomach at the prospect of his questions, when my thoughts drifted back to San Francisco. I thought about Eva and the children receiving their presents from England soon, and pictured Eva's face when she saw the real life St Paul's Cathedral on the postcard I had sent. When I thought of Eva, I couldn't wish her anything but the blessing of two parents who loved her. I had so wanted to be a part of Max's life but Eva still was. All I could hope for, I decided, was that Max would stay true to his family and not be tempted away again. Eva clearly idolised her father – for her sake he owed it to her to never repeat the mistake he had made with me . . .

On the Underground I turned my attention to my list of new suppliers I had found, each one of which had the potential to give the diner a real edge in the marketplace. By identifying and using a small number of specialist ingredients and a simple range of food options we could ensure quality without building too much cost, hopefully extending the menu as the popularity of the diner increased.

Aidan had told me that John was impressed with my thoroughness and attention to quality. He felt the diner would be in good hands – a fantastic compliment and a great boost to my confidence. While I knew he still had tough questions for me, I was looking forward to presenting the fruits of my considerable labours this afternoon.

Arriving at the expensive Marylebone High Street offices of Matthews Investments Ltd it was impossible not to be impressed by the beautifully lit, classically styled offices. Elegant glass chandeliers hung from the high ceilings in reception and John's office. Expensive brocade curtains hung from the large sash windows and every room was painted in a soft primrose yellow, which contrasted with the black ash of the furniture and desks.

John's PA escorted me into his office and returned moments later with a cafetiere of coffee and two slender silver and glass latte mugs.

'You've been working very hard,' John observed, handing me a mug of coffee. 'Aidan's been telling me about everything you've achieved. I must say I'm impressed. I don't usually get such commitment from prospective tenants.'

I flushed with pride. Coming from such an influential businessman this was a wonderful compliment. 'Thank you. I believe in this venture and I'm determined to make it succeed.'

'Good.' John's smile was warm and I could see where Aidan had inherited his from. 'You know, you've surprised me, Nell. And that rarely happens in this business. When you and Aidan were together I never had you down as a confident businesswoman. I always liked you, of course, and I confess I was disappointed when the two of you broke up. But I didn't realise you could be this driven.'

Hearing this from someone who had known me before was heartening to say the least. 'I think I've always had it in me. It was waiting for something to bring it out.'

'Quite. Sometimes we need life to give us a swift kick up the backside to push us out of our comfortable situations.' He picked up a stapled stack of papers from his desk. 'So, to business. I've looked at the list of suppliers you've put together. It's very good . . .'

'Thank you.' I was relieved to hear this.

'. . . but not for this business.'

His last sentence hit me like a boulder.

'Excuse me?'

'I appreciate your vision, Nell, and I understand how much this means to you. But we're not operating in Knightsbridge: this is Acton. It might be an up-and-coming area, but you have to remember what the diner will be taking the place of. The greasy spoon café wasn't pretty but it did solid business and gave the people what they wanted.' He flicked through the pages of my carefully prepared document and pointed at an item listed on it. 'I mean, artisan breads are all very well, but the cost is prohibitive. And sourcing eggs from another county when we have a perfectly good cash and carry five minutes up the road from the premises doesn't make sense.'

My pulse rate had increased, the work suit I had chosen for this meeting becoming uncomfortably hot. 'But I believe carefully sourced items can be great selling points,' I argued. 'The changing demographic in the area means young professionals are moving in with increasing expectations of quality, ethics and value for money. Nobody else in the area is doing this . . .'

'My point exactly.' John's expression was one of quiet patience and it made me feel utterly patronised. 'Nobody else is doing it. Times are tough, Nell, even for young professionals with their ethics and expectations. I bought the café because it was a good, honest investment offering a valued service for a large client base. I didn't want to turn it into a novelty business.'

Anger was beginning to pump adrenalin through my body. 'With respect, John, this diner wouldn't be a novelty. It would be a community hub . . .'

'I've heard that kind of rhetoric before, Nell. I'm not looking to build a community service. I'm looking to make money.'

'But it *will*!'

John let out a sigh. 'I didn't ask you here to argue. I'm telling you, we need to cut costs to make this a viable concern. It's my business, my premises, my investment.

You're the person who will make this work. I appreciate your vision but you've never run a business before. I have. Maybe in five years when the place is a success and you have the option to buy it from me you can do all of these noble things. But for now I need you to be more realistic. Work with what works, not what your ideal is.'

I couldn't believe what he was asking me to do. 'But I've worked so hard making this something that will be different.'

'I appreciate your efforts. Of course I do. But you're going to have to change how you see this business or else it won't be viable. I'm sorry for being blunt, but that's the deal.'

Slumped on the District Line tube train on the slow journey home, I stared at the list in my hand. How could I cut costs without sacrificing quality? I shoved the papers in my bag, feeling utterly deflated. John Matthews had been patronising and rude. I felt as if he'd taken something precious that I had invested hours in creating and attacked it with a chisel until it was reduced to its lowest common denominator, regardless of the character and quality that had been sacrificed in the process. Of course there needed to be compromise; of course not all of my plans would prove financially viable. I'd expected that. But to have the whole premise of my business destroyed in the name of a fast buck was devastating.

I had given so much already to making this diner a reality. But was I still willing to do it if it was somebody else's cheap imitation of my dream?

CHAPTER TWENTY-NINE

Compromise or die

'Are you OK, Nellie?'

'I'm fine, Dad.'

Dad threw a handful of bread scraps to the excited ducks floating in the shallows of the Thames and watched them bicker and fight. 'You don't seem very OK, sweetheart.'

Feeding the ducks with my parents was always fun as a child but as I grew up it became a by-word for important conversations when one or other of us had a crisis and needed to talk it through. 'Fancy feeding the ducks?' meant, 'I know you have something on your mind. Shall we go somewhere and talk about it?' When Dad had suggested it this morning I accepted immediately, even though I wasn't sure I wanted to discuss the cautiousness I was feeling about the diner-that-wasn't-my-diner.

I let out a sigh as a large swan waddled out of the water towards us to claim the best crusts. 'I'm just not sure about the diner.'

'Oh?' Dad tried not to stare at me, his attempt about as

successful as the small white duck that was quacking belligerently at the swan five times its size. 'How come, darling? I thought you were riding high with all guns blazing?'

'I was, but – now I just don't know.'

'What's happened, Nelliegirl?' The compassion in my dad's voice almost brought me to tears.

'I'm being asked to make changes to my plans. Which I expected, of course. But what I'm being asked to do changes the place so much that it bears no resemblance to my vision.'

'Can't you dig your heels in? Surely if they're asking you to compromise there's room for them to do likewise?'

'I don't think it works that way, Dad.' I tore off more pieces of bread for the greedy waterfowl and looked at the traffic crossing Richmond Bridge above us.

'Well, it should. You've worked so hard to make this happen. They should recognise the effort you've put in.'

'Thanks Dad.' A couple of courageous pigeons descended, risking the wrath of swans and ducks to claim some of the feast. Suddenly remembering my promise to Eva to 'feed the birds', I emptied the last of the scraps from the bread bag for them to take.

'Nell, at the end of the day you have to remember that this is your dream,' Dad said. 'Nobody has the right to dictate what that should be. And if you decide this opportunity isn't right – even at this stage – you know your mother and I will support you.'

I linked my arm through his and hugged him. 'I love you.'

'Feeling's entirely mutual,' he replied nonchalantly, his pride glowing as brightly as the carved stone of Richmond Bridge in the Saturday morning sunshine.

* * *

'Patronising git!' As usual, Vicky's summation of the current state of affairs was simple yet effective. 'What does John Matthews expect you to do? Put in all the donkey work so he can claim the profits?'

I laughed. 'That's kind of the point of the owner–tenant agreement. If he wanted to put the work in he wouldn't need me to manage the place.'

Vicky gave a loud tut as she held a striped t-shirt on a tiny coat hanger against Ruby's chest. 'Well it stinks. The bloke should be on his bended knees worshipping you for all the effort you've put into his project.'

'Hardly, Vix. John's a businessman. It's only natural he's going to be thinking of profit first. I'm just going to have to compromise, that's all. I was naive to think I wouldn't have to.'

Ruby was chatting to her teddy as Vicky steered her pushchair around the narrow gaps between the clothes rails in Next's children's section. 'So how are you going to do that?'

'I've already revised the supplier list and found three companies who can match the prices of the cash and carry near the diner. He has to be happy with that.' I held up two cute t-shirts, both of which Vicky dismissed.

'Maybe. But are *you* happy with that?'

It was a question I had asked myself over and over since my meeting with Aidan's father. If I wanted to be running the diner by Christmas I would *have* to be happy with it. 'I'm getting there.'

'Well, make sure you aren't just saying that, Nell. Because it's a heck of a commitment if you're not sure.'

'I know. I'll be fine,' I assured her, hoping with all my heart that I would be.

On Monday morning I met Aidan in the Richmond coffee shop to go over the changes I had made to the supplier list. He was looking tired, dark circles beginning to appear beneath the blue of his eyes.

'This is great work, Nell,' he said, running his fingers down my list of revised costings. 'Dad's going to be much happier with that. Oh, I meant to tell you there's been a problem with the flat-top hotplate you wanted for the kitchen.'

I didn't want to hear this now. 'What's happened?'

He smiled with weary sympathy but I already knew the news wasn't going to be good. 'We can't find a company to provide it within budget. Seriously, Nell, these guys are charging an arm and a leg for the things. Said there's been a rise in demand for them in the last twelve months and that's pushed the prices up. I've tried telling Dad this is a non-negotiable, but he won't budge. We're going to have to think of something else.'

'We could do without the burners,' I suggested, grasping at straws. 'At Annie's the chefs did most of the meals on the flat-top.'

'Like I said, Dad isn't going to go for that. We've already overspent on new fridges to replace the others and the construction work was more than the original estimate. If we're going to open in December we have to cut corners now.'

Frustrated, I threw my copy of the costings sheet on the table and sank back into my armchair. 'What else are we going to have to sacrifice to make this thing happen? I've worked and reworked the details so many times I can hardly remember what it is we're actually doing. I'm going to turn up on opening day and not know a thing about the diner I'm meant to be running.'

Aidan reached across and put his hand on my knee. 'I know you're annoyed, but this is the reality of business. Trust me, when this diner opens with your name over the door you'll forget all of this crap stuff. It'll be your dream and your achievement. I promise.'

Maybe he was right. Maybe all this frustration was necessary in the final stages before my business came into being. 'I'll take your word for it.'

'You should. I'm *very* good with words.' He considered me for a moment. 'And I'm also good at knowing when you need cheering up. What do you say we sack off the diner talk for the rest of the day and go and have some fun?'

The suggestion was just what I needed to hear. I was sick of battling lists and just wanted to be myself for a couple of hours. 'What do you have in mind?'

He grinned. 'You'll see.'

The very last thing I was expecting was a day trip to the seaside, but stepping off the train in Brighton that afternoon was a perfect antidote to the stress of recent weeks.

'I can't believe we're doing this,' I grinned as we headed down towards the sea.

'We deserve it. Remember when we used to come out here on Sundays in the summer?'

I did. It was one of the things I'd loved most when we were together, jumping on an early train and spending a lazy Sunday wandering along the promenade and eating fish and chips by the pier. Of course Aidan knew exactly what he was doing bringing me here today, but it was such a lovely thought that I didn't mind.

It was a little overcast and chilly on the beach but that didn't seem to deter the people walking, playing ball games and running around us as we crunched across the shingle. Aidan kept catching my eye, the deliciousness of our illegal day off making us giggle like naughty children.

'Whatever would your dad say if he knew where we were?'

'He'd be royally hacked off,' Aidan replied, holding up his mobile phone. 'In fact, I have three missed calls from him already.'

'Shouldn't you phone him back?' I imagined John Matthews storming around his elegant office with every call diverted to Aidan's voicemail.

'Nah. Let him stew.' He bumped the back of his hand against mine. 'Last one to the sea buys ice cream.'

I laughed as he sped away, running after him and loving the ease of it all. At the water's edge I knocked into him, sending him a few steps into the sea. Cursing, he grabbed my arm and tried to drag me into the water with him, laughing at my loud protests. After several attempts to soak one another we retreated to the shore and flopped onto the pebbled beach. I felt happy and peaceful as we dropped back into the rhythm of easy banter, the years of uncertainty falling away.

'Feel better?' he asked later, as we tucked into enormous sundaes in Vicky's favourite retro ice cream shop on Gardner Street.

'Much better. Thanks for this, Aidan.'

He shrugged. 'I think it's been good for both of us.'

I was aware of the weight behind his words. 'Yes, I think it has. Aidan, I'm sorry if I was cold with you when we met after San Francisco. So much had happened before I left and I blamed you for a lot of it. Wrongly.'

'It's understandable. Losing your job is a terrible thing to come to terms with.' He ate a large spoonful of ice cream. 'And there was the other guy . . .' Seeing my expression, he held his hand up. 'It's OK, Vicky told me. I take it things didn't end well?'

His sudden mention of Max unsettled me, as if two pieces of my life were colliding. 'No, they didn't. But then nothing was ever going to come of it.'

'Just a holiday fling?'

'Yes,' I replied, as his verdict stung. 'Just a holiday fling.'

Aidan reached over the table and rested his hand on my arm. 'I'm sorry you got hurt, Nell. You deserve to be happy.'

I looked away, the closeness between us suddenly uncomfortable. 'And I will be, when the diner is up and running and we can finally put the lists to bed.'

He took the hint and let go. 'Amen to that. Now do you think it would be *really* wrong if I bought us some of those amazing cupcakes for the journey home?'

Aidan's ability to cheer me out of my disappointment increased as we neared the start of November. He surprised me with dinner, walks along the Thames with takeaway cups of tea and a night at a new West End musical I wanted to see. Even though he must have been as tired as I was, he always made time to help me work through the ever-narrowing demands from his father and became intermediary, champion and chief problem-solver for the diner. I was aware I was leaning on him more and he seemed happy to take the strain.

From: LizzieS@SF-musictuition.com
To: nell.sullygirl@gmail.com
Subject: Thank you – and WOW!

Hi lovely

Forgive the delay in getting back to you – Tyler surprised me with a trip away in LA! His brother has a place out there and we stayed for a week. What it meant though was a stack of emails when I got back.

I just wanted to let you know how thrilled the S-O-S Club kids were with the presents you sent them. Thank you so much for doing that. Eva was beside herself with joy when she saw the postcard and snowglobe. I waited until it was time to go home to give it to her. Shanti sends her thanks, too. Sorry, I promised her I'd tell you – I know you might not want to hear it.

At least you and Aidan sound like you're getting along. That must be nice, after all the bad feeling that went along with losing your job. It sounds as if he's keen to make it up to you and I'm glad that you have somebody fighting your corner when his dad is being a right royal pain.

And as for the photos of your diner – wow! It looks amazing, Nell. Can you believe it was only a few months ago that you told me about your dream? And now you're about to make it happen for real. I'm unbelievably proud of you. The best bit is, I'll be there for your opening day! I can't wait to stand with you when you open for business. Getting emotional just thinking about it – but you know me! ☺

Good luck with the final preparations. See you in three weeks!

Lots of love

L xxxx

As autumn gave way to winter the initial pain of compromise began to dwindle and I could see how it would all work towards the greater good of the diner. I spent more time with Aidan, appreciating the peace his presence seemed to bring in any decision. He was becoming a constant in the ever-changing landscape of the diner plans, a consistent encourager who maintained my focus on the goal ahead.

On the first day of November, the countdown to opening day in four weeks' time began in earnest. In a bid to cut costs further, I had painted all the walls myself and was now doing the final decoration for the seating area, stencilling quotes from famous American movies around the walls. It was good to be contributing something physical to the diner, rather than lists of numbers and cost breakdowns. And touching the walls of what would soon be my workplace brought me back in touch with my ambition. I enjoyed letting myself into the unit while it was still dark outside and working uninterrupted as Acton High Street came to life outside the window. Several people stopped to peer into the former café to see the changes that had taken place, leading to some interesting conversations with locals I hoped would become customers in four weeks' time. Building links with local people was going to be vital to fuel the success of the diner and I was glad of the opportunity to start early.

Halfway up a paint-splattered stepladder putting the finishing touches to a quote from *Raging Bull*, I paused with a mug of tea to admire my work. The diner was different from my initial vision, but this aspect was exactly as I had imagined.

Nell's Place. That was the name that would be across the frontage of the diner when it opened in December. It was simple but it proclaimed to the world that this was Nell Sullivan's dream, inviting everyone in for awesome food, attentive service and a great cup of coffee.

Feeling a shot of excitement for the first time in weeks, I smiled at the empty shell of the diner. *My* diner, whatever John Matthews said. Soon it would be my everyday reality and none of the disappointments would matter.

'I thought you might be in need of these.'

Aidan grinned as I turned from the last section of the movie quote mural to see he was holding a tray with two Starbucks takeaway cups and a bag of doughnuts.

'Aidan Matthews, I love you.' I clambered down and claimed my breakfast, realising how hungry I was.

'If I'd known coffee and a bag of doughnuts was all

it took to get you to fall for me I'd have bought them years ago.'

I stuck my tongue out at him, enjoying our cheeky flirtation. 'A girl can love her cholesterol-heavy treats. You were just the conduit.'

'Ouch. Never been referred to as a conduit before.'

I gave him a sugary grin. 'A very attractive conduit.'

'Thanks. I'll put that on my Match.com profile.' He looked up at the almost complete mural. 'That looks so good, Nell.'

'I'm pleased with it. Makes everything feel more real.'

'I should hope so. You're going to be running the place in a few weeks. Excited?'

'I am now. Thanks for putting up with my flip-outs.'

'It was touch-and-go for a while there.' Aidan ran a hand through his blond hair. 'But even with your neurotic meltdowns it's all been worth it.'

'That's the nicest thing you've ever said to me.'

'Ever?' He laughed, the sudden, joyous sound of it echoing around the bare diner walls. 'Blimey, I was a really crap smooth-talker, wasn't I?'

I winked back. 'You weren't bad.' For the briefest moment, I glimpsed an image of the way we had been together – and was surprised at how warm it felt. 'So, did you say your dad wants to come down today?'

Aidan leant against the newly sanded counter. 'He said he might do later. But don't worry if you have other stuff to do. I'll stick around here this afternoon. I've got some paperwork to catch up on and it's quieter here than the office is.' He yawned and stretched his arms up over his head, revealing muscles in his upper arms I didn't remember being so defined.

For want of something else to look at, I quickly turned my attention to my painting. I was tired and clearly needed to be away from here. 'OK. I'm going to finish this and then go home for some sleep,' I said, taking a big bite of jam doughnut and enjoying the sugary rush it injected into my system.

'Mm, attractive,' Aidan chuckled.

'Sorry?'

'I'd forgotten how messy you get when you're eating doughnuts,' he laughed, putting his coffee cup on the counter and walking over to me. 'You have half of it smeared across your face. Come here.'

I stood obediently while he wiped jam from my cheek with a napkin, cradling my other cheek as he did so. Our smiles began to fade as the closeness hit home. The strokes of his fingers slowed, the pressure lifting to the lightest of touches. I could feel his quickening breath on my face, the rise and fall of my chest meeting the rhythm in response.

'Nell—'

I closed my eyes as his lips found mine, the taste of sugar claiming my mouth. His kiss was at once familiar and brand new, reawakening the old longings that had brought us back together time after time and confirming the new attraction that had been steadily building between us. Tired of fighting it and energised by the power of his kiss I gave in to the soothing emotion as it wrapped around us, as familiar as a favourite blanket, as fresh as the famous words spilling over the walls of the diner . . .

Our diner . . .

Wait – what was I doing?

Stunned, I pulled away, my breathing shallow and fast. He stepped away too, his stare filled with apology.

'Hell – I don't know what happened . . .'

'Don't apologise. It was me . . .'

'It was *both* of us.'

'That shouldn't have happened.'

'No.' He stared at me. 'But I don't regret it.'

Silence fell in the diner. I didn't know how to respond. It had felt right, but was that just because of the pressure we were both under? We had been here before: how could we know whether this was genuine now?

'I should go.'

'No, Nell, don't. Let's talk about this.'

'I don't know what to say, Aidan. I don't think it's a good time for . . .'

'No, of course. It felt good though, didn't it?'

I nodded slowly. There was no point denying it – I'd kissed him as much as he'd kissed me.

'What if,' he said, moving closer again, 'this was meant to happen?'

'Aidan . . .'

'Let me say it, Nell. Because the past few weeks I've just kept thinking: what if all this moving away and coming back we've been doing for so many years means we're supposed to be together?'

Our eyes met and for a while neither of us spoke. I had to admit what he said wasn't an awful suggestion. But as we stood in the place that would soon be my business, the question seemed too much to consider.

I touched his arm, my voice hushed and my words

tentative. 'Can we just focus on what we have to do? Maybe when Nell's Place is running and I'm settled into the routine we could discuss it then?'

He smiled. 'I think you're right. Let's not think about it now. Fancy a hug?'

Accepting, I stepped into his embrace, relieved that the moment had passed.

My journey home was arduously slow. Roadworks at almost every junction made me curse my decision to catch the bus rather than the Overground train. All I wanted was to get back to Mum and Dad's, have a hot bath and relax. It had been a confusing day so far and I wasn't sure my addled brain could compute all of it. To pass the time I took my mobile phone from my bag and opened the picture gallery, smiling immediately as a view of the Golden Gate Bridge from Crissy Field appeared. What I wouldn't give to be there now, enjoying the warm Californian sun and a good book as the great and good of San Francisco walked and jogged past. I could hear the sound of seagulls and lapping waves of the Bay waters, and almost taste the salt in the air. It seemed like a lifetime away and my heart sank when I raised my head to see the disgruntled expressions of my fellow passengers sitting in stoic isolation.

Much later that evening, after a soothing bath and a long sleep that restored some of my sanity at least, I suggested to Mum and Dad that I could take them out for dinner in Richmond. They had been so wonderfully supportive of me during the diner renovations and I wanted to show my appreciation.

'What a lovely thought,' Mum said as she collected her coat and scarf. 'It's very kind of you, darling.'

The November evening was clear and chilly as we walked along the High Street, considering the food options available to us. After some debate, we decided on a gastro pub near the Odeon cinema, the prospect of which pleased my parents greatly.

Over a hearty meal of pork belly, apple and parsnip mash, rich gravy and peas, I filled my parents in on the latest developments, carefully omitting my kiss with Aidan. Until I could make sense of it and what it meant for the future, I wasn't ready to try to explain it to anyone else.

'I'm certain your diner is going to be lovely,' Mum said, firmly. 'And after all the shenanigans that John Matthews put you through, you deserve all the success in the world.'

'Thanks Mum.'

'Bloody idiot for not trusting our daughter,' Dad said, and I loved him for his unfettered bias. 'You'll show him, Nelliegirl.'

The pub was warm and filled with loud conversation, music and laughter. I revelled in the treat of a meal out, liking the feeling of decadence it gave me.

When we were ready to leave I paid the bill and we walked out into the wintry night. The lights of the riverside bars were reflected in the black waters of the Thames flowing beneath Richmond Bridge, stars overhead emerging from the chill of the night sky. As we walked down towards the bridge, the bright lights of passing traffic turned the billows of our visible breath intermittently white and red.

'Are the swans out tonight, Doug?' Mum asked as we began to cross the bridge.

Dad peered over the stone edge. 'Can't see any yet. River's running fast this evening.'

I smiled. Since moving to Richmond my parents had developed a slight obsession with the Thames and it still amused me to hear them earnestly discussing the waterfowl and flow rates of the river.

Moving away from the edge, Dad linked his arm through mine. 'Now, I suggest home for cocoa and some of your mother's coconut macaroons. Sounds like a plan?'

'Sounds wonderful.'

My mobile buzzed in my coat pocket. Nodding at it, Dad let go of my arm.

'Tell you what, Mum and I will go on ahead and let you answer that. Bound to be something important for your great culinary adventure.' He kissed my forehead. 'Don't be too long, now. If they get annoying, pretend to be an answering machine. I do that quite a lot with some of my customers.'

The thought of my tall, matter-of-fact father pretending to be an inanimate object was very amusing and I giggled as I inspected the screen. I didn't recognise the number, but this was nothing new: during the last couple of months I had received more calls from suppliers, workmen and complete strangers than I had from people I knew.

'Hello, Nell Sullivan speaking.'

'Hi Nell – it's Max. Please don't hang up . . .'

CHAPTER THIRTY

Hello again, hello . . .

I couldn't move.

The cars sped past me across Richmond Bridge, people walked around me to continue their evenings out, but the only thing marking me out from the elegant glass lamps attached to the bridge were the short puffs of breath rising slowly into the night sky.

'Please say something.'

'How did you get this number?'

'Lizzie gave it to me.'

His answer set my nerves tingling. What was Lizzie thinking?

'Don't be mad at her. She had good reason.'

'Why?'

'I'm here. In London. Eva is with me.'

A stab at my heart caused me to take a deeper breath. 'And Shanti?'

There was a pause. 'Shanti's at home with her mother.'

'Why are you here?'

‘I have an exhibition – can you believe it? I thought about what you said about the sidewalk paintings and revealed my identity as the artist. The internet’s gone crazy with pictures of my work and it’s led to an invitation to London to speak at a street art conference. We have an exhibition in a hotel near the Millennium Bridge. Say you’ll come?’

‘Max, I can’t.’ Tears were stinging my cold cheeks as they fell.

‘Not for me, then. For Eva. You’re all she’s talked about since we arrived. She wants to see you.’

‘I don’t know . . .’

‘The exhibition opens Monday. Say you’ll come.’

I closed my eyes.

I didn’t say I definitely would. I had the weekend to decide. Max Rossi was in my city and I needed time to process the fact.

Aidan made no more mention of what had happened at the diner and for that I was immensely grateful. In turn, I didn’t mention Max’s phone call. He didn’t need to know. Besides, I probably wouldn’t go to the exhibition. There was too much to do at Nell’s Place. It could be confusing for Eva. It could be upsetting for me.

The sudden reappearance of Max Rossi played on my mind all weekend. Why had he chosen *now* to contact me? I had just managed to pack him away with my San Francisco memories – why jump out of the box now? I considered calling Lizzie but I was still angry with her for giving Max my number. I hadn’t talked about Max with my parents and didn’t intend to explain everything to them in order to discuss this latest turn of events. In the end, there was only one person who knew enough to tackle the latest development.

'You are having me on! When did this happen?'

'On Friday evening.'

'And he just called you out of the blue?'

'Yes. Lizzie gave him my number.'

'Why on earth did she do that?'

'I have no idea.'

Vicky blew out a long breath as a waiter brought an afternoon tea tray to our table. 'And you say his little girl's with him?'

'Yes. He said he was asking me to come for her, not him.'

'Dreadful! What kind of father uses his daughter as a bargaining chip?'

'The kind of father who lies about her existence and dates someone behind his partner's back, presumably.'

'Good point. Is Shanti with him?'

'No.' I could tell from her expression exactly what Vicky thought of this.

'Are you going to go?'

'No. Probably not.'

Vicky gave me a knowing look. 'Those are two very different answers. You're not considering it, are you?'

'No.' I picked up a fruit scone and broke it into pieces. 'I don't know, Vix. What do you think I should do?'

Vicky held up her hands. 'Don't ask me. I'm living with a bloke whose chat-up line was, "More wine, love?" My standards really are that low.' She gently took the pieces of decimated scone from my hands. 'Only you can decide what's best.'

'Thanks, that's not helpful.'

'OK, look at it like this: if you go, you might find some answers to be able to let him go and move on with your life. Alternatively, you might end up more confused. If you don't go, you could save yourself a lot of unnecessary heartache before the diner opens. Or you could regret it for years.'

In a nutshell, my best friend had summed up the kaleidoscope of questions whirling in my mind. Thinking about this wouldn't move me forward on it: I was going to have to trust my instincts.

Monday morning arrived with no clearer answer. I turned my attention to fulfilling the long list of tasks for the week ahead. I was keen to hear what John had made of progress on Nell's Place when he had visited on Friday, so I arranged to meet Aidan for lunch.

At a pub restaurant overlooking the Thames, we made slow progress through the to-do list, updating each other as we went. Aidan was still looking tired and his curt answers to my questions made me conclude that he, like me, was growing impatient of the endless planning.

'It'll be happening soon and then we can forget all this,' I smiled.

He gave a hollow laugh and rubbed his eyes. 'I hope so.'

'Are you OK? You look tired.'

'That's probably because I am. I was at the diner till late on Friday evening and spent most of yesterday thrashing out plans with Dad. I love my father but he really doesn't know when to give it a rest.' He observed me. 'How about you?'

'Oh, the same. I'd like to remember a time when I was

able to go to sleep without a million-and-one thoughts racing around my head.' I felt a pang of guilt at concealing the real reason for my lack of sleep.

Aidan's gaze held mine. 'It wasn't to do with – you know – what happened on Friday, was it?'

Now I felt even worse. Aidan had mistaken my reason for not sleeping for thinking about him, when in truth he'd barely entered my thoughts all weekend. 'No, not that. I think what we said about waiting until Nell's Place opens still stands.'

His smile was pure relief. 'Me too. Look at the pair of us, eh? If this is what Nell's Place has done to us before it even opens, I dread to think what we'll be like a month from now.'

A month from now Max will be back in San Francisco and I won't be debating whether or not to see him . . .

I returned Aidan's smile, pushing the thought of Max away. Instead I focused on the way that Aidan's gaze flipped my stomach. What happened last week was a mistake, but the memory of it remained. 'We'll be celebrating the successful launch of Acton's latest hot place to be.'

Aidan laughed and raised his pint glass. 'Here's to being the talk of Acton!'

As the day wore on, I tried not to think about Max and Eva, or the fact that they would both be at the exhibition, waiting. Aidan had suggested we go out for a meal in Kensington after work and, thinking this would solve the issue once and for all, I agreed. We now had a table booked for eight thirty p.m., across the city from the hotel where the exhibition was taking place. It would be impossible to do both in one evening and I had already accepted Aidan's invitation. In the meantime, I had plenty of tasks to keep me occupied. Q.E.D. – problem solved.

At three p.m. I called it a day, intending to catch a couple of hours' rest before I had to get ready to meet Aidan. But by the time I lay down in my room, however, I was wide awake. Frustrated, I rolled over and picked up a book from beside my bed. Something fell out from between the pages, landing on the bedroom floor. I leaned down to pick it up, my heart stopping when I turned it over: an iconic red suspension bridge across vivid blue water to green-blue hills at the far side of its expanse. The towers of the Golden Gate Bridge began to wobble and blur as tears filled my eyes.

And I knew what I had to do.

The Underground was a mass of swarming, jostling bodies as I waited for a tube train that would allow me to stand in it and still be able to breathe. With the departure of each packed train, more bodies pushed onto the platform. I checked my watch and felt like screaming. The next train arrived and I elbowed people out of the way, squeezing myself into the smallest imaginable space. I needed to see Max to finally put my feelings for him to rest. Only then would I know how I felt about Aidan . . .

As I changed lines the queues only seemed to grow, but I had come this far and there was no point turning back. Knowing I would have little time to spare between the two engagements, I had dressed in my black lace dress ready for my dinner date with Aidan, my red heels swinging in a carrier bag as I dashed across London in my ballerina flats.

Nearly two hours after I had left my parents' house I emerged from the Underground station and hurried across the road to the glass and steel hotel building where Max's exhibition was taking place. Pink and yellow lights blazed from within its translucent core, revealing a seven-storey floor-to-ceiling atrium served by glass lifts moving at high speed, like those I had watched travelling outside the uppermost floors of the tall green Westin St Francis Hotel in Union Square. Using the tinted glass of the street level windows as a mirror, I re-pinned the strands of hair that had worked loose from my ponytail and patted my cold hands against my cheeks to cool the redness from my sprint. Taking a deep breath of cold air, I entered the lobby.

I was directed to the seventh floor – the Wren Suite – where the exhibition was being held. I took off my coat in the lift and swapped my flat shoes for the heels. My stomach lurched as I neared the top floor and I couldn't tell whether this was due to a dizzying drop from the glass sides of the lift, or the imminent reunion with a man I'd thought I never wanted to see again.

Don't over-think this, Nell. Follow your heart, I instructed myself as the doors opened and I walked out onto the luxurious thick carpet of the hotel's premier suite.

'Can I take your coat, Madam?' the polite cloakroom attendant asked, as I neared the Wren Suite's opulent entrance. I handed it over, but held on to my bag, feeling the need for a barrier of some kind to protect myself as I walked through the doors – and saw him.

Max Rossi was wearing a white open-necked shirt and khaki trousers, his suntanned Californian skin contrasting with the pale English exhibition organisers with whom he was speaking. He didn't see me enter the room, deep in conversation about a large canvas unusually displayed at his feet, mimicking the wide grey sidewalks of San Francisco. It was transformed into a cracked Arctic ice floe ridden by a large white polar bear – just like the one I had seen with Lizzie near her apartment. Before I'd discovered the artist was Max. Before the lies had begun . . .

All around the wide suite, similar canvases bore the unmistakable evidence of his craftsmanship, each one eliciting delighted responses from the exhibition guests.

As I was gazing at one secret he had kept from me, another spotted me in the crowd and screamed at the top of her lungs.

'*NELL!*'

Max's head snapped upright as his daughter dashed across the exhibition floor to jump with a loud whoop into my arms. The force of her hug spun me three hundred and sixty degrees as Eva clung on to me for all she was worth, sobbing into my shoulder.

'Hello you,' I laughed, despite my increasing nerves as Max hurried over. 'It's so lovely to see you.'

'You came.' Max was standing next to me, his grey eyes wide.

'Eva wanted me to come,' I replied. *After all, that was the reason you gave me, Max . . .*

'Are you pleased to see Nell, honey?'

Eva's head nodded emphatically against my shoulder.

'I missed you,' her muffled voice said before she pulled her head back and grinned at me. 'I waited all day.'

'Well, I'm here now.' I avoided eye contact with Max, but I could feel the weight of his stare. 'So what do you think of London?'

'It's cool. Daddy took me on the bus with no lid and we saw Buckingham Palace and the Tower of London. We didn't see the Queen or Prince William, though.'

'Most rude of them not to say hello,' Max commented.

I kept my smile hidden. 'And what about your daddy's paintings? Do you like them?'

'Uh-huh. My daddy's very good at colouring, just like me.'

'I have a long way to go before I'm better than you, kid.'

Eva shrugged. 'I know. But I'll help you.' She wriggled back to the floor and took my hand. 'Wanna see the best thing?'

'Absolutely.' I let her lead me, expecting her to share her favourite chalk artwork, but instead she marched me past the exhibits, through a set of sliding doors and out onto the marble and steel balcony which ran the entire length of the top floor. It was freezing up here, with the lights along the Thames in the distance below. 'Is the view from here your favourite thing?'

'Not *just* the view,' she replied, looking to her left and pointing upwards. 'Look!'

Above her little hand, seemingly floating over the nearby rooftops, was the white dome of St Paul's Cathedral, floodlit and ghostly against the dark sky.

'That's beautiful.'

'Isn't it? I got so excited when I saw it. Daddy took me out here this morning when we came to get the room ready. I've seen the birds, too! They sit on here sometimes.'

I grinned at Eva, noticing that the little girl had begun to shiver. 'We'd better get you back inside. It's too cold to be out here without a coat.'

'It's cold here *all the time*,' she exclaimed as she led the way.

More visitors had arrived and the Wren Suite was already looking crowded as waiters dressed in the hotel's signature burgundy waistcoats traversed the room with trays of red and white wine. A large woman dressed head to foot in floating layers of chintz-patterned chiffon had cornered Max and appeared to be attempting to persuade him to paint a permanent artwork in the grounds outside her home. He was smiling politely, but his gaze drifted over her shoulder towards me. At the earliest opportunity, he made his excuses and joined us.

'Hey honey, can you help the organiser lady to hand out those flyers we brought? She's over by the waterfall picture, you see her?'

'I see her. And her name is *Kathy*, Dad.' Having corrected her father, she dashed off to attend to her task.

'I wanted to see you,' Max said, his body inches from mine in the crowded room. 'Thank you for coming.'

'Like I told you, I came to see Eva.' It was so difficult not to sustain eye contact with him and I began to feel hemmed in. I jumped as his hand touched my arm.

'I want to explain. There are things you don't understand.'

I wanted to walk away, to leave him here and never look back. But another part of me needed answers. Everything had ended so suddenly, with such devastating hurt, that I wanted to know why. I looked at my watch. It was almost seven p.m. If I was going to make it across town to meet Aidan, I didn't have long. 'Then tell me.'

Surprised, he looked around but found no corner of the room where we might talk. A queue of new visitors blocked the entrance and each exhibit was crowded. Then, he turned back. 'Wait, I have an idea.' Holding my arm to guide us through the guests, he propelled us in the direction of the balcony doors. The chill wind bit at my face as we stepped outside and I wished I had hung on to my coat, the thin lace-covered sleeves of my evening dress offering little protection from the plummeting November temperature.

'It's freezing out here.'

'I'm sorry. It's the only place we can talk.'

'Then talk quickly.'

He faced me, his body blocking some of the icy wind as I huddled against the side of the building. 'Nell, what you saw at Eva's club – it's not what you think it is.'

'You were picking your daughter up,' I returned. 'A daughter I didn't know you had. I've met her mother, Max! She's a wonderful lady – and all along I was having an affair with her partner while making friends with their child. Do you have any idea how that made me feel?'

'I should have told you . . .'

'Yes, you should. Before anything happened. Before . . .' *Before I fell in love with you*, I completed in my head. 'I thought you cared about me, Max.'

'I did. I still do!'

I couldn't believe he thought that would change anything. Did he even understand what he had done? 'You cheated on a woman you confessed to me you still loved. The mother of your child, Max! Don't you see how bad that is?'

'Nell, listen to me . . .'

'Why? So you can tell me more lies?'

'I never lied.'

His attitude stunned me. 'You didn't tell me about the paintings. You didn't tell me about Shanti. And you didn't tell me about your daughter. Three lies, Max.'

'I never lied to you!' Anger tensing every muscle in his face, Max moved closer. I could feel the air temperature rise between our bodies. 'Yes, I didn't tell you about the paintings. But I didn't tell anyone – not even my little girl. And you were right. I needed to reveal my identity as the chalk artist. It brought me here and it's bringing me the promise of good money to support my kid. I didn't tell you about Shanti because she's not my partner. We had ten years together and one beautiful child, but we broke up, eleven months ago. We're still friends. You asked me if I loved her and I said yes – because she gave me Eva. You don't spend ten years of your life with someone and not love them in some way. She's my friend and we're raising our kid as best we can between us. But not *together*.'

Could I believe him? He was inches away from me, the intensity of the way he looked at me greater than I had seen before. Had I made the biggest mistake by refusing to see him on my last night in San Francisco?

'I didn't know. I'm sorry.'

His hand rested on my shoulder, the warmth of his palm sending shivers down my arm. 'I wanted so much to tell you the truth. But when you wouldn't talk to me I thought I'd lost my chance. Eva said . . .' his voice faltered in surprise as I shook his hand away from me.

'Eva,' I repeated. 'Why didn't you tell me you had a child?'

'I – I don't know. Things were happening between us so fast I wanted to see where it was going . . .'

'I told you everything about me. Everything. There were things I could've held back, but I didn't because I wanted you to know me.'

He dropped his head, a gust of cold breeze hitting my face and neck when he moved. 'I love my little girl. I wanted to protect her. I haven't been a dad before – I'm going to make mistakes. And you were the first person I wanted to be with since Shanti. I was in new territory and I didn't know what to do. How was I to know you already knew her?'

'What difference does that make?' A clock chimed the three-quarter hour and I looked down at my red heels. 'I really have to go.'

'Nell, I love you. I think you love me too. And Eva loves you. I don't know if we can make this work, but I'm willing to try.'

My heart breaking, I looked into his eyes and saw the truth. Tears welled up and my heartbeat drowned out the sound of the wind. I thought about Nell's Place and all of the hours I'd invested in making my business a reality. I thought about Aidan, on his way to meet me now on the other side of London; of the closeness between us since my return from San Francisco; and how, even though I thought I loved Max, the hurdles between us were just too much to overcome.

His hand stroked my face and I wanted to stay . . . but I had a life here and a dream to fulfil.

'It's not enough. I'm sorry.'

'No!' A loud wail beside us caused us both to turn. To my horror, I saw the crushed expression of my little friend feet away from us. 'I *hate* you!' she yelled, running back into the room.

'Eva!' Max hurried after her.

Alone on the freezing cold balcony, I covered my face with my hands and sobbed. In one moment I had broken any bonds remaining between us. Once and for all, I had my answer: Max Rossi would never be a part of my life.

CHAPTER THIRTY-ONE

Back to reality

The distant church clock began to mark the hour and I hurried back inside, pushing through the crowd of visitors to collect my coat and blinking away tears as the lift descended. On the road outside I hailed a taxi, clambering into a black cab when it stopped for me.

'Kensington High Street, please.'

As the lights of London passed by, I dropped my head into my hands. I should never have gone there tonight. I could have carried on thinking Max had lied to me, shelving that episode of my life and moving on. I could have left things with Eva as her exciting occasional London correspondent, her happy memories of me intact and perfect.

Instead, I had lost Max all over again and broken Eva's heart when she overheard our argument. I would never forget the look of hurt in her eyes as she ran from the balcony. I knew the truth about Max and no matter what else happened in my life there would always be the question of what might have been. And now I was on my way to meet Aidan, feeling like I'd betrayed him already. It was a mess – and I only had myself to blame.

Nearing the restaurant address, I did my best to hide the evidence of my tears, trying to look as though the only stressful thing I'd dealt with this evening was over-crowding on the tube. I had to put this behind me, draw a line underneath it and focus on what I knew my life had in store: opening Nell's Place and working hard to make it a success.

Aidan was already at the table when I arrived. My heart ached as soon as I saw him, guilt and longing pulling me in two directions at once.

'Hi, sorry I'm late.'

'Everything OK?' he asked, rising to kiss my cheek. 'You look stressed.'

'The tube was horrific,' I replied, hating the excuse even though it was partly the truth. 'I gave up and caught a taxi but then we were stuck in traffic.'

'Ah, the joys of London. At least when Nell's Place opens your commute will be relatively easy.' He grinned. 'Now there's a scary thought: very soon you'll have a commute to your new business.'

His smile coaxed me back to life, the thought of something as mundane as the journey into work becoming a cause for excitement. 'I'll be able to call the diner my *workplace* – now that will be amazing.'

Aidan ordered a whisky on ice for him and a glass of red wine for me as we waited to be served. 'Do you know what you want?'

I was startled by his question until I realised he was

referring to the menu. 'Oh, something light I think. I'm not really hungry.'

'Fair enough. I won't be joining you in your small meal, I'm afraid. I'm ravenous.'

I watched Aidan eagerly scanning the menu and considered how much my opinion of him had changed since I came home. He had been there for me all the times I had needed support over the last few months and that had to count for something. I was lucky to have him.

We ordered food and Aidan asked for another whisky.

'Have you finished the last one already?' I asked, eyeing his glass.

'They serve a fantastic Speyside single malt here,' he replied. 'I just fancied another.'

'You'll be asleep before you know it, especially after your busy weekend.'

'Maybe you should join me,' he ventured, raising a suggestive eyebrow.

'Aidan!'

He gave his best impression of an innocent man. 'What? I was talking about whisky, Nell. What did *you* think I meant?'

I laughed in spite of the knot twisting my insides. 'Very funny.'

'It made you smile though, so that's a good thing. Listen, I know what happened last week was – unexpected,' he dropped his voice, 'but I still don't regret it. I believe there's more for us – I want there to be more.'

Determined to push any last memory of Max away, I let myself be charmed by Aidan's words. Maybe I wanted more too. Maybe this is how it should always have been between us. 'I hope so,' I replied, the words causing chills to tumble down my spine.

He reached for my hand and I let him hold it, taking a deep breath when I realised I was shaking.

'I promise you that when Nell's Place is open, we'll work out where we should be. And this time, I'm not letting you go.'

Wanting to bring the conversation back from such emotive territory, I changed tack. 'So, you were going to tell me what your dad thought about the progress at Nell's Place?'

Aidan groaned into his single malt as he released my hand. 'Let's just eat first, baby. We've talked of little else for months.'

The sudden swing in his mood was unwelcome and new. 'But it was your idea to discuss the diner over a meal,' I returned. 'You said we needed to spend every available opportunity double-checking everything.'

'I'm sorry. I'll just be glad when you're in there and it's operational.'

'Me too, I can't wait. So what did John say?'

Aidan swigged the remainder of his whisky. 'He had some concerns.'

Still? How could that be the case? 'Such as?'

'It's nothing we can't work through with some give-and-take.'

'Aidan. What concerns?'

He stared at his glass. 'The menu.'

That was a relief. If the only issue John Matthews had about Nell's Place was the design of the menu it was easily remedied. 'What doesn't he like about it? If he gives me a snag list I can chat to the printers . . .'

'All of it, Nell. Apart from the French toast varieties – he thinks that could be a good gimmick.'

I stared at him. '*Gimmick?* It's not a gimmick. It's an American diner classic – because the diner is an American diner . . .'

'Don't get hung up on the word, Nell. The whole concept is a gimmick, let's face it.'

'No, it's not. You know it isn't.' Adrenalin had started to pump as I noticed he was no longer making eye contact with me. 'What exactly is your father asking me to do?'

He began to spin his knife on the white cotton tablecloth. 'Change the menu back to what it was.'

'I don't understand.'

'Dad did some market research in Acton. People want the old café back. They don't want an American diner, no matter how carefully the food is sourced or how authentic it is.'

'No . . .'

He stared at me. 'You think I didn't say this to him? You think I let him dismiss all of our hard work without a fight?'

'*Dismiss* it?' I was gripping the edge of the table now, the tablecloth bunching beneath my fingers.

'I'm sorry, I wish it was different. But Dad's ploughed a lot of money into this café.'

'It's not a café, it's a diner. *My* diner!' My voice was lifting above the restaurant noise, but I didn't care. How dare John change his mind now! Did all the work that Aidan and I had put into the place mean nothing to him?

'Keep your voice down,' Aidan hushed me, glancing

in embarrassment at the other customers. 'We both knew there would be compromises.'

'I've done nothing *but* compromise,' I shot back. 'I've compromised on quality, ingredients, equipment, layout . . . Just what, exactly, does your father want this time?'

'Food that people recognise, Nell. Full English breakfasts, bacon sarnies, egg and chips, that sort of thing. Dad thinks you should sell jacket potatoes and panini for the more health-conscious, maybe some salads. You can still do the burgers – they fit the brief. And like I said, the French toast selection could be a great draw for the younger crowd. Oh and Dad *really* liked the movie quotes mural you've painted on the wall.'

I felt sick. Everything I had worked so hard for was being reduced to a greasy spoon café with fresher paint and less beer guts behind the counter. 'He'll be changing the name back too, will he?'

Aidan gave a weak smile. 'No, Nell. You've earned the right to have your name over the door. Nell's Place will be somewhere people can come to enjoy food they love, right on their High Street where it's always been.'

'And you agreed to this?'

He shook his head. 'Of course not. But given Dad's attitude, perhaps this is the best thing for now.'

'All your father is doing is ripping the heart out of everything we've worked for and sticking my name above the door!'

'Nell, listen to me. This is still your dream. But by doing it this way you gain experience of running the diner with a menu we know will sell. Dad will be happy and will leave you alone to get on with running the place.

Play his game, Nell, and then start to change it from within. Stick to his menu for a year and slowly start to introduce the other items on the specials board. The popular ones will stay, the others won't. It'll be like market research in real time.'

Our meals arrived, but I pushed my plate away. My appetite had disappeared along with the remaining pieces of my dream for Nell's Place. 'This isn't what I wanted. It's not what I've worked so hard for.'

'Honey, stop worrying and eat something. You're tired, you're disappointed, but you're still opening your own business in three weeks' time. And I'll be there to help you.'

But I *wasn't* opening my own business. I was managing somebody else's – somebody who cared about profit over service, and quick returns over community building. John Matthews was paying me a wage to run the business the way he wanted – that was the reality of it.

'I don't think I can do this.'

Aidan left his seat and gathered me into his arms as I broke down, this revelation the final straw in a day I wished had never happened. 'You *can* do this. You've already made a fantastic job of all the crap Dad's thrown at you! It will be a success because you have the determination to succeed. That's what matters.'

Having made a total prat of myself in front of an entire restaurant full of people, I made my excuses and hurried to the ladies' toilet. My mascara-streaked, flushed face stared blankly back at me. So John Matthews wanted to mess with all the plans I'd made, did he? Well, I had two choices. I could give up, postpone the dream and join the unemployment massive of London. I could let this beat me.

Or I could fight back by making my mark where I could, in any way, however small.

I drew deep breaths and steadied myself as I held the edge of the sink. Staring at my reflection, I looked deep into my own green eyes. This had to be possible. I hadn't come this far, risked this much and given all of myself to see the dream fall at the final fence. I thought of Ced with his Gothic coffee house, Rosita with her New Age store and Annie with her diner. None of them had started with the perfect conditions for a successful business, yet all of them were now Haight-Ashbury legends. And after them would come others, driven by a desire to do something different, to follow their dreams however ugly and out-of-shape they began life as. If they could do it, so could I.

Opening my handbag, I set about reapplying my make-up and straightening my hair. I would *show* John Matthews. Nell's Place was going to be a success.

Calmness settling once again on my shoulders, I pushed open the door to the restaurant and was walking back towards Aidan when my mobile rang. Seeing the number on the screen, I turned my back on Aidan and answered.

'Hello?'

'Nell – Eva's missing. I've searched everywhere but I can't find her.'

The panic in Max's voice made every hair rise to attention on the back of my neck. 'Stay there. I'm on my way.'

CHAPTER THIRTY-TWO

Little lost girl

Icy rain had begun to fall across the city, turning pavements into dark glass reflecting the lights from cars, shops, offices and buildings. The black cab sped through quieter streets, frustratingly finding every red traffic light between Kensington and Blackfriars Bridge. All I could think about was how upset Eva had been when I'd last seen her. In a hotel as vast as the Blackfriars Millennium there could be countless places for an eight-year-old to hide. Especially an eight-year-old who didn't want to be easily found. I checked my watch. It had been two and a half hours since Eva had left the balcony: had she been missing all this time? If so, how had Max lost sight of her when he knew how upset she was?

Max's number flashed up on my mobile phone and I answered it before it even rang this time. 'Any news?'

'No. The hotel people are doing a sweep of all floors. She could be anywhere.'

'What happened after –' I paused to carefully phrase my question '– after I left?'

'Eva was upset. She ran to the bathroom and locked the door. I talked her out after about twenty minutes. I thought I'd calmed her down. She said she was OK and I left her talking to the cloakroom attendant. But when I checked ten minutes later she'd disappeared. How could I let this happen? I promised her mother I'd take care of her . . .' His voice cracked and I could hear sharp bursts of breath as emotion swept over him.

'Max, keep looking. This taxi's taking forever but I promise I'll be there soon. We'll find her.'

I hadn't explained to Aidan where I was going, only that a good friend urgently needed my help. I'd refused his offer to join me, hailing a cab before he could pay the bill and leaving as he ran out onto the steps of the restaurant. It was another mess I would have to rectify when I next saw him, but tonight it wasn't important. Eva's safety and wellbeing were at stake and despite how things had ended with us earlier that evening, Max had called *me*.

Maybe Eva had taken the lift, got off on a floor she didn't recognise and become disorientated. Every storey of the Blackfriars Millennium was identical, with long, narrow corridors that seemed to stretch on forever in every direction and mirrored doors that confused your sense of direction.

I stared at my phone, willing it to ring with news of her safe discovery. Max was experiencing every parent's worst nightmare, in a city he didn't know. If she was in the hotel at least she was safe. But if she'd left it, with the Thames nearby and countless dark and unfamiliar streets snaking away from the Blackfriars Millennium, it didn't bear thinking about. A scared little girl in a strange city, at night, in the icy rain . . .

And then it hit me: I knew where she was.

'Wait!' I yelled, slapping my hand on the Perspex screen separating the driver from me.

'Oi, pack that in!'

'I'm sorry, mate. Change of plan. Take me to St Paul's, as fast as you can. It's an emergency.'

Grumbling, the taxi driver made a sharp U-turn, sped down a side street I was pretty sure was one way in the opposite direction, and joined another main road, the windscreen wipers battling with the heavy rain pelting the glass.

Hanging on to my seat belt as the taxi veered from left to right, I called Max but he didn't answer. Frustrated, I left a message and rang off. I would keep trying when I arrived, but for now all that mattered was that I found Eva.

The taxi screeched to a halt outside the South Transept steps of the cathedral – the view featured on the postcard I had sent Eva a few weeks ago. I stuffed a handful of notes from my purse into the driver's hand and dashed from the cab, gasping as freezing cold raindrops assaulted my body.

Holding my bag over my head I shouted, 'Eva! Eva, it's Nell!'

The marble of the famous cathedral glowed in the floodlights, caliginous shadows gathering between its columns as it rose like a giant from the street. The sight was daunting for me, but for a small, scared eight-year-old it could be terrifying. No Disney-style cuteness here: it was more like a scene from a Gothic horror film.

'*Eva!*'

Shielding my phone as best I could, I called Max again.

'*Max Rossi here, I'm not able to take your call but leave a message and I'll get back to you . . .*'

'Max, it's Nell again. I think Eva is at St Paul's Cathedral. I'm there now and I'm looking for her. As soon as you get this, call me.'

I looked up at the curve of the South Transept, the grand dome rising high behind it, and tried to remember the picture of St Paul's from *Mary Poppins*. I recalled Dad remarking once that the painting used in the film didn't look anything like the real thing. Blinking through the raindrops, I tried to think clearly. I *must* be missing something . . .

'Eva!'

Certain that these steps were deserted I turned left and ran the outside length of the church, my eyes scanning the periphery for any sign of her. In the floodlights of the surrounding buildings the rain was descending in undulating sheets. I couldn't feel my feet in my thin ballerina flats and my face was numb.

'Eva! Eva, it's Nell!'

The raindrops thundered against the bag I held overhead, crashing onto pavements painted an eerie pale orange by the streetlights. I ran on, my fear growing with every empty shadow.

I remembered getting lost on holiday one year when I was around Eva's age. We were staying in Torquay and Dad found out that a travelling funfair was visiting nearby. Walking around the stalls I somehow lost sight of my parents, suddenly realising that I was alone. As night closed in and the crowds grew, I remember the awful terror that gripped me, thinking I would never see my mum and dad again. I felt like I wandered around the funfair for days, scared out of my wits, although my parents reckon I was missing for around thirty minutes. When they finally found me, I was curled up beside the Hook-a-Duck stall because the jolly yellow plastic birds reminded me of the one I had for bath time back at home and that made me feel safe. But it was traumatic for me – and I didn't want this to be Eva's version of my experience.

'Spare a pound, love?' A man suddenly appeared in front of me, a sleeping bag wrapped around his body offering meagre cover from the rain.

'I'm sorry, I don't have any . . . Oh, wait . . .' I stopped running, dug in the front pocket of my bag and gave him a handful of coins. 'I'm looking for a little girl, eight years old, light African skin, black hair? I think she was wearing a red dress. Have you seen her?'

The homeless man shook his head. 'Seen no kids here tonight. You want to find her fast, though. This place ain't friendly.'

I was really scared now. I rounded the corner of St Paul's Churchyard and looked up. *That was it* – the grand classical entrance with columns, towers, stone staircase and dark dome above. The view from the film!

'*EVA!*' I screamed over the rainstorm, running towards the steps where the bird woman had fed her charges. As I neared them, it became clear that they were deserted. Frantically I scanned each step, remembering how small Eva was, how easy she would be to miss. But it was empty. Wiping the rain from my eyes I stared at the cathedral in disbelief, trying hard to catch my breath. I'd been so certain she would be here . . . If there was no sign of her in the hotel and none out here, where was she?

'Eva!' I called out again, but the only reply came from the drops of rain hammering down on the entrance to the famous cathedral. I began to ascend the steps slowly, lowering my handbag to my side as the freezing rain soaked into my hair and ran down my face and neck. At the top of the staircase a wide, black and white chequered tiled floor passed beneath giant dark shadows from the Corinthian columns. Gaining some shelter from the rain, I found my mobile and saw three missed calls from Max. What was I going to say to him? I had summoned him to a red herring – and what if my interference had caused a dangerous delay to the real search for his daughter?

A bus drove past on the road, its bright headlights casting new, temporary moving shadows across the carved stone columns. I followed their trajectory to the furthest end of the chequered floor.

And that's when I saw it.

A tiny huddled shape was hiding in the deep shadow of the final column, barely perceptible in the unnatural glow of floodlights. My heart was about to explode out of my chest as I sped across the tiles.

'*Eva!*'

The bundle didn't move and as I neared it I could see Eva's head bowed onto her knees, her little arms wrapped around her legs as she sat against the enormous column.

I fell to my knees beside her, throwing my arms around her shivering body and pulling her close to me.

'It's OK, baby, you're safe now. I'm here.'

'Nell . . .' she wailed, her voice tiny, terrified.

'*Shh*, I've got you.'

Slowly, she unfurled her body, wrapping her cold arms around my neck as she sobbed and I shifted position until I was sitting against the column with Eva on my lap, wrapping my coat around us and cradling her head against my shoulder.

'I was scared, Nell.'

'I know you were. Why did you run away, honey?'

She raised her head and stared at me, a pitiful expression on her face. 'You and Daddy were fighting. You said you didn't love me . . .'

'No, darling, you know I love you. You're my superstar.'

'I didn't think you did. And Dad shouted at me for running away.'

I brushed the dark curls of her soaked hair back from her forehead. 'I'm sure he didn't.'

'He did. He was angry because you ran away, too.'

My heart sank to the cold stone floor beneath us. Eva had heard me say the situation wasn't enough and she believed that I was talking about her – that she wasn't good enough for me to love her. It crushed me to think I might have said something that could damage her self-esteem.

'When you ran away, why did you come here?' I asked.

'I wanted to find *her*. The bird lady. I thought Daddy and you didn't want me but I knew she would. She feeds the birds, so she could look after me.' Her face crumpled. 'But I couldn't find her.'

'*Eva! Nell!*' Max's distant voice travelled through the rain.

'Over here! On the top step!' I yelled back, hugging Eva. 'Hey, your daddy's here.'

Fear shone in her dark eyes. 'He's gonna be mad . . .'

'No, he won't be. He's been very worried about you.'

'He's going to be sad again, isn't he?'

'He'll be very happy to see you.'

'He'll be sad. He's been sad for a long time. Until today, when you came. He smiled again when you came in. And then you had a fight.'

I couldn't speak then, the gravity of her words too much to take in.

'Eva!' Max skidded across the black and white floor, flinging his arms around us both, his kisses falling on his daughter's head as fast as the rain across St Paul's Churchyard. His wet hair brushed my cheek as he kissed his little girl and I could feel the tension shaking his body as his arm encircled me.

'I thought I'd lost you. I was so scared.'

'I love you, Daddy.'

'I love you, baby.'

He raised his head, water dripping from his hair and running down his face. In the pale orange half-glow of the colonnaded entrance, his eyes were as dark as the shadows.

'You found her.'

I nodded, acutely aware of how little distance stood between us.

'Thank you.'

Eva twisted her head to look up at both of us and I smiled. 'I'm just glad she's OK.'

His hand slid back to curl around my shoulder. 'You found me, too.'

'Max—'

'Don't let me go again.'

I didn't think, didn't debate, didn't plan. As his fingers travelled slowly up my spine, tangling in my hair at the nape of my neck and drawing me closer, I let instinct guide me. There, on the steps of St Paul's Cathedral, I kissed Max Rossi. And my questions were blown away like birds taking flight to the furthest corners of London.

CHAPTER THIRTY-THREE

Welcome to Nell's Place

'Move it to the left a bit. No, *left* . . .'

Vicky punched her hands onto her hips as she wobbled at the top of the stepladder. 'It's a Christmas tree, Nell. Not the bloody Eiffel Tower.'

I gave her a sheepish smile. 'Sorry Vix. I just want everything to be perfect.'

'And it will be. If you stop acting like a neurotic psycho. OK, hand me that tinsel. I'm going in.'

'Hey beautiful, the new sign looks great.' Max strolled in from the street and slipped his arm around my waist, planting a warm kiss on my neck. 'Mmm, I like Nell's Place already . . .'

'You're filthy, Mr Rossi.' Giggling, I moved my clipboard around his head to tick another item off my ever-present list. 'Diner sign – done. Great. I can't believe this is happening today.'

'You've worked hard to make it happen,' Vicky called from somewhere within the branches of the large, kitsch white plastic Christmas tree suspended by invisible thread from the ceiling.

Max grinned. 'She's right. What else do I need to do?'

'Stand there looking gorgeous,' Vicky offered.

'He's here to help, Vix, not stand around to be ogled at.'

'Well, that would help *me* . . .'

I rolled my eyes. 'Ignore my best friend. She's a letch.'

'Oh I dunno, I think she's kinda cute.'

'Ooh, I *like* your fella, Nell!'

Ignoring my best friend's outrageous flirtation with Max, I turned the page on my clipboard. There was so much left to do and barely half an hour until the official opening. So many decisions had been made about this place without me that during the last few days I was worried it wouldn't feel like mine, that the compromises would have robbed me of any pride I could feel in this new venture. Up until this morning, when I'd stepped into the darkened diner and turned on the lights and it hit me: this was *my* diner.

A shriek from the street was followed by Lizzie, breathless and clutching her sides. 'I just had the shock of my life,' she panted, giggling in between the gasps. 'Have you seen the picture on the pavement outside? I thought I was going to fall down a ravine!'

Max held his hand up in surrender. 'Guilty.'

'When did you do that?' I asked him.

'This morning. While you were arranging the kitchen.'

'My own Max Rossi original outside my diner – lucky me!' I wrapped my arms around him and kissed him. 'I love you. I'm so glad you could be here.'

'I wouldn't be anywhere else. So, what next?'

I checked my list. 'Can you set up the coffee filters? I know it's something I'll forget to do.'

'I'm on it.'

Lizzie linked arms with me. 'How are you feeling?'

'Nervous.' I'd woken at four that morning in a blind panic and written fifteen more items on my clipboard list. 'I almost had heart failure about napkins this morning.'

'You were born to run your own diner,' my cousin reassured me.

'Of course, it isn't *my* diner.'

'*Yet*. So what if you're a tenant for the time being? It's yours in every other respect. Name above the door, Nell Sullivan. That counts for a lot.'

Today of all days it meant so much to have my friends around me. Vicky had been a star – and Greg even more so for looking after Ruby while she was here. She'd only taken a few days off from her new job, but I appreciated the gesture more than she knew. Fortuitous timing meant that Lizzie was here too – and that brought a much-needed boost to my confidence.

As my friends prepared Nell's Place for its first day of custom, I cast my gaze around the diner. This was the first day of my new adventure – and I was eager for it to begin. I thought back to the unlikely catalyst that had set this whole course of events into action: one lime-green sticky note. Had it not been for the questionable logic of my Council superiors and the guilty actions of my former flame, I would never have jumped on a plane with my redundancy cheque, never taken a chance on a city I'd never visited and never found the determination to make this dream a reality. As it turned out, I owed a great deal to Aidan Matthews and his lime-green guilt-trip. Which is why it was a shame he wasn't here. One day I might tell him – when he was talking to me again, that is.

Now I was standing in the diner I'd dreamed of, on opening day. And by the look of it, my new customers were eager to share it with me.

'What time do you open?' asked an old man, his head appearing around the front door. 'We're waiting, you know.'

'Any minute now,' I called back. 'We're just putting the final touches to everything.'

'OK.' He ducked his head back outside. 'They're not ready yet.'

'What do you mean, they're not ready yet?' a woman's voice retorted from the street outside. 'Did you tell them we're waiting?'

'*Yes*, I told them we were waiting. How can I help it if they're not ready yet?' He reappeared, an apologetic look on his wrinkled face. 'Forgive me, Nell. My wife wishes to know when you will be ready.'

I exchanged looks with Lizzie. 'Tell Esther she's welcome to come and wait inside, Saul.'

Clasping his hands together in gratitude, Mr Alfaro gave me a wink. 'A thousand blessings on your head, Nell. *Mazel tov.*'

I sighed. 'So much for the big theatrical opening. Shall we just let everyone in?'

'It's your diner, Nell,' Lizzie smiled.

I grinned at the woman loading oranges into the

orange juicing machine behind me. 'Technically *not* mine.'

'You do what you like, Nell,' Annie Legado called back. 'I'm *delegating*, remember?'

I walked over to join her. 'And you're sure about this? I mean you could be sold up and relaxing on a Caribbean island by now.'

'Nah. Selling is overrated. Owning property is the future. If this works out and you buy the diner from me in five years, who knows? I might expand – build my portfolio. I could be bigger than Donald Trump.' Her half-smile stretched into a full beam. 'I'm proud of you, kid. And I'm glad you suggested this.'

'Nell! Can I take the orders?' Eva shouted from behind the counter. 'I'll write real big so you can read it.'

'You can help me, if you like.'

'Cool!'

The Alfaros were already settled at their favourite table. I could hear the buzz of voices from the line of customers beyond the door. It was time.

I stood in the middle of the diner and raised my voice. 'OK, is everyone ready?'

'As we'll ever be, boss,' Laverne replied, walking through from the kitchen to take her place behind the counter. Karin and Dom leaned through the serving hatch to give me their thumbs-up.

I looked down at the list on the clipboard. 'I think everything is done . . .'

'One more thing left to do,' Max said, grabbing the clipboard from my hands, opening the front door and tossing it out onto Haight Street.

'What did you do that for?' I protested.

My wonderful Max Rossi took both my hands and lifted them to his soft lips. 'You don't need that list. You have everything you need to succeed, right here.'

I couldn't argue with that. And so, with pride and emotion welling up within me, I looked around at the encouraging smiles of the people I loved, in the city I now called home.

'Right then. I declare Nell's Place open for business. Let them in!'

THE END

*Five must-see films set in San Francisco**

(*and why you should watch them . . .)

1. The Five-Year Engagement (2012)

I didn't actually see this until Bob and I returned from San Francisco and when I watched it I sobbed. *Sobbed.* Because it features all the San Franciscan places I loved in glorious Technicolor®: the setting for Alex and Suzie's wedding is The Palace of Fine Arts in The Presidio (Bob and I sat on a bench where the wedding scene happens); Tom proposes to Violet overlooking the Bay Bridge at night (*the* most beautiful setting, and where I set an important scene for Nell and Max in the book); and the final scene (I won't give away the ending in case you haven't seen it yet) takes place in Alamo Square Park, which I completely fell in love with because you can see the whole of San Francisco from the top of it. Watch it: you'll *love* it!

2. Mrs Doubtfire (1993)

Why should you watch this film? Because it's a classic. Because it has Robin Williams, Sally Field and Pierce Brosnan in it. But mostly because it has beautiful San Francisco in it. The city looks exactly like it does in the film – which is why it feels so familiar even if it's the first time you've ever been there. One more thing: when Miranda Hillard gives Mrs Doubtfire her address on the phone as '2640 Steiner Street', this is the *actual* address of the house used in the film. (I was so impressed by this fact – geek that I am – that I included it in Nell's birthday treasure hunt organised by Lizzie in the book.)

3. Serendipity (2001)

OK, I confess, this is a *bit* of a cheat because everyone knows *Serendipity* mostly takes place in New York. But the scene where Lars proposes to Sara with the trail of rose petals and boxes-within-boxes is in San Francisco and I'm a big John Corbett fan. Also, that scene begins with Sara on a boat in the Bay looking back at San Francisco, which is a fabulous way to see the city. And even though you *obviously* want Sara to find Jonathan because Lars is a bit of an idiot, John Corbett is a beautiful man. The Defence rests, Your Honour . . .

4. Heart & Souls (1993)

This is another geeky choice, but well worth checking out. It's a really sweet love story with a supernatural and retro twist and stars a very young Robert Downey Jr. He's fantastic in the film (no surprises there) and the four ghosts he helps are brilliantly cast. One of the scenes was filmed in The Conservatory of Flowers in Golden Gate Park, which isn't far from where I set Lizzie's Haight-Ashbury home in the book. It's A proper snuggle-in-front-of-the-telly-with-hot-chocolate, feel-good film.

5. Monsters vs Aliens (2009)

Yes, it's an animated film – but even in computer-generated action sequences, San Francisco looks amazing. Even when aliens are trashing it. The Golden Gate Bridge as a setting for a battle is brilliant and while, thankfully, no such epic battles took place when Bob and I visited, there is something profoundly impressive about the bridge, no matter which angle you view it from. And I'm not surprised that aliens chose San Francisco to visit – they might be evil baddies but they have fantastic taste!

My ten favourite places in San Francisco

San Francisco is an incredible city and completely stole my heart (you *may* have noticed this . . .). Here are my favourite places:

1. **Crissy Field,** the **Warming Hut** and **West Bluff** – just an amazing place to be. Awesome views of the Golden Gate Bridge, the San Francisco Bay and the city in the distance and definitely my favourite place.
2. **Union Square** – grab a coffee and just watch the world go by.
3. **Chinatown** – wander around the streets and soak up the atmosphere.
4. **Alamo Square** – the view from the top of the park is worth the scramble.
5. **Haight-Ashbury** – kooky, colourful, friendly and unlike anywhere else.
6. **Golden Gate Park** – you can easily spend hours here,

with the Japanese Tea Garden, the California Academy of Sciences with its Planetarium, the Conservatory of Flowers and acres of beautifully maintained parkland.

7. **The San Francisco Ferry Building** and **The Embarcadero** – a busy organic food market by day and the best place to see the lights of San Francisco and the Bay Bridge at night.
8. **Fisherman's Wharf, Pier 39** and **Ghirardelli Square** – fun, brash, colourful and wonderful. Ride one of the vintage trams – including one from Blackpool – and say hello to the lazy sea lions at Pier 39.
9. **The Palace of Fine Arts in The Presidio** – it's a crazy building that looks as if it's come straight out of Roman history and has to be seen to be believed.
10. **Market Street** – great shops, a buzzing atmosphere and it's fun to watch the cable cars being turned on the wooden turntable where Market Street meets the bottom of Powell Street.

Bob's Top Five Things to Eat in San Francisco

When Bob and I went to San Francisco to research this book (and also for our delayed honeymoon!), I took a list of places I wanted to see for key scenes in the story – and Bob took a list of food. This therefore makes him the expert on all things foodie, so here are the top five things he recommends for noshing when you're in the City by the Bay (and I agree with him):

1. **Cinnamon & Walnut French Toast** (with sliced banana and warm maple syrup, dusted with icing sugar).

2. **Mac Cheese** – an American classic, the one we had was made with white wine, onion and three cheeses.
3. **Clam Chowder** – from one of the outdoor stalls at Fisherman's Wharf, served in a hollowed-out bread loaf with crunchy oyster crackers.
4. **Omelettes** – made with four eggs, stuffed with cheese, bell peppers, sour cream and white onions and served with chilli-sautéed 'home fries'.
5. **Ice Cream** – from Ghirardelli Square. It's quite possibly the most amazing ice cream you'll ever taste!